THE
ILIAD

A TOM DOHERTY ASSOCIATES BOOK

NEW YORK

THE
ILIAD

HOMER

Translated by
RALPH BLAKELY

Foreword by
KEYNE CHESHIRE

THE ILIAD

A Forge Book
Published by Tom Doherty Associates, LLC
175 Fifth Avenue
New York, NY 10010

www.tor-forge.com

Forge® is a registered trademark of Tom Doherty Associates, LLC.

Library of Congress Cataloging-in-Publication Data

Homer, author.
  [Iliad. English]
  The Iliad / Homer ; translation by Ralph E. Blakely ; foreword by
Keyne Cheshire, Ph.D.—First edition.
    pages cm
  ISBN 978-0-7653-3168-7 (hardcover)
  ISBN 978-1-4299-9728-7 (e-book)
    1. Epic poetry, Greek—Translations into English.   2. Achilles
(Mythological character)—Poetry.   3. Trojan War—Poetry.
I. Blakely, Ralph E., translator.   II. Title.
PA4025.A2B5513 2015
883'.01—dc23

2015023348

Our books may be purchased in bulk for promotional,
educational, or business use. Please contact your local bookseller
or the Macmillan Corporate and Premium Sales Department
at (800) 221-7945, extension 5442, or by e-mail at
MacmillanSpecialMarkets@macmillan.com.

First Edition: December 2015

Printed in the United States of America

10   9   8   7   6   5   4   3   2   1

To the memory of Wilmer Hayden Welsh,
who lived always with the courage of the heroes

FOREWORD

These days, it is common for many institutions of higher learning to require that syllabi include a list of clearly stated goals. Of course, the achievement of some goals cannot be measured for years to come. For my current course on Homer's *Iliad*, one of these stated goals reads, "Befriend a work that for the remainder of your life may serve as palliative for grief and loss." A professor emerita auditing the course expressed delight at this promise, saying she had worried that *The Iliad* was just a violent war story. Violence does pervade the poem, it is true, but war as setting serves as a constant memento mori, raising the stakes of life and so rendering the characters' every word and deed all the more critical. More than a war story, *The Iliad* offers a treatment of the human experience so sublime that later Greeks viewed Homeric verse as the wellspring of all poetry to follow. There is even some evidence that a desire to preserve this poem may have inspired the invention of the Greek alphabet itself.

Imagine my excitement just last fall upon learning that a Davidson alumnus had undertaken the daunting task of translating this masterpiece. My first encounter with Ralph Blakely lasted several hours of an afternoon, and although he might tell you that he benefited some little bit by our meeting, I aver that I learned a tremendous lot that day. Translators of Homer tend to be philologists or poets, but Blakely is unabashedly neither. Instead, this gentleman, a self-proclaimed amateur, had spent more hours with *The Iliad* for the love of it than most scholars of classics will in their lifetimes, and he had in the process developed a profound and deeply personal relationship with the poem.

One aspect of this relationship is Blakely's certainty that

Homer was a keen observer of his time. Blakely provides a glimpse of this in his preface, where he discusses the nature of ash wood, and of the air and the sea around Troy. But he could also tell you what breed of dog must have accompanied the Homeric hero, and in what contexts the Greek word *hippos* ("horse") must in fact refer to a mare and not a filly. This kind of knowledge is often acquired not through ancient evidence but by consultation with modern experts in a range of fields beyond the classics. When my students and I came to *The Iliad*'s account of a remarkable war wound, where both of Cebriones's eyes pop from his head to land at his feet, we wondered whether this was the anatomical impossibility that M. M. Willcock asserts it is. I asked Blakely, of course, who assured us the wound was realistic. It turned out that he had consulted an oculoplastic surgeon about all the epic's eye wounds. It is this careful concern to understanding the realities of the world Homer describes that lies at the heart of Blakely's translation. It lends the work a most compelling authenticity and is one of its greatest strengths.

This commitment to authenticity is compatible with the decision to translate the poetry of *The Iliad* into prose. As Blakely suggests in his preface, rendering the work in English verse risks distancing the reader still further from the original. English marches to the rhythm of the stress accent, obedient above all to the volume with which we pronounce certain syllables. This is so fundamental to our language that relocating the stress of a word can even alter its meaning and grammatical function. Compare, for example, the noun *PRO-duce* with the verb *pro-DUCE*. The meter of Homer's Greek, by contrast, depends not on the loudness of syllables but on how long they take to pronounce. Translating that verse into poetry for the English ear, then, is in large part a conversion of time into decibels, a curious alchemy that may produce a poem, but a poem enjoyed in a manner surely alien to the original experience.

Instead of falling to that distance, Blakely brings us *The Iliad* in the language and idiom he grew up with, in part because he finds compelling parallels between the epic's agrarian society and his native Deep South. Make no mistake. This represents a conscious decision to personalize his translation, a critical move that benefits the lucky reader and models the practice of making the work one's own. Blakely's authentic and noble prose complements the authenticity of detail that he seeks out and carries forward from the Greek original.

In my friendship with Ralph Blakely, I have witnessed firsthand his intimacy with the poem. It has deepened and nuanced my own appreciation of Homer. Now, with this translation, Blakely invites his readers to cultivate a like intimacy with the work, a relationship of profound reward that will serve for years to come.

KEYNE CHESHIRE
Associate Professor and Chair of Classics
Davidson College

PREFACE

Soon after Alexander the Great died in Babylon in 323 BC, the Egyptian morticians who traveled with his expedition began their work. At the same time, goldsmiths began work on the coffin that was to contain the mummy. There seemed never to have been doubt that anything other than gold would have been proper for that remarkable man. A gigantic rolling catafalque was constructed to carry the coffin and its mummy across Asia back to Pella in Macedon. Placed beside the golden coffin was a smaller bejeweled casket, also of gold, containing Alexander's copy of Homer's *Iliad*, which he read from daily as his court progressed from Thrace across Asia to the Indian subcontinent and back to Babylon. It was the most valuable book of the ancient world, with critical comments in its margins written in the hand of Aristotle himself, who had presented it to his royal pupil.

Many teams of mules pulled the catafalque with its heavy burden along a way smoothed by hundreds of laborers, as the bells and cymbals attached to its frame jangled. Alexander's general Ptolemy hijacked the procession in Syria and led it to Alexandria in Egypt, the part of Alexander's empire Ptolemy claimed for himself. The golden coffin was placed in a great square in the city. Next to it, Ptolemy's son and successor built the famous library and installed Aristophanes of Byzantium as librarian, with the task of continuing the textual criticism of *The Iliad* begun by Aristotle. He was followed by a succession of scholars, Aristarchus of Samothrace, a pupil of Aristophanes, the most prominent of them. A competing library was later built in Pergamum. From both places text made their way to what eventually became Constantinople, and from there the text was passed along so that it comes to us with hardly any changes from about 200 BC, the most carefully preserved text from the ancient world.

Since the late eighteenth century there has been some debate over whether there really was someone named Homer, and whether the poem was the work of one person or a compilation of the works of many. The reader interested in learning current scholarly thinking about the war in the poem and the people involved in it should consult Eric H. Cline's excellent little book *The Trojan War: A Very Short Introduction*, Oxford 2013. After having spent much time with the work, I offer that it seems too consistent and too carefully crafted to have been a compilation. There is in some a grudging refusal to accept that there might be one among us who, as Cassius says in *Julius Caesar*:

"doth bestride the narrow world
  Like a Colossus, and we petty men
  Walk under his huge legs and peep about
  To find ourselves dishonorable graves."

I worked from the critical text of Thomas W. Allen published at Oxford in 1931, and reprinted by Sandpiper in 2000, so that I might be aware as I proceeded of the variants in the oldest copies of the text and papyrus fragments that are older still. Now thought by most scholars to have been written around 725 BC, *The Iliad* is still a gripping tale, and I have attempted to be very respectful of the text while moving the tale from Greek into English.

I am a native speaker of American English as spoken in the Deep South by the likes of William Faulkner, Robert Penn Warren, Eudora Welty, and Walker Percy. It is rich in imagery as they used it, and I have tried to convey Homer's imagery in that English, both the small images and the extended similes. There are aspects of the poem that can be translated and others that cannot. Greek is an inflected language, which is to say that nouns have stems to which are added endings or inflections that signify number and case, while verb stems have both inflections and prefixes called augments that signify number, voice, tense, and mood. Thus the poet had great flexibility of word order that allowed metrical considerations to be more important than English allows. For instance, a relative pronoun may be distanced from its antecedent by six or eight lines and yet be clearly understood because of its number and case. In English, such an orphaned pronoun would make no sense.

I have chosen prose to convey both the tale and the images into English, because verse translation seems a contrivance that further distances the English reader from the poem. It is for the reader to judge whether I have succeeded in conveying some of the grandeur and sweep of the text, as I have tried to do.

The nouns *Ilium* and *Troy* are used in the poem to designate the city of Priam. Some say that one means the lower city while the other the upper. I cannot find a clear distinction. For this reason and also because I have never heard anyone, academic or layperson, refer to the city in conversation as anything other than *Troy*, I use only *Troy*. However, there is a character central to the tale who has two names—Paris and Alexander. Additionally, he is called Parius and Dysparis. The first is a diminutive inflection conveying the idea that the person named is insignificant. The latter has the derogative prefix *dys-* conveying the contempt the Trojans felt for Paris. In the places where he is called Alexander, he behaves with greater dignity and valor, and for this reason I use both names. Eric Cline explains that the character in *The Iliad* is the conflation of two earlier separate myths about Paris and Alexander, while Troy similarly references two of the progeny of Dardanus, the founding ruler of the city—Tros and Ilus.

The epithets in epic poetry may be stumbling blocks for first-time readers. They must be translated the same way every time they appear. Often the poet's choice of epithet seems to have been made for the purpose of metrical scan and in some of those cases the meaning is jarringly inconsistent with the circumstances that surround the noun. I have omitted some of those.

There are some tautologies and pleonasm in the poem that I have omitted. They were certainly useful to the performers, or rhapsodists as they were called, who sang the poem in ancient times. Then the repetition reinforced certain things for the audience, but it now seems tedious to a modern reader.

Greek has a patronymic suffix to indicate the father (or sometimes mother) of a human or god. Homer uses those often. I translated them into English using patronymics familiar to us all: Thompson, Williamson, Wilson, Anderson, and the like. Where Homer uses *son of*. . . I have translated it literally.

To avoid using notes in certain places that require more information for a modern reader to understand the meaning, I have occasionally added expository material to the sentence to more fully explain, as in the following examples: V, 845, helmet of Hades *that makes its wearer invisible*; VI, 152, Ephyra, *or Corinth*, on a gulf *of the Ionian Sea*; VI, 403, *King of the City* following Astyanax as translation; VI, 428, with the sweet arrows *of a heart attack* to explain the metaphor; VIII, 306–7, Like an *opium* poppy in a field of grain *that bloomed in the fall and swelled with seeds in winter,* has its *seed* head bent over, when it is weighed down *on its slender stem* by a heavy spring dew; XIX, 72–73, But, I think some of them will welcome the chance to bend their knees, *as animals do when resting,* especially ones who might escape from the furious warring under my spear; XXIII, 684, well-made cords of the hides of oxen that live in the fields, *to be wrapped around the fists and so increase the damage inflicted by them.*

Lines VIII, 548 and 550–552 are missing from the text in all copies and fragments. Plato quotes them in *Alcibiades* ii,149D. They seem authentic, and as is custom, I have included them because the sense of the rendering is improved. X, 458–461 are likewise missing. Plutarch quotes them in *Moralia* 26F and they are included because they are essential to the sense of the rendering. On the other hand, XI, 543 is missing from all copies of the text, and I have not included it because it is incongruous. Plutarch quotes it in *Moralia*, and it could be translated thus: "Zeus was incensed at Hector because he would not fight against a better man."

Places mentioned in the poem that are now archeological sites identified on maps of the National Geographic Society and the *Oxford Atlas of the World* are given those authorities' spellings rather than transliterations of names in the text; for instance *Lyttus*, instead of *Lyctus*, II, 647.

Most of what is necessary to understand the story is contained in it. I offer just a few comments in explanation. The ancients recognized a relationship that is herein called *guest-friend*. When a man of noble rank traveled to the land of another of similar rank in a peaceful way, he was given lodging and entertainment in as grand a manner as the host could muster, often for weeks at a time. At parting, the two nobles exchanged gifts and made pledges of mutual amity that were binding on them and their offspring for generations to come. This relationship is described in Book III, 354.

The poet frequently uses the term *winged words*. I have read various explanations for this, but remain unconvinced about the meaning. I simply cannot figure from context just how words with wings differ from those without. So I have brought the term into English in the places where it occurs and will leave it to the reader to vex this puzzle.

Some mention should be made of arms and tactics, though there are many sources for more detailed information. The principal offensive weapon was the spear, and it was wielded from a chariot drawn by two or more horses. The shaft of the spear was made of ash, since its wood may be scraped and polished without throwing splinters the way wood from many species of trees does. It is thus easily handled. Tool handles are still fashioned of it for the same reason. The tip of the spear was fashioned of bronze and the spearhead held in place by a ferrule of soft metal, sometimes gold, which Homer delights in describing.

Armor choices then and now involved concern for mobility. The more protection offered, the less easily its wearer could move about. The spearmen and charioteers wore breastplates with girdles underneath and an apron over the genitals below that. All those parts had bronze plates fitted in front of brightly colored textile webbing. The shins were covered with greaves of tin, with ankle plates of silver hinged from them. Most warriors wore a helmet with cheek-pieces and a horsehair crest from which a plume nodded when the wearer's head moved. Archers, slingers, and the like wore little or no armor since they could not function while wearing it. Some heroes, like Oïlean Aias (II, 529), wore light, linen armor because their speed at running was their special skill. There are two types of shields described: a long one that covered most of the body and a smaller buckler. They were of laminated ox hide overlaid with bronze and were used offensively as well as defensively. There are elaborate descriptions of them found throughout the poem. All armor was intended to protect a warrior advancing. It offered no protection for anyone in retreat.

The chariot of the Bronze Age was a rickety affair. Its frame consisted of a single axle for two wheels joined to a pole. The free end of the pole was attached to the yoke for the horses. There was no suspension; the charioteer and spearman stood on the axle. Two types of enclosures are described in the poem as mounted on the axle. The one used in combat was framed of bent wood with a rail to grab and pegs to which the reins could be tied. Two of the chariots used for the race in the Patroclus games had wicker enclosures (XXIII, 335 and 436), likely for saving weight and increasing speed. Both types of chariots had bronze escutcheons applied to their fronts. Without any doubt it took no small amount of skill to drive one of them, let alone to accurately aim and cast a spear from a chariot while dodging slings and arrows the whole while.

Homer was a keen observer of the natural world. When I first began this project, I did not understand just how accurate he truly was. I was confounded by the frequent contrasting of the bountiful earth with the barren or sterile sea. The ocean off the coast of Charleston where I live is a veritable soup of life, with single-cell plants and animals up to whales and everything in between. I went repeatedly to the lexicon, thinking that somehow *atrygetus* had to have another meaning, but it doesn't. I found I wasn't the only person to have trouble with this. A. T. Murray and other translators fudged it to make it work. Further, Homer describes clouds descending onto mountaintops and pouring down the sides to settle in the hollows formed by the ribs or ridging. I'd seen clouds hover around peaks in the Appalachians, the Alps, the Pyrenees, the Andes, and other ranges, but I'd not seen what he describes. I decided a visit to Troy was necessary and went to see for myself. Troy is, as Homer says, windy. And apparently the wind is responsible for both the descriptions I couldn't understand. The water of the eastern Aegean has such a high saline content that there is no life to be seen in it; one can see down through it more than a hundred feet. The water is so salty I could float in it, standing upright with only the buoyancy provided by my extended arms. Clouds there do descend onto mountain peaks and appear to pour down the sides into hollows.

With the help of quite a number of experts in specialized areas, I verified that all the behaviors and phenomena in the natural world Homer describes are remarkably accurate. It was his special genius to create a parallel supernatural world of immortal beings whose interactions and behaviors explained with precision the natural world he saw.

It has been offered by many in the recent past that his representation of reality was somehow skewed, or even that his brain was not a fully developed modern brain. But I have not found either notion credible after examining the poem very closely. None of the characters is without flaws, not mortal, nor immortal. But then, how does that differ from reality?

The purpose of the great enterprise led by Agamemnon against Troy is explained from the mortal point of view as vengeance for an egregious violation of the guest-friend custom by Paris, while from the immortal point of view it is Paris's judgment on Mount Ida that Argive Helen was fairer than the two goddesses Hera and Athena. Either explanation seems a weak reed to support an invasion and siege of ten years. Paris is a strikingly modern character. He is seductive, charming, and remorseless. He does whatever the spirit of the moment moves him to do. In our world he would be said to be a psychopath. The historian James Westfall Thompson noted that after the Venetian entry into the Fourth Crusade in AD 1202, when the undertaking is viewed stripped of its piety, one sees the sordid atmosphere of modern imperialism. Scattered through *The Iliad* are references to another explanation for the expedition and siege of Troy, beginning with the description of Tlepolemus's remarkable good luck colonizing Rhodes in II, 667–70. References to the treasures of Priam and the evidence of the Acheans' developing tastes for oriental luxury goods, like silverware and carpets and other fine textiles, occur throughout the poem. I think that if one strips the tale of its piety, one would see the two purposes as pretexts for colonizing the Aegean coast because of its rich soil and trade with the East. The Hellenic Peninsula is covered with a thin layer of rocky soil. The beautiful buildings we admire in Athens and Delphi were paid for with profits from trade, especially with the colonies that were settled, not long after *The Iliad* was written, on the Aegean coast with its rich soil and mild climate.

It might be said that Professor Thompson was in error only in suggesting that there is a difference between old imperialism and the modern version. After all, one can find no better poster boy for imperialism than Alexander the Great. Perhaps it is part of our makeup. A penchant for war surely seems to be a part of us, and *The Iliad* is about war. Homer spares nothing in conveying the horror and violence of war, in his day the same as in our own. Each of the heroes is seized at some point with fear, and each learns that the root of fear is the fear of dying. That, too, has not changed from Homer's day to ours. The heroes arrive at the realization that courage is not the absence of fear, but persevering by relying on skill and training after facing that they will all die, but just when is not theirs to know.

In Homer's work we see ourselves and people we have known. His descriptions are lively and the problems his characters faced three thousand years ago remain problems still. And that is why we still read his work. There are lessons to be learned from it that we may use in our own time.

I have sought help from many people during this project and have been touched that not one refused my request. Some have been especially generous. My editors, Harriet McDougal, Miriam Weinberg, and Kelly Quinn, have been constantly patient in guiding me along. I am most grateful to two distinguished classicists, Professor Keyne Cheshire of Davidson College and Professor Robin Rhodes of the University of Notre Dame, for their comments and suggestions. I have been for Professor Cheshire like an unexpected and perhaps unwanted graduate student, though he has been too gracious to complain. I would also thank Professor Scott Denham of Davidson who, along with Professor Cheshire, invited me to be part of a course they taught together. I am grateful to Professor Mary B. Speer of Rutgers University for her help in setting up the editorial criteria and format for translation. She has been most indulgent with her brattish younger brother. Professor Stephen Price of Old Dominion University shared his great knowledge of the neural systems of reptiles with me. Dr. Layton McCurdy shared his considerable psychiatric knowledge. Professor Emeritus

George W. Williams of Duke University alerted me to the publication of Eric H. Cline's handy little introduction. Elizabeth Santen helped me by sharing what she had learned from a lifetime lived around horses. James A. McAlister, Jr., descended from a family that has handled the dead for many generations, shared his knowledge of practice and vocabulary specific to that work. I owe debts to some who are no longer seen among those who walk on the earth. John Alexander McGheachy, Jr., taught me how to learn to read Greek by using the wonderful little green books of the Loeb Classical Library, along with the indexes of the grammar and the lexicon. That opened the door for me to the treasure trove of work written in that language. I also owe a debt to one I never met, John Pickering, who compiled the lexicon that passed down to me more than forty years ago after it had been passed down through many hands since it was published in 1846. Mr. Pickering was, like me, an amateur in Greek studies. He did it for love. Unlike me, he was twice offered professorships at Harvard that he twice refused, staying in his position as a solicitor in Boston. He put a great deal of himself into his entries, so that I have come to feel that I know and like him, and share his passion for Homer. Perhaps because as solicitor he had seen just about everything, his work is devoid of the priggishness and prudery that sometimes mars the work of classicists. He has been a good companion for a long time.

CAST OF CHARACTERS

References are to the most detailed descriptions of the characters in the text.

Salamis

Aias Telamonson, King of Salamis, VII, 206–95. When Aias
Oïleusson and Aias Telamonson are together they are re-
ferred to as Aiantes, the Greek double.

Teucer Telamonson, Half-brother of Aias, best archer of the
Acheans, VIII, 265–99

Argos and Tiryns

Diomedes Tydeusson, Commander IX, 31-41

Sthenelus Capaneusson, Close friend of Diomedes

Sparta

Menelaus Atreusson, King of Sparta, brother of Agamemnon,
husband of Argive Helen, VII, 127–53

Ithaca and Cephalonia

Odysseus Laertesson, King of Ithaca, III, 214–24. Odysseus and
Copreus are two characters who are called by nicknames, as
the *-eus* suffix means *man of—*. In Odysseus's case, the meaning is man of anger, suggesting that his countenance was
stern and forbidding. For Copreus, Homer reserved a special
odium for some unspecified calumny toward Heracles, since
coprus means "excrement."

Eurybates, Herald to Odysseus

Crete

Idomeneus Deucalionson, King of Crete, IV, 257–64. It is possible that Idomeneus is also a nickname for one with particularly keen sight. If so, it adds the element of a pun to the spat
between Idomeneus and Oïlean Aias in XXIII, 475–88, something not at all out of character for the poem.

Meriones Molusson, Half-brother of Idomeneus

Phylace

Protesilaus, King of Phylace

Podarces Iphiclusson, Chosen successor to Protesilaus, II 698–710

Tricia and Eurytus in Oechalia
Asclepius, Healer
Podaleirius Asclepiusson, Commander skilled in healing
Machaon Asclepiusson, Commander skilled in healing

THE TROJANS AND THEIR ALLIES

Troy
Priam Dardanusson, King of Troy, XXIV, 631–33
Idaeus, Herald to Priam
Sons of Priam:
> **Hector,** VI, 390–496
> **Paris,** Husband of Argive Helen, also called Alexander
> **Deïphobus**
> **Helenus**
> **Polydorus**
> **Lycaon,** and others

Dardanians
Aeneas Anchisesson, II, 820–23
Archelochus Antenorson
Acamas Antenorson

Those from Lycia, on the southernmost part of the eastern Aegean coast from the Dalaman River southward
Other than the strange tombs they carved into the hillsides, nothing is known of the Lycians, other than what Homer tells.
Sarpedon, Son of Zeus, XII, 378–96
Glaucus, VI, 119–236

THE ROYAL HOUSE OF CALYDON
(simplified)

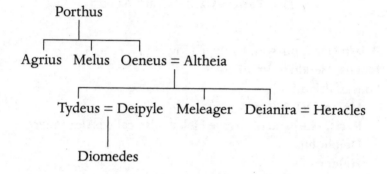

Porthus
├── Agrius   Melus   Oeneus = Altheia
                       ├── Tydeus = Deipyle   Meleager   Deianira = Heracles
                             │
                           Diomedes

Thoas Andraemonson

= indicates marriage

The Royal House of the Myrmidons
at Phthia, Thessaly
(simplified)

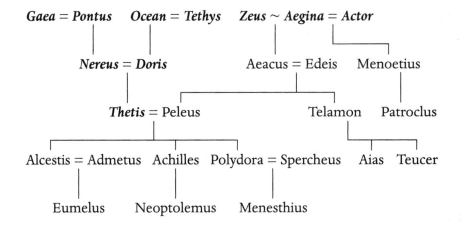

Bold Italic: names of Immortals
= indicates marriage
~ indicates liaison

THE ROYAL HOUSE OF TROY
(simplified)

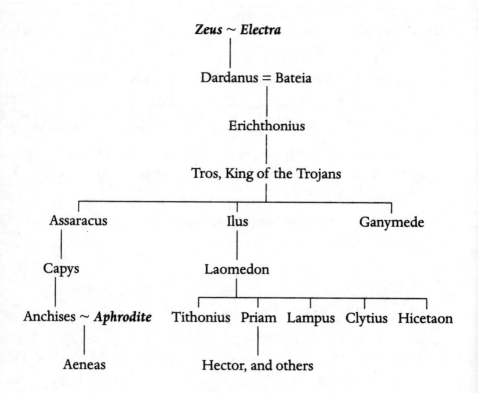

Zeus ~ Electra
|
Dardanus = Bateia
|
Erichthonius
|
Tros, King of the Trojans
|
Assaracus   Ilus   Ganymede
|
Capys   Laomedon
|
Anchises ~ Aphrodite   Tithonius Priam Lampus Clytius Hicetaon
| |
Aeneas   Hector, and others

Bold Italic: names of Immortals
= indicates marriage
~ indicates liaison

THE ROYAL HOUSE OF THE LYCIANS
(simplified)

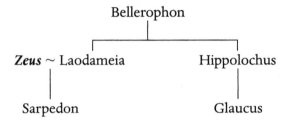

Bellerophon

Zeus ~ Laodameia   Hippolochus

Sarpedon   Glaucus

Bold Italic: names of Immortals
~ indicates liaison

The Immortals
(simplified)

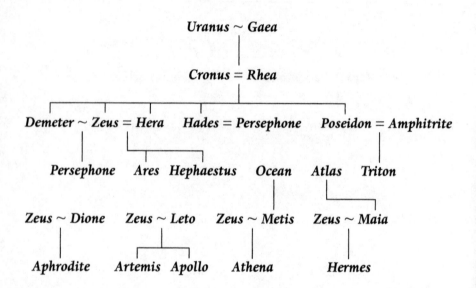

THE
ILIAD

Book 1

Sing, goddess, of the wrath of Achilles Peleusson, the ruinous wrath that brought immense pain to the Acheans and propelled many valiant souls of heroes down to Hades, and made them pickings for dogs and birds of all kinds, that the plan of Zeus might be brought to completion. Tell why they were first separated in quarreling, the son of Atreus, the Supreme Commander—Agamemnon—and noble Achilles. 8

And which one of the gods brought them together to fight in a quarrel? It was the son of Leto and Zeus; he grew angry with the king and raised up a terrible plague upon the camp, and the troops perished. This he did because the son of Atreus dishonored Chryses, Apollo's priest. 10

Chryses came to the swift ships seeking the release of his daughter, and brought with him a priceless ransom. He held in his hands the wreath from the head of far-shooting Apollo, mounted atop a golden staff. And Chryses pleaded with all of the Acheans, most especially with the two sons of Atreus, Marshals of Troops:

"Sons of Atreus, and others of you well-armed Acheans, the gods who dwell in palaces on Olympus might permit you to sack the city of Priam and to return home safely, but you should release to me my dear daughter and receive the ransom. In so doing, you would show reverence for Apollo, the far-shooting son of Zeus." 21

At that, all of the rest of the Acheans applauded the proposal both to pay reverence to things sacred and to receive the magnificent ransom. But this did not please the heart of Agamemnon Atreusson, who profanely dismissed the priest with a harsh command:

"Do not let me find you among the hollow ships, old man,

hanging around now, or coming back in the future. The staff and wreath of the god will not protect you. I will not free your daughter until she grows old in our house in Argos, far from her homeland, weaving at her loom and keeping me company in my bed. Get lost! Do not cross me, if you want to get back home safely!"   32

So Agamemnon spoke, and the old man grew fearful, and he obeyed the order. He walked silently along the splashing waves on the beach. When he had gone far off, the old man prayed:

"Lord Apollo, child of fair-haired Leto, hear me, silver bow! It is you who have defended Chryse and sacred Cilla and you who rule mightily in Tenedos. If ever I pleased you who rid Sminthia of rats, when I roofed your shrine, or if ever I burned fat thighs of bulls or goats, fulfill my wish, I implore you. Avenge my tears with your arrows on the Danaans!"   42

So he spoke in prayer, and Phoebus Apollo heard him, and bounded down from the peaks of Olympus with a furiously raging heart. The god had his bow about his shoulders, and his covered quiver. The arrows within rattled as his shoulders shook with anger. His going was like the night.   47

Then Apollo sat down afar off from the ships and dispatched an arrow among them. Dreadful was the twang that came from the silver bow. The mules were the first to drop, and the swift dogs. Then others were hit by the deadly darts he fired off. Constant were the dense fires burning the corpses of those he took down.   52

For nine days the shafts of the god rained upon the camp, and on the tenth, Achilles called for an assembly of the troops. The white-armed goddess Hera placed the idea in his mind, as she was concerned for the Danaans when she saw so many of them dying.   57

And when the assembly was convened, fleet-footed Achilles stood up and addressed them, saying, "Son of Atreus, I think that now we should retrace our steps and return home, if indeed we plan to escape death, for surely both war and plague beat down the Acheans at the same time. But, come now, let us ask of some diviner, or priest, or interpreter of dreams, for a dream is certainly from Zeus, what he might say as to why Phoebus Apollo is so angry. Perhaps there was some error in prayer or in offerings and we might somehow, with smoke of rams or of goats, find a plan to save us from destruction."   67

So, you may be sure, he spoke and then sat down. Calchas Thestorson stood from among them. He was, by far, the best at divining meaning from the behavior of birds; he could tell the things that were, and those that are, and those that are to come. He guided the ships of the Acheans to Troy, using the gift of prophecy that Phoebus Apollo had given him. With a sound mind, he addressed them, saying, "Oh Achilles, dear to Zeus, you tell me to explain the wrath of the far-shooting Lord Apollo. I ask of you directly that you swear to me that you will readily back me up with words and hands if I speak frankly. I think that a man will be very angry, a man who is great in power over all of the Acheans. He is a mightier king when he is angry at a lesser man. Even if he chokes down his anger today, in the future he will retain the fury. In the end it will surface as it would remain in his heart. You must declare that you will save me if that happens."   83

Fleet-footed Achilles spoke in reply to him.

"Take great courage and tell what you know of the prophecy. By Apollo, dear to Zeus, to whom you pray and who reveals prophesies to you, Calchas, I swear that as long as I live and look about on the earth, none at all of the Acheans will put his heavy hands on you near the hollow ships, not even Agamemnon who would likely be the one you're talking about. He now claims to be the best by far of the Acheans."   91

At that, the exceptional diviner took heart and spoke out.

"The god is not unhappy because of errors made in prayers or sacrifices to him, but rather because Agamemnon dishonored Apollo's priest, and did not accept the ransom or release his daughter. On account of that, the far-shooting god delivered misery and still continues to do so. He will not put off the constant suffering from the Acheans until they give back the bright-eyed daughter to her dear father, without ransom or compensation. She must be led back to Chryse accompanied by a sacred offering. Only then, having obeyed him, will we appease him." 100

You may be sure that having spoken thus, he sat down. Up among them stood the hero Agamemnon Atreusson, the eminent prince. He was furious; a black rage filled his heart. His eyes were like a blazing fire. Looking first of all at Calchas, he growled, "You prophet of evils, what you have said does not please me at all. Your heart's delight is to constantly preach evil. You never say anything worthwhile, nor do you accomplish anything. And now among the Danaans, you talk about a prophecy that the far-shooting one has brought them suffering because I did not wish to accept the magnificent ransom for the daughter of Chryses. This, because I very much want to take her back home and I intend to, since she is inferior to my lawful wife Clytemnestra neither in her body nor her face. Nor is she inferior in her spirit, nor her skill. However, even so, I wish to give her back if it is better to do that. I definitely prefer that the troops remain safe than perish. But I must procure for myself a prize immediately, or I would be the only one of the Acheans without one. That would not be seemly. Look around, all of you, and see that the prize comes to me from another source." 120

The noble, fleet-footed Achilles replied to him.

"Most glorious son of Atreus, you are the greediest man alive! How could the greathearted Acheans give you a prize? We don't know of anything at all lying around that is common property. The things from the cities we sacked have been divided. It would not be just for the troops to gather everything together a second time. You must send your prize back to the god. Later, we Acheans will allot to you three or four times as much of

the spoils if Zeus grants us the plunder of the well-fortified city
that Troy is."   129

Prince Agamemnon responded to Achilles, saying, "Godlike
Achilles, brave as you are, in this you rob your mind of sense.
You will neither surpass me nor will you persuade me. You want
to keep a prize for yourself while I, on the other hand, would
sit without one. Are you asking me to return the girl? Then let
the robust Acheans give me a prize that suits me and right the
inequality. If they do not, I myself am going to choose your
prize, or that of Aias, or of Odysseus. Having seized it, I shall
carry it away. The man I come to will be furious. But Achilles,
you be sure to give these matters some thought and we will get
back to them. But now come, let us pull a black ship to the glistening sea, and muster a sufficient number of rowers in it, and
put in the offering. And we will go up with the pretty-cheeked
daughter of Chryses herself. And there should be a captain for
it, a man of sound judgment, either Aias, or Idomeneus or noble
Odysseus, or perhaps you, Peleusson, most magnificent of men.
These things we should do so that the one who works from
far off will be appeased by our pious rites."   147

Scowling, fleet-flooted Achilles spoke up to him once more.

"Oh, damn! How shameless, how disgraced, you are! You're
in this for your own gain. How would any of the Acheans who
is sound of mind obey your commands, be it setting up an ambush or fighting strenuously against men? Certainly, I didn't
come here because Trojan warriors were making war against
me, since there are no reasons for that. They have not been
driving off my cattle, nor my horses. Never have they eaten my
grain in rich-soiled Phthia, sustainer of men, since it is far from
here, between the hazy mountains and the crashing sea. Instead,
O great, shameless one, I followed you in front of the Trojans
to please you, to restore the honor of Menelaus, you dog! For
the Trojans, you have no apparent regard and don't care.   160

"You even threaten that you yourself will seize my prize that
the sons of the Acheans gave me for my hard work. Whenever

the Acheans may sack the teeming city of the Trojans, I will not have a prize equal to yours, even though my hands have directed more of the dreadful fight. Whenever the division comes, your prize will be far superior. I will go with a trifle in my ships, but something I care about, since I am tired of war. Now I shall go to Phthia, since it would be much better that I return home with my beaked ships. I don't intend to stay here to pile up wealth and riches for you without honor." 171

The Supreme Commander Agamemnon answered him, "Run away if your heart is so determined. I will not beg you to stay because of me. There are others who will stay beside me; they revere me, especially Zeus, the counselor. To me you are the most obnoxious of the highborn kings of the Acheans. Your love is for constant conflict, wars, and fighting. If you are so powerful, maybe it is because some god gave you that gift. Order your Myrmidon comrades to go home with your ships. I don't care about you, and your anger does not bother me. 181

"I will command you at your peril thus: since Phoebus Apollo is taking away from me the daughter of Chryses, I shall send her with my ship and my comrades. But, I shall go to your hut and I myself will lead away sweet-cheeked Briseis, your prize, so that you will know that I am more powerful than you. Also, so that any other man would be loath to claim that he is my equal and compare himself to me in front of my face." 187

So Agamemnon spoke. Grief rose up in the son of Peleus. Within the heart inside his hairy chest, his thoughts ranged back and forth considering his dilemma: would he draw the sharp sword hanging on his thigh and slay Agamemnon as he stood among them, or would he check his spirit and curb his anger? He pulled the great sword from its scabbard. Athena came down from the sky; she came on behalf of white-armed Hera. Both of them loved and cared for Achilles equally. She stood behind him and grabbed his orange-red hair. He was aware of her, but none of the others saw her. 197

Achilles was astonished and turned toward her. Instantly, he recognized Pallas Athena, so terribly did her eyes flash. And he spoke to her with winged words, saying, "Why have you who bears the aegis come here, child of Zeus? Is it so that you might see for yourself the arrogance of Agamemnon Atreusson? But I ask you how it will come out, though I think he will soon perish for his insolence."   205

And the sharp-eyed goddess spoke to him.

"I came from the sky to rein in your ardor, if you listen. I came on behalf of white-armed Hera. We both love and care for you equally. But, come, leave off the fighting. Don't raise the sword in your hand. Instead, heap abuse on Agamemnon with words, for that is how it ought to be. I declare to you this is how it will come to pass. And, at some time he will place before you magnificent gifts, threefold as much as this. Hold off, and obey us."   215

Fleet-footed Achilles said to her, "I should be restrained by your command, goddess, and especially so since I am very angry at heart, for it is better this way." He held the silver hilt in his brawny hand and quickly shoved the great sword into its scabbard, in obedience to Athena. But she had already gone to Olympus, and the palace of Zeus who bears the aegis, to be among the other deities.   222

Immediately, the son of Peleus spoke up to the son of Atreus with scathing words, as he had not at all lessened his rage.

"Drunkard, you with the face of a dog and heart of a deer, you never put on armor with the troops for war, nor lie out in ambush with the best of the Acheans. You've not endured suffering in your spirit. This you know in your heart. There is one far braver in the wide army of the Acheans—me—who speaks out to your face, for seizing the gift. You are a king who ravages his own people. You rule over weaklings. And now, son of Atreus, you would stoop to something so low.   232

"But I declare that on account of you I shall swear a great oath. Yes, I swear by this staff that will never sprout any leaves and branches left in the mountains when it was first cut. Now,

the sons of the Acheans bear it in their fists for the administra-
tion of justice, those raised up in front of Zeus who presides
over justice. On it there will be a great oath, on your account,
Agamemnon. At some time a longing for Achilles will come to
all the sons of the Acheans. They will be unable to ward off
great grief, when many have fallen, struck by man-killing Hector. You will claw at your heart in regret that you failed to show
respect to the best of the Acheans." Having so spoken, the son
of Peleus thrust the staff, mounted with gold devices, down to
the ground and sat himself down. Opposite him the son of
Atreus seethed with anger.   247

And among them rose up Nestor, lucid and eloquent orator
from Pylos. His voice flowed from his tongue sweeter than
honey. Two generations of mortal men had been born and
raised by him before, and then perished in sacred Pylos. He
ruled now over the third.

With careful thought, he addressed them, saying, "Oh blast!
What great misery visits on the land of the sons of the Acheans! Ah, yes, Priam and the sons of Priam will be gleeful, and
the other Trojans will have great joy in their hearts, if they
learn that you two are squabbling over all this, you who outstrip all of the Danaans at counsel and at fighting.   258

"Instead, trust me. Both of you are younger than I am. When
I joined others who were better than you in warring against
men, I was never looked down on. Never have I seen men such
as there were then nor shall I see them in the future. Such men
as were Peirithous and Dryas, Shepherds of the Troops. There
were Caeneus, and Exadius, and godlike Polyphemus. And
there was Theseus Aegeusson, equal of the immortals. Such
were the mightiest of the men brought up on all the earth; they
fought the exceedingly powerful Centaurs who dwell in the
mountains. Those men brought upon the Centaurs the most
terrible destruction.   268

"I went from Pylos to muster with them. Theirs was a far-
distant land, a long way off from Pylos, but they singled me out

to call on me. And I fought by myself. There are not now men on earth who could do battle with the Centaurs as they did.   272

"But they listened to my counsels and were persuaded by my words. Even you should obey, since obedience is more worthy. Agamemnon, you should not take away the girl, though you are brave, as she was given as a prize by the sons of the Acheans. Nor should you, son of Peleus, wish to quarrel against a king, because that shows a lack of respect for the sceptered king whose rank Zeus gave. If you are braver than he, perhaps it is because your goddess mother bore you thus. Yet, Agamemnon is more powerful than you because he rules over more men. Son of Atreus, stop this power struggle! I beg you to end your anger against the son of Peleus, who has been a bulwark for the Acheans in battle!"   281

Mighty Agamemnon replied to him, "Yes, old man, all the things you said are proper, but this man here wants to be greater than anybody else. He wants to be more powerful than everybody, to rule them all and give them orders. I do not think he will obey your words. If the eternal gods made him a warrior, did they, for that reason, put inside him this hateful speech?"   291

Interrupting, noble Achilles said to him, "I would be called cowardly and even worthless were I to submit to you in everything as you say. Order around the others that way, but you do not direct me. I don't think I am yet ready to obey you. But I will tell you something else, and you should fix it firmly in your mind. I shall not raise my hands to fight you over the girl, neither you nor anyone else who takes away what was given me. But no other things of mine that are among the swift black ships will you carry off, seized from me against my will. But come, try it and there men will know. If you do, your dark blood will at once gush out around a shaft."   303

Thus, the two men faced off battling with words. They dissolved the assembly of the Acheans. The son of Peleus went to the huts and the balanced ships with both the son of Menoetius and his other comrades.   307

The son of Atreus dragged a swift ship forth into the sea.
He chose twenty rowers for it and placed a sacrificial offering
for the god in it. He led up into the ship the sweet-cheeked
daughter of Chryses. And the ever-cunning Odysseus went as
captain.   311

And when they had sailed along their watery way, the son
of Atreus ordered the troops to purify themselves by washing.
That done, they cast the dirt they had removed into the sea.
They made sacrifices to Apollo, bulls and goats, beside the beach
of the barren sea. The smell of burning fat spiraled heavenward
in the smoke.   316

The troops worked at chores in the camp. But Agamemnon
had not put to rest the quarrel from when he first threatened
Achilles. He summoned both Talthybius and Eurybates. The
two were his heralds and capable attendants: "Go to the hut of
Achilles Peleusson. Take sweet-cheeked Briseis by the hand and
lead her away. If he does not give her up, then I will go there myself with more men to take her. And then it will be more chilling
for him."   325

Having laid on a stern order, he sent them off. Reluctantly,
the two men strode along the beach of the barren sea. They
came upon the huts and ships of the Myrmidons. They found
Achilles sitting beside both his hut and his black ship. Achilles
was not pleased at seeing the two men. They stood in fear and
respect for the king, neither saying anything, nor speaking. But
Achilles knew in his mind why they were there, and said, "Greet-
ings, heralds, messengers of Zeus and of men! Come closer.
You I do not blame, no one but Agamemnon. You two have been
sent because of the girl Briseis. Rather, come here, Patroclus,
born of Zeus, fetch the girl and give her to them to lead away.
They themselves are witnesses before both the blessed gods and
before mortal men, and also before him, this cruel king. If ever
again need arises for me to ward off limitless destruction from
others, Agamemnon may rage with destruction in his heart. He

knows nothing to consider then, in the past or in the future, about how the Acheans might fight safely beside the ships." 344

So he spoke, and Patroclus obeyed his dear friend. He led Briseis out of the hut and gave her over to the heralds to lead away. The two immediately went off along past the ships of the Acheans; the girl went with them reluctantly. Weeping, Achilles moved away off from his comrades and sat down on the beach of the gray sea. He gazed out over the limitless deep, and prayed earnestly to his dear mother with his arms outstretched.

"Mother, since you bore me for but a brief existence, loud-thundering Zeus, the Olympian, granted that my honor be increased on account of my life's brevity. But now he values me only a little. The eminent Prince Agamemnon insulted me when he seized my prize, taking her for himself." 356

So he spoke, eyes welling tears. His revered mother heard him; she was sitting in the depths of the sea beside her father, the Old Man of the Sea. Hurriedly, she rose up out of the gray waters like a vaporous mist. She sat down in front of him as his tears flowed down. She caressed him with her hand, addressed him by name, and said, "My child, why do you weep? What grief has come into your heart? Out with it! Keep nothing hidden in your mind from me."

Groaning deeply, fleet-footed Achilles said, "You know. Why is it that you know everything I tell you? We went to Thebes, the sacred city of Eetion. We sacked it and brought everything here. The sons of the Acheans carefully divided up the spoils among themselves. For the son of Atreus, they chose the sweet-cheeked daughter of Chryses. He is a priest of far-shooting Apollo. Chryses came to the ships of the brazen-shirted Acheans with a priceless ransom seeking the release of his daughter. He had in his hand the wreath from the head of far-shooting Apollo made of gold, mounted atop a scepter. 374

"He pled for her release before all of the Acheans, especially the two sons of Atreus, the Marshals of the Troops. All of the other Acheans there applauded, agreeing to venerate the priest and to receive the magnificent ransom. But that did not please the heart of Agamemnon Atreusson. He laid on Chryses a harsh command and cruelly sent him away. The old man went home angry. And he prayed to Apollo, who heard him, since the god loved Chryses dearly. Apollo sent an evil arrow onto the Argives. The troops died one after another; the shafts of the god fell everywhere in the widespread camp of the Acheans.   384

"A very knowledgeable seer told us that the troubles came from the far-shooting one. Immediately I proposed that we propitiate the god. The son of Atreus was seized by anger. Right away he stood up, saying sarcastically what would come to pass. The bright-eyed Acheans sent the daughter with a swift ship to Chryse, bearing gifts for the lord god. Then heralds took Briseis from my hut leading the girl away, when the sons of the Acheans had given her to me.   392

"If you are able to, defend a just son. Go to Olympus and plead with Zeus, reminding him that once, some deed of yours brought joy to his heart. Often, I heard you boast in your father's palace that you alone of the immortals warded off limitless misery from the son of Cronus, who darkens the clouds. When the other Olympians, Hera, Poseidon, and Pallas Athena, went to truss him up, you, goddess, went to break his bonds. You summoned to Olympus the hundred-handed god, who is called Briareus by the gods; all men know him as Aegaeon. His father Poseidon is no more powerful than he is. Briareus sat close beside the son of Cronus, taking pleasure in his power. The blessed gods were unable to bind Zeus because they were afraid of Briareus.   406

"Sit beside him now and clasp his knees, reminding him. Perhaps, in some way, he might wish to give aid to the Trojans. They could hem in the Acheans around the sterns of their ships, killing them near the sea, so that they could all enjoy the benefits of their king. Then would the eminent Prince Agamem-

non Atreusson know that he did not honor the best of the
Acheans at all, because of his blindness."   412

Eyes pouring with tears, Thetis answered him.

"Oh my dear child! Why then, having given birth to you
cursed, did I bring you up? I wish that you were sitting near the
ships, not weeping, and free from harm, since it is your destiny
to have a brief life. But now there are at the same time both a
bitter fate to come, and present misery beyond all imagining.
Thus it was for a baneful destiny that I bore you in our halls.
This request of Zeus, who delights in thunder, I shall make. I am
going myself to the cloud-gatherer on Olympus to find out if he
might be persuaded to grant it. Meanwhile, remain with the
ships, with your wrath for the Acheans, but refrain altogether
from fighting. Zeus left yesterday to go along Ocean to a feast
thrown by the exceptional Ethiopians. All the other gods followed along after him. But in twelve days he will go again to
Olympus. Then, I shall go the bronze floor of Zeus to make
your case, clasping his knees, and I think I will persuade him."
Having so spoken, she went away. She left Achilles fuming over
the buxom woman taken away from him against his will.   430

Meanwhile, Odysseus neared Chryse with the sacred offering. When they came into the deep-water harbor, they struck
the sail. They stowed it in the black ship. Quickly loosening the
stays, they lowered the mast to rest on the crutch. Then they
rowed the ship into its mooring. The sailors tied the anchor
stones securely to the stern and cast them out. And they stepped
off onto the rugged seashore. They unloaded the sacrificial animals for the sacred offering to Apollo and from the seagoing
ship, out went the daughter of Chryses.   439

Then the ever-cunning Odysseus led her to the altar, and
said, "Oh Chryses, the Supreme Commander Agamemnon
charged me to bring your child to you. I am to make holy sacrifices to Phoebus on behalf of the Danaans in propitiation to
that lord, who now sends much grievous suffering to the Argives."   445

Having so spoken, Odysseus gave her into her father's hands. Chryses joyfully received his beloved child. Quickly they led the sacrificial animals to stand near the well-built altar. They washed their hands and held up coarsely ground barley over the offering. Chryses made a great prayer for them with his arms outstretched.

"Hear me, silver bow, you who have protected Chryse and Cilla, and ruled powerfully in holy Tenedos. You have always listened to my prayers, and you honored me when you brought great affliction on the Achean troops. And even now, fulfill my wish! Spare the Danaans now from this horrible plague." 456

Thus he spoke in prayer and Phoebus Apollo heard him. Then, they prayed and sprinkled the course-ground barley over the victims. They turned the heads up and slit the throats. They flayed them and cut out pieces of thighs. They wrapped those in two layers of fat and placed raw pieces on the fat layers. The old man burned them over kindling and poured out a libation of dark wine. The youths beside him held out five-pronged spits. When they had burned the thighs completely, they tasted the entrails. 464

They butchered the rest, skewering the pieces on the spits. These they roasted with great care, pulling them all off when done. They dined, and the spirit wanted for nothing at the proper feast. When they had sent away their desire for drink and food, the youths turned their attention to the mixing bowl for drink and moved about from place to place, as all had begun the libations from cups. All day long the Achean youths propitiated the one who works from afar with dance, beautifully singing the hymns to Apollo. Hearing them was a delight to Apollo's mind. 474

After that the sun went down and twilight came. Then they laid themselves down to sleep beside the ship's stern cables. As soon as rose-fingered Dawn, born of the morning, appeared, they set sail for the wide camp of the Acheans. Far-shooting Apollo sent them a fair breeze. They raised up the mast and on it they stretched out a white sail and the wind bellied it out. A great dark-purple swelling of waves smacked loudly on both sides of the prow as the ship made way. She raced against the waves. 483

When they arrived at the wide camp of the Acheans, they dragged the black ship onto the dry land, and underneath propped the long stays. They themselves scattered to both ships and huts. 487

Fleet-footed Achilles Peleusson, born of Zeus, remained by his seagoing ships, with his wrath. He went neither to the assembly, where men win glory in drills for war, nor did he enter into the fighting. He was wasting away his own heart, and he was longing for both the war cries and the warring. 492

But when the sun rose on the twelfth day from this, the eternal gods all went together to Olympus, with Zeus leading the way. And Thetis did not forget the request of her son. In the early-morning mist, she rose up from the swelling waves of the sea, and went up to the great heavens and Olympus. She found the far-seeing son of Cronus sitting apart from the other gods on the tallest peak of craggy Olympus. She went over and sat down beside him. She clasped his knees with her left hand, and grasped under his chin with the right. She addressed the Lord Zeus Cronusson, pleading, "Father Zeus, if ever I was of benefit to you among the immortals at some time or by some deed, grant me this wish. Give honor to my son who carries the swiftest fate of death among all men. Recently, the Supreme Commander Agamemnon insulted him by arrogantly taking away for himself a prize that was my son's. Pray honor him, Olympian Zeus, counselor, in this way: give strength to the Trojans for a time until the Acheans value my son more highly and show him respect." 510

So she spoke. Zeus the cloud-gatherer made her no reply, but sat silently for a long time. Thetis sat clasping his knees, and as she clung more tightly to him, asked again.

"Promise me truthfully and lower your eyebrows in assent

or refuse me. Don't worry that I might learn just how much
I am held in the lowest esteem of all the gods."   516

Groaning loudly, Zeus the cloud-gatherer replied to her.

"What a pernicious deed this is. Surely it will precipitate
quarreling with Hera, when she abusively provokes me. She is
ever scolding me about things among the immortal gods, and
she claims that I help the Trojans in battle. But now you go back,
and so prevent Hera from knowing anything about it. I will
consider just how I might accomplish what you ask. But come
now, if you have persuaded me and I nod my head in assent, this
would be thought among the immortals the ultimate proof. I
do not change my mind, nor am I deceitful, nor leave a thing
unfulfilled that I nod my head to."   527

And the son of Cronus nodded with his bushy eyebrows, and
the ambrosial locks of the mighty lord swayed from the immortal head. It caused a temblor on great Olympus.

The two of them, having thus conspired, parted. Thetis then
went from shining Olympus to the farthest depths of the sea.
Zeus went toward his palace. All the other gods who had been
seated apart from him stood up from their seats at once. No one
dared remain seated as he walked along; all stood in greeting
as he sat down on his throne.

Hera was not unobservant when she saw him making plans
together with silver-footed Thetis, daughter of the Old Man of
the Sea. Immediately she viciously addressed Zeus Cronusson.

"Which one of the gods, O treacherous one, have you been
making plots with? You have always loved to keep such things
from me. You make decisions and hide your thoughts, and you
have never dared to speak your mind with me in a straightforward way."   543

The father of both men and gods then replied, "You ought
not to wish to know all my thoughts. Hard they would be for
you to know, though you are my wife. Such of my thoughts
as are suitable for you, you will hear and none of the gods and
no men will know before you. What I plan without consulting

gods you ought not inquire about or dig around for, searching
out every particular." 550

The revered and lovely-eyed Hera answered him.

"Most dreaded son of Cronus, what do you mean? I never in
the past have inquired or dug into anything. Rather, I advise on
matters very gently such as you might wish. But I am dreadfully
afraid that she has persuaded your mind, silver-footed Thetis,
daughter of the Old Man of the Sea. Early this morning she sat
beside you and clasped your knees. I think you nodded truthfully to her that you would grant honor to Achilles by destroying many of the Acheans beside the ships." 558

Zeus the cloud-gatherer answered.

"You miserable wretch, you're always conjecturing, but I
conceal nothing! You cannot do anything at all but distance
yourself from my heart, and it will be more chilling for you. If
it is thus, it seems to me acceptable. Obey my commands. As
many gods as there are on Olympus, they would be unable to
protect you if I were to put my hugely powerful hands on you." 567

So he spoke and lovely-eyed, revered Hera was fearful. She
sat quietly, gnawing at her own heart. Up in the palace of Zeus
the heavenly gods groaned. Of them the highly-skilled Hephaestus was first to speak, trying to humor his dear mother, white-
armed Hera. "This will be toxic business and certainly it will
no longer be tolerable if you two fight like this about mortals.
You two are inciting a noisy brawl among the gods. Our excellent feast will not be pleasant, since evil will win. I advise my
mother, and you know it yourself, to do pleasant things for dear
father Zeus, lest our father again become angry at her and turn
our feast into a feud. If he so wishes, he will cast us out of our
seats on starry Olympus, for he is by far the most powerful.
Rather, wheedle him, and then the Olympian will soon be gentle
with us." 583

So he spoke. He raised a two-handled cup and placed it in
the hands of his dear mother and said to her, "Take courage, my
mother. Bear up under the stress, so that I do not see you whom

I love thrashed before my eyes. Then I could do nothing to ward off your suffering. It is difficult to stand against the Olympian, as at another time I was eager to come to your aid, when he took me by the foot and hurled me from the sacred threshold. I was falling the whole day. When the sun set, I had been thrown to Lemnos. I had hardly any life left in me. There the men of Sintia cared for me after my fall."   594

Thus he spoke, and white-armed Hera smiled, and continued smiling as she received the two-handled cup from her son. He handily poured out wine, the sweet nectar, for all the other gods from the mixing bowl. There rose up unquenchable laughter among the blessed gods as they watched Hephaestus bustling about in the palace.   600

For the whole day until the sun set they feasted. Their spirits wanted for nothing at the sumptuous banquet. Nor was anything wanting from the beautiful lyre of Apollo who sang in response to the Muses with his beautiful voice.

When the glowing light of the sun went down, they went back home, each to his own house that the famous Hephaestus, lame in both legs, had built with knowing skill. Thundering Zeus went to his bed, where the Olympian always lay when sweet sleep found him. There he went up to sleep, and Hera of the golden throne was by his side.   611

Book 2

The other gods and the mounted warriors slept the whole night, but sweet sleep did not hold Zeus. He cycled around in his mind just how he might bring honor to Achilles and destroy many of the Acheans beside the ships. Then the best plan was revealed to him in his mind: to send Agamemnon Atreusson a bad Dream. He addressed the Dream with winged words.

"Bad Dream, go quickly to the Acheans' swift ships, and when you come to the hut of Agamemnon Atreusson tell him faithfully everything I tell you. Order him to arm the long-haired Acheans with the greatest of haste. Now is the time he might take the city of wide streets, that of the Trojans. Because of Hera's pleas, the immortals living on Olympus are no longer divided in their thinking. She has turned them all, and ruin threatens the Trojans."

So he spoke, and when the Dream had heard his order, he went off. Soon, he arrived at the swift ships of the Acheans. He searched for Agamemnon Atreusson and came upon him in his hut. Around him had been poured ambrosial sleep. The Dream stood over Agamemnon's head, taking the likeness of Nestor Neleusson, since Agamemnon valued Nestor most of the old sages, and said to him: "You sleep, son of the warlike, noble horseman Atreus. It is not necessary for a warrior in command to sleep all night during the time when the troops are entrusted to his care and there are urgent concerns. Now, understand me quickly. I am a messenger of Zeus, who though far from you, cares greatly for you. He orders you to arm the long-haired Acheans with the greatest of haste. Now is the time you might take the city of wide streets, that of the Trojans. Because of Hera's pleas, the immortals living on Olympus are no longer divided in their thinking. She has turned them all, and ruin from

Zeus threatens the Trojans. Keep those things are in your mind and don't forget them, as the city should be taken when gentle sleep might release you." 34

So saying, the Dream departed and left him there. Agamemnon was considering in his heart the things he was not about to accomplish. He was actually convinced that he could take the city of Priam that day. What a fool he was! For this certainly was not what Zeus had on his mind, you may be sure. He was still about to set the greatest imaginable pain on both the Trojans and the Acheans in a furious conflict. 40

Agamemnon awoke from sleep. The divine oracle poured all around him. He sat up straight and put on a soft tunic, beautiful and newly made. And around him he tossed a great cloak. He bound his beautiful sandals underneath his oiled feet, and around his shoulders he threw his silver-studded sword. And he chose his paternal scepter, which was ever incorruptible. He went with it along the ships of the brazen-shirted Acheans. 47

The goddess Dawn approached blessed Olympus, disclosing light to Zeus and the other immortals. After that, Agamemnon ordered the heralds, with their resonant voices, to cry out to summon the long-haired Acheans to assembly. They did their cry, and quickly were they gathered around him. First seated was the council of greathearted elders beside the ship of the Pylian-born King Nestor. And Agamemnon set out his important plan.

"Listen my friends, a Dream from a god came to me in sleep during the ambrosial night. Most especially did it look like noble Nestor in size, and vigor, and it was the closest resemblance. It stood over my head and spoke to me saying: 'You sleep, son of the warlike horseman Atreus. It is not necessary for a commander with a plan to sleep all night at a time when the troops are his responsibility and there are urgent concerns. Now, understand me quickly. I am a messenger to you from Zeus, who though far from you cares greatly for you. He orders you to arm the long-haired Acheans with all possible haste, for now might you take the city with wide streets, the city of the Trojans. Because of Hera's pleas, the immortals who have dwellings around Olympus are no longer divided in their thinking. She has turned them all, and ruin from Zeus threatens the Trojans. But keep these things in your mind.' 70

"Having spoken thus, the Dream left, flying away. Sweet sleep let go of me. But come now, let's get the sons of the Acheans into their armor, but first I shall test this with words. That is the proper thing to do. I shall order them to flee with the many-benched ships. You restrain them verbally one way or another." Indeed, so spoke Agamemnon, and then he sat down. 76

Nestor, king of sandy Pylos, rose up among them. With careful thought, he addressed them.

"O beloved Argive kings and princes, if someone else among the Acheans recounted such a dream, we would declare it false and shun it. But this time the one who has seen it claims to be by far the best of the Acheans. So come, let us get the Acheans into their armor." 83

So spoke Nestor. He led the procession out of the council. The kings with their scepters stood up, yielded to the Shepherd of the Troops, and dispersed like dense swarms of bees streaming from a rock hollow in spring, constantly surging in clusters, flying among the flowers. They flew from here to there in swarms, many bands of soldiers going here and there from the ships and from the huts in front of the deep sea, marshaling for assembly. Rumor, the messenger of Zeus, went like fire among them, urging them on. They were brought together, and there was murmuring in the assembly and the troops groaned as they sat down on the ground underneath them. A din arose. Nine shouting heralds restrained those who were making noise so they might hear the kings, cherished by Zeus. The heralds promptly reined in the troops, who ceased the clamor. 100

The Lord Agamemnon stood up holding the scepter that Hephaestus had fashioned with much care. Hephaestus gave it to the Lord Zeus Cronusson, who gave it to his messenger

Hermes, slayer of Argos. And Lord Hermes gave the scepter to the horseman Pelops. Then Pelops again gave it to Atreus, Shepherd of the Troops. At his death, Atreus left it to Thyestes, owner of many sheep. Finally, Thyestes left the scepter to Agamemnon that he might carry it, since he ruled over many islands and all of Argos.   108

Leaning on it, Agamemnon spoke to the Argives, saying: "O beloved Danaan heroes, attendants of Ares, Zeus has greatly bound me up in an impenetrable blindness. He is heartless! He did this when earlier he promised me and nodded in assent to the sack of high-walled Troy and a return home afterward. Now he sent me a plan that is evil and deceitful. He orders me to return to Argos empty-handed, since so many of the troops have been wiped out. This somehow seems to be a good thing to almighty Zeus, who has demolished the high citadels of many cities, and will destroy even more. He is mightiest by far.   118

"This is and will be shameful for the troops of the Acheans: to learn that they have come so far and done so much for no purpose. Theirs is an unfinished war after fighting and doing battles with fewer men. It is not how it was revealed that the enterprise should come out. Though, if both the Acheans and the Trojans would wish it, we might swear a great oath, counting out on both sides. On the Trojans' side the oath would be taken by such citizens as could be gathered together and we would marshal the Acheans by tens in formation. We would choose a Trojan warrior to pour wine for each decade of Acheans, but many would lack a wine-pourer.   128

"I declare that the sons of the Acheans outnumber the Trojans, but the others of the many valiant allies of the city hinder me greatly. And though I am desirous of sacking the well-populated city of Troy, they will not allow it.   133

"Nine years of Great Zeus have passed. The wood of our ships has rotted, and their cables are unsound. Our wives and small children sit in our houses still waiting to receive us home. The work we came here to do is unfinished. But come now, let us all be persuaded. Let us flee with our ships to our beloved homeland, for we will never take Troy, with its wide streets." 141

So he spoke. He stirred up the spirit in the breasts of all those among the throng who did not hear what he said in the council of elders. That spirit moved along the gathering like a long wave in the Icarian Sea that rises up driven on by both East Wind and South Wind from the clouds of father Zeus. It was like what happens when West Wind seizes the tips of a stand of rich grain that sway wildly, the ears bent over. In such a way did the speech move the whole assembly. They gave a loud shout and rushed toward the ships. Dust rose upward from underneath their feet into the air. Urging each other on, they grabbed the stays underneath the ships. Then they dragged them toward the shining sea along the channels hollowed out in the sand. A shout went up toward the sky, as they were overjoyed at the prospect of returning home. 154

Thus might the Argives have made their return home, contrary to fate, had not Hera said to Athena: "Oh damn, indomitable child of Zeus, who bears the aegis! Is this how the Argives are now returning to their beloved homeland over the broad back of the sea? You people would leave Argive Helen behind and give Priam and the Trojans something to boast about. It is because of her that so many have perished in Troy, so far from their beloved homeland. So, Athena, hold back no longer, but go now to the brazen-shirted Acheans. Calm down each man with your soothing words, and do not allow them to drag their ships into the sea." 165

So Hera spoke. And the sharp-eyed goddess Athena obeyed her and set off, sprinting down from the peak of Olympus. Quickly she came to the ships of the Acheans. There she found Odysseus, equal to Zeus at counsel, standing. He was not holding on to the well-benched black ships, since grief had come to his heart and spirit. Sharp-eyed Athena stood close to him and said: "Ever-cunning Odysseus Laertesson, born of Zeus, is this how you are fleeing to your beloved homeland, falling into your many-oared ships in defeat? And you would leave Argive Helen with Priam and the Trojans? Was it not on account of her that many troops of the Acheans perished far from their beloved homeland? But go down quickly to the troops of the Acheans, and do not hold back. Calm them down, each man with your soothing words, and do not allow them to drag the ships to the sea." 181

So Athena spoke. Odysseus, hearing the goddess's voice, threw down his cloak and ran off. The herald Eurybates of Ithaca took care of the cloak as he attended Odysseus, who himself went over in front of Agamemnon Atreusson and took from him the patriarchal scepter that was ever incorruptible. With it he ran down along the ships of the brazen-shirted Acheans. 187

Whichever king or eminent warrior Odysseus met, he calmed with soothing words.

"Friend, it is not like you to be a coward in the face of fear. So, sit yourself down and get the rest of the troops to do the same. You've misunderstood the mind of Agamemnon. He is now putting on a trial, but will swiftly punish the sons of the Acheans. In our council we didn't at all hear what he just said. Take care that Agamemnon, being angry, might do some mischief on the sons of the Acheans. Great is the spirit of the highborn kings. They possess the honor from Zeus; Zeus, the counselor, loves them." 197

Those warriors that he came to as he pushed along carrying the scepter, to them he shouted again the same speech.

"Friend, sit still and listen to the command of others who are better than you. You are cowardly and weak, and cannot be counted on in battle or in council. That is not at all how we will rule here over the Acheans. It is not good to have a multitude of kings; there ought to be but one, the only king. To him, the son of crooked-dealing Cronus has given both the scepter and the law, so that he may rule over them." 206

So, acting as commander, he swayed the camp. They soon

rushed out from their huts and ships to the assembly with
Odysseus in the lead, as when a sloshing, foaming wave crashes
onto a great headland and reverberates across the deep of
the sea.   210

The others sat down, restrained in their seats. Only Thersites
babbled on, chattering like a jackdaw. He had in his mind
foul words that were at the same time very numerous and
quite pointless. Without justification, he constantly quarreled
with the kings. What he said seemed utterly ridiculous to the
Argives.   216

Thersites was the ugliest man who came to Troy. He was
bandy-legged and lame in one foot. Both his rounded shoulders
contracted over his chest. And above that his head was cone-
shaped, bald, but with a ring of woolly nap around it. Thersites
was despised most especially by Achilles and Odysseus since
he rebuked both whenever he could; but now he shouted harsh
criticisms at noble Agamemnon. The Acheans despised Ther-
sites.   224

While everyone else sat calmly, Thersites, with a loud voice,
shouted a taunt at Agamemnon.

"Son of Atreus, again it is you who would complain, and
what do you want? Your huts are full of bronze and lots of
captive women that we Acheans gave you earlier when we
took cities. Even so, you want the gold that one of the sons of the
Trojans, the noble horsemen, will bring as ransom for a son
whom I or others of the Acheans might bring in. Or if it might
be a young girl, so that you could fuck her, you would keep her
away from the others for yourself, wouldn't you?   233

"It is not right that a leader has visited so much trouble on
the sons of Acheans. O mates, you're lily-livered; you're
Achean women and not Achean men anymore. Let's go back
home in our ships and leave him here in Troy to digest his prizes.
That way he will learn whether we provide for and assist him
or not. Now he has dishonored Achilles, a far better man
than he, by arrogantly taking his prize. But there is no anger in

Achilles's mind. Instead, he is just sitting around. Otherwise, son of Atreus, you would be committing your last act of depravity."

243

So Thersites spoke, taunting Agamemnon, Shepherd of the Troops. Quickly Odysseus went to stand beside Thersites and delivered a harsh rebuke.

"Thersites, you babble pointlessly. Even though you speak in a clear voice, hold your tongue, you should not be the only one wishing to quarrel with the kings. I think that no other man among those who came to Troy with Agamemnon is sorrier than you. You should hold your tongue and not harangue against the kings, nor utter insults. Instead you say outrages and defend a flight for home. We do not know clearly how things will turn out, but bravely or cowardly we will return home.

253

"Now, you sit viciously reviling Agamemnon, Shepherd of the Troops, because the Danaan heroes give him a very large amount of the spoils. But, I ask of you, what is the point of this, if we still find you behaving like an idiot? Never while there is a head on Odysseus's shoulders, nor when he is called father by Telamachus, will there be a time when I don't seize you and strip off the cloak and tunic that conceal your genitals, and send you in tears to the swift ships, after thrashing you in the assembly with humiliating blows."

264

So Odysseus spoke, and he struck Thersites with the golden scepter on his back and shoulder. Thersites writhed around and copious tears poured out. A bloody welt rose up on his back. He sat down in terror, experiencing sharp pain, and with a helpless look, wiped away his tears.

269

Though they were upset, the men laughed heartily at him. And one of them who saw it would have said to another close by in the throng:

"Did you see that? Odysseus has done many good things as counselor and chief. He is brave in war and a worthy prince. This time, what he's done to this miscreant is the best thing that's happened among the Argives. I'll bet you Thersites won't

feel the urge again to rail against the kings in such a high-handed
way." 277

So spoke many in the throng. Odysseus, sacker of cities, stood
up with the scepter. Beside him stood sharp-eyed Athena, in the
guise of a herald, silencing the troops so that each and all of
the sons of the Acheans might hear and understand the plan.
Candidly, Odysseus addressed them and said: "Son of Atreus,
the Acheans intend for you to know, O king, that they are the
shabbiest of human animals, and will renege on the promises
they made on coming here from horse-raising Argos. They
stood in battle order, and promised that they were ready to
sack well-built Troy and then return home. Like little children and widowed women, they now whine to each other about
going home. 289

"Yes, no doubt, the toilsome work makes return difficult.
Even one month spent apart from his wife makes a man uptight
when on a many-oared ship he is confined to a harborage as winter storms rise up. For us this is the ninth revolving year we've
been stuck here. I do not blame the Acheans for being frus-
trated beside the beaked ships. But, because we have remained
firm for so long, it would be disgraceful to return having accomplished nothing. 298

"Take courage, dear friends, stay long enough for us to learn
whether Calchas prophesied the truth or not. Thus, we will
know well in our hearts as we are all witnesses, those whom
the fates have not carried off in death. Why, it was just yesterday or the day before, when the Acheans' ships converged on
Aulis to begin the campaign against Priam and the Trojans. We
gathered around the spring to make sacrifices on the sacred
altar to the immortals. The clear water of a spring flowed from
under a beautiful sycamore tree. There was revealed a great
sign. A hideous snake with a blood-red back was drawn to the
light by the Olympian himself. From inside the altar it rushed
out and slithered up into the tree. There on the highest branch
of the tree were young sparrows, baby chicks. There were eight

of them, cowering under the leaves. Together with the mother who hatched them, there were nine. The snake devoured the miserable chicks even as they shrieked aloud. The mother flew around wailing for her beloved brood. But the snake coiled around to seize her by the wing. She gave out a loud cry, but it devoured her along with her chicks. The god who manifested the snake, made it disappear; the son of crooked-dealing Cronus turned it into stone.   319

"We stood there struck dumb with amazement that a dreadful monster of the gods had come to our sacrifices. Calchas immediately pronounced his divination.

" 'Why are you silent, long-haired Acheans? Counselor Zeus has revealed a great sign, late in coming, signifying that our goal will be late in fulfillment, but the glory of it will never die. The snake devoured eight sparrow chicks and the mother, herself, making nine; that is how many years we shall be fighting there. In the tenth, we shall take the city of wide streets.'   329

"So Calchas spoke, and now what he prophesied has come to pass. But, come, all you well-armed Acheans, stay in place until we take the great city of Priam!"   333

Thus he spoke. The Argives gave up a great shout and all around the ships reverberated the awesome roar from the Acheans' cheering at the speech of noble Odysseus. And to them spoke Nestor, the Geranian horseman.

"Woe! You certainly are babbling like children when the concern is the toil of war! How will our agreements and oaths be carried out? In the councils men make plans with libations around fires where both the able and the weak obey those agreements. When we argue like this, we're not discovering any plan of action, though we have been here a long time. Son of Atreus, earlier you led the Argives here with a firm plan for fierce fighting. As for those who make plans different from yours, let those one or two go to ruin. They will accomplish nothing. The Argives want you to command them, nonetheless.   347

"Their plan is to set off for Argos before learning whether the promise of Zeus, who bears the aegis, was false or not. I think that the almighty son of Cronus nodded in assent that day when the Argives set off in their swift-sailing ships to bring death and calamity to the Trojans. The lightning bolt on the right side revealed the portentous signs. Thus no one should scramble to return home before sleeping with a Trojan wife, or being rewarded for the troubles and groaning caused by Helen. But if someone urgently desires to return home, let him take hold of his well-benched black ships so that he can meet death and his fate before the rest. You, O king, plan carefully and listen to another man. This would be the order I might give, Agamemnon, and do not lightly set it aside. Sort out the men into tribal groups and families. Group them tribe with tribe, family with family. If you do this, the Acheans will obey you. You now know who of the leaders and who of the troops are cowardly, and who are valiant. Hence, divide them up to fight. You will find out whether it is divine will that you not sack the sacred city, or whether it is because you have cowardly men or ones unskilled in warfare."   368

Prince Agamemnon replied to Nestor, saying: "Certainly, old man, you again excel at speaking over all the sons of the Acheans. I wish, by father Zeus, and Athena, and Apollo, that I had ten such advisers among the Acheans; then the city of Lord Priam would quickly bend over under our hands and we would sack it. However, the son of crooked-dealing Cronus, Zeus, who bears the aegis, gave me pain. He cast on me pointless wrangling and quarreling. And Achilles and I are quarreling over a girl. I started it, provoking him. But, if we are ever again agreeing on the same plan, it will not do to procrastinate on harassing the Trojans, not even a little bit.   380

"But now we must take on food so that we can join with Ares, making war. Everyone should sharpen his spear carefully and put his shield in good order. It is good that someone give fodder to the swift-hoofed horses. It would be well if somebody gets the chariots ready, inspecting them all around. A man should think about war. That way, we are ready to contend with Ares in furious battle the whole day.   385

"There will be no time out, nor slacking off unless nightfall stops the fury of the warrior, not for an instant. He will sweat all over the sword belt around his chest and on the whole-body shield. Around the shaft of the spear his hand will be fatigued. The horses will sweat from pulling the well-polished chariot. I will be well aware of anyone who might want to escape the fighting and stay back beside the ships. He will not be able to escape the dogs and birds that feed on the dead."   393

So spoke Agamemnon. And the Acheans shouted as when a wave comes against a high cliff, driven by South Wind against a steep rock projection. But the waves do not recede as they are driven by winds from all directions, which make more waves here and there.   397

The troops stood up and rushed away, splitting off toward their ships. They kindled fires among the huts, and they took their meal. They made prayers to the various eternal gods that they might escape death and tame Ares. The Supreme Commander Agamemnon sacrificed an ox, a fat five-year-old, to the almighty son of Cronus. He summoned the old aristocrats of all the Acheans: Nestor, by far the first; and Lord Idomeneus; then the two Aiantes and the son of Tydeus; and eighth was noble Odysseus, equal to Zeus at counsel. On his own came Menelaus, good at the war cry. Menelaus was aware in his heart what his brother was up to.   409

They stood around the ox and held up coarsely ground barley over it. Praying for them, the Prince Agamemnon said: "Most glorious, most powerful Zeus of dark clouds, who dwells on high, do not permit the sun to set, nor allow darkness to come until I have torched Priam's gates with blazing fire and thrown down his sooty great hall. I would shred the shirt of Hector with bronze, leaving it in tatters. I would leave many of his comrades facedown in the dust, biting the dirt."   418

So prayed Agamemnon. But the son of Cronus did not yet fulfill his request. Instead, he received the sacrifices and added to the onerous toil going on. 420

And, after the prayer, they tossed on the coarsely ground barley. First, they positioned the victim for the sacrifice and then slit its throat and flayed it. They cut a thigh and enclosed its pieces within two layers of fat. On top of that they placed some raw meat. They set fire to a pile of wood split from leafless branches. They held the spitted entrails over the fire of Hephaestus. When the thigh and entrails were completely burned, they cut the other parts into small pieces and stuck them on spits. They roasted these with great care and then pulled them all off. They ate heartily and the proper feast lacked nothing. 431

When the desire for food and drink was gone away from them, Nestor, the Geranian horseman, led off in speaking to them.

"Most glorious Supreme Commander, Agamemnon Atreusson, we ought not to lie around here long. We should not procrastinate in the work the god has given us to do. So, come, heralds of the brazen-shirted Acheans: hail and roust them out from around the ships. We ought to go as a group through the wide camp of the Acheans so that we can sooner raise up the sharp-edged Ares of war." 440

So spoke Nestor. And the Supreme Commander Agamemnon did not disobey him. Immediately, he ordered the loudvoiced heralds to call the long-haired Acheans forth to war. The heralds went about announcing the call and the men rousted out very quickly. The sons of Atreus and the highborn kings rushed around arranging them into formation. And among them was sharp-eyed Athena with the highly esteemed aegis that is ageless and immortal. From it hung a hundred tassels fashioned altogether of gold. All were tightly twisted, each worth a hundred oxen. With the aegis, she darted about the troops of the Acheans at the speed of light, shaking it as she went. She urged them on, increasing might in each, an

unflinching will to fight and make war. War became sweeter
to them than return in the hollow ships to their beloved homeland.   454

It was like a flash fire in a huge forest on the peaks of a mountain. The bright light shines far off from it. In such a way the
light shining off the blazing bronze shone up to the ethereal
heavens. And it was like when many flocks of birds, cranes and
geese and long-neck swans, fly over the meadows of Asia around
the streams of Caÿstrius. They fly from place to place, rejoicing
that they can fly. They make loud, clacking noises when they
land, which reverberate over the meadows. So it was with the
Acheans as many bands of them went from the ships and from
the huts onto the plain where the Scamander flows. An awful
din was raised by the pounding on the ground of the men's feet
and the hooves of the horses. They stood on the Scamandrian
meadow with its myriads of flowers, and saw that leaves and
flowers were just coming out.   468

They were like the many swarms of flies that one sees
swarming around a sheepfold in the springtime when milk is
poured into a bucket. In such a way did the long-haired Acheans stand in the plain eager to wipe out the Trojans completely.   474

Just as in a widespread herd of goats, the goatherds go about
separating the goats to move them to pasturage, so the squad
leaders got their men in order here and there to proceed into
battle. Among them stood the Lord Agamemnon; his face and
head looked like Zeus, who delights in thunder, his waist like
Ares, and his chest like Poseidon. Just as in a herd of cattle the
bull stands out as superior to all the others, in such a way did
Zeus cause the son of Atreus on that day to stand out from all the
others; he seemed clearly the best, by far, of the heroes.   483

Speak to me now, you Muses who have dwellings on Olympus. You are goddesses; you are present, and you know everything. We hear only rumor but know nothing. These were some
of the chieftains and kings of the Danaans. I shall not recite them
all for I do not know them all. Not even were I to sing with ten

tongues and have ten mouths, an untiring voice, and if my heart were of bronze. But, such as the Olympian Muses, daughters of aegis-bearing Zeus, give me to know, I shall tell of all those leaders and ships that came to Troy. 493

Peneleos and Leïtus led the Boeotians, as did Arcesilaus and Prothoenor, and Clonius. There were those who lived in Hyria and rocky Aulis, and Schoenus, and Scolus, and heavily forested Eteonus, and ancient Thespeia, and Goraea, and spacious Mycalessus. There were those who lived near Harma, and Elesion, and Erythrae, and those who held Eleon, and Hyle, and Peteon, and Ocalea, and Medeon, that well-built city. There were those from Copae, and Eutresis, and from Thisbe, a place with many pigeons. There were those from Coroneia, and grassy Haliartos. There were those who held Plataea and those who lived in Glisanta and those who held Lower Thebes, that well-built city, and sacred Onchestus, where the magnificent grove of Poseidon was. There were those who held Arne, a place with many vineyards. They were there from Midea, and sacred Nisa, and Anthedon on the coast. These went with fifty ships and in each were a hundred and twenty Boeotian youths. 510

Those living in Aspledon and Minyeian Orchomenus were led by Ascalaphus and Ialmenus, sons of Ares. Astyoche, who was a venerated virgin, but went up the stairs to the women's chamber with mighty Ares. He slept with her in secret. She bore Ascalaphus and Ialmenus in the palace of Actor Adzeiusson. With them came thirty hollow ships in battle order. 516

Schedius and Epistrophus led the Phoceans. They were the sons of greathearted Iphitus Naubolidusson. They held Cyparissus, and rocky Pytho, and sacred Crisa, and Daulis and Panopeus. With them came men living around Anemorea and Hyampolis, who live along the noble river Cephisus; as well as those who hold the Lilaea beside the headwaters of the river Cephisus. Accompanying these men were forty black ships. The Phoceans were instructed to stand armed in ranks close by the Boeotians on the left-hand side. 526

Swift Aias, commanded the Locrians. He was known as the
Oïlean or lesser Aias since he was nowhere near so large as Telamonian Aias. He wore light armor, but he had a farther spear
cast than all of the Hellenes, even the Acheans. With the Locrians, came men living in Cynus, and Opoeis, and Calliarus, and
Bessa, and Scarfe, and even lovely Augeiae. Also, came they
from Tarphe, and Thronium, and those from around the steams
of the river Boagrius. The Locrians living across from sacred
Euboeia came with Aias in forty black ships.   535

The Fire-Breathing Abantes hold Euboea, and Chalcis, and
Eretria, and Histiaea, with many vineyards, and Cerinthus, by
the seaside, and the high citadel of Dion. Those who hold Carys-
tos and those living around Styra were led there by Elephenor
Chalcodonson, scion of Ares, greathearted ruler of the Abantes.
There followed behind him the Abantes, fast, long-haired warriors eagerly stretching out their ashen spears to tear through
breastplates, with fire in their hearts. With Elephenor came
forty black ships.   545

And there were those who held illustrious Athens, and the
district of greathearted Erechtheus. He was raised by Athena,
daughter of Zeus, though the bountiful Earth gave birth to
him. Athena placed him in Athens where there was a wealthy
temple dedicated to her. There the Athenian youths propitiated
her with offerings of bulls and sheep year after year. Menestheus, son of Peteus, ruled after Erechtheus. There was never
on earth such a man as Menestheus. He excelled in driving
chariots and shield handling above all others save Nestor, who
was older than he. With Menestheus followed fifty black ships. 556

Aias led twelve ships from Salamis. His men stood wherever
the Athenian formations were placed.   558

Those who held Argos, and walled Tiryns, and Hermione,
and Asine, which surrounds a gulf, and Troizen, and Eïone, and
Epidaurus, with many vineyards, and the youths of the Acheans
who hold Aegina Mases. These were led there by Diomedes,
of the shrill war cry, and Sthenelus, the beloved son of the

celebrated Capeneus. Along with them came a third godlike man, King Mecisteus Talusson. Diomedes was their overall leader with eighty black ships. 578

Those holding Mycene, that illustrious city, and rich Corinth, and illustrious Cleone, and Orneae, and lovely Araethyrea, and Sicyon, where Adrastus first ruled, and those holding Hyperesia, and even lofty Gonoessa, and Pellene, and those living around Aegium and the Aegialus and all around broad Helice. These Prince Agamemnon Atreusson led with a hundred ships. With him followed the most by far and the best of the troops. And he, himself in his shining armor, stood out among all the heroes since he was by far the best and was the leader of the most troops by far. 580

Those who held hollow Lacedaemon, with its corrugated mountain walls, and Pharis, and Sparta, and Messene with its many pigeons, and Augeiae, and those living in lovely Bryseia; those who held Amyclae and Helos, the seaside city; those who held Laas and those living around Oetylus; all these Menelaus, Agamemnon's brother, led in sixty ships. They put on their armor a ways off, and trusting in Menelaus, as he went around, rousing themselves for battle with an eagerness to fight. He had most earnestly set his heart to avenge Helen, for the deep offense done him and for all his suffering. 590

Those who dwell in Pylos, and those living around lovely Arene, and Thryus, a ford on the river Alpheus, and those living in well-built and lofty Aepy, and Cyparissia, and Amphigeneia, and Pteleo and Helus, and Dorium. There the Muses met Thamyris the Thracian singer from Oechalia, and put an end to his singing as he was going along away from the home of Erytus in Oechalia. He boasted to the Muses, daughters of Zeus, who bears the aegis, that he could way outdo them at singing. Furious, they maimed him, destroying his heavenly voice even as he played his harp. All of these were now ruled by the Geranian horseman Nestor, and with him followed ninety ships in formation. 602

Those who held Arcadia under steep Mount Cyllene and near the grave mound of Aepytus, where warriors do battle in close combat, and those living around Pheneus and Orchomenus, which has many sheep, and Rhipe, and Stratia, and windy Enispe. Those who held Tegea, and lovely Manteneia, and Stymphalus, and also those living in Parrhasia; all these King Agapenor, the son of Ancaeus, led in sixty ships. The many Arcadian warriors who sailed in each ship were skilled in fighting. But, since they were not accustomed to seafaring, the Supreme Commander Agamemnon himself gave them the hollow ships to cross over the wine-red sea.   614

Those from Buprasium, and as many as live near Hyrmine in shining Elis, and the rock outcropping that forms the farthest borders of Myrsine and encloses within it Olen and Alesium, there were four rulers over them and ten swift ships followed with each of those men. Many Epeans went from Elis. Amphimachus, and Thalpius, grandsons of Actor, led them. The former was the son of Cteatus, the latter of Erytus Actorson. Diores Amarynceusson also was a leader, and the fourth was the godlike Polyxeinus, son of King Agasthenes Aygeusson.   624

Meges Phyleusson, equal to Ares, led those from Dulichium, and the sacred islands of the Echinades, which are situated across the sea before Elis. Meges was born to Phyleus, a horseman beloved by Zeus, but for some time lived apart from his father in Dulichium, because Meges provoked anger in his father. With Meges followed forty black ships.   630

Now, Odysseus led the greathearted Cephalonians who held Ithaca, and leafy Neritum. Those living around Crocyleia, and rugged Aegilips, and those who held Zacynthus, and those living around Samos, and those who held the mainland and those living on the opposite side, Odysseus, equal to Zeus in counsel, also led. With him followed twelve ships with red-ocher prows.   638

Thoas, son of Andraemon, led the Aetolians. They lived around Pleuron, and Olenus, and Pylene, and Chalcis, close to the sea, and rocky Calydon. But the sons of greathearted Oeneus were no longer living, nor was Oeneus himself. Red-haired Meleager also died and so the royal succession among the Aetolians came to an end. With Thoas followed forty black ships.   644

Idomeneus, famed for the spear, commanded the Cretans, those who held Knossos, and walled Gortyn, and Lyttus, and Miletus, and white Lycastus, and Phaestus, and Rhytium, well-populated cities. The others living around a hundred Cretan cities, Idomeneus, famed for the spear, and Meriones, equal to warlike, man-killing Ares, commanded. With them followed eighty black ships.   652

Tlepolemus Heraclesson, worthy and big, led nine ships of the princely Rhodians from the island of Rhodes. Those living around there are divided into three districts: Lindus, and Ialysos and white Cameirus. Tlepolemus, famed for the spear, ruled over them. Astyochia bore him to mighty Heracles. Heracles led her from Ephyre, carrying her away from the river Sellenes, as he was sacking many cities of highborn young men. After Tlepolemus had grown up in the well-built palace, all of a sudden, he killed his father's beloved uncle Licymnius, scion of Ares, who had already become aged. Immediately, Tlepolemus constructed ships, gathered together troops and sailed off, in flight, over the sea, since the other sons and sons of sons of mighty Heracles threatened him.   666

After wandering around for a time, and experiencing many troubles, he arrived at Rhodes. There his men settled, organizing into three tribes, and because of love from Zeus, who rules over gods and men, heavenly riches were poured on them.   670

On the other hand, Nereus led three balanced ships from Syme. Nereus was the son of Aglaea and King Charopus. He was the handsomest man of all the Danaans who came to Troy, after the exceptional son of Peleus. But he was irresponsible, so few troops followed him.   675

Those who held Nisyrus, and Carpathus, and Casus, and Cos with its city of wide gates, and the islands of the Sporades, them Phidippus and Antiphus commanded. They were two sons of

King Thessalus Heraclesson. With them thirty hollow ships came in battle formation. 680

Now, then, such of the Pelasgians who live in Pelasgian Argos, those who hold Alos, and Alope, and those living around Trachina, those who hold Phthia, and those from Hellas, known for its beautiful women, the people who are called Myrmidons, and Hellenes, and Acheans. Achilles was their leader and they followed him in fifty ships. But they had no notion of participating in the terrifying din of war, because there was no one to lead them into formation. Fleet-footed Achilles lay among the ships. He was angry over Briseis, with beautiful hair. He captured her from Lyrnessus after much trouble in the sack of Lyrnessus and walled Thebes. He took out Mynte and Epistrophus, experts at throwing the spear. They were sons of King Euenus Selapisson. On account of his anger over Briseis, Achilles lay back, but he was about to recover. 694

Those who held Phylace and flowery Pyrasus, the grove of Demeter, and Iton, the mother of sheep, and Antron by the sea, and grassy Pteleus, them warlike Protesilaus once led while he lived. But at the time of my song, the dark earth held him down. He had left behind his wife, with her flesh torn all around in her distress at his leaving, in his half-completed palace in Phylace. A Dardanian warrior killed him as he leapt from his ship, and he became the very first of the Acheans to die. But not for long were they leaderless, for they wanted someone in command. Podarces, scion of Ares, son of Iphiclus Phylacusson, who owned many sheep, marshaled the men. He was greathearted Protesilaus's own younger brother. The hero, warlike Protesilaus was older and more capable, but the troops hoped for a commander who was worthy. With Podarces followed forty black ships. 710

Those living around Pherae beside Lake Boebeïs, and Boebe, and Glaphyrae, and illustrious Iolcus, them Eumelus, dear son of Admetus led in eleven ships. Eumelus was born to Admetus by his wife Alcestis, known for her virtue, the prettiest of the daughters of Peleus. 715

Those from Mathone, and those living around Thaumacia, and those who hold Meliboea and rocky Olizon, them Piloctetes, highly skilled with a bow, led in seven ships. There were fifty rowers in each. Highly skilled with bows, they had gone into fierce combat. But on the sacred island of Lemnos Philoctetes lay, suffering great pain. The sons of the Acheans left him in great distress from the bite of a deadly water snake, and there he lay in agony. King Philoctetes was constantly in the minds of the Acheans around the ships. But they were not leaderless for long; they wanted a commander. Medon, the bastard son of Oïleus, marshaled them. Rhana bore him to Oïleus, sacker of cities. 728

Those who held Tricca, and Ithome, with its steep cliffs, and those who held Oechalia, the city of Eurytus in Oechalia, them the two sons of the famous healer Asclepius led, Podaleirius and Machaon. With them followed forty ships in formation. 733

Those who held Ormeneus, and those holding the spring of Hyperia, and those who held Asterium, the white peaks of Titanus, them Eurypylus, the glorious son of Euaemon, led. With him, they followed in forty black ships. 738

Those who hold Argissa, and those living around Gyrtone, those who hold both Orthe, and Elone and the white city Oloosson, them the intrepid Polypoetes, son of Perithous, led. Perithous was born of immortal Zeus. Polypoetes was born to Perithous of the famous Hippodamia. Polpoetes was conceived on the day when they were celebrating with the hairy Centaurs on Pelion. Perithous drove them from there and pushed them on farther to Aethices. But he was not alone; with him went Leonteus, scion of Ares, son of greathearted Coronus Caenesson. 747

Gouneus led twenty-two ships from Cyphos and with him followed the Enienes and the stalwart Peraebi. Some of them make their home around stormy Dodona and others tend fields on both sides of the lovely river Titaressus that shoots out beautifully flowing water onto the river Peneus, but it doesn't mix

with the silvery-swirling Peneus. Instead, it flows along on top
of it like olive oil. This is because it is a tributary of the river
Styx, that terrible boundary.   755

Prothous, son of Tenthredon, commanded the Magnesians,
who live around the river Peneus and leafy Pelion. Swift Prothous was their leader, and they followed him with forty black
ships.   759

And these were the leaders and commanders of the Danaans.
Tell me, Muse, which of them was the best of all, themselves
and their horses, who followed the sons of Atreus?   762

The best horses were those Eumelus Pheresson drove. Fleet
of hoof, like birds they were. They were of the same age, with
backs as even as a plumb line when they ran. Both were mares,
and Apollo, the silver bow, raised them in Pereia. They drove
along as though routed by Ares. Of the men again, the best was
huge Telamonian Aias, on account of Achilles's wrath. Achilles
was a far better man, and he drove the horses of the exceptional
Peleus. But he lay among the beaked ships, nursing his anger at
the Shepherd of the Troops, Agamemnon Atreusson. His troops
were beside the seashore amusing themselves tossing discuses,
throwing javelins, and practicing archery. Their horses, which
were to pull the chariots, were munching on lotus and parsley
growing in the marshes while the chariots lay folded up in the
huts of their masters. Each of the men longed for a war-loving
leader as they were wandering around here and there through
the camp. But the Myrmidons did not fight.   779

The Acheans were going along like a fire spreading out
all over the ground. The earth groaned underneath as when a
lightning bolt of Zeus lashes the ground around Typhoeus in
Arimus, where they say Typhoeus makes his bed. In such a way
did the great earth groan under their feet, for very swiftly did
they make their way across the plain.   785

The messenger, swift Iris, fast as the wind, came to the Trojans from beside Zeus, who bears the aegis, with a distressing
message. They were gathered in assembly near Priam's gates.

They were all clustered close together, young and old. Swift-footed Iris stood close to them and spoke in a voice like that of Polites, a son of Priam. Polites was posted as a lookout, at the top of the grave mound of old Asyatas, to gather information about whenever the Acheans might be advancing from the ships. Iris, swift of foot, in his likeness, said to Priam: "Oh, old man, your advice is unfailingly kind and uncritical, whether we are at peace or rising up for terrible war. Very often I have seen warring men, but never have I seen so many troops as this; they are as numerous as leaves or grains of sand. They come across the plain toward the city for battle. 801

"Hector, I have directions specifically for you as to what you should do. Get our many allies down from the great city of Priam. They speak one language or another of many diverse peoples. Make certain that each commander understands what he is supposed to do. Then, have him get his own citizen-soldiers marshaled into formation." 805

So she spoke, and Hector understood completely the directions of the goddess. Immediately, he dismissed the assembly and they put on their armor. All the gates were opened and the troops rushed out, foot soldiers and horses. And a great roaring noise rose up. 810

In front of the city on the plain a ways off is the high mound with open spaces on both sides. Men call it the Bramble. The immortals call it the burial marker of the nimble Myrine. There the Trojans and their allies were getting into order. 815

Mighty Hector Priamson, with the shining helmet, commanded the Trojans. With him were the very best and most numerous troops, armed with their spears and eager. 818

Aeneas, the worthy son of Anchises, ruled the Dardanians at that time. Aphrodite bore him to Anchises, the goddess having taken to bed a mortal in the forests of Ida. But Aeneas was not alone. With him were the two sons of Antenor, Archelochus and Acamas, both very skilled in the arts of war. 824

Those living in Zeleia under the most distant foot of Ida, the

Troes, had plenty of dark drinking water from the river Aesepus. Pandarus, the magnificent son of Lycaon, led them. And,
Apollo himself had given Pandarus his bow.

Those who held Adrasteia and the district of Apaesus, and
those who held Pityea and the high mountain of Teria, both
Adrastus and light-armored Amphius, the two sons of Merops
of Percote, led them. Merops was the most revered of all proph-
ets and never allowed his sons to marshal for murderous war,
but the two obeyed him not at all. The fates of black death led
them on. 834

Those living around both Percote and Practius, and those
who held Sestus, and Abydus, and shining Arisbe, Asius Hyrtacusson, master of men, led. Great fiery horses brought Asius
Hyrtacusson from Arisbe, from the river Selleis. 839

Hippothous led the tribe of Pelasgeans, experts at throwing
the spear. They were living in fertile Larisa. Both Hippothous
and Pylaeus, scion of Ares, commanded them. They were the
two sons of the Pelasgian Lathus Teutamusson. 843

Acamas and the hero Peirous led the Thracians, as many as
are bounded by the impetuously flowing Hellespont. 845

Euphemus was the commander of the Ciconian spearmen.
He was the son of Troizenus, the noble-born son of Ceas.

Pyraechmes led the Paeonians, with curved bows. They
were from far-off Amydon, from the wide-flowing Axius, the
prettiest water on earth. 850

Shaggy-hearted Pylaemenes commanded the Paphlagonians.
He was from the Enetians, where there is a breed of wild mules.
They held Cytorus, and lived around Sesamus, with notable
dwellings on both sides of the river Parthenius, and in Cromna,
and both Aegialus, and lofty Erythini. 855

Odius and Epistrophus commanded the Halizones. They
were from far-off Alybe, the birthplace of silver. 857

Chromius and Ennomus, a diviner of birds, commanded the
Musonians. But the auguries did not spare Ennomus from black
fate. He was struck down by the fleet-footed grandson of Aeacus

in a river, when Achilles went on a rampage against the Trojans and others.   861

Phorcys, and the godlike Ascanius led the Phrygians. They were from far-off Ascania, but they were eager for furious fighting.   863

Further, both Mesthles and Antiphus commanded among the Maeons. Both were sons of Talaemeneus that a nymph of Lake Gygaea bore. They ruled the Maeons who were born under Mount Tmolus.   866

Nastes commanded the Carians who spoke a foreign tongue. They held Miletus, and the heavily forested mountain of Phthires, where the Maeander flows, and they held the high peak of Mycala. Amphimachus and Nastes both commanded them in the beginning. They were the magnificent sons of Nomion. Amphimochus even went in the fighting wearing gold like a girl. What a fool! But in no way did it protect him from miserable destruction. He was struck down by the hand of the grandson of Aeacus in a river. Warlike Achilles took care of the gold.   875

Sarpedon and the exceptional Glaucus led the Lycians, who were far from Lycia, away from the swirling Xanthus.   877

Book 3

Now, when all of the Trojan units were marshaled with their leaders, they shouted a great war cry. It was as when birds take off, like the shout of cranes that goes up toward the heavens. When they escape from winter and endless rains, they fly across currents of Ocean, to take death and fate to the Pygmies when they engage in shameful conflict at dawn.　　7

At the same time, the Acheans were going along silently. Breathing fervently, they were eager in their hearts to help one another. As when South Wind pours out a misty cloud over the peaks of the mountains, it is not something shepherds love. But it is loved more by the thief than night, since a man can see ahead of him only as far as he can throw a stone. So it was, that from underneath the Acheans' feet a cloud of dust rose up into a storm as they went. They rushed forward over the plain.　　14

And when the two sides were drawing closer to one another, godlike Alexander was moving to the front line of the Trojans, wearing a leopard skin and carrying his curved bow over his shoulders, along with a great sword. Brandishing two bronze-tipped spears, he challenged all the best of the Argives to fight opposite him.　　20

Then Menelaus, beloved of Ares, recognized Paris as he was coming from the throng to the front in long strides. Just as when a hungry lion rejoices greatly when he happens on the carcass of an antlered buck or wild goat, he lustily gobbles it down, even if swift dogs and energetic young men rush on him. In such a way did Menelaus rejoice on seeing godlike Alexander. Menelaus was intent on avenging the wrong done him. Immediately, he jumped from his chariot to the ground with his armor.　　29

And so godlike Alexander recognized Menelaus as he appeared in the front line. Alexander's own heart was stricken with panic. He retreated back in among his comrades, to avoid fate. As when someone jerks back on suddenly seeing a snake in a glen in the mountains. His knees are seized with trembling, and he retreats backward, and the flesh of his cheeks pales. So godlike Alexander retreated back into the throng of the Trojans in fear of the son of Atreus.   38

Embarrassed at seeing this, Hector scolded him.

"Shameless Paris, though you are handsome, you are an adulterous, woman-crazed man. Oh, how I wish that you had never been born, or that you had perished unmarried! It would have been much better than this, since you are a disgrace and the object of suspicion by the others. Without doubt, the long-haired Acheans are laughing their heads off that you appeared in the van among the chiefs shaking in fear, but you only did it to show your pretty face, since you have neither strength of character nor fortitude.   45

"Was it with this sort of bravery that you got together your usual cronies and sailed across the deep in your seafaring ships? Among foreigners, you screwed one of their beautiful women, a daughter of brave warriors. And you brought her here from a faraway land. You've done great harm to our father, to those in the city, and all in the district. Do you realize what a delight it is for the enemies to see you like this? Could you not stand up to Menelaus, beloved of Ares? You would then realize from what sort of man you took a vibrant wife. Your lyre and the gifts of Aphrodite will not protect you when your long locks and your pretty face are mingled with the dust. There are some very cowardly Trojans, otherwise you would have worn a stone tunic for what you did."   57

And godlike Alexander replied.

"Hector, you have upbraided me in a way that was fair, but not beyond that. Courage is always for you like an ax that never dulls. An ax that slices through wood when wielded by a shipwright. It increases the strength of the man. So the force in your chest is fearless. But, you may not throw back at me the gifts of love that golden Aphrodite gave, since no one may refuse the glorious gifts of the gods. Such gifts as they themselves give, no one would willingly choose for himself.   66

"Now then, if you wish me to fight a duel, have the other Trojans and all of the Acheans sit down. In the middle, between them Menelaus, beloved of Ares, and I will come together to fight over Helen and all her treasure. Whichever of us proves braver would win and justly choose many women and treasure to take home. The rest would swear solemn oaths of friendship, those living in fertile Troy, and those living in horse-raising Argos and Achea, known for beautiful women."   75

So spoke Paris, and Hector was overjoyed by the proposition he heard. He went into the midst of the Trojans to hold back the ranks, holding his spear midway along the shaft's length. He ordered them all to sit down. The long-haired Acheans drew their bows on him, aiming arrows, and throwing rocks. But the Supreme Commander Agamemnon shouted loudly: "Hold off, Argives, Achean youths, don't throw anything. Hector, with the shining helmet, maintains that he has something to say."   83

So he spoke, and they held off on fighting and quickly grew quiet. Hector spoke to all those on both sides.

"Hear me, Trojans and well-armed Acheans, as I tell you the proposition of Alexander. It is on account of him that this dispute came up. He says that the rest of the Trojans and all of the Acheans should set their handsome arms on the bountiful earth. Then Alexander and Menelaus, beloved of Ares, will fight in between us by themselves for Helen and all her treasure. Whoever proves the braver wins. He rightly chooses all the treasure and women to take home. All the rest of us are to swear solemn oaths of friendship."   94

So spoke Hector, and all grew very quiet. And among them spoke Menelaus, good at the war cry.

"Hear me now, as the pain has come chiefly to my heart. I believe that both the Argives and the Trojans should be separated, since they have suffered so much on account of the dispute between Alexander and me, though he started it. Whichever of us death and fate strikes will die. Quickly, let the others be separated.   102

"Bring two lambs, one a white male and the other a black female, both for Earth and Sun. And we shall bring yet another for Zeus. Fetch mighty Priam so that he may swear the oath himself, since his sons are unscrupulous and untrustworthy. No one ought to break or transgress against an oath to Zeus. The younger men always seem unsteady in their minds. While those older may make plans, since they can look at what was before and what will be, and thus, bring forth the best possible plan for both sides."   110

So Menelaus spoke, and both the Acheans and the Trojans rejoiced in the hope that the dreadful warfare might cease. They drew the chariots up into ranks, the men went from them and took off their armor and placed it on the ground close by, and there was little space around them. Hector sent two heralds off quickly toward the city to fetch the lambs and to summon Priam. Prince Agamemnon went to Talthybius whom he ordered to go to the hollow ships and bring back a lamb. And, Talthybius did not disobey noble Agamemnon.   120

The messenger Iris went to white-armed Helen. Iris took on the appearance of Laodice, her sister-in-law, the wife of Antenor's son. Helicaon Antenorson married her, the best looking of Priam's daughters. Iris found Helen in the hall. She had been weaving at a large loom a two-ply purple fabric. On it Helen was embroidering scenes of many struggles suffered on her account at the hands of Ares by the noble horsemen Trojans and the brazen-shirted Acheans.   128

Fleet-footed Iris stood close to Helen and said to her: "Come here, dear sister-in-law, so that you may see the astonishing thing that has happened. The noble horsemen Trojans and the brazen-shirted Acheans earlier brought to each other warring Ares, which causes many tears, in dreadful, terrible fighting on the plain. But now, they have stopped fighting and sit quietly.

Their shields lean up against their long spears that are fixed together. Alexander and Menelaus, beloved of Ares, are to fight
against each other with long spears over you. The one who wins
would claim you as his beloved wife."   138

So spoke the goddess and she thrust into Helen's heart a
sweet longing for those things that formerly were hers: her husband, her city, and her parents. Immediately, Helen took up a
white veil and covered her face with it and went out from her
chamber, her eyes welling tears as she went. But she did not go
alone. With her followed two chambermaids, Aethra, daughter
of Pittheus, and lovely-eyed Clymene. Very soon they arrived at
the Scaean Gate.   145

The elders of the district were sitting around Priam near the
gate: Panthous, and Thymoetes, and Lampus, and Clytius, and
Hicetaon, along with Ucalegon, scion of Ares, and Antenor, both
prudent men. They were old men who had stopped going to war
long ago, but they were excellent at speaking, like crickets in a
forest tree sending out a sound that is lilylike in its stateliness
and sweetness. So the leaders of the Trojans were who sat on
the tower. When they saw that Helen was coming toward them,
they whispered to each other with winged words.

"It is not retribution for crimes by this woman that the Trojans and the well-armed Acheans have suffered pain for so long.
Awfully like an immortal goddess's is her face. But, even though
she is like a goddess, she ought to return home in the ships, so
that our grandchildren don't inherit calamity."   160

So the old men spoke. But Priam called out to Helen in his
resonant voice: "Come here and sit beside me, dear child, so that
you may look out over those who were before your husband,
your kin, and your friends. In no way do I blame you for what
has happened, but rather it is the gods I blame. They urged the
Acheans to make war, which causes many tears, on me.   165

"Tell me the name of that gigantic man who seems to be
both an excellent Achean warrior and huge as well. Certainly,
some of the others are taller than he is, but he is as handsome,

such as I have not seen before. I have never seen one so worthy
of respect. He appears to be a king over the warriors." 170

Helen, goddess among women, answered him: "Beloved
father-in-law, you are both venerable and awesome to me. How
I wish death had come to me. It would have pleased me more
than the evil that has befallen me since the time I followed your
son and left my relatives, my earlier-born children, and my
lovely contemporaries. I would not remember them, nor would
I melt into tears crying. 176

"But, you ask me who this man is who rises up above the
others assembled: he is Agamemnon Atreusson, eminent prince.
He is, at the same time, both a worthy king and a mighty warrior. He was once my brother-in-law, if ever such a one as I had
such a husband as Agamemnon's brother." 180

So Helen spoke. The old man admired him and addressed
him: "O blessed son of Atreus, you lucky man, born under happy
stars, many Achean youths are now under your command. As
well as those who came from Phrygia, with its many vineyards.
I saw the most Phrygian warriors with their dappled horses I have
ever seen, the troops of Otreus and the godlike Mygdon, when
they were encamped along the bank of the river Sangarius. I was
with their allies, sleeping among them, when the Amazonian
viragoes came. But those with me then were not so numerous
as the Phrygians who are with the bright-eyed Acheans now." 190

Next, the old man caught sight of Odysseus and asked:
"Come, tell me whose beloved son is that one who is a head
shorter than Agamemnon Atreusson, but appears wider across
the shoulders and chest. His armor is lying on the bountiful
ground, while he himself is walking around the formations of
men like a lead ram. I liken him to a ram with a thick fleece at the
head of a big flock of white sheep." 198

Then Helen, begotten of Zeus, answered him: "This one is
the son of Laertes, ever-cunning Odysseus. He was raised in the
district of rocky Ithaca. He truly knows both all manner of
deceits as well as having many sound ideas." 203

At that point, prudent Antenor, sitting opposite, said to her: "O woman, this description you have given is very accurate. When noble Odysseus came here with Menelaus, beloved of Ares, in an embassy on your account, I gave them guest-friend hospitality in my palace. I came to know both in regard to stature and careful thought. When they were intermingling with the assembled Trojans, Menelaus stood taller and with broad shoulders. When seated, Odysseus looked more distinguished.   211

"When everyone began to weave ideas and plans, Menelaus spoke rapidly, with few words, but very clearly. He was not overly wordy, nor did he digress. And after him came Odysseus. When that ever-cunning man fixed his eyes on the ground, he held his scepter so that it was neither behind, nor in front of his face. He grasped it like a man of no experience. His face looked angry and witless. But then came the deep sound of his voice from his chest and words came out like snowflakes in a winter storm. Afterward, being amazed at his performance, no other man challenged Odysseus."   224

Then, the old Priam saw Aias and asked: "Who is that man, who is both excellent and huge? He is biggest by far of the Acheans in height and his wide shoulders."   228

Helen, of the long veil, goddess among women, answered him: "This is the giant Aias, bulwark of the Acheans, and Idomeneus stands on the other side of him with the Cretans, like a god. Their leaders have gathered around him. Menelaus, beloved of Ares, extended guest-friendship to Idomeneus whenever he came to Sparta. Now, I see many others among the bright-eyed Acheans.   234

"Some I knew well and remember their names. I am not able to see two who were file leaders of the troops. Castor, who trained horses, and Polydeuces, good at boxing, were brothers born of the same mother, who was mine as well. Either they did not come from lovely Sparta or they followed in the ships, which sail over the sea. Maybe now they do not intend to go

into battle for fear of embarrassment among the warriors, or
they may be very upset with me." 242

So spoke Helen. But at that time Sparta held fast both Castor
and Polydeuces in the fertile earth of their beloved homeland. 244

The heralds ran up to the city with news of the solemn
oath. They were joyful as they selected the two lambs and put
the exhilarating wine and grain from the fields into goatskin
bags. The herald Idaeus brought the shining mixing bowl
and the golden cups. He stood beside the old man, roused him
up, and said: "Rise up, son of Laomedon. The best of the noble
horsemen Trojans and of the brazen-shirted Acheans summon you to go down to the plain in order to swear a solemn
oath. Alexander and Menelaus, beloved of Ares, will fight with
long spears over the woman. Whoever is the winner gets both
her and her property. The rest are to swear a solemn oath of
friendship, those living in fertile Troy, and those living in horse-
raising Argos, and those living in Achea, known for beautiful
women." 258

So the herald spoke and the old man shivered. But he ordered his attendants to harness his horses, and they promptly
obeyed him. Up stepped Priam and he stretched the reins
down behind. Antenor mounted the beautifully wrought chariot and stood beside him. The two of them went through the
Scaean Gate driving the fast horses onto the plain. 263

When they arrived at the space between the Trojans and the
Acheans, they stepped off the chariot onto the bountiful
ground. Immediately, the Supreme Commander Agamemnon
rose up, along with ever-cunning Odysseus. The illustrious heralds brought along the offerings to confirm the oath to the
gods and the bowl for mixing wine. They poured water over
the hands of the kings. Agamemnon drew out the dagger that
always hung beside the scabbard of his great sword. He cut some
hairs from the heads of the lambs, which the heralds distributed
to the best of the Trojans and the Acheans. Before them the

son of Atreus raised up his hands grandly in prayer: "Father
Zeus, who rules from Ida, most glorious, and greatest; and
Sun, who looks out over all and hears all things, Rivers and
Earth, and those underneath who avenge men who are done
with toil, those who would breach solemn oaths; be witnesses
for us and defend our solemn oath. Should Alexander kill
Menelaus, he himself will retain Helen and all her property,
and we will return home in our seagoing ships. But, if red-
haired Menelaus slays Alexander, the Trojans will then give
back Helen and all her treasure, and pay back to the Acheans
some compensation, such as is just and customary among men.
Should Priam and the sons of Priam not wish to pay me compensation when Alexander is struck down, I will stay and fight
on as punishment, until I reach the end of the war."   291

And he slit the throats of the lambs with the pitiless bronze
and cast them down on the ground, gasping as their breathing
stopped. The bronze took away their life force. They filled the
cups with wine poured from the mixing bowl and raised them
up in prayer. This is what one of the Acheans or the Trojans said:
"Zeus, most glorious, greatest, and you other immortal gods,
you who would take vengeance on whichever side might be first
to violate the oath: May their brains pour out upon the ground
just as this wine now does; strike them down, and also their
wives and children."   301

So they spoke, but the thundering son of Cronus was not yet
inclined to bring about what they swore. Among them, Priam,
descended of Dardanus, said: "Hear me, Trojans and well-armed
Acheans. You may be sure that I am going back to windy Troy,
since there is no way that I could endure watching while my
beloved son fights against Menelaus, scion of Ares. Though Zeus
knows, and the other immortal gods, which of them is destined
to meet his end."   309

And the man equal to a god placed the lambs into his chariot. Then he himself stepped up and stretched out the reins.

Antenor mounted beside Priam and the two of them returned home to Troy along the way that they had come. 313

Hector, son of Priam, and noble Odysseus first measured out the place for the contest. Then they selected lots to be shaken in a bronze helmet to determine which man would first cast a brazen spear. The assembled troops stood with their hands raised up to the gods. In this way one was praying: "Father Zeus, who rules from Ida, most glorious and mightiest, who determines the outcome of the combat between these men, grant to him who perishes entry in the House of Hades. May the solemn oath bring about friendship again for us here." 324

So they were praying. Great Hector shook the helmet, looking back away as he did. The lot of Paris quickly popped out. Then the troops sat down, each in his place in formation. Where the nimble horses stood, the various armor lay also. Noble Alexander, husband of long-haired Helen, armed himself handsomely. First, he put his beautiful greaves around his shins. They were fitted with silver ankle guards. Next he got into the breastplate and corselet. They had belonged to his brother Lycaon, but had been fitted for Paris himself. Around his shoulders he tossed a great brazen sword with silver studs. He took a buckler, large and stout. He set on his valiant head a helmet, with its horsehair crest. Dreadfully did the plume nod as he moved. He chose a sturdy spear fitted for his hand. In like manner Menelaus dressed himself with the armor of war. 339

And when they had armed themselves, they came out from each side of the throng into the middle between the ranks of the Trojans and the Acheans; they were gleaming most terribly. Their appearance sent a shock of awe throughout the noble horsemen Trojans and the well-armed Acheans. The two men stood at close range opposite one another in the marked-off place, scowling at each other and brandishing spears. Alexander cast his long spear forward. It struck against the shield of the son of Atreus; a shield that was balanced all around. But the

bronze did not penetrate: the spear tip was bent by the sturdy
shield.   349

And next up to raise his bronze spear was Menelaus Atreusson who prayed as he did to father Zeus: "Zeus, master, give
me revenge for the evil noble Alexander has done me first, and
smite him under my hands. Thus anyone, even distant descen-
dants, would shiver in fear at doing evil to one who offers hospitality and friendship."   354

He cast his long spear and it struck against the balanced
shield of the son of Priam. Through the burnished shield the
sturdy spear went. It fixed itself in the brilliantly wrought corselet, piercing through and rending Alexander's tunic beside his
belly. He leaned over, avoiding black fate. The son of Atreus
pulled out his silver-studded sword and raising it up, crashed it
down on the crest of Paris's helmet. But the sword shattered into
three or four pieces that all fell around Menelaus. The son of
Atreus groaned and looked toward the wide heavens and said:
"Father Zeus, is there some other god more destructive than
you? I was intending to take revenge on Alexander for the worst
evil he has done me. But now, I have in my hand a broken sword
and my spear, already cast, is useless. And I did not get him."   368

Menelaus rushed in and grabbed the helmet with its
horsehair plume. He turned Paris around and dragged him in
among the well-armed Acheans and choked Paris with the
elegantly embroidered strap under the soft part of his neck.
Menelaus tightened his hold on Paris's neck under the helmet.
And even now might he have gained everlasting fame had not
Aphrodite, daughter of Zeus, taken quick notice. With her might
she broke the strap made from the hide of a slain ox. Menelaus
held the empty helmet in his powerful hand. The hero turned
and tossed it violently toward the well-armed Acheans and his
bellicose comrades picked it up.   378

Again, Menelaus sprang forward, intending to slay Paris with
a brazen spear, but Aphrodite snatched him out of there. You
see, that is very easily done by one who is a goddess. She envel-

oped Paris with a dense fog and transported him to his fragrant bedchamber. Then she went to summon Helen. The goddess found her on top of the high tower, where a crowd of Trojan women had gathered together. Aphrodite took hold of Helen's soft, ambrosial gown and shook it. So that she could speak to Helen, the goddess took the likeness of an old woman born long before who lived in Sparta and carded beautiful wool. Helen had a special love for her. With the sound of the old woman's voice, Aphrodite said: "Come here. Alexander has returned home and is calling for you. He is in your chamber in the lathe-turned bed, and he is shining and handsomely dressed. He does not look like one who has come from fighting with a warrior, but as one going to a dance, or who has just sat down after the dance has ended." 394

So spoke Aphrodite. Helen's heart beat faster in her chest. But suddenly, she recognized the goddess because of her gorgeous neck, and her shapely breasts, and her dazzling eyes. In amazement at what she had realized, Helen spoke: "O spirit, why do you deceive me with such longings? You appear to me as one who lived well in my former city of Phrygia, or lovely Maeonia. It seems that someone there of living men is dear to you. Is it because Menelaus has defeated the noble Alexander and wants to lead me, wretched, back home, so that now you stand here beside me telling me lies? 405

"Since you have not turned your feet toward Olympus, you go and sit beside him, but not like one of the gods who is always around Paris, protecting him lest he suffer somehow. Instead, make yourself into his wife or some slave girl. But, I will not go there. It would be the cause of outrage if I were to cherish him in bed if he ran away from the fight. All the Trojan women will taunt me afterward. I have the most anguished of hearts." 412

Becoming furious at Helen, Aphrodite spoke in her own voice: "Do not try my patience, slut, because in anger I might desert you, and utterly despise you, I who extravagantly loved you! Provoke me in this way and I will devise a horrible agony. Be careful, so that you do not die most miserably in the middle of the Trojans and the Danaans gathered all around."   417

So the goddess spoke, and Helen was terrified of her. Silently, she covered herself in her soft, radiant white veil and she went, escaping the notice of all the Trojan women. The goddess led the way.   420

When they arrived at the exceedingly beautiful palace of Alexander, the chambermaids quickly went about their work, and Helen went through the women and up to her lofty chamber. Laughter-loving Aphrodite took a chair for her and carried it across the room, placing it opposite Alexander. Helen, daughter of Zeus, who bears the aegis, sat down in the chair. She turned away her eyes and chided her husband with a lecture. "You have come from the fight. Oh, how I wish that you had died, brought down by a mightier man, who used to be my husband. Earlier, you boasted that you were stronger and better with a spear than Menelaus, beloved of Ares. So, go now and call out to him so that you may resume fighting each other. However, for my part, I urge you to stop fighting, the pointless making of war and doing battle with red-haired Menelaus, so that he does not quickly defeat you with his spear."   435

Paris made reply with a lecture of his own: "O woman! Do not upbraid me with your harsh talk. Now, Menelaus is victorious with help from Athena, but another time I will best him. There are also gods on our side. But come now, let us make mad, passionate love together. I have never been so consumed with feelings for you, not even back when first I snatched you from lovely Sparta to sail in my ships, which go over the sea, and on the island of Cranae slept with you entwined in lovemaking. In such a way, now do I love you and the sweet fog of passion rises." And he led his wife to the bed.   447

So as those two were sleeping on their bed, with a frame bored to hold a web of rope, the son of Atreus was frantically wandering around the throng like a wild animal for some glimpse of godlike Alexander. But none of the Trojans nor their illustrious allies could show Alexander to Menelaus, beloved of Ares, nor would any of them have hidden him because of affection for him. All of them despised him as much as they did black death.   454

Among them the Supreme Commander Agamemnon spoke: "Hear me, Trojans, and Dardanians, and allies. It was surely clear that Menelaus was the victor. You must hand over Argive Helen and all her treasure with her. And furthermore, you must pay a suitable ransom, such as is customary among men."

So he spoke, the son of Atreus, and the other Acheans cheered.   461

Book 4

The gods were gathered together, sitting near Zeus on his golden pavement. Among them revered Hebe was pouring nectar, as they toasted one another with golden goblets while looking out over the city of the Trojans. Soon, the son of Cronus started bickering sarcastically, but deviously, with Hera: "Two goddesses are assisting Menelaus, Argive Hera and Athena, the protector. They are taking their ease as they sit looking on. But then again, Aphrodite, who delights in laughter, constantly goes to the aid of another and spares him his fate, and has now rescued him from death. Certainly, Menelaus, beloved of Ares, is the victor. Let us consider what may happen. Either we rouse them up again for evil fighting and the dreadful cry of war, or we cast over them friendship all around. If it might become all love and sweetness for everybody, surely King Priam's city would be inhabited on the one hand, and Menelaus could take Argive Helen back, on the other." 19

So Zeus spoke. Athena was quiet and said nothing. She was angry at father Zeus, and that anger grew into wild rage at what he said. But Hera didn't hold back the anger in her breast. Instead, she spoke out: "Most terrible son of Cronus, such a plot you are talking about! How you wish to set in place useless and never-ending misery! My horses are tired, covered with sweat and more sweat from their toil as I gather up troops to go against all such evil as is done by Priam and his sons. Do what you like, but none of us other gods will praise you for it." 29

Greatly annoyed with her, cloud-gathering Zeus said: "You miserable wretch! How is it now that Priam and the sons of Priam are doing such terrible things to you that you are constantly working to destroy the well-built city of Troy? If you go inside the gates and the long wall and gobble down Priam, and his children, and the other Trojans raw, maybe that would cure your anger. Do whatever you want, or the quarreling between you and me might generate a huge wrangle. But, I'll tell you something, and get it firmly fixed in your head. At such time as it pleases me to destroy a city where men you love were born, do nothing to lessen my anger. For I have given you what you want even though I didn't wish to. 43

"There are many cities of mortal men who dwell under the sun and starry heavens, and of those sacred Troy, and Priam and the skilled spearmen of Priam, have especially pleased my heart. They have never failed to offer both libations and burning fat at my altar when they were at their proper feasts. That is the honor we immortals receive from mortal men." 49

At that point, lovely-eyed Hera replied: "Indeed, there are three cities that are dearest of all to me: Argos, and Sparta, and Mycene, with its wide streets. Sack them whenever your heart is angered against them, and I will not oppose your plan, nor will I become incensed. I will not be grudging in any way, because I cannot prevent you from destroying the cities, as you are much more powerful than I. Even so, my doings ought not to be futile, because I too, am a god, born of the same family as you. Crooked-dealing Cronus sired me to be the eldest, most respected goddess. Equally because of family and because I am called your wife, and you rule over all the immortals, it is right that we yield to each other, I to you, and you to me, so that the other immortal gods will follow suit. You should immediately urge Athena to go into the dreadful combat of the Trojans and the Acheans, and to arrange it so the Trojans are the first ones to commit violence against the glorious Acheans, in breach of the treaty." 67

So spoke Hera, and the father of both men and gods did not disobey her. Immediately, he spoke to Athena with winged words: "Go with all haste to the camps of the Trojans and the Acheans, and try to get the Trojans to be the first ones to breach the treaty." 73

So speaking he urged on Athena who had already been impatient to go. She went rushing down from the peaks of Olympus, like a gleaming star the son of crooked-dealing Cronus sends as a sign for sailors or to a wide camp of troops. Many sparks of fire come from it. It was like that when Pallas Athena rushed to the ground. She leapt down into the middle between the two sides and the Trojans, noble horsemen, and the well-armed Acheans were astonished. In such a way was one of them saying to another close by on seeing her: "Either war, and evil, and dreadful war cries are back again, or Zeus is setting in place friendship all around since he is the dispenser of war among men."   84

And Athena, taking the likeness of Laodocus Antenorson, a mighty warrior, went into the throng of the Trojans. She was looking around, hoping to find godlike Pandarus. She found the illustrious and mighty son of Lycaon standing among the brave ranks of shield-bearers who followed him from the streams of Aesepus. She stood beside him and said: "Warlike son of Lycaon, would you now trust me in a matter. If you dare to send a sharp arrow toward Menelaus, it might excite joy in all of the Trojans and win glory for yourself from all of them, especially from King Alexander. He might be the first of all to bring you magnificent gifts if he were to learn that warlike Menelaus Atreusson, vanquished by your dart, was going onto a flaming funeral pyre. So come, shoot an arrow at glorious Menelaus. Vow to wolf-born Apollo, renowned archer, that you will make a glorious sacrifice of firstborn lambs to him when you return home to the sacred city of Zelea."   103

So spoke Athena, and she convinced Pandarus. Immediately, he unsheathed his well-polished bow made from a leaping ibex. It was a goat he himself had shot in the chest from a blind. When hit, the goat fell on a rock, belly side up. The horns that grew from its head had a span of sixteen palms, or five feet. An experienced finisher of horn fashioned them into a bow. The tips he covered with highly polished gold.   111

Pandarus bent the bow against the ground to slot and stretch the bowstring. His worthy comrades held their shields in front of him so that the warlike sons of the Acheans could not rush him before he got off a shot at Menelaus Atreusson. He took the cover off his quiver and drew an arrow from it that had never been sent forth to cause dark torment. He prayed to Apollo, vowing to make a glorious offering of firstborn lambs when he returned home to the sacred city of Zelea.   121

Pandarus notched the arrow into the ox hide string. At that moment the string was at his nipple, the iron arrowhead beside the bow. Then he took aim with the powerful, bent-back bow. There was a loud twang, as the bowstring smartly snapped, and the sharp-pointed arrow eagerly flew up into the throng.   126

But the blessed gods who are immortal did not forget Menelaus. The daughter of Zeus, goddess of spoils, stood in front of him warding off the painful dart. She held it back from his flesh just as a mother keeps away a fly from her child, held by sweet sleep, lying in bed. Athena herself carried the arrow past the gilded armor plates where they meet doubled over the chest. The bitter arrow struck the fitted armor belt and went through the shiny plates which protect the flesh and serve as a bulwark against darts. All those are protection, but the arrow pierced even them. The very tip end of the arrowhead scratched the man's flesh. Immediately, blood the color of a thundercloud flowed from the wound.   140

Just as when a woman in Maeonia or Caria stains some piece of ivory purple in making the cheek-pieces for horses that are destined to lie in a treasure chamber—many a horseman prays that his horses might wear them, since they are both an embellishment for the horse and a glory for his charioteer, but instead, the cheek-pieces lie in a treasure chamber, a trophy for a king—in such a way, Menelaus, blood stained on his well-developed thighs and dripped down his shins to be seen below on his handsome ankles.   147

The Supreme Commander Agamemnon shuddered when he

saw the dark blood flowing from the wound, and even Menelaus, beloved of Ares himself, shuddered. But when he saw that both the string that holds the arrowhead in place and the barbs were on the outside of the skin, his spirit flowed back into his chest. Prince Agamemnon, holding the hand of Menelaus, shouted to his comrades in a deep voice: "Dear brother, it was for your death that I previously made a treaty and positioned you by yourself in front of the Acheans to hold off the warring of the Trojans. Since they hit you, they have trampled upon the solemn oath. But it was not for nothing the oath, and the blood of the lambs, and the libations, and right hands clasped. Certainly, even if the Olympian will not pass his judgment right away, in time he will fulfill his promise, by exacting a heavy price on the Trojans, and their wives and children. This I know well, for it is just in both mind and spirit. The day will come when he will destroy sacred Troy, and Priam, and those troops, the skilled spearmen of Priam. Zeus Cronusson, who dwells in the firmament, who holds the scales of justice, will shake the terrible aegis against them all. Such is his anger at deceit. These things will not be left unfinished. But there will be awful grief for me, Menelaus, if you should die. Even I, most shamefully, would head for parched Argos, since immediately after your death, the Acheans will remember the land of their fathers. According to the boast of Priam and the Trojans, we will abandon Argive Helen. Your bones will rot, lying in a field in Troy, and our work will remain unfinished.   175

"And someone of the haughty Trojans, jumping up onto the tumulus of famed Menelaus, will say: 'How I wish that everything that comes from the anger of Agamemnon could turn out this way, since now the army of the Acheans he led here had no longer any purpose. So, he went back home with his empty ships, leaving behind good Menelaus.' So one may say. By that time, the ground will gape wide to hold me."   182

But, lifting Agamemnon's spirits, red-haired Menelaus replied: "Take heart, there is nothing for the troops of the Achaeans to worry about. The sharp arrow is not stuck in a mortal wound. It passed alongside the polished armor plate that the bronze-workers made, and both of the belts below." 187

Prince Agamemnon made his reply, saying: "O, dear Menelaus, I hope this is the way it is. A healer can assuage the wound and put herbs on it that would stop the dark pain." 191

And Agamemnon said to the godlike herald Talthybius: "Talthybius, go as quickly as you can to summon Machaon, son of the renowned healer Asclepius, so that he can see warlike Menelaus, son of Atreus. One of the highly skilled archers of the Trojans and Lycians hit him with an arrow. For the archer there is glory, but for us there is grief." 197

So spoke Agamemnon. And hearing him, the herald did not disobey. He went out among the brazen-shirted Acheans, peering around looking for the hero Machaon, and recognized him where he stood. Around him were the mighty ranks of the shield-bearing troops who came from Trica, where they raise horses. The herald stood close to Machaon and addressed him with winged words: "Up, son of Asclepius, Prince Agamemnon summons you, so you might see Menelaus, the warlike king of the Acheans. One of the Trojans or Lycians hit him with an arrow. It is a cause of grief for us." 207

So the herald spoke and Machaon set off through the throng to the wide camp of the Acheans. When they arrived at the place where the wounded Menelaus was, the herald and Machaon found him surrounded by a circle of leaders who were among the most distinguished. The godlike man stood beside Menelaus in the middle of the circle and immediately pulled the arrow from the girdle. As he pulled it back the sharp barbs broke off. He loosened the beautifully ornamented breastplate and the belt underneath and the under-armor that bronze-workers had fashioned. Then he saw the wound the bitter arrow made when it hit. Machaon sucked the blood out of the wound and skillfully applied a plaster of soothing herbs that Chiron once gave to his father as a friendly gesture. 219

While they went about tending to Menelaus, good at the war cry, the ranks of the shield-bearing Trojans advanced. The Acheans got back into their armor, recollecting their martial ardor.   222

It is not for you to know whether noble Agamemnon ever slept after eating, or if ever he felt fear, or if there were some time he didn't feel like fighting. Instead, you should know that it is in eagerly pursuing combat that a man gains fame.   225

Agamemnon permitted his attendant to hold his panting horses and chariot, with its many-colored bronze work, behind him. His attendant was Eurymedon, the son of Ptolemy Peiraeusson. Eurymedon was under strict orders to stick close lest fatigue should seize Agamemnon's limbs as he went on foot through the ranks of men, giving the orders a general must. Those he knew of the Danaans, who have swift horses, he urged on: "Argives, never shrink from furious valor. Father Zeus will be no accomplice to lies. The Trojans were first to do violence in breach of the treaty. Now, count on it, buzzards will feast on the soft flesh of these very men, while we return home again with their wives and young children in our ships after we sack the city."   240

There were some he saw who were shrinking back from war. Those he scolded angrily: "Disgraceful Argive archers, have you no shame? Why do you stand there like startled fawns weary from running around a plain? They stand there and not one mind among them is the source of any valor. You just stand there the same way, startled, and don't fight! Are you really waiting for the Trojans to come closer to the sound-sterned ships on the beach of the gray sea, hoping that maybe then you might see if the arms of Cronusson are extended above you in protection?"   249

In such a way did Agamemnon go about among the ranks of men, doing what generals do. As he was going along through the throng of men, he came to the Cretans. They were arming themselves around warlike Idomeneus, while Idomeneus was in the front lines of the fight, as he had strength like a boar, and Meriones was urging on those farthest back in the formation. Seeing them, the Supreme Commander Agamemnon rejoiced. Immediately, he spoke to Idomeneus in a genial way: "Idomeneus, I value you most of the Danaans, who have fast horses, when we are in battle, or doing some other chore, or at feasting, or even when the best of the Acheans are stirring the dark wine in the mixing bowl for the council of elders. If, for the others of the long-haired Acheans, there are rations of drink, yours would always be a full cup, the same as mine. You may drink as the spirit moves you. But roust the men out to war in the same way as those who went before us boasted that they did." 264

And Idomeneus, leader of the Cretans standing face-to-face with Agamemnon, replied:

"Son of Atreus, I will be to you an especially agreeable companion, just as when I stood among the first ranks and nodded in agreement. But now, rouse the other long-haired Acheans to go quickly into battle. The Trojans made a treaty, and in the future there shall be death and destruction for them, since they were first to commit violence in breach of it." 270

So Idomeneus spoke and the son of Atreus moved along the close formation of warriors with a contented heart. He came to the Aiantes. The two of them were preparing for battle, and a cloud of dust from the foot soldiers followed them. It was like when a goatherd from his lookout post sees a storm cloud coming across the sea on a blast from West Wind. From far off it appears darker than pitch as it moves over the deep, and it is the front edge of a huge cyclone. The shepherd trembles on seeing the storm, and drives his flock into a cave. In such a way did the two Aiantes shepherd their youths into the flames of battle, rousing them into close, dark formations brandishing shields and spears. 282

And seeing them, the Lord Agamemnon rejoiced and spoke to them with winged words.

"Aiantes, both of you are main leaders of the brazen-shirted Argives. None is your equal in preparing men for the fight, so I have no orders for you. You yourselves give the orders to troops in battle. Would that father Zeus, and Athena, and Apollo kindle in all such spirit as is in your chests. Then the city of King Priam will quickly sink to ruin, taken by your hands and sacked." 291

Having so spoken, Agamemnon left them and went on among the others. There, he chanced upon Nestor, the eloquent orator from Pylos. Gathered around him were great Pelagon, and Alastor, and Chromius, and Aemon and Prince Bias, Shepherd of the Troops. Nestor was arranging the men in order for battle and urging them to fight. In the front he positioned the horses and chariots. In the rear, he placed the bravest foot soldiers as a bulwark in the fighting. Then he drove along the cowards into the middle so they would fight even if they didn't want to, but because they had no choice. He gave orders to the best charioteers, telling them to hold back their horses lest they bolt from confusion in the throng: "No one should be in such a hurry to fight that he gets out alone ahead of the others in the fight against the Trojans, relying just on his skill at driving horses. The others behind him might turn back around and then the loner would be very vulnerable. A warrior who meets another chariot opposite him should cast his spear, since that would be much better. In this way those in the past destroyed cities and walls, as they had the skill and the spirit in their chests." 309

So the old man, who had known so well the skills of war for so long, roused them up. Seeing him, Prince Agamemnon was glad, and spoke to him with winged words: "Old man, would that your knees might follow the spirit that lives in your own chest. Then you would be firm in your strength. But age has worn you down in this way. I wish that one of the other warriors had what you have, and that your spirit were in those men who are younger." 316

Nestor, the Geranian horseman, replied to him, saying: "Son of Atreus, I would like very much to be who I was when I killed noble Ereuthalion. But that is not how it is. The gods give to mankind all the things they give, but not at the same time. Then I was a youth; now age has caught up with me. But I am here among the horsemen and I give orders and counsel. It is the reward of old men to teach the younger ones to wield the spear, and those young men rely on their strength."

325

So Nestor spoke, and the son of Atreus went on along happily. He found horse-training Menestheus, the son of Peteus, standing with the Athenians, masters of the war cry, around him. Close by stood the ever-cunning Odysseus and around him the formations of the Cephalonians. They were not weak men, but they had not yet heard any war cry rise from among the troops. After all, both the Trojans, noble horsemen, and Acheans were just now set into motion. The Cephalonians and the Athenians stood waiting for whenever another battalion of Acheans might come to rouse them to commence the fight.

335

And when the Supreme Commander Agamemnon saw them he scolded them: "Son of noble-born King Peteus, how cowardly and deceitfully you hold back in your own self-interest. Why do you hunker down in fear, waiting for others? You ought to be among those at the front, urging on the fiery fighting. At the feast you were the first to hear my call when the Acheans were preparing it for the elders. Then there was wonderful roast meat and cups filled with sweet wine, as much as you two wanted. Now, you would happily watch ten battalions of Acheans stand in front of you in battle with pitiless bronze."

348

Frowning, the ever-cunning Odysseus replied: "Son of Atreus, what crazy idea escaped from the fence of your teeth? What the hell do you mean that we are holding back when the Acheans are rushing to engage the Trojans, noble horsemen, in furious Ares? You will see, if you might care to, and I assure you that you will be able to, that the loving father of

Telamachus is serious about engaging the Trojans in the front
line. What you say is nonsense!"   355

Chuckling, the Lord Agamemnon smiled when he realized
that Odysseus was angry and answered him, taking back what
he had said: "Ever-cunning Odysseus Laertesson, born of Zeus,
I am not going to scold you exceedingly, nor am I ordering you
to do anything. Because I know absolutely that the spirit in your
friendly chest knows effective schemes. That you are of sound
mind, I declare absolutely. So, go ahead with what you're doing, we shall reconcile down the line if some ill is spoken now.
The gods make all such things into breezes."   363

Having so spoken, he left them there and moved on among
the others. He found the super-hearted son of Tydeus, Diomedes. He was standing near his horses and framed-wood
chariot. Beside him stood Sthenelus, the son of Capaneus. And
Prince Agamemnon, seeing him, chided Diomedes: "O my son
of the warlike, noble horseman Tydeus! Why hunker down like
a frightened bird? Why are you staring so intently at the space
between the armies? Tydeus would not have looked kindly on
such cowering, but would have been very much in the fiery fight
for his own comrades. So say those who saw him at work. They
say Tydeus came to Mycene without fighting. He was a guest-
friend of godlike Polynices, who was raising up troops. They
were then encamped in front of the wall of sacred Thebes.
They pled urgently with their illustrious allies to give aid, and
they were desirous of giving it as requested. But Zeus turned
back the helpers by revealing an inauspicious sign.   381

"It happened as they were leaving, and they saw it ahead on
the path. They arrived at Aesepus, thick with reeds and long
grass. There, the Acheans prepared to send an embassy with
Tydeus. Thereupon, he went and found the many sons of Cadmus feasting in the palace of mighty Eteocles. As the knight Tydeus was not a guest-friend of Eteocles, he was fearful, since he
was alone among the Thebans. He challenged the others to con-

test with him and vanquished them all easily since Athena was his helper.   390

"The Cadmeans, who lash horses, were angered by this. They laid on a sneaky ambush for Tydeus's return trip. They had fifty youths with two leaders: Meon Haemonson, very like unto the immortals, and the son of Autophonus, intrepid Polyphontes. Tydeus sent them to their shameful fate; he killed them all. That is all but one, who returned home. Meon, he sent away in obedience to a sign from the gods. Of such stuff was Tydeus the Aetolian. He fathered a son who happens to fight less well than he, but is better at talking."   400

So Agamemnon spoke, but mighty Diomedes said nothing to him. He respected the king and remained modest at the reproach. But the son of glorious Capaneus replied to Agamemnon: "Son of Atreus, do not lie when you know the truth. We claim that we are certainly far better than our fathers. We even took the seat of seven-gated Thebes with fewer men, warring under the wall. We trusted the signs of the gods and Zeus was our helper. The Thebans perished in their insolence. You should not hold our fathers in honor equal to both of us."   410

Frowning, mighty Diomedes said to Sthenelus: "Sit quietly, man, and trust what I tell you. I don't resent Agamemnon, since, as Shepherd of the Troops, he is only trying to rouse up the well-armed Acheans so they can fight. In this way either glory will be his if he takes the warlike Trojans and sacred Troy, or to him will come great sadness if the Acheans are vanquished by fire and sword. But come now. Let's the two of us give thought to valor."   418

Diomedes jumped down from the chariot with his armor. A terrible clang of bronze plates rose up from his lordly chest. Even one who was resolute would have been seized by fear upon hearing it.   421

As when an ever-rolling wave of the sea comes onto the shore, rising again and again, powered by West Wind—first it forms peaks as it moves across the deep, then crashes onto the mainland with a great, thunderous noise. The swollen caps surround the high cliffs and the sea spits out foam. So it was then with the unending formations of the Acheans, one after another moving toward war. The leaders of each formation called out orders. The troops did not move accompanied by the sound of their voices, as you might expect; they went silently, for fear of their squad leaders. Their multicolored armor gleamed all around as they made their formations.   432

But the Trojans were like ewes in a rich man's sheepfold, where countless numbers of them stand, waiting to have their white milk drawn. They bleat while listening for the sounds of their lambs. So from the Trojans arose war cries across the wide camp. It was not the same voice from all, but a mixture of languages, as they were warriors assembled from many places.   438

And Ares stirred up the Trojans, while sharp-eyed Athena stirred the Acheans. And Fear, and Rout, and Strife, of insatiable ardor, accompanied them. Strife was the sister and concubine of man-killing Ares. She, at first was a little bit like the rising caps on the waves of the deep, but then she fixed her head in heaven as she went about the earth and cast a brawl into the middle of the throng that increased the groaning of men.   445

When the Trojans and the Acheans met together, the warriors thrust at each other with shields and spears against bronze armor. Their bossed shields smacked against one another, and a great clamor arose. There was, at the same time, the wailing of lamentation, and the triumph of men, the deeds of those slaying and those slain. Blood flowed onto the earth, as when the winter snowmelt runs into the rivers in the mountains. The rushing water flows into converging valleys and thence from the great peaks into a steep hollow ravine. A shepherd hears the crashing sound from a long way off. So it was that from among those in combat came both shouting and toil.   456

Antilochus was first to take a valiant Trojan warrior in the forefront of the fighting. Echepolus Thalusisson was first hit

in the crest of his horsehair-plumed helmet. The bronze spear
tip smashed into his forehead and pierced bone. Darkness enveloped his eyes and he fell like a tower under heavy siege.
After he fell, Elephenor, son of Chalcodon, leader of the greathearted Abantes, grabbed his feet and pulled him out from under the spears, hoping that he might quickly strip off the armor.
But his enterprise was cut short. As he dragged the corpse,
greathearted Agenor caught sight of Elephenor's flank exposed
beside his shield as he stooped over. Agenor jabbed with his
bronze-tipped, polished shaft and loosed Elephenor's limbs. His
spirit left him, and over him the Trojans and the Acheans became locked in struggle. They were like wolves rushing at one
another, as man thrashed against man.   472

Then, Aias, son of Telamon, struck the son of Anthemion,
the valiant youth Simoeisius, whom his mother bore on the
banks of the Simois as she was coming down from Ida, where
she had gone with her parents to watch over their flocks. It was
on this account that men called him Simoeisius. But he had not
even paid the recompense a man pays to his parents for his
rearing, as his life span was so brief. He was taken down by
the spear of greathearted Aias as he was going along the front
line. The bronze spear first struck Simoeisius in the chest beside the right nipple and then went completely through the shoulder. He fell to the ground in the dust, like a black poplar tree that
grows large in a damp marsh, with smooth bark, and sprouts
branches at its crown. The tree is cut down with shining iron
by a man who bends the branches into the wheel rims of a very
beautiful chariot. The trunk lies on the bank beside a river drying out. In such a way Simoeisius, son of Anthemion, lay when
noble-born Aias slew him.   488

Antiphus, a son of Priam, with a multicolored breastplate,
cast at Aias from the throng with his sharp spear. He missed,
but the spear struck Leucus, a valiant comrade of Odysseus.
It hit him in the groin as he was pulling a corpse to the other
side. He fell on it and the corpse dropped from his hands.

Odysseus's heart was greatly distressed over Leucus's death, and he went through the front lines armed with his helmet of glowing bronze. He stood and cast his shining spear. Then he looked around at the Trojans, who had pulled back, to see if he had made a strike. His cast was not for nothing: he hit Democoon, a bastard son of Priam who had come to him from Abydus, from Priam's stable of fast horses. In his anger over the death of Leucus, Odysseus hit Democoon in the temple. The bronze spear point pierced though one and out the other temple. Darkness enveloped Democoon's eyes, and he fell down with a thud. His armor crashed about him. The front lines and glorious Hector gave ground on account of it. The Acheans gave a great shout and advanced much farther, pulling away the corpse as they went.   506

Apollo, looking down from Pergamum, was displeased. He shouted to the Trojans in a loud voice: "Rise up, Trojans, noble horsemen; do not retreat from the Argives. Their skin is of neither stone nor iron, to repel javelins of flesh-cutting bronze. Besides, Achilles, son of lovely-eyed Thetis, is not in the fight, but nurses an anger that pains his spirit by the ships."   513

So shouted the terrible god from the fortress of Pergamum. Then the most glorious daughter of Zeus, born of his head, roused the Acheans. She went into the throng wherever she could see them giving ground.   516

And fate shackled Diores Amarynceusson. He was hit in the ankle by a jagged rock thrown by a chief of the Thracian warriors, Peiros Imbrasusson, who came from Aenus. It hit Diores's right shin. The shameless stone crushed tendons and bones almost completely. He fell faceup in the dust with his arms outstretched to his beloved comrades, gasping for breath. And Peiros ran over and stabbed him with a spear beside the navel. His guts poured out onto the ground, and darkness enclosed his eyes.   526

But as Peiros withdrew, Thoas the Aetolian hit him with a spear in the chest above the nipple. The bronze stuck in his lungs. Thoas came up closer to Peiros and yanked the huge spear from his chest, and then pulled out his great, sharp sword and stabbed him in the middle of the stomach. His spirit was so dispatched. But Thoas did not strip the armor, because the man's long-haired Thracian comrades were standing around him with long spears in their hands. Thoas was exceedingly large and powerful, but the Thracians pushed him away from them. Thus two men, both commanders, were stretched out beside one another in the dust. For sure, the one was of the Thracians and the other of the brazen-shirted Epeans. Very many others lay dead around them. 538

No man, on coming to that place, would ever have made light of the toil. If there was anybody going around in it sound and unscathed by bronze, it was because Pallas Athena led him by the hand and shielded him from the barrage of spears, for many of the Trojans and of the Acheans lay facedown, stretched out beside each other in the dust, that day. 544

Book 5

At that point Pallas Athena again invested Diomedes Tydeusson with strength and courage so that he would stand out among all the Acheans and win worthy fame. She ignited on his helmet and shield an inexhaustible fire, like the autumn star, which glows with special brilliance when it has been bathed in Ocean, as she roused Diomedes's strength to the middle of the fighting.   8

And there was one among the Trojans, a rich man, the exceptional Dares. He was a priest of Hephaestus. He had two sons, Phegeus and Idaeus. Both were quite skilled in all aspects of war. They separated from the formation and challenged Diomedes. Both of them were in their chariot, while Diomedes proceeded on foot. They advanced, and Phegeus was first to cast his long spear at the son of Tydeus. The point of the spear passed above Diomedes's left shoulder without hitting him. Diomedes was next in raising bronze. Not for nothing did the javelin flee from his hand; it struck Phegeus in the chest between his nipples; he fell from the chariot. Idaeus leapt off, leaving the beautiful chariot, but he did not dare approach his dead brother. Although there was no way that he could escape his dark fate by himself, Hephaestus enclosed him in a cloud of night and saved him, so that old Dares would not lose everything.   24

The greathearted son of Tydeus drove off the brothers' chariot and gave it to his comrades to convey to the hollow ships. When the greathearted Trojans saw that one son of Dares was retreating, but that the other had been killed beside his chariot, they were all deeply upset.   29

Bright-eyed Athena took furious Ares by the hand and said: "Ares, Ares, misery of mankind, stained with death, destroyer of fortresses, should we not abstain from aiding the Trojans and the Acheans in fighting, so that father Zeus can give glory to whichever he pleases? Let us both back off now, so that we might avoid his wrath." 34

Having so spoken, she led furious Ares away from the fighting and sat him down beside the river Scamander, with its hilly banks. And the Danaans put the Trojans to rout. Each of their leaders took a man. First of all, the Supreme Commander Agamemnon knocked great Odius from his chariot. He was the leader of the Halizones. As he turned around to flee, a spear smashed into his back, between the shoulders. It drove through his chest and he fell with a thud. His armor crashed on top of him. 42

Idomeneus struck Phaestus, son of Borus the Meonian. He came from Tarne, which has rich soil. Idomeneus, famed for the spear, hit him with his long spear in the right shoulder as he was mounting his chariot, and he fell from it. Miserable darkness seized him. Then Idomeneus's attendants stripped him of his armor. 48

Menelaus Atreusson took Scamandrius, son of Strophius, with his sharp spear. Scamandrius was an excellent hunter taught by Artemis herself to take all manner of wild game that live in the forests of the mountains. But neither Artemis, who delights in archery, nor his skill as an archer, excellent though he'd been, was any help as he withdrew. Menelaus Atreusson, famed for the spear, struck him in the back between the shoulders before he could escape. The spear drove through his chest and he fell facedown, and his armor crashed on top of him. 58

Meriones slew Phereclus, son of Tecton Harmonson, who was skilled in making all sorts of wonderful things with his hands. Pallas Athena loved him more than all others. He crafted the balanced ships for Alexander that began all the trouble for the Trojans, since he knew nothing except what the gods gave him to know. Meriones pursued him and struck him in the right buttock. The spear tip went all the way through the bladder

under the bone. Phereclus groaned as he fell to his knees, and
death closed in around him.   68

Antenor killed Pedeus, a bastard son of Meges. The eminent
Theano carefully reared him like his legitimate siblings to please
her husband. The son of Phyleus, famed for the spear, closed in
on Pedeus and struck him in the back of the head with a sharp
spear. The bronze cut through under the tongue, above the
teeth. Pedeus fell in the dust, chewing on cold bronze.   75

Eurypylus Euaemonson took Hypsenor, the noble son of
super-hearted Dolopion, a consecrated priest of Scamander. He
was prized in his district as though he were a god. The magnificent son of Euaemon took Hypsenor, chasing him as Hypsenor was running away. Eurypylus drove his sword slashing
into the shoulder, cutting off a heavy arm. The bloody arm fell
to the ground. Dark purple death seized the eyes of Hypsenor;
his was a violent fate.   83

And so it was as they went about the fierce fighting. But you
would not have recognized Diomedes, the son of Tydeus, as he
moved around among the Trojans and the Acheans in the
throng. He rushed over the plain like a river overflowing with
the runoff from the melting snow of winter. It flows swiftly,
sweeping away bridges. Even sturdy, well-built bridges cannot
hold it back, nor can dikes hold the water back from the fruit-
ful orchards. It comes suddenly when a heavy rainstorm of Zeus
pours down. Many fine crops the young men planted fall down
in ruin under the flood. So it was when the son of Tydeus slashed
against the dense ranks of the Trojans. And none could stand
against him, even though there were many.   94

The magnificent son of Lycaon saw him as he was rushing
around the plain harassing the formations in front of him.
Quickly, Pandarus drew his curved bow, and the swift shot
struck the son of Tydeus in the right shoulder, lodging in a seam
of his armor. The sharp arrow flew all the way through the
armor, staining it with blood. The magnificent son of Lycaon
gave a very loud shout: "Rise up, greathearted Trojans, who lash

horses! The best of the Acheans has been hit, and I doubt that
he can survive the cruel dart for long. Lord Apollo, son of Zeus,
urged me on when I came from Lycia." 105

So he boasted. But the swift dart did not get the best of Diomedes. Instead, he drew back and stood in front of the horses
and chariot. He said to Sthenelus, son of Capeneus: "Move it,
brother! Get down off your chariot so you can pull this bitter
arrow out of my shoulder." 110

So he spoke. Sthenelus jumped down onto the ground. He
stood beside Diomedes and yanked the dart out of the shoulder
all at once, and blood spurted through the mail shirt. Diomedes,
good at the war cry, prayed: "Hear me, child of Zeus, who bears
the aegis, born of his head, if ever you stood favorably beside
my father or me in burning war, now again, show your love to
me, Athena! Grant that I may raise up my spear to challenge
the one who wounded me, and now boasts about it. He claims
that it will not be long before I can't see the glowing light of the
sun." 120

So he spoke in prayer, and Pallas Athena heard him. She
made his knees and feet nimble, and his hands dexterous. She
stood close to him and spoke with winged words: "Take courage now, in your fight against the Trojans. The limitless strength
of your father has come into your breast. You have as much as
the shield-handling horseman Tydeus. I took away the cloudy
mist before your eyes that was there before, so that you may
easily recognize those who are gods, as well as men. Now, if a
god comes and challenges you, remember you must not fight
all out with the immortal gods as you would with mortals. But
if Aphrodite, daughter of Zeus, ever comes into the fight, wound
her with sharp bronze." 132

Sharp-eyed Athena went away. The son of Tydeus went back
again to the forefront of the fight. Though he had been eager
in fighting the Trojans before, now he had three times the
strength. When a shepherd with his woolly sheep wounds a lion
that vaults fiercely from a pinnacle into the sheepfold, but does

not take it down, the lion's strength increases, and then it is impossible to keep it away from the farm. It slinks about the stalls
and the sheep, who are abandoned, take flight and bunch tightly
together. So eager was mighty Diomedes to mix it up with the
Trojans.   143

There, he took Astynous and Hypiron, Shepherd of the
Troops. The former, he struck above the nipple with his brazen
spear. The other he struck with his great sword on the collarbone beside the shoulder and cleaved the shoulder from the neck
and from the spine.   147

He left them behind and came upon Abantes and Polyidus,
the sons of Eurydamas, an old diviner of dreams. The old
man ought to have judged from his dreams that they would
not be coming back, since mighty Diomedes slew them. And
Diomedes went near Xanthus and Thoon, who were both late-
born sons of Phaenops. Phaenops was worn down by the misery
of age. He had no other son or offspring to inherit his wealth.
There, Diomedes killed them, taking away the life from both.
He left to their father sorrow and misery, since he would not
receive them home alive from war. The next of kin divided his
property.   158

There he grabbed hold of two sons of Priam Dardanusson.
Both Echemmon and Chromius were in one chariot. Just as a
lion leaps and grabs hold of the neck of a calf or a cow in a herd
grazing in a thicket, in such a way the son of Tydeus savagely
pulled both of them off their chariot, though they resisted. Then
he slew them, and stripped off their armor, and gave the chariot to his comrades to drive back to the ships.   165

Aeneas saw Diomedes ravaging the ranks of soldiers, and
went about through the fighting and clashing of spears looking
for godlike Pandarus. Upon finding the excellent and mighty
son of Lycaon, he stood in front of him and said: "Pandarus,
where are your bow and feathered arrows, and your fame? No
man here rivals you, nor is there anyone in Lycia who boasts
that he is better than you. So come now, raise your arms to Zeus

and shoot at this man who does so much vicious harm to the Trojans. He has loosed the knees of many valiant men. Maybe some god is angry at the Trojans. Harshest of all is the wrath of a god."

178

In return, the magnificent son of Lycaon said: "Aeneas, counselor of the brazen-shirted Trojans, that man seems to be the son of Tydeus, who is always warlike. I recognize his crested helmet and plume, and his shield, and his chariot. I do not know if he is actually a god, but I think this warlike son of Tydeus is not unlike a god the way he rages about. For already I shot an arrow at him and hit him in the right shoulder, and it went through a seam in his breastplate. I was certain that I had sent him to Hades. Some one of the immortals sticks close by him, holding a mist about his shoulders. It was this god who turned away the course of my sharp arrow. At any rate, some god is now angry.

191

"There is no chariot close by for me to mount, though somewhere in the great halls of Lycaon there are eleven beautiful chariots, newly made and covered with fluttering draperies. Beside each one of them stands a yoked pair of horses feeding on white barley and spelt. And the old warrior Lycaon gave me many instructions as we were preparing to leave his elegant house. He told me to go in one of the chariots to lead the expedition into heavy fighting on behalf of the Trojans. But I didn't listen to him, though it would have been more profitable if I had! I was concerned for my horses, afraid there might be a shortage of food for them. Crowded among the horses of friendly warriors, mine might not get enough to eat. So I left them at home and came on foot to Troy, trusting in my bow and arrows. But it doesn't seem to me to have been a good idea, after all. I tell you, I shot two of the best of the Acheans, the son of Tydeus and a son of Atreus. From both I drew real blood, but I only riled them up more. It was a cursed omen, for sure, that day when I took my curved bow off its peg and brought it with me to lovely Troy to please noble Hector.

211

"When I do get to return home and see my homeland and

my wife and my great palace with its lofty roof, I deserve to have
some enemy quickly cut off my head if I do not break the bow
into bits with my own hands and throw it into a blazing fire. It
has been a useless companion."   ·   216

Aeneas, leader of the Trojans, answered him back: "Don't
talk like that. It will not get any better until the two of us go
in strength against this man with our horses and chariot and
put him to the test of arms. Come now, get onto my chariot,
so that we can see what the horses of Tros can do on the
plain. They race wildly about here and there, in pursuit or in
flight. They will bring the two of us safely back to the city, if
Zeus grants glory to Diomedes Tydeusson. Either take the
whip and handsome reins, so I can get down from the chariot
and fight, or you wait to receive him and I'll look after the
horses."   228

The magnificent son of Lycaon spoke back to him: "Aeneas,
you should hold the reins for the horses yourself. It is far better
that the curved-front chariot carry a charioteer with whom the
horses are comfortable if we have to flee from the son of Tydeus.
Then the horses won't be too frightened to take us away, for
they will be longing for the sound of your voice. And then the
son of Tydeus will rush upon us and kill us both, and drive off
your solid-hoofed horses. So you drive your own chariot and
horses, and I will ride with you in it, to stand against his sharp
spear."   238

So saying, they mounted the many-colored chariot, energized for the pursuit of the son of Tydeus with the swift horses.
Sthenelus, the magnificent son of Capaneus, saw them and
instantly addressed the son of Tydeus with winged words:
"Diomedes Tydeusson, great joy of my heart, I see two threatening warriors anxious to fight with you since they have immense power. One is Pandarus, well skilled in archery, who
claims to be the son of Lycaon. The other is Aeneas, the illustrious son of Anchises, who claims that the mother who bore
him is Aphrodite. So come! Let us pull back with our horses,

and stop raging through the front lines, so that your loving
heart does not perish."   250

Scowling, the mighty Diomedes answered: "Do not speak in
fear! You will never persuade me. I was not born to retreat from
a fight. My strength is always firm and I won't turn back the
horses. Instead I will go against both of them. Pallas Athena
does not allow me to tremble.   256

"As for them, their swift horses will not carry both of them
away from us, even if one or the other might escape. And, I'll
tell you something else, and get it set firmly in your mind. If
the ever-wise Athena grants me the glory to kill them both, you
are to pull the reins of your own horses tight, and fasten them
to the hitching pins. Remember to rush to the chariot of Aeneas,
and drive it away from the Trojans toward the Acheans. His
horses are from the breeding stock of horses given Tros by Zeus
as recompense for Tros's son Ganymede. On that account they
are the best of all horses under either dawn or sun.   267

"Anchises, the Supreme Commander, stole from the stock,
by setting his mares under Laomedon's stallions without his
knowledge. From them six foals were born in Anchises's great
halls. Of these he kept four for himself, and raised them in his
stable. Two of them, those that inspire fear, he gave to Aeneas.
If we take those horses in this way, we will win worthy fame."   273

In such a way Diomedes and Sthenelus spoke to each other.
The other two quickly closed in on them, driving their swift
horses. The magnificent son of Lycaon addressed Diomedes
first: "Warlike, stubborn son of illustrious Tydeus, indeed the
blow of the sharp arrow didn't take you out! But now I will try
again with a spear, to see if I get a hit."   279

Pandarus raised up his hand and cast his long spear and hit
the shield of the son of Tydeus. The spearhead sailed through
his shield and passed close to his breastplate. At that, the magnificent son of Lycaon gave a loud shout: "I have hit him, stab-
bing him completely through his belly. I don't think he will stay
standing for long! O Great One, you have granted my wish!"   285

Mighty Diomedes, standing without fear, replied to him: "You missed me! I don't think that you two can be stopped until one or the other is lying in so much blood that it will satiate even Ares, who endures any beating to stay in the fight."

So saying, he made his cast. Athena guided the spear to Pandarus's nose near the eye. It punctured his white teeth, and the never-tiring bronze spearhead cut off the base of his tongue, exiting through the lowest part of the chin. He fell from the chariot, and his gleaming, multicolored armor crashed about him. There, both his soul and his strength were set free.

Aeneas rose up with his shield and long spear, fearing that somehow the corpse might be dragged off by one of the Acheans. He went around it like a lion that trusts in its valor. In front of him he held his spear and sturdy shield, eager to kill anyone who came in front of him, shouting in a terrifying manner. But Diomedes grabbed a rock in his hand. It was a great effort by the son of Tydeus, as two men could not have lifted that rock. But such a man was he that he easily handled it by himself. He hit Aeneas with it on the hip where the head of the femur turns in the hip joint, which they call a socket. The jagged stone ripped up the skin and shattered that socket and tore the tendons on both sides, and Aeneas, hero that he was, fell to his knees and stretched out his powerful hands on the ground. Dark night folded in around his eyes.

And then might Aeneas, Supreme Commander of the Trojans, have perished, had not his mother Aphrodite, daughter of Zeus, taken keen notice. She had borne him to Anchises when he was herding cattle. She threw her white arms around her beloved son and wrapped about him the folds of her dazzling gown, which served as protection lest one of the Danaans, who have swift horses, strike him in the chest with their bronze, taking his breath away.

Aphrodite carried her dear son away from the fighting. But the son of Capaneus didn't forget the inspired directions that Diomedes, good at the war cry, told him to fix in his mind. He

289

296

310

317

pulled up his swift-hoofed horses away from the din of battle and tightly fastened their reins around the pegs on the rim of the chariot. He took the horses of Aeneas, with their beautiful manes, and he drove them from the Trojans into where the well-armed Acheans were clustered. He gave them to Deipylus, a friendly comrade of his same age, so that he could drive them back to the hollow ships. Deipylus was one he valued above all others because Deipylus was as sound of mind as he was. Then the hero Sthenelus went back and regained the shiny reins of his chariot and immediately drove his horses with powerful hooves, following after Diomedes with great zest. 329

Diomedes went along armed with pitiless bonze, and recognized Aphrodite. He understood that she was a weak god and not one of those who go about giving orders in the fighting—that is to say, neither Athena nor Enyo, sacker of cities, is weak. But when the greathearted son of Tydeus came upon Aphrodite, following close to her from the great throng, he leapt up, stretching out his arm through the ambrosial gown the Graces made for her, and wounded her slightly on the edge of her hand with his sharp spear. The wound was on the base of the palm near the wrist. From the wound flowed divine ichor, which flows in the veins of the blessed gods, instead of blood. They eat no bread, nor do they drink dark red wine. On this account, they are bloodless and called immortal. 342

From Aphrodite came a loud cry. She dropped her son, but Phoebus Apollo pulled over him a black cloud with his hands, in protection, to prevent one of the Danaans, who have fast horses, from striking him. Diomedes, of the shrill war cry, shouted at Aphrodite in a loud voice: "Get out of here, daughter of Zeus, go away from the fighting. Is it not enough that you seduce helpless women? If you go about peddling strife, I think in the future you will shudder even if you just hear the word 'war.'" 351

So Diomedes spoke. And, becoming hysterical, Aphrodite went away. She was terribly worn down. Iris, swift as the wind, took her by the hand and led her away from the throng. She was suffering pain as her lovely flesh turned black. Then, on the left of the fighting she found furious Ares sitting. His spear was leaning up against his swift chariot. She fell to her knees before her dear brother, pleading, asking for his horses, which have bridles with golden headbands: "Dear brother, take care of me and give me your horses, so that I can get to Olympus, the seat of the immortals. I suffer greatly since a human warrior, the son of Tydeus, wounded me. He would now make war even against father Zeus."   362

So she spoke, and Ares gave her the horses. She mounted the chariot with grief in her own heart. Iris went up beside her and took the reins into her hands. She snapped the whip and drove off. The two horses willingly took flight. Soon, they arrived at steep Olympus, seat of the gods. There, Iris, swift as the wind, brought the chariot to a stop. She unhitched the horses and tossed alongside them some ambrosial fodder.   369

Divine Aphrodite fell at the knees of her mother Dione, who took her daughter in her arms, and, caressing her with her hand, spoke to her and called her by name: "Dear child, which of the sons of the heavens has done this to you so pointlessly, as though you were doing something evil quite openly?"   374

And then Aphrodite, fond of laughter, replied to her: "Diomedes, son of greathearted Tydeus, wounded me because I was carrying my dear son Aeneas, who is to me the most beloved of all, away from the fighting. To be clear, it is no longer just fighting between the Trojans and the Acheans in the terrible din; the Danaans are even fighting against the immortals!"   380

And then Dione, regal among goddesses, replied: "Endure it, my child, and bear it though it is painful. Many of us who dwell on Olympus suffer the pain of men while causing harsh pain to one another. Ares suffered when Otus and powerful Ephialtes, sons of Aloeus, bound him tightly and kept him in a brazen jar for thirteen months. Then might Ares, insatiable of war, have perished had not the stepmother of Otus and Ephialtes, the ever lovely Eeriboea, sent a message out to Hermes, who stole the distressed Ares away. But harsh were the bonds that held him. 391

"Hera endured when the powerful son of Amphitryon hit her in her right nipple with a three-barbed arrow, and unremitting pain took hold of her. Hades suffered in this way, also, when that same man, son of aegis-bearing Zeus, struck him in Pylos, when he was among ghosts, with a huge, sharp arrow that caused him pain. He went to the palace of Zeus, on blessed Olympus, with a grieving heart, pierced through with pain, for the arrow had fixed firmly in his stout shoulder. Paeeon spread soothing herbs on the wound and healed Hades, so that nothing caused his death. It is shameful for a man to be violent and carelessly do wicked deeds such as these with his bows and arrows, a man who makes pain for the gods who hold Olympus. Sharp-eyed Athena visited this on you. 405

"He is a fool, the son of Tydeus! He doesn't realize that one who fights against the immortals hasn't very long to live, and little time for children on his knees calling him Papa when he comes for war and terrible conflagration. But now, son of Tydeus, mighty though you are, consider that someone who is better may fight against you. Then far away might Aegialeia, prudent daughter of Adrastus, valiant wife of the noble horseman Diomedes, wake her kindly house servants from their sleep, moaning in sorrow for her youthful husband, the best of the Acheans." Dione wiped the ichor from both of Aphrodite's hands. At that, the wounded hand was healed and the intense pain abated. 417

As they looked on, both Athena and Hera resumed their sarcastic quarreling with Zeus Cronusson. Sharp-eyed Athena was first to speak: "Father Zeus, will you be angry at me in any way for what I say? It is indeed so that Aphrodite has been urging the Achean women to follow after the Trojans, for she now loves them excessively. In caressing one of the well-dressed Achean women, she scratched her slender hand on her golden belt buckle."

425

So Athena spoke and Zeus, father of both men and gods, smiled. Summoning her, he said to golden Aphrodite: "Dear child, it was not given to you to pursue the deeds of war. Instead, you should be about the sensual exploits of the bedroom. It will be for dark Ares and Athena to take care of all feats of war."

430

In such a way were the gods speaking to each other. But Diomedes, of the shrill war cry, rushed at Aeneas, although Diomedes was aware that Apollo held his hands above Aeneas. He showed no respect for the great god, but struck at Aeneas repeatedly. Three times he rose up intent on killing Aeneas, and three times was he repelled by the dazzling shield of Apollo. When on the fourth try, he charged like a demon, Apollo, who works from afar, shouted angrily: "Think on it, son of Tydeus, and back off! You ought not to consider yourself equal to the gods in any way. A race of men like unto the immortal gods has never come upon the earth and never will."

442

So Apollo spoke, and the son of Tydeus backed off a bit, avoiding the wrath of far-shooting Apollo. The god moved Aeneas away from the throng to sacred Pergamum where a temple had been built for him. There, in the great sanctuary, Leto and Artemis, who delights in archery, healed Aeneas and gave him glory.

448

Thereupon, Apollo of the silver bow fashioned himself into a likeness of Aeneas, so that he looked like him wearing his armor. Around that image the Trojans and noble Acheans raged at each other with ox hide shield and light bucklers fluttering about on both sides. Then Phoebus Apollo spoke to furious Ares: "Ares, Ares, bane of mankind, stained with death, destroyer of fortresses, could you not go in and pull that warrior, the son of Tydeus, from the fighting? He would even fight against father Zeus. Earlier he closed in on Aphro-

dite and wounded her hand near the wrist. And since then, he
has come at me like one possessed." 459

So spoke Apollo, and removed himself to sit on the spire of
Pergamum. Ruinous Ares went about in the guise of swift Acamas, leader of the Thracians, urging on the formations of the
Trojans. He called to the noble-born sons of King Priam: "Why
do still you allow the Acheans to kill the troops? Will they be
allowed to fight around the well-built gates? There is a man lying there whom we value as highly as Hector, Aeneas, son of
Anchises. Come out of the din of battle so that we may save this
valiant comrade." 469

So Ares roused up strength and spirit in each man. But Sarpedon scolded noble Hector: "Hector, where did the strength you
once had go when it vanished? Maybe you were thinking that
you could hold the city alone with your brothers and your
brothers-in-law without troops and allies. But now, I don't see
that happening. Instead, they cower like frightened dogs around
a lion. It is we who are fighting, even though we are here as allies. And I have come from a long way off in Lycia by the rippling river Xanthus. There I left behind my dear wife and young
son, and much property, things that anyone who doesn't have
longs for. Instead, I rouse up the Lycians here and am steadfast
myself in the fight. But there is nothing of mine here that the
Acheans might carry off or drive away. And you just stand
there without ordering the other Trojan troops to stand against
the Acheans and save their own wives, so that they do not become
caught up in a net that catches everything, and become booty
and prey for enemy warriors. The Acheans will quickly sack your
teeming city. It is necessary that you consider these things day
and night. You ought to plead with the leaders of the allies to
hold their positions, and so refute their harsh criticism of you." 492

So spoke Sarpedon. What he said stung Hector, and immediately, he jumped down from his chariot with his weapons.
Brandishing a sharp spear he went about the entire army

urging them on in the fight, and raised up a terrible din of war. He then circled back around to where the Acheans stood opposite. The Argives held a closely packed formation to withstand assault and were not put to rout. Just as when the wind carries chaff away from the sacred threshing floor when the threshers are at work, when red-haired Demeter separates the grain from the chaff, by lifting up the chaff into the wind, white piles of it accumulate: in such a way did white come onto the Acheans in clouds of dust that rose toward the firmament, which abounds with bronze. Dust poured from the brazen hooves of the horses pounding in the fight underneath the cloud.   506

Furious Ares enclosed all around in darkness, aiding the Trojans. He went about everywhere. Phoebus Apollo, of the golden quiver, gave Ares his directions, as it was Apollo who told Ares to urge on the spirit of the Trojans, after he saw Pallas Athena leaving; she had been helping the Danaans.   511

Apollo himself sent Aeneas back from the wealthy shrine at Pergamum, casting strength into the chest of the Shepherd of the Troops. And, as Aeneas stood among his comrades, they rejoiced on seeing him alive and hale, even robust. But they asked him no questions, as the struggle that the god of the silver bow urged on man-killing Ares and Strife, with unceasing zealotry, did not allow time for that.   518

The two Aiantes, and Odysseus, and Diomedes urged on the Danaans in the fighting. Neither they nor any others showed fear of the might of the Trojans or of the din of war. Instead they held their positions like the mists the son of Cronus fixes around mountain peaks when the wind is calmed; they were steady as when the strength of North Wind sleeps and the other violent winds are stilled, the winds who are ever scattering about the misty clouds with their shrill gusts. In such a way did the Danaans stand fast against the Trojans without fear.   527

The son of Atreus walked about the throng giving many orders: "O friends, be brave and let valor take hold of your heart. Hold each other in respect through the fierce combat. More of those who are respectful are saved than perish, but from those who flee soars neither fame nor valor." And he made a quick cast of his spear. He hit the front warrior, greathearted Deïcoon Pergasusson, a comrade of Aeneas. The Trojans valued him as much as they did the sons of Priam, since he was swift in the front lines of the fighting. Prince Agamemnon hit his shield with the spear, but the shield did not protect Deïcoon. The bronze went through it into his belly, driving through his girdle and into his stomach. He fell with a thud, and his armor crashed on top of him.   540

Then in return Aeneas took two of the best Danaan warriors, sons of Diocles, Crethon and Orsilochus. Their father lived in famous Phare; he was rich and had much livestock. His family line was from the river Alphius that flows wide through the land of the Pylians. The river fathered a son Orsilochus, ruler over many men. Orsilochus was father to Diocles and of him were born twin sons, Crethon and Orsilochus. They were highly skilled in all manner of martial arts. When they arrived at manhood, they followed the Argives to Troy in black ships. They were like a pair of lions in the high mountain peaks who were raised by their mother in a forest thicket. They prey on cows and fat sheep, ravaging the farms of men, until the men kill the lions with sharp bronze hurled from their hands. In such a way Crethon and Orsilochus were vanquished under the hands of Aeneas. They fell like tall fir trees in a high forest. Both sought to earn rewards from the sons of Atreus, Agamemnon and Menelaus, but both found their end in that place, enveloped by death.   560

Menelaus was deeply saddened at their fall. He went through to the front line armed with his deep red bronze, brandishing a spear. Ares roused up strength in him because of the two slain at the hands of Aeneas. Antilochus, the greathearted son of Nestor, saw Menelaus and went through the front line, running fast toward the Shepherd of the Troops, for fear some harm might come to him. Then the Acheans would be mired in their struggle with no purpose for being there. Antilochus stood very close beside the Shepherd of the Troops. Both men had spears in their hands and, standing opposite Aeneas, they were both eager to fight. And Aeneas did not hold his position, though he was keen for fighting, when he realized the two men stood firmly together as they pulled the corpses toward the Acheans, tossing those two wretches into the hands of their comrades while they themselves turned toward the front of the battle. 575

There the two slew Pylaemenes, equal of Ares, the ruler of the greathearted, shield-bearing Paphlagonians. Menelaus's spear pierced Pylaemenes's collarbone. Mydon, his attendant and charioteer, was the esteemed son of Atymnias. As he turned back his horses, a flying rock hit the middle of his forearm. The white, ivory-handled reins fell to the ground, into the dust. Rushing on him, Antilochus drove his great sword into Mydon's temple. Gasping for breath, Mydon fell headfirst from his well-built chariot and landed on his head and shoulders. For a long time his body remained upright, as he had fallen into deep sand, until his horses kicked him and knocked him down. Antilochus cracked his whip and drove the horses toward the camp of the Acheans. 589

Hector noticed Antilochus and Menelaus among the formations and rushed at them, yelling. The mighty ranks of the Trojans went with him. Leading them were Ares and the revered Enyo. She was with Tumult, the shameless, most ferocious. Ares held a gigantic spear that he brandished. At one time he was seen ahead of Hector, and then at another, behind him. 595

Upon seeing Hector, Diomedes, of the shrill war cry, shivered. He was like a man who goes over a vast plain and stops unprepared beside a swift river where it flows into the sea. It roars along, raising up foam. On seeing it, the man runs back upriver. In such a way, then, the son of Tydeus gave ground and spoke to his men: "O friends, how we marvel at noble Hector, a spearman courageous in warfare! But constantly alongside him is one of the gods, protecting him from destruction. And now beside Hector is Ares, who has taken on the likeness of a human. Facing the Trojans, you should be always pulling back. Do not be eager to struggle against gods."   606

So Diomedes spoke. And the Trojans came much closer to them. There, Hector killed two men in the same chariot who were known for their martial skills. They were Menestheus and Anchialus. Great Telamonian Aias was saddened at their fall. He came close to them and cast his shining spear. And he hit Amphius, son of Selagus, who lived in Paesus and had much property and many fields, but was led by fate to be among the allies of Priam and his sons. Telamonian Aias hit Amphius in his girdle; the long spear passed into his gut and fixed in his stomach. He fell with a thud. Glorious Aias ran over to strip off his armor. But the Trojans rained down spears on him, sharp and gleaming all around. His buckler took many hits, and with his heel on the corpse he retrieved his brazen spear, but he was not able to remove the handsome armor from Amphius's shoulders. The number of missiles increased. Aias became concerned that he might be surrounded by the many Trojans as they came in together. They were prodigious with their spears fixed. Huge, and powerful, and valiant though he was, and he was more so than they, they pushed him back and he retired.   626

So they toiled in heavy fighting. A powerful fate roused Tlepolemus Heraclesson, who was worthy and big, to go against godlike Sarpedon. They came close to one another, one a son, the other a grandson of Zeus the cloud-gatherer. Tlepolemus was first to speak, saying: "Sarpedon, counselor of the Lycians, of what need is there for you to be flitting about here, as you are a man unskilled in warfare? They are lying when they say you are the offspring of aegis-bearing Zeus, since you are much the inferior of those men who were earlier born of Zeus. Such men as they say mighty Heracles was. He was my father, valiant in mind and lionhearted. He once came here solely because of the horses of Laomedon. With only six ships and fewer men, he sacked the city of Troy and made its streets desolate in pursuit of those horses. But you have a cowardly spirit; your troops are perishing. While you have come from Lycia to be a bulwark for the Trojans, I do not think that you will achieve it. And you are not especially powerful, so beaten by me, you will arrive at the Gates of Hades."   646

Sarpedon, leader of the Lycians, spoke back to him: "Tlepolemus, indeed Heracles did destroy sacred Troy on account of that famous Laomedon who scolded harshly even one who had done well for him, but he did not give Heracles the horses he came so far to get. I declare that I shall bring about death and black fate for you here. You will be brought down by my spear. That will give me something to boast about, and your soul will be in Hades, celebrated for horses."   654

So spoke Sarpedon. And he raised his ashen spear. They cast the long weapons at the same moment. Sarpedon hit Tlepolemus in the middle of the neck. The painful spear point went straight through. Dark night enveloped his eyes. The long spear of Tlepolemus struck Sarpedon in the left thigh. Moving with eagerness it passed close to the bone, though Sarpedon's father Zeus still kept death away from him.   662

The noble comrades of godlike Sarpedon carried him off from the fighting, as he groaned at the long spear torturing him. No one paid attention, so nobody thought to pull out the ashen spear, so he could stand up. They were in a hurry and worked hard in caring for him.   667

On the opposite side the well-armed Acheans carried the body of Tlepolemus off from the fighting. Noble Odysseus watched with a suffering spirit, his loving heart distressed. He turned around in his mind and spirit, back and forth, how he might pursue the son of loud-thundering Zeus; how he might take the spirit out of him when he was in the midst of many Lycians. But it was not fated for greathearted Odysseus to kill the valiant son of Zeus with sharp bronze.   675

Athena turned his mind onto the Lycian throng. Odysseus

took Ceranus, and Alastor, and Noemon, and Prytanus. And he would have killed even more of the Lycians, had not great Hector, of the helmet with a waving plume, observed closely. He went through to the front in his deep red bronze armor bringing fear to the Danaans. Sarpedon, son of Zeus, was pleased as Hector came near, and spoke pathetically to Hector: "Son of Priam, do not allow me to become spoil for the Acheans as I lie here. Instead, protect me so that my life might leave me in your city. It will not be mine to return home to my beloved homeland and make my dear wife glad as well as my young son."   688

So spoke Sarpedon, but Hector said nothing to him in reply. Instead, he rushed off immediately, so that he could push back the Argives with the greatest speed and take away many of their lives.   691

The noble comrades of Sarpedon placed him underneath the lovely oak tree of aegis-bearing Zeus. Mighty Pelagon, who was his dear comrade, pushed the ashen shaft of the spear out through the exit wound. Sarpedon's breath left him and a dark mist poured over his eyes. Yet, when a breeze of North Wind passed around him, it revived his breathing again, after his spirit had cruelly expired.   698

The Argives were under the domination of brazen-helmed Hector and Ares. They were unable to drive the fighting toward the black ships, nor could they turn it back; they were constantly giving ground after they learned that Ares was among the Trojans.   703

Who were the first killed by Hector, son of Priam, and brazen Ares, and who the last? Hector slew godlike Teuthras, the exceptional horseman Orestes, and the Aetolian warrior Trechus, and Oionomaus, and Helenus, the son of Oenopus, and Oresbius with the apron of many colors, who lived in Hyle, greatly abounding in riches. Hyle lay alongside Lake Cephisis. Other Boeotians lived nearby and were very rich.   710

White-armed Hera took note of the slaughter of the Argives

in the fierce fighting. Immediately, she spoke to Athena with winged words: "Oh damn! Indomitable child of aegis-bearing Zeus, it was useless, the promise we made to Menelaus that he could sack well-fortified Troy before returning home, if we permit deadly Ares to rage in this way. Come now, let's the two of us set our minds on impetuous valor!"

So Hera spoke and Athena, the bright-eyed goddess, did not disobey. Hera, elder goddess, daughter of great Cronus, went about preparing the horses with their bridles that have golden headbands. Hebe put the bent wheels with eight spokes of bronze on both sides of the chariot. They turned around an axle of iron. Indeed, the rim of the wheels was of incorruptible gold, and the tires fitted on them were of bronze. It was amazing to see. The hubs of the wheels circling around about were of silver. The double seat and the two sides curved about were of gold and the whip had been extruded of silver. The pole by which the chariot was pulled was silver and bound to its tip was a beautiful yoke of gold. In that were beautiful golden collars. Hera led the swift-hoofed horses under the yoke; they were eager for strife and the cries of battle.   732

Athena, the youthful daughter of aegis-bearing Zeus, spread out her soft gown of many colors, which she had woven and stitched with her own hands, on the floor of her father. She put on the tunic of Zeus the cloud-gatherer, along with his battle armor that brings many tears. Around her shoulders, she tossed the terrible, tasseled aegis. It was decorated all over with likenesses of Fear, and of Strife, and of Valor, and of Rout, which gives men a freezing shudder. There was the head of the Gorgon, the terrible monster; it was the dreadful and horrifying signification of Zeus. She set on her head a helmet, embossed all around, with four horsehair plumes. It was fashioned in gold of value sufficient to maintain the armies of a hundred cities. Athena stepped into the flaming chariot and grabbed her huge spear, strong and stout. With it she could vanquish files of warrior heroes, those who brought anger to the one with the powerful father.   747

Hera snapped her whip and the ever eager horses swiftly set off. To the Hours are delegated the maintenance of the lofty heavens and Olympus. They decide whether to open the dense cloud lying around it, or close it. The gates of the heavens, held by the Hours, opened of their own accord, their hinges grating as the gates opened, when Hera drove her horses, responsive to the goad, through the clouds. The two goddesses found the son of Cronus sitting apart from the other gods on the highest of the many peaks of Olympus. Hera, the white-armed goddess, reined in her horses and went up to supreme Zeus Cronusson and spoke to him: "Father Zeus, are you not displeased that Ares is killing so many Acheans? It is not in accordance with the proper order of things. It grieves me. They are being quiet and peaceful, both Aphrodite, who delights in leisure, and silver-bowed Apollo. They are taking their ease, after having set loose this stupid idiot who does not realize which things are just! Father Zeus, would you be angry at me if I were to inflict a painful wound on Ares and chase him from the fighting?"   763

Zeus, the cloud-gatherer, replied: "All right, I will allow Athena, who gathers in spoils of war, to go in close to him and inflict pain on him, as she is especially wont to do."   766

So Zeus spoke, and Hera. The white-armed goddess cracked her whip over her horses, and the two of them flew, not grudgingly, in between the starry heavens and earth. The distance was about as far as a man can see with his eyes when situated in a watch point looking out through the atmospheric vapor over the wine-red sea. So far did the neighing horses of the goddesses go in one leap. When they came to Troy, where the rivers Simois and Scamander meet, Hera, the white-armed goddess, reined in her horses. She loosed them from the chariot and covered them over with a dense mist. The Simois caused ambrosia to rise for them to graze on.   777

The two goddesses went with steps like cowering pigeons, eager to assist the Argive warriors. And when they came to the place where the most and best of them were standing around mighty Diomedes, the noble horseman, they were pressed in tight together like lions, who eat raw meat, or wild pigs, whose strength was not weakened. There, white-armed Hera stood, taking the likeness of greathearted, brazen-voiced Stentor whose voice makes as much noise as fifty other men.　　786

"What a scandal is this! How disgraceful! The Argives seem to be low-life cowards! You were wonderful for as long as noble Achilles was with you in the fight. The Trojans never went far afield when defending the Dardanian Gate, because they were afraid of his mighty spear. But now, they fight far from the city, by the hollow ships."　　791

Speaking in this way, Hera roused the strength and spirit in each one. Bright-eyed Athena sought to rouse the son of Tydeus. She found the chief beside his horses and chariot. The wound from Pandarus's arrow was being fanned to keep him cool. He was sweaty from weariness under the wide strap of his well-curved shield. He was worn down and his arm was injured. He had a bandage on it and was wiping away dark-clotted blood. The goddess grabbed hold of the horses' yoke and spoke: "Well, you scarcely look like a son born to Tydeus. Certainly, Tydeus was short in stature, but what a fighter! And when I was fighting beside him he had no equal, even when I did not allow him to fight or to run around like a madman. When he went as a messenger away from the Acheans to Thebes, the city of Cadmus, I ordered him to feast in the great hall peacefully. Since he had a powerful presence, the young Thebans near him challenged him in martial contests, but he easily beat them all, for I was the one who came to his aid. Indeed, I am set firmly beside you, too, and I protect you. I command you to promptly get in the fight against the Trojans. But sickness has rushed into your limbs. Maybe, you have now fear and have become faint

of heart. If so, you are not the offspring of Tydeus, the warlike
son of Oeneus."   813

Mighty Diomedes spoke to her in reply: "Goddess, I recognize you, daughter of Zeus, who bears the aegis, so I will gladly
talk with you, and I will conceal nothing. Fears do not hold me
at all and I am not faint of heart. And there is no hesitation. But
I remind you that in the orders you gave me that you expressly
said that you would not allow me to fight all out against any of
the blessed gods. But if Aphrodite came into the fighting I was
to wound her lightly with sharp bronze. Now, on account of
your orders, we have pulled back from the other gods and I
gave orders to the Argives to remain here all close together.
I recognize that Ares is in command of the fight."   824

The sharp-eyed goddess Athena replied: "Diomedes Tydeusson, you who have brought joy to my heart, fear neither Ares,
nor any other of the immortals, for I am your aid in the fighting.
When you get closer, strike and have no reverence for furious
Ares as he rages. He is perverse mischief, now on one side and
then on another. He recently was talking with both Hera and
me and he promised to fight against the Trojans and assist the
Argives. But now he is among the throng of the Trojans, having forgotten the Argives."   834

So speaking, she pushed Sthenelus aside on the chariot, and
he forthwith bounded to the ground. Athena pulled back the
reins in her hands and the ever eager goddess drove off in the
chariot beside noble Diomedes. There was a loud thundering
from the beechwood axle under her mighty thrust. Awesome,
they were, as they drove along, the best of both gods and men.   839

Pallas Athena immediately drove the horses straight toward
Ares. He was stripping the armor from the giant Periphas,
the best by far of the Aetolians. He had been the magnificent
son of Ochesius. Ares, stained with death, had slain him. Athena
donned the helmet of Hades, which renders its wearer invisible, so that mighty Ares would not recognize her.   845

At that point, man-killing Ares caught sight of noble Diomedes, and first off moved back from huge Periphas and left him lying where his breath rushed out of him. From there, Ares made straight for the noble horseman Diomedes. When he got closer, as they were advancing toward each other, Ares reached forward under the yoke and reins with his bronze spear, eager to take Diomedes's life. But Athena seized it in her hands and pushed it from underneath, making Ares's assault useless. Next, Diomedes, good at the war cry, advanced with his bronze spear. Pallas Athena guided it so that it pierced Ares in the belly and through to the stomach at the place where the lower armor belt was, below the girdle. It was there that Ares was hit. The tip tore through his lovely flesh. Immediately, Diomedes pulled out the spear. Brazen Ares made a thunderous cry. It was as great a noise as would be made by nine thousand or ten thousand men struggling in war. In fear, both the Acheans and the Trojans trembled. So thunderous was the shout of Ares, insatiable of war.   863

Just as when a darkness appears in the air driven by gusts of a hot wind, so brazen Ares appeared to Diomedes Tydeusson going toward the wide heavens. Quickly, he arrived at the peak of Olympus, seat of the gods. He sat down beside Zeus, the son of Cronus, with a grieving heart. Ares showed Zeus the ambrosial ichor flowing from his wound and, sobbing, spoke to him with winged words: "Zeus, Father, are you not upset on seeing such violent acts? We gods are constantly enduring the most horrible things from each other while we bring joy to men. But we all fight against you, because you have fathered a witless, destructive girl—Athena—who is always eager to do things that are not right. All the other gods on Olympus are obedient and subservient to you. But you never oppose that girl in word or deed. Instead you goad her on; you begot a child who is smoldering with havoc. Just now, she allowed Diomedes, the arrogant son of Tydeus, to strike against immortal gods! First, he closed in on Aphrodite and wounded her hand. Then he rushed on me—me, you understand! He was demonic. My fast feet carried me off or for a long time I would have suffered the outrageous indignity of being underneath piles of hideous corpses, or since I was just barely alive, I could have been struck with bronze." 887

Looking sternly at Ares, Zeus the cloud-gatherer said: "You, who are first on one side and then on another, should not sit next to me and whine about anything. You are the most obnoxious to me of all the gods who dwell on Olympus. For you are always in love with conflict, wars, and fighting. From your mother Hera you get the unstoppable strength that is intolerable. Her, I carefully subdue with words, but I think it is because of her that you experienced these troubles. But you certainly ought not to suffer pain for a long time. After all, you were born of me. Even if you knew another one of the gods to be destructive in such a manner, so what? You have been for a long time the least of all the celestial beings." 898

So spoke Zeus, and he summoned Paeeon to heal Ares. When he came, Paeeon applied a poultice of pain-relieving herbs. The wound had not been lethal. So quickly as the sap of a fig tree curdles white milk when mixed into it and quickly stirred around, that quickly was furious Ares healed. Hebe bathed him and dressed him in pleasing garments. And then he sat beside Zeus Cronusson, rejoicing in his glory. 906

Hera and Athena, powerful protectors of the Argives, returned again to the great palace of Zeus, having stopped man-killing Ares from slaughtering men. 909

Book 6

L eft to themselves, the Trojans and the Acheans continued their dreadful combat. Many of them raced about in the fight on the plain, attacking each other with bronze spears in between the currents of the Simois and the Xanthus. 4

Telamonian Aias, bulwark of the Acheans, smashed a formation of the Trojans, setting a light of example before his comrades. He killed a man who was the best of those born among the Thracians, Acamas, son of Eussorus. Acamas was worthy and big. Aias first hit the crest of his helmet with its horsehair plume. The spear fixed between his eyes and the bronze tip pierced through the bone. Darkness enveloped his eyes. 11

Diomedes, of the shrill war cry, slew Axylus Teuthrasson, who lived in well-built Arisbe, rich in livestock. Axylus was loved by Arisbe's people. Everybody who went along the way past his house shared his hospitality. But none of them could protect him from miserable death when it chanced upon him. And it found not only him but also the spirit of his attendant Calesius, his charioteer, as well. The two of them entered the earth together. 19

Euryalus killed Dresus and Ophelius. He went at Aesepus and Pedasus, whom the Naiad nymph Abarbarea once bore to the exceptional Boucolion, eldest born son of famous Laomedon. When Boucolion was out tending sheep, he and Abarbarea lay together, commingling in love. She became pregnant and was delivered of twin sons outside the royal succession. Euryalus loosened the strength and handsome limbs underneath both. The son of Mecisteus stripped their armor from their shoulders. 28

Intrepid Polypoetes killed Astyalus, and Odysseus slew Pidytes the Perconian with his bronze spear, and Teucer killed noble Aretaon. Antilochus Nestorson killed Ablerus with his polished shaft, and the Supreme Commander Agamemnon took Elatus, who lived by the banks of the river Satnioeis, which flows clear and sparkling on steep Pedasus. The hero Leïtus took Phylacus as he fled, and Eurypylus slew Melanthius.   36

Then, Menelaus, of the shrill war cry, took Adrastus alive. When his horses took fright going across the plain, Adrastus was snagged by a tamarisk branch that caught the pole of the curved chariot. He was heading for the city, as were the others who were frightened. When he was thrown from the chariot and was lying facedown beside a revolving wheel with his mouth down in the dust, Menelaus Atreusson stood beside him with his long spear. Adrastus clasped Menelaus's knees, pleading: "Take me alive, Menelaus, and you will receive a worthy ransom. Great treasure lies in the vaults of my father: bronze, and gold, and beautifully crafted iron. My father will pay beyond counting on learning that I am alive beside the ships of the Acheans."   50

So Adrastus spoke and persuaded the heart in the chest of Menelaus. He was just about to give Adrastus to his attendant to lead immediately back to the ships, but Agamemnon came running up in front of him, shouting in an angry voice: "Oh you softhearted man, Menelaus! Why do you care about such men? Have they done especially good things to your family on behalf of the Trojans? Let none of them escape a miserable death at our hands, not one carried in the belly of a young mother, not any of them. Let all from Troy perish completely! Let them be unmourned, disappearing from sight!"   60

So speaking, the hero changed the mind of his brother since what he said was right. Menelaus pushed the hero Adrastus away from him and Prince Agamemnon stabbed Adrastus in the abdomen. He collapsed, and the son of Atreus went over to him, placed his heel on the chest, and retrieved his spear with its shaft of ash.   65

And Nestor shouted to the Argives in a loud voice: "O friends,

Danaan heroes, attendants of Ares, no one should stay behind to strip the armor from the fallen so as to take back the most spoils to the ships. Let us focus on slaughtering warriors, and strip trophies from those we kill when there are only corpses on the plain."   71

So speaking, he roused the strength and heart of each one. At that point, the Trojans, beloved of Ares, would have gone up into the fortified city of Troy in cowardly fashion, having been vanquished by the Acheans, but for Helenus Priamson. He was the best by far of those who make divinations from birds. Helenus stood beside Aeneas and Hector and said: "Aeneas and Hector, it is because of you the Trojans and Lycians who are not so special have retreated from the struggle. As you are the best, you should be first in the fight and first in counsel. Stay here, and hold the troops before the gates, going everywhere among them, before they run away into the arms of their wives, bringing joy to our enemies. For now, rouse up all the ranks hereabouts. Standing here, we will fight against the Danaans. Even though we are weary, push forward.   85

"Hector, you go into the city and then tell our mother, yours and mine, that she should select a flowing gown which seems to be most pleasing and the finest woven that she has in the palace, and which she loves most. Then she should gather the old women, and they should go to the temple of bright-eyed Athena in the high city. Mother should open the door of the sacred dwelling with her key, and place the gown on the knees of fair-haired Athena and promise her twelve yearling bullocks that have not known the goad as an offering in her temple. This, if she would have mercy on both the Trojan wives and the young children, so that she would remove the son of Tydeus from sacred Troy. He is a beastly warrior, a powerful master of rout. I think that he has become the most powerful of the Acheans. We have never feared Achilles, the regimental commander, so much as Diomedes, though they say Achilles was born of a god-

dess. But this man rages terribly and no one is able to match
him in strength." 101

So, Helenus spoke—and Hector did not disobey his brother.
Immediately, he jumped down from his chariot with his armor.
Brandishing his sharp spear, he went all around the army, urging the soldiers to fight. He raised up a furious din. The Trojans
turned around and made a stand against the Acheans. The Argives pulled back and held off on the slaughter, thinking that
one of the gods had come down from the starry heavens to
assist the Trojans, and that was why they had turned about. 109

Hector shouted to the Trojans in a loud voice: "Super-hearted
Trojans and celebrated allies, you must be warriors, friends!
Keep your fierce courage, so that I might go up to the city and
speak to the elders, and the counselors, and our wives to promise offerings to divine beings so that they will lend us their help
in battle." Having so spoken, Hector, with the helmet with a
waving plume, set off. On both his ankles and his neck bumped
the black hide that ran around the rim of his bossed shield as
he went. 118

Glaucus, the son of Hippolochus, and the son of Tydeus came
together in the middle of the fighting, eager to do battle with
each other. As they grew closer, Diomedes, of the shrill war cry,
spoke first: "Who are you, mightiest one among mortal men?
I have never seen you before in the fighting that ennobles men.
But now you have come far out from among all the others to
stand bravely against my long spear. Very unhappy are the children of those who stand against me. But if you are one of the
immortals who have come down from heaven, I do not fight
against heavenly gods. Not at all!

"Lycurgus, mighty son of Dryas, was a long time in his struggle with heavenly gods. Once, when he was rushing around
most sacred Nysa, he became angry at the nurses of Dionysus.
Man-killing Lycurgus shouted threats of thrashing Dionysus
with an ox goad, and Dionysus's nurses spilled all the sacred

implements of Bacchus on the ground. Dionysus, trembling in fear of the mighty warrior, dived into a wave of the sea, but Thetis took him into her bosom fearfully. Then the living gods became angry at Lycurgus. The son of Cronus struck him blind. He did not last long, since he was despised by all of the immortal gods. And so, I would not wish to fight against the blessed gods. But, if you are one of the humans who eat the grain of the field, come closer, so that you may sooner come into the noose of ruin."

143

And the glorious son of Hippolochus replied to Diomedes: "Greathearted son of Tydeus, why do you ask of my birth and family? It is a tribe of men that produces as many as there are leaves. Some leaves are scattered by the wind over the grounds, while others are sprouting out in the forest, when they are brought forth in the season of spring. In such a way, it is with generations of men, either they flourish or they cease to be. But if you wish, learn such things so that you might know my family well. Many men know it.

151

"There is a city named Ephyra, or Corinth, on a bay of the Ionian Sea in horse-raising Argos. There Sisyphus was living. He was born the slyest of men. Sisyphus Aeolusson, he was. To him was born a son named Glaucus and the son of Glaucus was the exceptional Bellerophon. To him the gods gave handsome good looks and sensual manliness. It happened that Antea, the wife of Proetus, to whom Zeus gave the scepter of subjugation in the district, became mad with passion for Bellerophon and proposed a clandestine sexual affair. But he, being virtuous and brave, could not be persuaded. Antea lied to King Proetus saying: 'Either you die, O Proetus, or you kill Bellerophon. He wants to go to bed with me, though I do not wish it.' So she spoke, and anger took over the king because of what he heard. Proetus plotted evil in his heart for Bellerophon and drove him away from the land of the Argives since he was far more powerful than Proetus.

166

"He had scruples against murder as it went counter to his re-

ligious beliefs, so Proetus sent Bellerophon to Lycia, providing
him with a murderous inscription written on a folded wooden
tablet. Proetus ordered him to show it to his father-in-law, the
Lycian king, so that the king would kill Bellerophon.   170

"Bellerophon went quickly to Lycia under a prestigious es-
cort of the gods. When he arrived in Lycia, where the Xanthus
flows, he was honored with enthusiasm by the king of wide
Lycia. He was treated to nine days of guest-friend hospitality, and
nine bulls were sacrificed. However, when rose-fingered Dawn
appeared on the tenth day, the king asked to see whatever message Bellerophon might have brought from the king's son-in-
law, Proetus. When the king received the evil message of his
son-in-law, he first ordered Bellerophon to kill the invincible
monster Chimaera. She was of divine origin, not of men. She
had the head of a lion, the middle of a she-goat, and a rear end
like a snake. She breathed out a dreadful, burning fire. But,
trusting in the signs of the gods, Bellerophon killed her. Next,
he was ordered to fight against the famous Solymi. This he said
was the fiercest fight he ever entered into among men. In a third
trial, he killed the Amazon viragoes.   186

"The Lycian king wove a devious plot for Bellerophon on his
return. He selected men for an ambush from among the best of
wide Lycia. But not one of them returned back home; Bellerophon killed them all. When the king realized that Bellerophon
was the brave offspring of some god, he spared him. He gave
Bellerophon his daughter in marriage and the value of half his
kingdom. The Lycians carved out a royal estate that was the best
by far with beautiful vineyards and fields so that he might remain there.   195

"His wife bore to warlike Bellerophon three children:
Isander, Hippolochus, and Laodameia. Counseling Zeus slept
with Laodameia and she bore Sarpedon of the brazen helmet.
However, even Bellerophon became detested by all the gods
when he avoided the footsteps of men while wandering around
the Aleion plain, eating his heart out. Ares, insatiate of war,

killed Isander, his son, who was fighting with the famous
Solymi, and Artemis, of the golden reins, killed Laodameia in
anger. Hippolochus sired me; it is from him I claim my descent.
He sent me to Troy, charging me often to always be superior to
others, so that I do not become a source of shame to the family
of my fathers. They are by far the best born of Corinth and of
wide Lycia, too. I boast that I am of that family and blood."   211

So Glaucus spoke, and Diomedes, of the shrill war cry, rejoiced. He fixed his spear in the bountiful earth. Then he spoke
jauntily to the Shepherd of the Troops: "You are a guest-friend
of my father's family of long standing. Once noble Oeneus
received the exceptional Bellerophon as a guest in his great
halls, where he stayed for twenty days. They gave to each other
beautiful gifts of friendship. Oeneus presented a dazzling purple
girdle of armor, while Bellerophon presented Oeneus a two-
handled goblet made of gold. I left it behind in my palace when
I came here. I have no memory of Tydeus, since I was but a little thing when he left me and died with the troops of the Acheans at Thebes. So I am a guest-friend to you when you are in
middle Argos, and you to me when I come to your district in
Lycia. We shall avoid each other's spears, even in the throng.
There are many Trojans and many of their famous allies, and it
is my duty to kill such as the gods give to me and those I happen upon while on foot. And there are many Acheans for you
to kill. I think we should exchange armor with each other in
recognition of our claim to be guest-friends of our fathers' families."   231

So his voice resonated, and Diomedes jumped down from his
chariot. They grabbed each other's hands and made a pledge.
At that moment Zeus Cronusson snatched away Glaucus's judgment. He handed over to Diomedes Tydeusson his golden
armor in exchange for bronze, a trade of the value of one hundred oxen for that of nine.   236

As soon as Hector arrived at the Scaean Gate and the oak
tree, the wives and daughters of the Trojans gathered around

him asking about their sons, and brothers, and friends, and hus-
bands. And then he told them to pray to the gods for all who
were away from them. Sorrow clung to many of them.   241

The palace of Priam was very beautiful, handsomely built,
polished to a gleaming finish. Inside it were fifty sleeping chambers of polished stone, close to each other for the married sons
of King Priam to sleep beside their lawful wives. Opposite,
across the courtyard, were twelve upper chambers of polished
stone near to one another for the married sons-in-law of King
Priam to sleep beside their glorious wives. When Hector arrived
at the palace, his mother Hecuba came to him leading Laodice,
the prettiest of her daughters. She took his hands in hers and
spoke and called him by name: "My child, why did you leave
the bold fighting to come here? The detestable sons of the
Acheans are surely wearing down our men fighting around
the city. Your heart sent you up here so that you might go up
to the high city to raise your arms to Zeus. But stay until I have
brought honeyed wine for you so that you may pour libations to
father Zeus and the other immortals first. Then it would be a
good thing for you to drink some yourself. Wine increases
the strength of warriors who are tired. Do this so that you can
defend your friends."   262

Great Hector, of the helmet with a waving plume, replied to
her: "Revered, sweet-tempered mother, don't raise up honeyed
wine for me, or I might become weak in the knees and forget
valor. I don't pray to Zeus by pouring libations of dark red wine
with unwashed hands; it is not reverent to pray to the dark-
clouded son of Cronus with palms slimed with blood and gore.
Instead, choose a gown that is one most especially precious to
you and the finest woven in the great hall, by far the best in it.
Then gather together the elder women and go to the temple of
Athena, who gathers in the spoils of war, with incense, and place
the gown on the knees of beautiful-haired Athena, promising
her that we will sacrifice twelve yearling calves, females who
have not known the goad, in her temple if she might show mercy

on the city and to both the wives and young children of the Trojans, and if she were to remove the son of Tydeus from sacred Troy; he is a savage and powerful warrior, who inspires fear. 278

"While you go to Athena's temple, I'll go in search of Paris so that I can summon him if he wants to hear what I say. How I wish the earth would suddenly gape open and swallow him. The Olympian has laid a great fate on the Trojans, and on great-hearted Priam and his children, because of Paris. I would like to see him go down to shining Hades; then my own heart might forget the miserable suffering he has caused." 285

So Hector spoke, and Hecuba left and summoned her chambermaids to the great hall and told them to gather the old women from the lower city. She herself went down into her scented chamber. In it were her many-colored gowns, the work of the women of Sidon. Alexander had brought them back from there himself, sailing across the wide deep, on the same journey when he had brought back Helen, daughter of a noble father. Hecuba lifted up one of the gowns that lay at the bottom of the others, choosing it as the gift for Athena. It had the most beautiful ornaments and was also of the finest weave. It gleamed like a star. Then she set off with many old women following along. 296

When they arrived at the temple of Athena in the high city, pretty-cheeked Theano opened the doors for them. She was the daughter of Cisses and wife of the noble horseman Antenor. The Trojans placed her in the position of priestess of Athena. All the women raised their hands and wailed loudly while pretty-cheeked Theano took the gown and placed it on the knees of Athena. She prayed to the daughter of great Zeus: "Revered Athena, protector of the city, noble goddess, break the spear of Diomedes, and deliver him fallen facedown in front of the Scaean Gate, and we will immediately sacrifice twelve calves in your temple. They will be yearling females, untouched by the goad. This we shall do if you would have mercy on the city, and on the wives and children of the Trojans." 310

So, she spoke, and in like manner the old women prayed to the daughter of great Zeus. But Pallas Athena shook her head in refusal. 312

Meanwhile, Hector had gone to the beautiful palace of Alexander. Paris had built it himself, along with men who were the best craftsmen in rich-soiled Troy. They built for him a sleeping chamber, a dining room, and a courtyard close to both Priam and Hector in the high city. Hector, beloved of Zeus, entered with a spear in his hands eleven cubits in length, or seventeen feet. At the tip of the shining shaft was a bronze spearhead, and around that ran a golden ring that held it on to the shaft. Hector found Paris in his bedchamber adjusting his curved bow. His armor and shield were collected around him. Argive Helen sat among her servants and chambermaids directing their exacting work. On seeing Paris, Hector scolded him: "You rascal! It is not a pretty thing that you nurse some grudge like this, hiding out while the troops are perishing in the fighting around the high city and the fortress wall. It is because of you that both the shouts and the war burn as they do around the lower city. Besides, even you would give a hard time to somebody shirking hateful warring. So get up, I am afraid that the city might be burned up in a blazing fire." 331

And godlike Alexander replied: "Hector, since you have scolded me according to what is right and have not gone beyond that, I will tell you, and think about what you hear from me. I am not sitting around in the bedchamber with a grudge against the Trojans, as you claim. I want to heed the shouts, and just now my wife was talking to me in gentle words, urging me into the battle. That seems to me the better course. Victory switches back and forth between warriors. But come, I will stand in the fight; I shall enter the armor of Ares. Go ahead. I will join you. I think I will even beat you there." 341

So Paris spoke, but Hector said nothing back to him. Helen spoke to Hector calmly: "O brother-in-law, what a trouble-making wanton I am. I shudder at the thought. It would have

been better if, on the day when first my mother bore me, I had
been taken to a mountain to face a bad windstorm or had been
cast into a wave of the thundering sea. The wave would have
washed me away before any of this happened. Ever since, the
gods have concocted so much evil because of me. I wish that
my husband were a braver man, for I have known the reproach
and disgust of many people because of him. Paris's resolve is
not firm now, nor will it be in the future. And he will reap the
fruits of it. But come in and sit here on the couch, brother-in-
law, since you have worked hard to defend the city because of
the bitch that I am and because of the blindness in the mind of
Alexander. On account of those things has Zeus placed an evil
fate on us, though we will be celebrated in the songs of men
now and in the hereafter."   359

Great Hector, of the helmet with a waving plume, replied:
"Don't make me sit down, Helen. Even though you are welcoming, you will not persuade me. Already my heart urges me on
so that I can protect the Trojans. They need my presence. Instead, hurry Paris along, as he ought to himself. That way, he
can meet up with me in the city. I'll go home to see my servants,
my wife, and my son. I still don't know if I will return again, or
whether the gods will take me down under the hands of the
Acheans."   368

So speaking, Hector left. Soon, he arrived at his comfortable
palace, but he did not find white-armed Andromache in the halls.
Not finding his wonderful wife, he stood at the entrance and
asked of his servants: "Come, tell me truthfully, servants, where
did white-armed Andromache go when she left? Has she gone
to visit one of my sisters or one of my well-dressed sisters-in-law?
Or, did she go to the temple of Athena with the other fair-
haired Trojan women to propitiate the terrible goddess?"   380

The diligent housekeeper answered: "Hector, since you especially charged us with speaking the truth, I tell you that she
is not with your sisters or your well-dressed sisters-in-law, nor
has she gone to the temple of Athena with the other fair-haired

Trojan women to propitiate the terrible goddess. Instead, she went to the great tower of Troy, so that she could hear the Trojans being worn down by the powerful Acheans. She felt the urge to get to the wall as she was justly concerned and agitated. She took the child with her." 389

The housekeeping girl spoke, and Hector rushed out of the house, going along the same route back along the well-kept avenues straight through the great city, and came to the Scaean Gate. He was about to pass through it into the plain when his generous wife came running up to him. Andromache was the daughter of greathearted Eetion, who had lived at the base of wooded Mount Placus in Thebes-under-Placus. He was the king of the men of Cilissia. She approached him then and with Andromache came a nursemaid with an infant child at her breast. He was the beloved son of Hector and he was as beautiful as a star. Hector called him Scamandrius, but others called him Astyanax, king of the city, because Hector was Troy's only protector. 403

Hector smiled quietly on seeing his son. Andromache stood close to Hector, her eyes gushing tears. She took his hands in hers and spoke to him: "My dearest one, your might will waste you. Have pity for your tender child and unlucky me. So quickly will I become your widow. Charged up as they all are, the Acheans will quickly kill you. It would be better for me to be buried in mother Earth if I lose you. Never again will I feel the warmth that comes when we lie next to each other, nor will I experience the pleasure that comes from that. After you meet your fate, I will have only grief. 413

"I have neither father nor revered mother. Indeed, my father was killed by noble Achilles when he sacked lofty-gated Thebes, that teeming city in Cilissia. Achilles killed Eetion, but he did not strip his body. He was too scrupulous for that, and instead burned it with its gleaming armor on and erected a mound over it. The mountain nymphs, those daughters of aegis-bearing Zeus, planted elm trees around the mound. 420

"There were seven of my brothers in our halls. All of them went down to Hades that day. Noble Achilles, fleet of foot, slaughtered every one of them among the cloven-footed oxen and white sheep. My mother succeeded as ruler of the land at the base of Mount Placus. When Achilles brought her here to this place with all her other possessions, he took a vast ransom in exchange for her release. Artemis, who delights in archery, shot her with the sweet arrows of a heart attack in your father's palace.   428

"Hector, you are my father and my revered mother, and my brothers, and my ardent companion in our bed. So come, take pity on me, and stay here now on the tower, for I fear that you might make your son an orphan and your wife a widow. Position the troops near the fig tree. That is the place where the wall that runs around the city is most easily scaled. Three times the best of them have made a try at the wall there. Both of the Aiantes, and famous Idomeneus, and both the sons of Atreus, and the valiant son of Tydeus have tried. Either someone very knowledgeable gave them inside information, or maybe their own hearts directed them."   439

Great Hector, of the helmet with a waving plume, spoke back to her: "O woman, all of those things concern me now. I have a terrible dread for the harm that might befall the Trojan women and their mothers, who wear gowns with long trains, if I shy away from fighting for them. And it is not that my heart drives me to do it, but rather that I have learned to be brave at all times and to fight in the vanguard of the Trojans, so that I may both vindicate my father and win great glory there for me. I know well in my heart and mind that is the right thing to do.   447

"There will be a day when sacred Troy may be destroyed, along with Priam and Priam's troops of spearmen. But such suffering in the future will not be on my account, nor the suffering of Hecuba herself nor of King Priam, nor that of my brothers. Many of the valiant ones would have fallen in the dust at the hands of the Achean enemies. And so for you on that day, it might be that one of the brazen-shirted Acheans would lead you away weeping far from the freedom of your homeland. And you might be in Argos weaving at another woman's loom or fetching water from the fountains of Messeis or those of Hyperia in Thessaly, under duress, weighed down by hard necessity. And perhaps, someone seeing your eyes welling tears might say: 'I recognize her as the wife of Hector. He was the bravest of the noble Trojan horsemen at the fighting around Troy.' Whenever somebody might say that, your pain will return anew. That's what would happen if there is want of a warrior to ward off the day of entering slavery. I would rather be dead, enclosed by the earth under a marker, than hear your screams as they drag you off."   465

So speaking, glorious Hector stretched out his arms to his son. Immediately, the child jerked back against the breast of his buxom nurse, screaming in fright at the sight of his father wearing the bronze and the horsehair plume. He watched in terror as it nodded from the top of the crest. At that, both his loving father and revered mother laughed. Glorious Hector quickly took the helmet off his head and set it on the ground, gleaming all around. Then, he took his son into his arms, caressing and kissing him, and said in prayer to Zeus and the other gods: "Zeus and you other gods, grant that my son may be as I am, the very best among the Trojans, in strength and virtue, and that he may rule powerfully in Troy. Grant also that someday one may say that he is much braver than his father as he returns from battle. Grant that he may carry off the gory arms of prized trophy after killing a hostile warrior. May he be the delight of his mother's life."   481

So speaking, he placed his son in the arms of his dear wife. She received the baby into her scented bosom, crying as she laughed, realizing that her husband did take pity on her. Hector stroked her hands, and spoke to her, and called her by name: "Dear heart, don't let yourself grieve so much for me. It would not be unreasonable for someone to send me to Hades. I assure you that there is no way for men to escape death. Whether to a good man, or a bad one, it comes even to the very best of men. But, go home and get about your household chores, weaving and directing the servants in their work about the house. War is for all men, especially for me. To be sure, I was born for it in Troy."   493

So speaking, glorious Hector seized his helmet with the horsehair plume. His beloved wife stood for a moment, then turned and went back, weeping copious tears. Quickly she arrived at the comfortable palace of man-killing Hector. There she found many servants and roused them all to groaning in sorrow. They were sorrowful, though Hector was still alive and had been in the house. For they believed that he would not return from the fighting, escaping the might and arms of the Acheans.   502

Paris did not linger long in his lofty palace. Instead, having put on his famous armor of multicolored bronze, he hurried through the city, giving over himself to his nimble feet. It was like when a horse, feeding in a stable, breaks loose from his halter and runs through the plain with hooves pounding, elated at bathing in the widely rippling familiar river. He holds his head high, and his mane flows around his shoulders, and he gives himself over to his own magnificence, his leaping knees carry him along as it is the nature and habit of horses.

In such a manner Paris Priamson came down from the high citadel. As he went, his gleaming armor shone like the sun. He chuckled in exhilaration as his speedy feet carried him along.   514

He met up with noble Hector, his brother, as Hector was about to turn away from the spot where he had just had his tender exchange with his wife. The godlike Alexander spoke first: "Yes, sir! I wasted no time, but dressed in my armor right away as you ordered. Have I not come at the proper time?"

Hector of the helmet with the waving plume replied to Paris, saying: "Man, you may be sure that no fit warrior would be scorned in the toil of battle for being bold. You may go on, willingly or not, as you wish. It gripes my heart when I hear of your shame from the Trojans; they have much trouble because of you. But let's go. We can reconcile these matters down the line, if Zeus, along with the everlasting gods in the heavens, should grant us the might to stand firm in freedom in our halls and drive the well-armed Acheans away from Troy."

529

Book 7

Having so spoken, glorious Hector went through the gates with his brother Alexander. Both were ready to fight. It was like when some god gives sailors a wind when they desperately need it, when their limbs are exhausted with fatigue at their oars worn slick from handling as they plow across the deep. So it was when the pair showed themselves to the Trojans, who so earnestly longed to see them.   7

Paris took Menesthius, the son of Areithous, king of Arne. Areithous was one who fought with the mace. Menesthius was born to Areithous and lovely-eyed Phylomedusa. Hector hit Eïoneon with his sharp-tipped spear in the neck under the sturdy, bronze helmet, and his limbs were loosed. In the furious fighting, Glaucus, son of Hippolochus, the leader of Lycian warriors, hit Iphinus Dexiusson in the shoulder, as he leapt from his swift chariot. Iphinus fell to the ground and his limbs were loosed.   15

When the sharp-eyed goddess Athena noticed that the Argives were perishing in the intense fighting, she came down from the peaks of Olympus, rushing to sacred Troy. Seeing her, Apollo rushed from Pergamum because he wanted victory for the Trojans and stood in front of her beside the oak tree. The Lord Apollo, son of Zeus, spoke first to Athena: "Daughter of great Zeus, why have you come breathlessly back from Olympus? Was your heart greatly agitated, or is it so you could give the Danaans a questionable victory in the battle, since you have no pity at all for Trojans who are perishing? If you were to trust me a bit, it would be much more profitable. Now, we shall stop the war and destruction for today. When they fight again they will find a suitable end to the endeavor when it pleases the hearts of us immortals; at that time the city will be sacked."   32

The sharp-eyed goddess Athena spoke back to Apollo: "That works for me, one who shoots from afar. I thought about that and other plans as I came from Olympus to the Trojans and the Acheans. But, come now, how do you want us to stop the men's fighting?"   36

The Lord Apollo, son of Zeus, replied: "We rouse up the mighty strength of noble horseman Hector, so that he can challenge the Danaans to have one of them fight against him in mortal combat. The brazen-shirted Acheans will be startled by his offer and sink into consternation to find someone to fight against noble Hector."   42

So he spoke, and the sharp-eyed goddess Athena did not disobey. Their plan found favor with the counseling gods, and they put it into the mind of Helenus, a dear son of Priam. He went and stood beside Hector, and told him what had been revealed: "Hector, son of Priam, counselor equal to Zeus, will you listen to something from me now, as I am your brother? Have the other Trojans and all the Acheans sit down, and challenge the one of the Acheans who is the bravest to fight against you in mortal combat. It is not your fate to die this way. So I heard in an omen from the gods, who live forever."   53

So Helenus spoke, and Hector was much taken with what he heard. He took his spear by the midpoint of its length and went into the ranks of the Trojans and made them all sit down. Accordingly, Agamemnon, and Athena, and Apollo, of the silver bow, made the well-armed Acheans sit. Their dense ranks sat with their shields, and helmets, and bristling spears. It was like when West Wind first starts to blow across the dark of the deep, it raises up rough undulations across the surface of the sea. That is how the ranks of the Trojans and the Acheans looked as they were sitting on the plain. Seated, they were like buzzards in a lofty oak of Zeus, who bears the aegis, taking pleasure at the thought of feasting on warriors.   66

Hector stood up with them all around him and spoke: "Hear me, Trojans, and well-armed Acheans. I say what my heart

directs me. The son of Cronus, who weighs human affairs on
high, did not fulfill our treaty. Instead, intending to do harm,
he has ordained for us both that either you take well-fortified
Troy or are yourselves vanquished beside the ships that sail over
the sea. There are among you the bravest of all the Acheans. If
the heart of one of those now tells him to fight against me, let
him come here as challenger to noble Hector. Thus, I swear,
and let Zeus be our witness, that if he takes me with his drawn-
out bronze, he may strip off my armor and carry it to the
hollow ships. My body would be returned back home, so that
the Trojans and the Trojan wives might give me my share of
the funeral pyre. But if Apollo gives me the glory, and I take
him, I will strip off his armor and carry it to sacred Troy and
hang it in front of the temple of far-shooting Apollo. His corpse
will be returned to the well-benched ships, so that the long-
haired Acheans can give it funeral rites and build a burial
mound over it beside the wide Hellespont. And, at some time,
even in generations yet to come, someone sailing in a ship, with
many oars, across the wine-red deep might say: 'That is the
burial mound of one long dead, defeated and killed by glorious
Hector.' That way my fame will not die."   91

So Hector spoke, and all became quiet. Embarrassed at de-
clining, still the Acheans were afraid to take him up on his
proposition. After a while, Menelaus, with much groaning
in his heart, stood up and mocked them jeeringly: "Oh my soul!
You pretentious windbags, Achean girls! There is no longer any
Achean man who would return his taunts. If there is no Danaan to go against Hector now, this will go from bad to worse.
You are nothing but water and dirt, sitting here lifeless and
inglorious like this. Fine, I will arm myself for it. Above us, the
verdict of victory is held by the immortal gods."   102

Having so spoken, he put on his beautiful armor. Then would
Menelaus have met his end, since Hector was a far better warrior than he. But the Achean kings rose up to restrain him. The
great Prince Agamemnon Atreusson himself seized Menelaus's

right hand and spoke to him, calling him by name: "Highborn
Menelaus, you are crazy! There is no need for you to behave so
rashly. You have cares enough, as it is. You have no business
fighting a man better than you, such as Hector Priamson, on
account of rivalry. The others dread him, too. Even Achilles,
who is much braver than you, would shudder at going against
this one in honorable combat. So sit down now in the band of
your comrades. Another one of the Acheans will take Hector's
challenge. Even though Hector is fearless and insatiable of war,
I think he will gladly bend his knees to rest if he escapes the
red-hot flames of battle and hateful combat."   119

So Agamemnon spoke. Since the hero justly spoke to his
heart, his brother obeyed him. Then, Menelaus's attendants
happily took the armor off his shoulders. Nestor stood up and
addressed the Argives: "A huge grief has truly come to the
land of the Acheans! The noble horseman Peleus would raise
a great lamentation, he the most excellent in Thessaly at planning and speaking. Once he asked me, in his house, the birth
and genealogy of all the Argives. And now, if he were to hear
they cower in front of Hector like frightened birds, he would
raise his arms up to the immortals, praying that his spirit depart and enter the House of Hades.   131

"Oh, would to father Zeus, and Athena, and Apollo, that it
be as when in my youth I was with the assembled Pylians and
Arcadians, experts at throwing the spear, when they fought near
the currents beside the swiftly flowing Celadon, next to the wall
of Pheia, on account of Jardanus. Ereuthalion was in the forefront
of them, a man like a god, with the armor of King Areithous
around his shoulders, noble Areithous, the 'mace-man.' That is
what the warriors and buxom women called him, because he
fought not with bow and arrows, nor with the long spear, but
with an iron mace. He could wipe out ranks of soldiers with it.   141

"Lycurgus killed Areithous. He did it with cunning, not at
all with might. Anticipating Areithous at a narrowing in a road
where his mace could not protect him from destruction,

Lycurgus pierced him in the middle with his spear. Areithous slumped to the ground faceup, and Lycurgus stripped the armor, which Ares provided to Areithous, from his body. And Lycurgus wore the armor himself in the struggle of Ares. When he passed into old age in his halls, he gave the armor to Ereuthalion, his beloved attendant, to wear. Wearing the armor of Ares, Ereuthalion challenged many of the bravest. But with much trembling and fear, none dared take up his challenge. However, my heart was fit for much daring and courage. Even though I was youngest of all, I fought against Ereuthalion. Athena gave me the glory. He was certainly the tallest and most powerful man I killed, and there he lay with limbs sprawled out.   156

"Ah, would that I were a young man at the prime of manhood, and my strength were steady! If both were so, I would quickly take up the challenge to fight against Hector, of the helmet with the waving plume. Though some of you are the best by far of all the Acheans, it appears that none is especially eager to go against Hector."   160

So the old man rebuked them, and nine men in all stood up. The first, by far, was the Supreme Commander Agamemnon, and then the mighty Diomedes Tydeusson stood. Beside them stood the two Aiantes, clad in zealous bravery. And, beside them stood Idomeneus and Meriones, the attendant of Idomeneus. Meriones was equal to man-killing Enyalius. And Eurypylus, the magnificent son of Euaemon, stood. Up stood Thoas Andraemonson and noble Odysseus. They all wanted to fight against noble Hector. Nestor, the Geranian horseman, spoke to them again: "Now, destiny will come by lot, thoroughly shaken. It will benefit the well-armed Acheans, and will benefit the heart of the one whose lot is chosen, if he escapes the red-hot flames of battle and hateful combat."   174

So spoke Nestor. Each of those standing marked a lot with his sign and tossed it into the helmet of Agamemnon Atreusson. The troops lifted up their arms to the gods and prayed. This

is what one, looking to the wide heavens, was saying: "Father
Zeus, may destiny come either to Aias, or the son of Tydeus, or
to himself, the king of Mycene, rich in gold."   180

So they prayed. And Nestor, the Geranian horseman, shook
the helmet and a lot popped out, which they all hoped was that
of Aias. A herald carried it around to all in the throng, showing
it in his right hand to the chiefs of the Acheans, but none of
them recognized it as the one each of them had marked with his
sign. But when the herald carrying the lot came and stood beside Aias and showed it to him, he recognized his mark on it. It
was the one illustrious Aias had written on and thrown into
the helmet. Aias was elated. He threw the lot to the ground beside his foot, and shouted: "Oh friends! This is for sure my lot
and I am very pleased in my heart, since it will fall to me to dress
down noble Hector. But, come, while I put on my battle armor,
pray to Lord Zeus Cronusson. You may pray silently so that the
Trojans don't hear, or openly, since we have nothing whatever
to fear. There is nobody with strength so great that he can run
over me if I don't allow it. Nor is there anybody with the skill
to do it either, since I hope I am not an untrained novice at this,
being as I was born and reared in Salamis."   199

So Aias spoke. The troops prayed to the Lord Zeus Cronusson. This is how one was speaking, as he looked to the wide
heavens: "Father Zeus, who rules from Ida, most glorious and
greatest of all, give victory to Aias that he may earn unsurpassed
fame. But if you love Hector and care especially for him, grant
to them both equal might and glory."   205

So they spoke and Aias put on his helmet of gleaming bronze.
Next, he covered all of his flesh with armor. Then he rushed out
like monstrous Ares, who enters among warriors brought together by Zeus to fight in mind-crushing combat. In such a way
did Aias rise up to be a formidable bulwark for the Acheans,
with a smile on his awe-inspiring face. Beneath him, he left footsteps far apart, his stride great as he went. He brandished a
long spear. Seeing him brought joy to the Acheans, while

terrible fear and trembling seized the limbs of each Trojan. In his own chest, Hector felt the pounding of his heart. But there was no way he could back off now, or slip back into the throng of the troops, since it was he who issued the challenge for the fight.   218

Aias came closer carrying a shield that was like a battle tower. Tychius had fashioned it. He was the very best of those living in his home area of Hule who worked with hides. He made the many-colored shield from seven laminated layers of ox hide skinned from the best-raised bulls. Over that he worked an eighth layer of bronze. Holding the shield in front of his chest, Telamonian Aias stood very close to Hector and taunted him, saying: "Now, you may see clearly one from among those who are both the best of the Danaans and next after lionhearted Achilles, who smashes whole ranks of men. But he lies beside the beaked ships, nursing a grudge against the Shepherd of the Troops, Agamemnon. There are many of us who could stand against you, so begin the fight."   232

Great Hector, of the helmet with the waving plume, answered him: "Noble-born Aias Telamonson, company commander, do not rile me as you would a callow boy or a woman who knows nothing of the deeds of war. I well know both how to fight and to kill men. I am skilled in parrying the shield of tanned oxen to the right and I know how to shift and parry to the left. I can withstand the blows of fighting. I know how to drive a fast-charging chariot, and I know the dance of Ares in the heat of close combat. But I don't want to throw at you while you are hiding like this, peering out behind your cover. I would prefer to throw at one in the open."   243

Even so, Hector raised the long spear and cast at the terrible shield of seven layers of hide topped with bronze in the eighth. The tireless, dazzling bronze went through six layers, and in the seventh hide the shield held. Next, noble-born Aias raised up his long spear and cast it back at the son of Priam, striking against his shield that was balanced all around. The massive, shining

spear passed through the shield and through the highly polished
and fitted breastplate. The spear went completely through, close
to Hector's flank, rending his tunic. Hector ducked and eluded
black fate.   254

Both of the men pulled out the spears, each using both hands.
At that point they fell on each other like lions that eat meat raw,
or wild hogs, whose might is not meager. Next, the son of Priam
struck the middle of Aias's shield with his spear, but the
spearhead bent. Noble-born Aias hurled and struck Hector's
shield. The spear point went through, startling Hector by its eagerness. The point sheared across Hector's neck as it passed, and
dark blood spurted out. But Hector, of the helmet with the
waving plume, didn't back off from the fight. Giving up a little
bit of ground, he grabbed a stone with his brawny hand. It
had been lying on the plain, black, and jagged, and big. He
hurled it against the dreadful, seven-hided shield of Aias. It
struck the middle of the boss. But the bronze held tight against
it. After that, Aias raised up a stone that was very much larger
and threw it with great speed. Hitting against Hector's shield, the
rock, which was like a millstone, smashed it to bits. It knocked
Hector's own knees out from under him. As he lay stretched
out faceup, a remnant of his shield wobbled near him. Apollo
immediately set Hector upright.   272

At that point they would have fought each other with swords
in close combat had not heralds, messengers of Zeus and of men,
come over from the Trojans and the brazen-shirted Acheans.
They were Talthybius and Idaeus, both men of sound judgment. They came in between the two men with their scepters.
The herald Idaeus spoke his thoughts: "My beloved sons, fight
and do battle no longer. Zeus, the cloud-gatherer, loves the two
of you equally. You both are warriors, and we all know that.
But to be sure, night falls, and it is a good thing to obey the
night."   282

Telamonian Aias responded to him saying: "Idaeus, you
ought to tell Hector to say those things, because he himself, first

challenged all of the bravest. He started it. I will gladly obey if
this man does as well."   286

And great Hector, of the helmet with the waving plume, said
back to him: "Aias, for sure, it was some god that gave you great
size, and might, and good sense. You are the best, by far, of the
Acheans with a spear. Now, we shall cease the fighting and
ferocious combat for today. We shall fight again in the future if
fate decrees it for us; and may it give one of us victory. Night is
falling. It is proper that we obey the night, so that you may bring
joy to all the Acheans around the ships, especially your clans-
men and comrades. I shall go to the great city of King Priam
and delight the Trojans and the Trojan women, who wear gowns
with long trains, who prayed to the god for me to enter the contest. We ought to give each other extravagant gifts so that one
of the Acheans or the Trojans might say that we fought in the
contention that destroys the mind, but that we were separated
in friendship and goodwill."   302

Having spoken thus, Hector gave his silver-studded sword
and scabbard as a prize, along with its handsomely worked baldric. Aias gave Hector his resplendent girdle of Phoenician scar-
let. The two men parted and one went among the Achean
troops, while the other went into the noisy band of Trojans.
They had had no hope that Hector would be safe and rejoiced
at seeing him coming toward them alive and hale, having escaped the invincible hands of Aias. They joyfully led him off
to the city. The well-armed Acheans led Aias away from his
comrades to noble Agamemnon, overjoyed at his victory.   312

And when they were inside the hut of the son of Atreus, the
Supreme Commander Agamemnon sacrificed for them an in-
tact bull five years old to the son of Cronus, who surpasses all
in might. They flayed him and butchered the carcass and cut it
up into small pieces. Those, they pierced and mounted on spits
and roasted carefully. Then they pulled the meat off the spits.
When they had stopped their work, they set about a feast. And
the spirit wanted for nothing at their proper feast. The hero, the

great Prince Agamemnon Atreusson, presented as a prize to Aias the entire chine of beef, the tastiest part close to the base of the ribs. And when any desire for food or drink had left them, Nestor spoke to them. It was he, the old man, who in the past had woven for them the very best of plans. Now, he addressed them with wisdom, saying: "Son of Atreus, and you others who are the best of all the Acheans, many long-haired Acheans have died. Keen Ares has scattered their blood around the amply flowing Scamander. Their souls have gone down to Hades. On this account, Agamemnon, it is necessary that you cease the fighting of the Acheans at dawn. We shall circle around and gather their corpses and load them into wagons drawn by horses and mules. That done, we shall give them their share of fire out a little ways in front of the ships, so that each man may take the bones to their children whenever we return home to our homeland. We will set one fire for all together without distinctions and build a funerary mound out from the plain.   338

"In front of that mound we should quickly build a fortification that rises high up in the air, as protection for both the ships and ourselves. We should put well-fitted gates in the wall so that chariots may pass through on a roadway. Out from the wall we will dig a deep trench close by, which will protect us from both troops and chariots, at such time as the haughty Trojans rush toward us."   343

So Nestor spoke, and all the kings praised him. Meanwhile, the Trojans were gathered together in the high city, and there was loud murmuring near the palace of Priam. Prudent Antenor was first to speak: "Hear me, Trojans, and Dardanians, and allies. I say the things the heart in my breast tells me to say. Bring Argive Helen here, and bring her possessions with her so that we may give them to the sons of Atreus. Because if we fight now, we will be in breech of our solemn oath. Doing so, we can hope that things might turn out better than what now is not good. We ought to do this."   353

Certainly, you may be sure, he said that. Afterward, he sat

down. Among them stood Alexander. The husband of fair-haired Helen answered him with winged words: "Antenor, what you said just now did not please me. You ought to have a better idea than that. Perhaps, you spoke in haste, or maybe the gods have destroyed your mind. I declare to the Trojans, noble horsemen, that I absolutely will not give up the woman. I would, though, give up that property of ours I brought back from Argos. I wish to give all that and anything else taken from our possessions."   364

So Paris spoke, and sat down. Among them stood up Priam Dardanusson, who was counselor equal to the gods. Thoughtfully, Priam addressed them and said: "Hear me, Trojans, and Dardanians, and allies, since I say what the heart in my breast orders me to say. Now, let us take our dinner down from the city, as we have in the past. But post sentries and have each of them remain awake and watchful. At dawn, let Idaeus go to the hollow ships to tell the sons of Atreus, Agamemnon and Menelaus, the proposition of Alexander, since it is because of him that this conflict has arisen. Also, let him present a serious proposition—they might wish to cease the horrible fighting so that we may burn the corpses. Later on, we can resume the battle, if some deity decrees it so for us. And he may give one or the other victory."   378

So spoke Priam. They heard him and readily obeyed. They took their dinner throughout the camp. At dawn, Idaeus went to the hollow ships. He found them, the Danaans, attendants of Ares, in assembly beside the stern of Agamemnon's ship. He stood in the middle of them and the loud-voiced herald called to them in his resonant voice: "Sons of Atreus, and you others of the best of all the Acheans, Priam and the other illustrious Trojans order me to speak, though hoping that it might be pleasing and felicitous to you. They ordered me to tell you of a proposal from Alexander, because of whom the conflict has arisen: The property that Alexander brought to Troy in his hollow ships—Oh, how I wish that he had perished!—all that

property, he wishes to give up and other things of his possessions. The girl who was the wife of Menelaus, he swears he will
not give up, though the Trojans told him to.   393

"The Trojans ordered me to make this proposal—they hope
that you would wish to cease the horrible fighting in order that
we may burn the corpses. We can resume fighting down the line
if some deity decrees it for us; may he give to one or the other
victory."   397

So Idaeus spoke. Everyone became silent and said nothing.
After a long while, Diomedes, of the shrill war cry, spoke
heatedly to them: "Let nobody receive the property of Alexander, nor that of Helen. Even a silly fool knows the noose of
destruction is fastened on the Trojans."   402

So he spoke, and all the sons of the Acheans shouted in
agreement with what the noble Diomedes said. And then, the
Lord Agamemnon said to Idaeus: "Idaeus, surely you have heard
yourself the mind of the Acheans as your answer. Such as it is,
it pleases me greatly. But the burning of the corpses, that I do
not refuse. No one should be sparing in the observances for the
dead. When they die, quickly appease them with fire. Let Zeus
the thunderer, husband of Hera, be witness that I made this
pledge."   411

So speaking, Agamemnon held up his scepter to all the
gods, and Idaeus went back to sacred Troy by the way he had
come. The Trojans and Dardanians sat in assembly, all gathered together to receive Idaeus whenever he might return. He
did arrive and delivered his message, standing in their midst.
They very quickly got ready both to gather in the dead and
to gather in wood, as well. The Argives rushed from the well-
benched ships, some to gather up their dead, and others to gather
wood.   420

The next day, Sun shot forward from deep currents of Ocean,
going up afresh over the tilled lands of the earth into the heavens. Then, they met each other as they identified every warrior.
It was onerous. Nonetheless, they washed off the bloody gore

with water, gushing hot tears as they lifted the corpses into the wagons. But great Priam would allow no weeping. His men silently heaped up piles of corpses for the fire with grieving hearts. They set flame to the pyre and went into sacred Troy. So also the long-haired Acheans piled up heaps of corpses apart from the Trojans, with grieving hearts. They set flame to the pyre and went to the hollow ships.   432

At a moment when it was not yet dawn, but when night was dwindling into gray, a select corps of the Acheans gathered around the pyre. They measured it and heaped a single tumulus mound around it, separated off from the boundless plain. In front of it they built a wall and high towers as protection for the ships and for themselves. In them they set well-fitted gates so that there could be a roadway for chariots. Out in front, they dug a deep, wide trench, and in the ditch they drove a palisade of sharpened stakes. The gods sitting near Zeus, the thunderer, took a look at the great work of the brazen-shirted Acheans. Poseidon, the earth-shaker, was first to speak: "Father Zeus, are there still any mortal men on the boundless earth who would announce to the immortals what was on their minds or seek counsel from them? Do you not see that the long-haired Acheans have done it again? They built a fortification in front of their ships, and around it they excavated a ditch. And they failed to give the gods glorious offerings. Glory and fame for such a thing will be spread all about at dawn. Men will forget the hardship Phoebus Apollo and I endured in the city building we did for the hero Laomedon."   453

Zeus, the cloud-gatherer, was annoyed with Poseidon, and said to him: "O ever-powerful earth-shaker, what are you saying? Some other of the gods might be afraid of this idea, one who is much weaker than you are in both hands and might. But so much glory will come to you, spread all about at dawn! Come now. When the Acheans return home with their ships to their beloved homeland, you may smash the fortification to pieces and have the sea pour all over it. It will be swallowed again up

by the sands of the grand shore. This is how you may destroy
the great fortress of the Acheans."   463

Thus they spoke to each other. The sun went down, and the
Acheans' work was finished. They slaughtered an ox and
took their dinner among their huts. Many ships had come in
from Lemnus carrying wine. Euneus Jasonson had sent them
out. Hypsipyle had born Euneus to Jason, Shepherd of the
Troops. The son of Jason set apart and gave the sons of Atreus,
Agamemnon and Menelaus, a thousand measures of the wine
to have for themselves. Afterward, the others of the long-haired
Acheans purchased wine from Euneus, some with bronze, but
others with glistening iron, while others traded shields, and others slaves, and oxen. They set out a handsome feast. Then the
long-haired Acheans feasted the whole night.   476

The Trojans and their allies were down from the city. All
night long counseling Zeus planned evil for them, with terrifying thunder and lightning. The fear that turns men pale seized
them. They poured wine from their cups onto the ground, and
none dared drink anything until they offered their libations to
the almighty son of Cronus. They went to their beds, and chose
the gift of sleep.   482

Book 8

Dawn spread her saffron gown over the earth. Zeus, who delights in thunder, gathered together the gods on the highest peak of many-ridged Olympus. He spoke to them, and all the gods heard him: "Hear me, all gods and all goddesses, as I say what the heart in my breast urges me to say. Let no one, whether goddess or god, try to disobey my command. Instead, let all give their assent, so that I can quickly bring an end to these matters that I have given my nod of approval. I will notice any god who wants to go away from the gods to the assistance of the Trojans or the Danaans. He will be struck by lightning and will return to Olympus battered and bruised; I will seize him and throw him down to gloomy Tartarus—ever so far away— where there is the deepest chasm underneath the earth. There are iron gates and a floor of bronze. It is as far below Hades as the earth is from heaven. That god will know then just how much more powerful I am than all others.   17

"But, just so all gods understand, if you try to disobey, you will be suspended from heaven by a golden chain. Any god or goddess who tries to pull you from heaven or the plain will be prevented by Zeus, the supreme contriver, even if they were to work at it with a vengeance. But should I wish to pull the chain, then I could pull them with the very earth and even the very sea and I might fasten the chain around the highest peak of Olympus. After that all those would become heavenly bodies. This I can do because I am above all gods and above all men in might."   26

So Zeus spoke and everyone became silent. They were stunned by what he said, for he had spoken so forcibly. After a time, the sharp-eyed goddess Athena spoke up: "Oh, our father, son of Cronus, you rule supremely; we know well that none is now equal to you in might. Nevertheless, we feel pity for the Danaan warriors, who, in fulfilling your plan, must die so miserably. We will certainly hold back from fighting as you command. But we will advise the Argives of a plan that will help them in some way, so that they don't all perish because you are angry." 37

Smiling at her, Zeus the cloud-gatherer said to Athena: "Take courage, my beloved child, born of my head. What you propose is not contrary to my plans. I wish to be kind to you." 40

Having so spoken, he yoked his pair of brazen-hoofed horses to his chariot. They were swift of gait with long golden manes. Zeus clad his own flesh with gold. He grabbed his handsome golden whip and mounted his chariot. With a snap of the whip he drove off. The horses were not hesitant, and they flew to the midpoint between earth and starry heaven. He arrived at Mount Ida, mother of beasts, on the peak of Gargarus, where there are many springs. There was in that spot an altar to him where men offered sacrifices and incense. There, the father of men and of gods stopped. He loosed his horses from the chariot and poured a thick mist over them. He sat himself down on the peak and, taking pleasure in his own glory, looked out over both the city of the Trojans and the ships of the Acheans. 52

The long-haired Acheans took their meal hastily around their huts and armed themselves. Some distance off, the Trojans also armed themselves up in their city. Though there were fewer of them, they were eager for fearful combat, driven by necessity. They fought for their children and their wives. They threw open all the gates and through them passed the troops, both foot soldiers and men in chariots. There arose a huge clamor. 59

When the Acheans and the Trojans arrived at one place together, they thrust with their shields, with spears and the might of warriors wearing brazen breastplates. As bossed shields smacked against one another, a monstrous din arose. In that noise there were together the wails of suffering and shouts of triumph. There were men slaughtering and being slaughtered, and the earth ran with blood.   65

All through the dawn and while the sacred day was waxing, many on both sides were hit by missiles and the troops fell. When Sun had climbed to the middle of heaven, even then the father stretched out his golden balance. And in it he placed two fates for death, which extends sleep, one for the Trojans, noble horsemen, and the other for the brazen-shirted Acheans. Taking it by the middle, he raised it. The balance tilted downward, as the fate of the Acheans sank down to the fertile ground, while that of the Trojans rose up toward the wide heavens. The god himself hurled a monstrous bolt from Ida. The lightning flash came down among the troops of the Acheans, shooting flames. Seeing it, they were terrified, and the fear that turns men pale seized them all.   77

At that point, Idomeneus did not dare to stand firm, and neither did Agamemnon, nor the two Aiantes, attendants of Ares, stand firm. Only Nestor, the Geranian, guardian of the Acheans, stood his ground, but not because he wanted to: one of his horses was stricken, hit by an arrow shot by Alexander, husband of lovely-haired Helen. The arrow struck the horse where the hair of the mane starts to grow, an especially deadly hit. In pain, the horse panicked, with the arrow stuck in his head. It terrified the horse next to him and they turned the brazen chariot around. The old man rushed with his sword to cut the ties to the paired horses. Meanwhile, Hector's swift horses were bringing the bold horseman in pursuit. And then might the old man have perished, had not Diomedes, good at the war cry, realized what was going on. He shouted in a dreadfully loud voice to alert Odysseus: "Odysseus, noble-born son of Laertes, ever cunning, why are you running away and driving like a coward to the back of the throng? Do you not realize that one who flees is likely to be struck by a spear in the back? Instead, rein in your horses so that we can save the old man from that savage warrior."   96

So Diomedes yelled, but the very daring, noble Odysseus did not hear. Instead he raced on to the hollow ships of the Acheans. Since the son of Tydeus was himself mixing it up in the forefront of the fighting, he went and stood in front of the chariot of the old son of Neleus, and shouted to him in winged words: "O old man, young men are wearing you down terribly in the fight. Your strength is gone. The troubles of age beset you. Your attendant is incompetent, and your horses are slow. So come, get up into my chariot so that you can see how the horses of Tros are at going about on the plain. They rush headlong this way and that, chasing and running away. They are the ones I took from Aeneas, master of fear. Let the two attendants take care of these horses, so the two of us may drive straight toward the Trojans, noble horsemen. That way, Hector can see my spear raging as I brandish it in my hand."   111

So, yelled Diomedes, and Nestor, the Geranian horseman, did not disobey him. And so the two attendants, broad-shouldered Sthenelus and Eurymedon, who loved manly things, took care of Nestor's chariot. Nestor and Diomedes together mounted his chariot. Nestor took the shining reins in his hands, and cracked the whip over the horses. In no time they got close to Hector. Eagerly, the son of Tydeus made a cast straight at him, but he missed, hitting instead his charioteer and attendant, Eniopeus, son of greathearted Thebaeus. Eniopeus was holding the reins of the horses when he was hit. He fell from the chariot, and the fleet-footed horses swerved to the side. Both his breath and his strength abandoned him.   123

An awful grief piled up heavily upon Hector's mind at the loss of his charioteer. But grieving though he was for his comrade, he left him lying there, and went in search of a brave charioteer. Not for long did his horses want for a driver. Quickly, Hector found brave Archeptolemus Iphitesson, who then mounted the chariot with its fleet-footed horses. Hector gave over the reins into his hands.   129

At that point might misery and irremediable harm have

befallen the Trojans. They would have been bottled up in the city like lambs, had not the father of both men and gods taken notice. Thundering terribly he hurled a dazzling white lightning bolt that landed on the ground in front of Diomedes's horses. Fearsome flames of burning sulfur rose up. The two horses contracted in fear under the chariot behind them. The shining reins slipped through Nestor's hands, and with fear in his heart he said to Diomedes: "Son of Tydeus, hold back, the solid-hoofed horses are afraid. Do you not realize that stamina from Zeus is not with you? Now, Zeus Cronusson grants glory to this man, according to his omen. Later on, he will even give it to us, if he might wish it. There is nothing a man can do, even if he is very powerful, to stave off the intent of Zeus, because he is ever so much mightier."   144

At that, Diomedes, of the shrill war cry, replied: "Yes, for sure, old man, all the things you say are proper. But terrible grief comes to my heart because of it. Someday, Hector will claim to an assembly of the Trojans: 'The son of Tydeus got to the ships after being routed by me.' So, he will taunt. Then I would wish that the ground would gape wide open to swallow me up."   150

Nestor, the Geranian horseman, answered him back: "Son of warlike Tydeus, what nonsense you speak! If, as you say, Hector claims that you are cowardly and inept, the others will not believe him. The Trojans, and Dardanians, and the wives of the greathearted, shield-bearing Trojans whose valiant bed partners you thrust into the dust, will not believe him."   156

So saying, Nestor turned the solid-hoofed horses back away from pursuit and toward flight. The Trojans and Hector, with divine assistance, rained down deadly missiles. Great Hector, of the helmet with the waving plume, shouted to Diomedes in a loud voice: "Son of Tydeus, the Danaans, who have swift horses, held you in higher regard than anybody. You knew that yours was the best seat at the table, the cut of meat, the full cup. Now they won't be honoring you. You have become a woman. So get lost, silly girl! No longer will you rush against me, or go against our walls, and you will not lead off our wives in your ships. I will deliver your fate to you before that happens."

166

So Hector spoke, and the son of Tydeus weighed in his mind the dilemma: whether to turn the chariot back toward the furious fight or not. Three times Diomedes thought about it, and three times, Zeus the counselor hurled omens from the peaks of Ida, showing that he was giving the advantage to the Trojans.

171

Hector yelled to the Trojans in a loud voice: "Trojans, and Lycians, and Dardanians, who fight hand to hand, you warriors are my friends. Bear in mind your ardent courage. I am certain that the son of Cronus has nodded in assent to grant me victory and great glory. That is a disaster for the Danaans. They were foolish to build that worthless, flimsy fortification. It will not ward off my might, and our horses can easily leap over the trench they've dug. But when I get to the hollow ships, there will be something to remember when the hot fire begins. Because I shall kindle the ships and kill the Argives beside them, as they panic under the smoke."

183

So speaking, he gave orders to his horses: "Xanthus, and you, Podargus, and also you, Aethon and noble Lampus, it is now time for you to pay me back for your keep, which often, in the past, Andromache, daughter of greathearted Eetion, placed before you when her spirit urged her: delicious wheat and mixed wine to drink. She did it for me, since I claim to be her ardent husband. I urge you to rise up and be quick so that we can grab hold of Nestor's shield. Its fame reaches the heavens, as it is entirely made of gold, straps and all. And we will take from the shoulders of Diomedes the dazzling breastplate that Hephaestus made. If we take those two, we hope the Acheans will sail off on the swift ships this very night."

197

So, Hector yelled, boasting. The revered Hera became furious, quaking on her throne, and high Olympus trembled. She said to the great god Poseidon opposite her: "Powerful earthshaker, is it not even now something deplorable to the heart in your breast that the Danaans are perishing as they are? They brought many gifts to you in Helice and Aege, and you were greatly pleased. You used to work on a plan for their victory. You could still, if we could figure out how we might help them and save them from the Trojans, and ward off loud-thundering Zeus. He sits all alone on Ida, plotting misery."   207

Annoyed with Hera, the lord earth-shaker said: "Hera, such bold words you speak! But there is no chance that I would wish that all of us fight against Zeus Cronusson, because he is far, far stronger than we are."   211

And in such a way did they converse with each other. The place near the trench in front of the wall built in front of the ships filled up, crowded with chariots and shield-bearing warriors alike. Hector Priamson, equal of swift Ares, crowded them in, since Zeus gave him glory. And, at that point he would have ignited the balanced ships with a glowing fire, had not revered Hera placed a warning to the mind of Agamemnon. Because of it, he hurried to rouse the Acheans. He went along the huts and the Acheans' ships with his big purple cloak in his meaty hand. The huts of Telamonian Aias and that of Achilles were at the far ends of the formation of ships. They depended on only themselves for protection, confident of their manliness and the strength of their hands. Agamemnon stood close to the big black ship of Odysseus in the middle so that his shout might reach both ends. He shouted to the Danaans in a loud voice they could understand: "What a disgrace! You are worthless cowards, though you are wonderful to look at. What happened to the boasts you made claiming to be the best? On Lemnos, you spouted such empty bragging. After eating much meat from straight-horned oxen, and drinking mixing bowls brimming with wine, you claimed that you could each stand against a hundred, two hundred Trojans in battle. But, now we have not a single one who is as worthy as Hector, who very soon will ignite the ships in blazing fire.   235

"Father Zeus, have you ever wounded one of the powerful

kings with such blindness of heart as this and taken away great glory from him? I swear that I never passed by an exceptionally beautiful altar of yours in my many-oared ship on the way to this destruction. I burned fat and thighs of oxen at every one of them, in my zeal to sack well-fortified Troy. But Zeus, at least fulfill this request of me. Permit them to escape and be spared, and do not allow the destruction of the Acheans by the Trojans."   244

So spoke Agamemnon, and the father took pity on him, his eyes welling tears. He lifted his eyebrow so that the troops might be saved. Immediately, he sent an eagle, the most reliable of birds for divining. It held a fawn in its talons, the offspring of a swift doe. The eagle threw down the fawn beside the beautiful altar of Zeus, where the Acheans were sacrificing to the source of oracles and omens. Seeing that the bird came from Zeus, they remembered their martial spirit, and were much charged up to leap on the Trojans.   252

Though there were many Danaans there, none claimed that he took his chariot and drove it out from the trench to fight against their opponents before the son of Tydeus. He was the very first to take an armed warrior when he took Agelaus Phradmonson, who had turned his chariot to escape, and as he turned back, Diomedes smashed his spear into Agelaus's back, midway between the shoulders, and drove it through his chest. He fell from the chariot and his armor crashed on top of him.   260

After Diomedes, others joined in the impetuous bravery: the sons of Atreus, Agamemnon and Menelaus, and after them the Aiantes, and Idomeneus and his shield-bearer Meriones, equal of man-killing Enyalius. After them was Eurypylus, the magnificent son of Euaemon. Teucer came as the ninth man, drawing his curved bow. He stood covered by the shield of Aias Telamonson. Aias would first carry the shield into a place, then the hero peered out, looking around. When he saw a target he shot an arrow into the throng, hitting it. The target fell, his breath taken from him. Then Teucer would dart back under the

protection of Aias, as a child would under its mother, and the
gleaming shield hid Teucer from sight.   272

And who were the first ones of the Trojans that the exceptional Teucer took? Orsilochus, he killed first, then Ormenus,
and Ophelestes, and Daetor, and Chromius, and the godlike
Lycophontes, and Amopaon Polyaemonson, and Melanippus.
All met the fertile ground in rapid succession. Watching him,
the Supreme Commander Agamemnon, was overjoyed that
ranks of Trojans perished because of Teucer's mighty bow. He
went and stood beside Teucer and said: "Teucer, dear soul,
son of Telamon, leader of the troops, if ever there was anyone
shooting like this, he would become a light to the Danaans and
to your father, Telamon, who reared you when you were but a
little one. Even though you were a bastard, he took care of you
in his household, and though he is far from here, your fame
should reach him.   285

"And I will tell you what is to come if Zeus and Athena give
it to me to sack Troy, that well-built city. First, I shall place the
prize gift from me into your hands. You shall have a tripod, or
two horses with chariot, or a woman who would jump into the
same bed with you."   291

The exceptional Teucer replied to Agamemnon, saying:
"Most glorious son of Atreus, why do you urge me to hurry
along so? You may be sure that I am not to be stopped as long
as I have the energy. From the time when we first turned them
back toward Troy, I have been hiding as I kill warriors with my
bow and arrows. Eight sharp-pointed arrows have been launched
from the bow, and all slashed the flesh of warlike young men.
But, I am unable to hit this man, Hector. He is a mad dog."   299

Just then, he let fly an arrow from his bowstring straight at
Hector, aimed at his heart. But it missed him. Instead, Teucer
struck the illustrious Gorgythion, a fine son of Priam, in the
chest with the arrow. A married mother from Aesumethe gave
birth to Gorgythion. She was the beautiful Castianeira, who had
a body like a goddess. Like an opium poppy in a field of grain

that bloomed in the fall and swelled with seeds in winter has its seed head bent over when it is weighed down on its slender stem by a heavy spring dew, so the head of Gorgythion bent over to one side weighed down by the helmet.   308

Teucer fired off another arrow from his bowstring straight at Hector, his heart eager for a hit. But, yet again, he missed— Apollo had deflected the arrow's flight. Instead, Teucer hit Hector's charioteer, brave Archeptolemus, as he was going about the fighting. Teucer hit him in the chest. He fell from the chariot and the swift-hoofed horses swerved to the side. In that place his soul and strength departed. Hector felt a terrible grief heavily in his heart for his charioteer, but he left him there, even though he mourned the loss of his comrade. Hector ordered his brother Cebriones, who was close by, to take the horses' reins. Cebriones heard him and obeyed.   320

Hector, himself all glistening in his armor, jumped down from the chariot onto the ground with a terrifying shout. He grabbed a rock in his hand and made straight for Teucer, whom his heart directed him to hit. Indeed, Teucer was then removing a sharp arrow from his quiver and notching it onto his bowstring. Hector hit him, as he raised the bow to his shoulder. The sharply pointed stone hit where the clavicle leaves the joint of the neck and chest. A hit here is especially deadly, and it was there Hector intended the jagged stone to hit. The rock severed the bowstring, and Teucer lost the sensation in his hand and wrist. He froze and fell to his knees. His bow fell from his hand. Aias did not miss what was happening with his brother. He ran over to him and covered him with his shield. Two of Teucer's affable companions, Mecisteus, son of Echius, and noble Alastor, crept underneath the shield and carried Teucer to the hollow ships, while he groaned loudly.   334

Once again, the Olympian roused strength in the Trojans, and they pushed the Acheans straight toward the deep trench. Hector went in the vanguard, jubilant in his might. It was as when one of a pack of dogs presses hard on a wild boar or a lion from behind on the flank or hip, chasing it going fast, while keeping a wary eye out for fear that the animal might wheel about. In such a way did Hector go in hot pursuit of the long-haired Acheans, constantly killing them from behind, as they fled from him. When they went through the trench and the stockade in flight, many were taken down under the hands of the Trojans. But they were restrained and made a stand by the ships. They called out to one another and to all the gods, each holding up his hands and praying mightily. Hector was every-where driving his beautifully maned horses; his eyes were the eyes of Gorgon or man-killing Ares.   349

Hera, the white-armed goddess, saw what was happening and took pity on them. Immediately, she spoke to Athena with winged words: "Aegis-bearing child of Zeus! Will we still not allow the final destruction of the Danaans? They are fated to a most hideous death wrought by just one man. Hector Priam-son rages in a way that is no longer bearable, for he has done so much harm."   356

The sharp-eyed goddess Athena answered her, saying: "I wish very much that this man might lose his might and spirit, wasting away under the hands of the Acheans in his home-land. But my father rages with a mind that is not right; it is horrible. He always is destructive and constantly getting in my way. Zeus does not remember how many times I saved his son Heracles when he was worn down by the trials of Eurystheus—how he did cry out to heaven! Zeus sent me down from heaven often to help him. If I had just known in my cunning mind, when Eurystheus sent Heracles to Hades, whose gates are kept in good order, to bring from Erebus, the dog of hateful Hades, he would not have escaped the deep currents of the water of the Styx. But, for now, Zeus despises me, as he fulfills his plan for the son of Thetis. She kissed his knees and tugged on his chin with her hand, begging him to honor Achilles, sacker of cities. Yes, at some time it will be that he might speak of his love for the sharp-eyed one. But for now, prepare your solid-hoofed horses for us, while I go to the palace of aegis-bearing Zeus and put on the armor of war. This, so I might see whether Hector, son of Priam, he of the helmet with the waving plume, will rejoice when both of us are revealed above the ranks of the fighting. Certainly, more than one of the Trojans will satiate the dogs and birds with his fat and flesh, fallen beside the ships of the Acheans."   380

So she spoke and Hera, the white-armed goddess, did not disobey. The elder goddess Hera, the daughter of great Cronus, brought out and made ready the horses that have bridles with golden headbands. But Athena, the young daughter of aegis-bearing Zeus, spread out her finely woven gown, which she had woven and stitched with her own hands, on the floor of her father. She put on the tunic of Zeus, the cloud-gatherer, and put on his armor for war, which makes men weep. She grasped Zeus's heavy, stout spear and stepped with her feet onto the flaming chariot.   391

Hera cracked her whip over her fast horses. The gates, which the Hours have charge of, creaked as they opened on their own accord. Great heaven and Olympus are entrusted to the Hours' care and it is they who either open the thick cloud or close it. Through those gates Hera and Athena drove the horses.   396

When father Zeus saw this from Ida, he became terribly angry. He roused Iris, his golden-winged messenger: "Iris, go swiftly. Turn them around and do not allow them to come face-to-face with me. It is not proper that we engage in combat. I will say this. The thing must play out to its end. I will cripple both horses harnessed to the chariot, and hurl Hera and Athena from the chariot and smash it to bits. And not until ten years of the sun's cycle drag by will they be healed, if my bolt of lightning hits them. This, I would do so that the sharp-eyed one might learn during that time when to fight against her father. I have no such vexation and anger toward Hera, since she is forever interfering with what I propose to do."   408

So Zeus spoke, and Iris, the messenger, swift as a storm, went from the mountains of Ida to the peak of Olympus. In front of the carefully fashioned gates of Olympus, she stood to detain them: "Which way are you two planning to go? Why do you both keep rage in your hearts? The son of Cronus will not permit you to protect the Argives. The son of Cronus threatens it will turn out this way. He will cripple the swift horses harnessed to your chariot and thrust you from it and smash it to bits. And not before ten years of the cycles of the sun drag by will the two of you be healed, if he strikes you with a lightning bolt, not until you learn, sharp-eyed one, when to fight against your father. He is not so vexed or angry with Hera, because she is forever interfering with what he proposes to do. However, you are blasphemous—you most terrible bitch—if you actually dare to raise your huge spear in opposition to Zeus!"   424

So spoke fleet-footed Iris, and went away. After a time, Hera spoke to Athena, saying: "Oh my, child of Zeus, who bears the aegis! I will no longer allow us to fight against Zeus because of mortals. Let him waste some of them, and strengthen others whom he touches. He can make his judgment on such things as his heart thinks wise about both the Trojans and the Danaans. That is fair."   431

Having so spoken, she turned around her solid-hoofed horses. The Hours unhitched the beautifully maned horses and tethered them by their ambrosial mangers. They leaned the chariot against the polished inside wall of the vestibule. Hera and Athena themselves sat on golden couches mingling with the other gods, but they were sad at heart.   437

Father Zeus went from Ida in pursuit with his sound-wheeled chariot and horses. When he arrived at the meeting place of the gods the famed earth-shaker loosed the horses for him and put the chariot on a stand. Poseidon unfolded over the chariot a fine linen cloth. Olympus trembled under the mighty feet as he went, and then loud-thundering Zeus sat himself down on his golden throne. Sitting away from him were only Athena and Hera. They said nothing to him, nor did they ask anything of him. He knew what they were saying in their hearts: "Why are you so sad, Athena and Hera? Surely you two are not weary of killing off Trojans in the fighting, which brings men honor, as your anger toward them is awful. But I am unique in my strength and my invincible hands. As many gods as there are on Olympus, they will not turn me about. For you two though, in the past trembling seized your glorious limbs before you saw the horrible deeds of war. But, this I will tell you, and this is how it would have played out. Had your chariot been struck by a lightning bolt, you could not get back to Olympus, seat of the immortals."

456

So spoke Zeus, and both Athena and Hera grumbled. They sat close to each other planning evil for the Trojans. Athena was quiet and said nothing as she frowned at her father Zeus, seized by savage anger toward him. But Hera did not hold her anger in her breast. Instead, she said to him: "Most hateful son of Cronus, you make no sense! We know very well now that your might is not harmless. But, in any event, we have compassion for the Danaan warriors. Theirs is to perish most horribly. But we will hold off from fighting, since you so order. We shall, instead, think up a plan that might help the Argives, so that not all of them die because of your anger."

467

Zeus, the cloud-gatherer, replied to her, saying: "At dawn you will see the overwhelming might of the son of Cronus, if you care to, lovely-eyed Hera. There will be much destruction of Argive warriors in their camp. But powerful Hector is not to be stopped from fighting, until the fleet-footed son of Peleus stands upright beside the ships. On that day they will fight at the sterns of the ships, shriveling most terribly over the dead Patroclus. This is ordained. I do not care about your anger, if you should end up at the farthest limits of the earth and the deep, where both Japetus and Cronus dwell, where there are neither the rays of Hyperion Sun, nor pleasing breezes. It would not be possible for you to avoid going there. And, I do not care whether you scowl, since no one else is bitchier than you."

483

So he spoke and white-armed Hera said nothing in response. And the radiant light of the sun fell into Ocean, pulling black night onto the cultivated earth, which gives grain. For the Trojans the setting of light was met with reluctance, but for their part, the dark night was welcomed by the Acheans, who had three times prayed for it.

488

Glorious Hector gathered an assembly of the Trojans far away from the ships, leading them to a clean place beside the swirling river, where the dead were clearly visible. The Trojans stepped off their chariots onto the ground to hear Hector, beloved of Zeus, speak. In his hand was a spear that was eleven cubits in length. At the end of the shining shaft was a spear point of bronze, and around it ran a golden ring that held the point on to the shaft. Leaning on the spear, Hector made his speech to the Trojans: "Hear me, Trojans, Dardanians, and allies. I have been saying that now is the time for the destruction of the ships and all the Acheans, and then we would return back to windy Troy. But that was before dusk came. It is a special salvation to the Argives and their ships beside the craggy seashore. But surely we must now obey black night and prepare our suppers. Unhitch our beautifully maned horses from their chariots and throw down beside them their feed. From the city, bring quickly both oxen and fat sheep, and sweet wine from the vintner and bread from the palace halls. Gather a lot of wood so that we can burn many fires all night long until dawn is born in the morning. The gleams from the fires will reach toward the heavens so that the long-haired Acheans don't rise up during the night and flee on the broad back of the sea. Yes! If we are careless at our watch, they might leave in their ships without any interference. Rather, let it be as if one of these was hit by some missile while cooking at home, be it an arrow or a sharp spear, as we leap upon the ships. So, such a one and others would dread the Trojans, noble horsemen, who bring Ares, of many tears.

516

"Heralds, friends of the messengers of Zeus, go up to the city to tell the boys and gray-haired old men to gather on the forti-

fication towers around the city, the towers whose foundation
was blessed by the gods. But the women should burn great fires
in their own palaces, and let all keep close watch so that troops
don't come to the city in ambush.   522

"It should be so, greathearted Trojans; the plan I explained
is sound. And I will speak again to the Trojans, noble horsemen,
in the morning. Praying to Zeus and the other gods, I hope that
we may drive from this place those dogs who bring death, whom
the fates brought in their black ships. But, for sure, let us keep
watch through the night to protect ourselves. In the morning,
at dawn, we will suit up in our armor and raise keen Ares
beside the hollow ships. I shall see whether mighty Diomedes
Tydeusson will push me back in front of the wall, beside the
ships, or whether I will carry off his armor as a trophy covered
with gore, after slaying him with bronze. In the morning will
his courage be proven, if he makes a stand against my spear as
I advance. But, I think that, having been hit, he will lie in the
vanguard surrounded by many of his comrades in the morning
as the sun rises. Oh, how I wish that I were immortal and would
have undying fame forever! I would be honored as Athena and
Apollo are honored, as now this day brings evil to the Argives."   541

Such was Hector's speech, and the Trojans shouted loudly.
They loosed their sweating horses from their yokes and tethered them with their harnesses, each beside its chariot. From
the city, they quickly brought oxen and fat sheep, and wine from
the vintners, and bread from the palace halls, and they gathered
wood. They performed sacrifices to the immortals, and the
sweet scent of burned and roasted fat wafted toward the heavens, born by the winds. But the blessed gods wanted no part of
the offering, as they greatly detested sacred Troy, and Priam,
and Priam's troops of spearmen.   552

And great were the spirits on the field of battle, as they sat
around the many fires that burned all night. It was as when
glittering stars surround the moon in a glorious display when
the air is still. Light is radiated from all the lookout posts and

headland peaks and valleys. And from heaven, a limitless ethereal space opens up. All the stars can be seen, and the shepherd
is delighted. So midway between the ships and the flowing
Xanthus were many burning fires of the Trojans and many
were seen before Troy. There were a thousand fires on the
plain, and around each sat fifty men, lit by the fire's radiance. The horses fed on white barley and spelt as they stood
beside their chariots, waiting for Dawn, the goddess of the
beautiful throne.

565

Book 9

And so the Trojans kept watch. However, a divinely inspired panic, that chilling companion of fear, gripped the Acheans. All of the best men were hit by unbearable misery. It was as when two winds, North Wind and West Wind, stir up the sea, full of fish. Both of them suddenly come from windblown Thrace. Together, they make crests of a dark wave, blowing many white caps on the sea that spits out seaweed beside it. In such a manner was the ardor of the Acheans rent from their breasts.

8

A great anguish gripped the heart of the son of Atreus. He went about ordering his deep-voiced heralds to call the men to assembly, while he himself dealt with the most prominent ones. They were to do so by speaking to each one, but not shouting. They sat in their assembly, feeling sorry for themselves. Agamemnon stood up, gushing tears, as though dark water from a spring, or turbid water flowing from the cliff of a rock mass. So, with deep groaning, he spoke to the Argives: "O friends, chiefs, and counselors of the Argives, great Zeus Cronusson has bound me up in profound blindness—shameful! Once, he promised me leave to sack well-fortified Troy and to return home afterward. But now, he intends an evil deceit for me, and orders me to arrive at Argos disgraced from losing many troops. This must please almighty Zeus in some way since he has cast down the high places of many cities and will continue to do so. There is none with more strength than he. But, come now, I say that we should all obey, and escape with the ships to the beloved land of our fathers, since we will no longer take Troy, with its wide streets."

28

So Agamemnon spoke, and all grew silent. For a long time, the sons of the Acheans were sad and quiet. At length, Diomedes, good at the war cry, said: "Son of Atreus, it is right in assembly that I be first to quarrel with you, because you are not thinking straight, Commander. You should not become angry because I speak out. When you scolded me earlier about valor among the Danaans, you claimed that I was unwarlike and incompetent. But we Acheans, young and old, know better. The son of crooked-dealing Cronus has given you a dilemma. On the one hand he has honored you above all others with the gift of his scepter. But on the other, he did not give you courage, which is the greatest strength. But, damn it, do you really believe the sons of the Acheans to be as unwarlike and incompetent as you have suggested? If the notion of returning has entered into your heart, go! The way is beside you; your ships are close to the sea, the many that followed you from Mycene. But, the rest of us long-haired Acheans will stay until we sack Troy. Even if the rest flee with the ships to the beloved homeland, Sthenelus and I both got here with the help of some god, and we will fight on to reach Troy!"

49

So he spoke, and all of the sons of the Acheans shouted in amazement at the words of the noble horseman Diomedes. And Nestor stood and spoke: "Diomedes, you are by far the mightiest in war and the best at counsel among all of your contemporaries. You speak with good sense to the kings of the Argives, since what you say accords with what is right. There is none among the Acheans who would challenge what you have said. But you do not address the point of the issue. You are younger than my youngest son. But, come now, I claim to be older than you. I have spoken about many things and deliberated over many problems, and nobody would treat me without respect, not even Prince Agamemnon.

"Only an outlaw, one who respects no customs, who has no property, loves pestilential, bone-chilling war! However, now we must obey the black night. We should get about preparing supper. The sentries should sleep at their posts beside the trench we dug, outside the wall we built. I will give instruction to the young men. You, son of Atreus, as you are the most exalted king here, should be the founder of a feast for the elders, if it seems comfortable for you, but not if it is odious. There is plenty of wine in your huts, since they bring it from Thrace daily in ships across the wide deep. It is a worthy thing that all receive wine from you since you rule over so many who have come together, and trust you to give the best counsel. It is especially necessary that all of the Acheans be brave and band together when so many fires burn close to the ships. Would not such a thing please you? Tonight, either the army is annihilated or it is saved." 78

So spoke Nestor, and those who heard him readily obeyed. The sentries rushed out with their armor, gathering around Thrasymedes Nestorson, Shepherd of the Troops; and around Ascalaphus, and Jalmenus, sons of Ares; and around Meriones, and Aphareus, and Deïpyrus; and around noble Lycomedes, son of Kreon. These were the leaders of the guard and a hundred youths followed each one. They proceeded in order carrying their long spears. And they went to the middle of the trench in front of the wall and took their stations. There they set a fire and each prepared his supper. 88

The son of Atreus led the elders of the Acheans together to his hut, and set beside them a sumptuous feast, and they set their hands to the food that was laid before them. And when they had put away the desire for food or drink, Nestor, far and away the foremost of them, who had previously revealed such excellent counsel, began to weave for them a plan. He spoke thoughtfully, saying: "Most glorious Agamemnon Atreusson, Supreme Comander, I shall address you first because you are the ruler of many troops and because Zeus has granted to you his scepter and the code of custom, so that you may pronounce judgment on those troops. It is necessary that you above all listen, and then speak, and it is you who should accomplish whatever someone else might begin. 102

"And so I will tell you what seems best to me to do, since there is no one else with a better plan in mind at any point. The problem still persists; from when, O noble-born one, you went and seized the girl Briseis from the hut of angry Achilles without thinking about us. I did particularly try to dissuade you from going there. But you gave rein to an arrogant heart. You insulted the best one—Achilles, whom the immortals honored beyond all others—by dishonoring him and taking his prize. However, even now we must figure out how we might persuade him to a reconciliation with cordial gifts and charming words."   113

The Supreme Commander Agamemnon replied back to him, saying: "O, old man, there is no lie in what you said about my blindness! I did injury to him and I myself failed to praise him. Instead, he is the man of the many troops dearest to Zeus, who now honors Achilles by smiting the troops of the Acheans. But, since you have persuaded me that I did him harm because of my wayward heart, I wish to give back to him a huge ransom so that we may reconcile. I will list for you all of the extravagant gifts in that ransom: seven tripods, untouched by fire; ten golden talents; twenty shining caldrons; twelve compact, prizewinning horses, which earned winnings in races with their hooves. Those solid-hoofed horses never lost gold in my wagers on any races so their owner will not become poor. And, I will give him seven Lesbian women skilled in exceptional handiwork, whom I chose as mine when Achilles himself took wellbuilt Lesbos. They are a race with only beautiful women. With them will be one I took away, the girl Briseis. I will swear a solemn oath that I have not taken her to bed and had sex with her, as is customary for men and women. All these things will be carried over to him immediately. Then, if the gods grant that we may sack the city of great Priam, he may take great piles of gold and bronze to his ships on the sea when we Acheans divide the spoils. He may choose for himself twenty of the Trojan women who are the most beautiful after Argive Helen.   140

"If we get back to Argos and the rich Achean soil, he could become my son-in-law. I will prize him as an equal of Orestes, who was born late to me and reared with every luxury. I have three daughters in my well-crafted palace, Chrysothemis, Laodice, and Iphianassa. He may choose the one he likes and lead her to the home of Peleus without paying a bride price. I will also give a rich dowry, such as is never given for a daughter: seven well-populated cities, Cardamyle, and Enope, and grassy Hire, and sacred Pherae, and Anthea, with its many beautiful meadows, and Aepia, and Pedasus, with its many vineyards. All of them are close to the sea, on the outskirts of windy Pylos. The men who live in them have many sheep and many oxen and they will honor him with gifts as though to a god. And under his scepter, his judgments will find prosperous fulfillment.   156

"I will bring all this about if he lets go of his anger. Achilles must submit, though! Hades, like him, is unyielding and will not submit. On that account he is the most despised by men of all the gods. And Achilles must be under my command, because I am a higher level of king than he is, and because I claim that I am older."   161

And then, the noble Geranian horseman Nestor replied to him: "Most glorious Agamemnon Atreusson, Supreme Commander, the gifts that you would give to the Lord Achilles are not at all contemptible. Come now, if I am to pick them out, let them consent, and go quickly to the hut of Achilles Peleusson. First of all, Phoenix, beloved of Zeus, he should lead them. Then let great Aias and noble Odysseus go. Odius and Eurybates will accompany you as heralds. Bring water for the hands and order them to wash for good luck, so that if Zeus Cronusson might take pity on us, he will help us."   172

So Nestor spoke, and what he said pleased them all. Right away, the heralds poured water over their hands, and the youths stirred wine in the mixing bowls. They went about filling the cups to their brims. After pouring their libations, they drank as much as their hearts desired. Then they set out from the hut of Agamemnon Atreusson. Nestor, encouraged them

enthusiastically as they passed by, winking at each one, especially at Odysseus, in hopes that they might persuade the exceptional son of Peleus.   181

The two of them went along the shore of the sea where the
waves lapped along. They prayed intently to the one who surrounds the world, the earth-shaker, that they might easily persuade the great heart of the grandson of Aeacus. They came to
the huts and ships of the Myrmidons, and found Achilles taking pleasure with his clear-toned lyre. It was dazzlingly beautiful, with a silver bridge. He had taken it from the spoils after
the sack of the city of Eetion. It delighted his heart to sing of
the famous deeds of men. Alone, Patroclus sat silently opposite,
waiting for Achilles to stop his singing. With noble Odysseus
in the lead, the two men stepped forward, and stood in front of
Achilles. Surprised, he rose and left the lyre on the seat where
he had been sitting. Patroclus also stood when he saw the men.
Taking them by the hand, Achilles, fleet of foot, said to them:
"Welcome! Do come in, warrior friends. Surely this is some
special necessity. Even in my angry state you two are the ones
I most love of the Acheans!"   198

Having said that first, noble Achilles led them into his hut
with its crimson carpets. Right away he spoke to Patroclus, who
was close by: "Son of Menoetius, set out the larger mixing bowl
and stir the undiluted wine. Fill a cup for each, since these warriors, who are my most beloved friends, are under my roof!"   204

So Achilles spoke, and Patroclus obeyed his dear companion.
He set down a large meat tray in the light of the fire. On it
he placed the chines of a sheep and of a fat goat, and a chine of
a fatted pig, rich with oil. Automedon held the tray while noble
Achilles cut the meat. When cut into pieces, these were stuck
onto spits. The great son of Menoetius, who was like a god, vigorously stoked the fire. After the fire burned and the flames
died down, he spread out the spits over the coals. He sprinkled
salt of the god over the holders for the spits. When they had been

roasted, he spread them out on the cutting tables. Patroclus took bread and portioned it on the table in pretty baskets, while Achilles divided the meat. He ordered Patroclus to make obeisance to the gods, and his comrade threw the portion saved for that purpose onto the fire. Achilles seated himself across from godlike Odysseus next to the opposite wall. They thrust their hands into the prepared victuals that lay before them, and when the desire for food and drink had left them, Aias nodded to Phoenix. Noble Odysseus caught his cue, and with a filled cup of wine he toasted Achilles: "Cheers, Achilles! You lacked nothing in this proper feast. We were in the hut of Agamemnon Atreusson and now here, for this sumptuous spread. However, the concern at hand is not about agreeable feasting, but rather that we are very much afraid of a huge disaster you may have been observing, noble-born that you are. It is doubtful whether we will save the well-benched ships, if you do not suit up in courage. The Trojans and their much-celebrated allies are situated in a place near the ships and the wall. They are burning many fires in their camp and they say that they will not hold back much longer, but will fall on the black ships. Zeus Cronusson hurls lightning bolts on the right-hand side revealing a sign to them. Hector, gloating in his strength, rampages about outrageously, trusting Zeus; he shows respect neither to men nor to gods. A violent madness has got into him. He prays that shining Dawn will show herself soon. He vows that he will cut off the high figureheads of the ships and torch them, and then cut down the Acheans beside them who would be sent into confusion by the smoke. I am afraid of these awful things in his heart, for fear that the gods might realize his threats. It might be our fate to perish in Troy, far from Argos, where they raise horses. 246

"Get up, if you want to. Even after such a long time, you could rescue the sons of the Acheans who have been worn down under the onslaught of the Trojans. Grief will come to you on account of their ruin, and you will find no remedy for it once the mischief is done. Remember how often in the past you staved off the day of destruction for the Danaans. O, dear friend, your father Peleus instructed you on the day when he sent you from Phthia to Agamemnon: 'My son, Athena and Hera will give you might, if they want to. But you must restrain the proud spirit in your chest. Remember that it is better to be friendly and let go of pernicious quarreling, so that you will be especially prized by the Argives, young and old.'   259

"That was what the old man told you, but you forget. So, even now, stop; let go of the anger that corrodes your heart! Agamemnon will give you worthy gifts if you do." And then Odysseus recited the many gifts promised by the Supreme Commander.   298

"These things happen for you if you let go of your anger. If you hate the son of Atreus in your heart too much to care about his gifts, at least take pity on the rest of the Acheans who are all worn down in the camp. They revere you as they would a god. You would win great glory among them, if you were to take out Hector now, since he would come very close to you in his murderous madness. Now he claims there is none who is his equal among those of the Danaans the ships brought here."   306

But, Achilles, fleet of foot, replied to him saying: "Noble-born, ever-cunning Odysseus Laertesson, I will cut to the chase and respond now to Agamemnon's offer frankly, telling you how I believe things will come out, so that you people don't waste your time, going from one thing to another, sniveling at me. That man would conceal one thing in his mind and say something else. He is as odious to me as the Gates of Hades. So, I will tell you what seems best to me. But, I don't think he will persuade me, either the son of great Atreus or the other Danaans, since there was never any acknowledgment for my endless and unrelenting pursuit of burning fires of war against men. The fate is the same for the man who holds back as for the one who fights with zeal. The coward and the brave man leave with the same reward. Death is the same for the lazy man as it is for the one who works very hard.   320

* * *

My efforts laid up no treasures for me, since I suffer pain in my heart from constantly risking my life in the fighting. It is as when a bird carries off food to the mouths of her un-fledged chicks as soon as she captures it. It goes badly for her. In such a way, did I spend many sleepless nights after I finished days of bloody fighting. I fought against men because of their bed partners. I sacked twelve cities with my ships, and I claim that I took eleven when on foot around Troy, with its rich soil. From all of those cities, I carried off much treasure and fine it was. And I brought all of it and gave it to Agamemnon. He received it beside his swift ships and thereafter parceled out small amounts to others, but held on to most of it. But, he did give prizes to the best men and to the kings. Their prizes lie safely with them. But from me, alone of the Acheans, he took mine, my wife, the love of my heart! Let him take pleasure ly-ing beside her! Why do the Acheans have to make war against the Trojans? Why did the son of Atreus gather the troops and lead them here? Was it not because of fair-haired Helen? Are the sons of Atreus the only ones in all humanity who love their wives? Because there was a certain man who loved and cared for one of his own, as I did, loving her from my heart, even though she was a trophy of war. But, since Agamemnon has now taken my prize from my hands and cheated me, he dare not challenge me, as I know well what he is! And he will not persuade me!   345

"Instead, Odysseus, you and the other kings together ought to consider how to protect the ships from fire. Certainly, Agamemnon has accomplished a lot without me. He both built a wall and ran the trench in front of it that is wide and deep, and drove a palisade down into the trench. Yet, he is un-able to curb the strength of man-killing Hector. As long as I was fighting with the Acheans, Hector had no urge to rush into battle in front of the wall. Instead he went only as far as the Scaean Gate and the oak. Only once he made a stand

there against me and escaped my assault only by the tiniest
bit.   355

"But, since I now have no desire to fight against noble Hector, I will make prayers to holy Zeus and the other gods in the
morning tomorrow, and load up my ships. Then I will drag
them to the sea. If you have both the desire and the energy, very
early in the morning, you will see my ships, sailing in the Hellespont, full of fish. In them, my men will be vigorously rowing
and if the famed earth-shaker might grant us easy sailing, I
can make Phthia, with its rich soil, on the third day. There are
many things of mine that I left there to come here, but I will
carry there for myself more gold and reddish bronze, buxom
women, gray iron as were allotted to me. But, my prize, though
he gave her to me, Prince Agamemnon in his arrogant pride
has taken back. Tell him openly all we talked about, so that the
rest of the Acheans will be outraged if he ever tries to cheat
others of the Danaans, for he is always dressed in insolence. He
would not dare look me in the face, dog that he is. I will not
discuss with him any plans and I will not work for him since he
has cheated me, committed a crime against me. Never again
will he deceive me. But, enough of him! He ought to get lost
quietly. Counseling Zeus has taken away his good sense. His
gifts disgust me. They are worth to me a single strand of hair
cut from my head.   378

"I wouldn't have them even if he were to offer ten or twenty
times as many as he now does; even if they were to come from
some other place, not even such as would approach that of
Orchomenus, or as much as Egyptian Thebes, where the most
wealth lies in their palaces. In that place there are one hundred
gates and through each two hundred warriors go out with their
horses and chariots. I would not have them if his gifts were as
numerous as grains of sand or particles of dust, and Agamemnon does not yet in any way persuade me, until he compensates
me for his utter disgrace and the pain at heart he gave me.   388

"And I will not ever marry a daughter of Agamemnon Atreusson, not even if she were to rival golden Aphrodite in beauty and equal sharp-eyed Athena in skill at handiwork. Let him choose some other one of the Acheans for that, someone who might be his equal as a higher level of king. Perhaps, if the gods deliver me and I get back home, Peleus will pick a wife for me, since he handles that himself. There are many Achean women, and many up in Hellas and Phthia, who are daughters of the best men, who protect the small cities. I might want one of them as my beloved wife. There my brave spirit very often urged me to actively court a bride who would be a suitable wife, and to enjoy the possessions old Peleus acquired. My possessions will not be at all equal in value to what they say was accumulated in well-populated Troy, earlier in a state of peace before the sons of the Acheans came. Nor are they of equal value to the great treasure the stone flagging of the archer, surrounds in Phoebus Apollo's rocky Delphi. Both oxen and fat sheep may be plundered, and tripods and horses with yellow manes can be purchased. But, the soul of a man should come back where it came from, neither as plunder, nor captured, when it has passed the barrier of his teeth.   409

"My mother, the silver-footed goddess Thetis, tells me the double fates that lead me to the end of death. If I remain here fighting around the city of the Trojans, my return home is wiped out, but my fame will be eternal. If I go back home to my beloved fatherland, worthy fame for me is erased, but my life will be long. The end of death will not speedily find me. And I encourage those others to sail on toward home, since you will not realize the goal of lofty Troy. Loud-thundering Zeus surely has it in the care of his own hands, as he has emboldened its troops.   420

"Instead, go to the best of the Acheans and tell them what I said. Because it is the mark of honor of old men, they will have to come up with another plan in their minds, one that is better, which will save both the ships and the troops of the Acheans beside the hollow ships. This they must do, because the plan they have now isn't working, and I will not relent in my anger. Phoenix ought to remain here to sleep with us so he can accompany me in my ships to our homeland in the morning, if he wants to. He is not under duress at all; I will not take him that way."   429

So Achilles spoke, and they all became silent and said nothing, astonished by what he said, especially the harshness of his words. After a time, the old horseman Phoenix said to him with tears welling up because of his concern for the Acheans' ships: "Glorious Achilles, if return is firmly set in your mind and you wish to do nothing at all to save the ships from destructive fire because of the unyielding anger in your heart, how could you leave me behind here, my beloved son? The old horseman Peleus sent me with you on the day he sent you to Agamemnon from Phthia. You were but a callow boy, knowing nothing whatever about the arts of war or speaking in assembly, the things noble men do to distinguish themselves. Peleus sent me along so that I could teach you all that. I was to be both your tutor in rhetoric and your drill instructor for combat. So, my beloved son, I would not want to be left behind by you, not even if a god were to promise to smooth the wrinkles of my age and make me youthful anew. Then I would be as I was when I first left Hellas, that city with beautiful women, to escape the anger of my father, Amyntor Ormenusson. He was furious with me over a concubine with beautiful hair, whom he loved himself. In loving her, he dishonored his wife, who was my mother. Mother constantly pled at my knees that I seduce the concubine, so that she would despise my father's decrepitude. I obeyed her and did it. My father immediately suspected what I'd done and laid many curses on me. He called out to the hateful Erinys that never would a beloved son born of me sit on my lap. The gods Amyntor swore by carried out the curse— infernal Zeus and dreaded Persephone. I planned to kill him with sharp bronze. But one of the gods reined in my anger, placing an oracle within my heart, and besides, many men in the district warned me that I would not want the Acheans calling me a patricide.   461

"The spirit in my heart could no longer keep me resident in my angry father's palace. To be sure, there were many friends and relatives who surrounded me, pleading with me to stay. They slaughtered many fat sheep and cloven-footed, crooked-horned oxen. There were many fat, oiled hogs stretched out roasting over the flames of Hephaestus. There was much wine drunk from the old man's jars. Nine nights they stayed through the night around me there. On the one hand, the guards changed, but on the other, the fire was never extinguished. There was one under the portico of the well-guarded courtyard, and another in the vestibule in front of the chamber doors.   473

"But on the tenth day when the dusk of night came, I smashed the thick, fitted chamber doors and leapt easily over the court-yard fence, without the notice of either the male guards or serv-ing women. Then, I fled across the broad expanse of Hellas far away, and arrived at the court of King Peleus in Phthia, rich in fields, mother of fruit. He received me enthusiastically and be-friended me, as would a father with many possessions receive an only son, born late in his life. And he made me rich, and granted me rule over the troops of Dolopians who dwell near the outer boundaries of Phthia. And, such as you are, I reared you like one of the gods, Achilles, loving you from my heart. Whether going to a feast or just eating in the great hall, you never wanted to be with anyone else. Back then, I cut up meat and sat you on my lap, filling you up with it, and held out wine for you. Often, when you were eating, you spit up wine on the chest of my tunic in little-child upset.   491

"So, you see, I have experienced a lot and had some hardship on your account. It was not in the minds of the gods that a child was to be got from me, but I made you into my son, Achilles, a son like unto the gods. I did it so that you would later protect me from a horrible death. But you must tame that great resent-ment! It is not at all necessary to have a pitiless heart. Even the gods themselves are flexible, though they are better than you in virtue, honor, and strength. When men have gone astray, they supplicate the gods with incense, and mild prayers, and libations, and the greasy smoke of sacrifices, for a transgression or a sin. Ate is blindness of spirit. She is strong and nimble, and far outruns everyone, getting ahead of them all over the earth. She disables men. And there are the Prayers who are daughters of mighty Zeus. They have arthritic joints, and wrinkling of the skin, and squinty eyes, the hardening of the lens in middle age that prevents compensation. They go along behind Ate tending to things, healing men after she disables them. He who reveres the daughters of Zeus as they come closer, to him they give a great redemption and hear his prayers. But, if there is one who refuses, and sternly rebukes them, they plead with Zeus Cronusson so that he will have Ate remain with the man, and exact the full price for his injury.   512

"Achilles, even you should obey the daughters of Zeus and pay them homage, especially she who bends the minds of other brave men. Had the son of Atreus not offered the gifts just listed, and instead remained persistently insulting in his behavior, I would not urge you to toss aside your wrath and defend the Argives who are stuck and need your help. But he would give you now many gifts, and promises more in the future, pleading for you to go in the vanguard with the ranks of the best of the Achean troops. Those men love you most of all the Argives. You should not resent their words or the actions of their feet. Before, they did not blame you for being angry. So it was back in the past, as we learn from stories of the exploits of heroes, that when someone brought furious anger on another, that he would appease with bribes and conciliatory words. I remember one such deed, a long time ago. I will tell all you friends here about it. The Curetes and the courageous Aetolians were at war, battling each other around the city of Calydon. The Aetolians were acting in defense of lovely Calydon, while the Curetes were rampaging like Ares eager to sack it. Artemis, of the silver throne, was urging on the Curetes because she was angered by King Oeneus of Calydon, who did not place the first fruits of his vineyard on her knees. He made sacrifices to the other gods in feasting, but not her alone, the daughter of great Zeus. He either forgot or he didn't know to do it, being greatly blinded in spirit. She, the child of a god, who delighted in archery, became angry. She roused up against Oeneus a wild boar with white tusks, which could do much damage, visiting Oeneus's vineyard often. It plowed the ground with its tusks, tossing up many long vines and their roots, together with the blossoms of the fruit. Meleager, the son of Oeneus, gathered together hunters and their dogs from many cities, and killed the boar. It was not brought down by a few men, as it was so large. And many were piled up on the miserable funeral pyre. 546

A round the carcass Artemis raised a great din and much shouting over the head and bristly hide of the boar between the Curetes and the greathearted Aetolians. As long as Meleager, beloved of Ares, was in the fight, things went badly for the Curetes. And though there were many of them they were unable to make a stand in front of the fortified wall. But when anger entered Meleager, things went the other way. It was anger of the kind that swells up with rage in the breast, even in those of sound mind. His heart hardened against his own mother Althea. Althea had prayed to the gods in anguish over the death of her beloved brother at the hand of Meleager. She violently pounded the fertile earth with her fists, calling on Hades and dreaded Persephone, imagining clasping their knees as tears poured down on her breasts, while pleading that they give death to her son. A hardhearted Erinys heard her from Erebus and quickly rumbling and clattering arose from the Curetes fighting around the gates and walls. Meleager left the fighting to lie beside his beautiful wife and sleeping partner, Cleopatra. Cleopatra was the daughter of the nymph Marpessa, with beautiful ankles, daughter of Euenis, and of Idas, born the mightiest of men dwelling on the earth at that time. King Idas had chosen to draw a bow against Phoebus Apollo because of the nymph Marpessa, who had beautiful ankles. In their palace, Cleopatra's father and revered mother called her by the name Halcyone, because her mother met with misfortune like the exceedingly sad halcyon-bird, the kingfisher. And Marpessa wept when Phoebus Apollo, who works from afar, snatched her daughter up.   574

"The elders of the Aetolians made supplications to Meleager. They sent the highest priests of the gods to go and promise a great gift. They directed him to choose a spot on the fertile plain of lovely Calydon, and section off fifty acres, which was half vine-yards, and half forests for cutting and arable land. The old noble horseman Oeneus went up to the threshold of Meleager's high-ceilinged bedchamber. He banged on the door made of joined planks, quietly pleading with his son. Meleager's sisters and his revered mother earnestly pled with him. But he abso-lutely refused to return to the fighting. Many of his comrades, those who were the most respected and the most concerned, begged him. But they were unable to convince his spirit. Until the Curetes were beating against his chamber and about the towers and started to set the city on fire, but then his buxom wife pleaded with Meleager, wailing because of her concern for all the people living in the city. There were those who might be captured. The men would be killed. Fire would reduce the city to ashes. The captors would lead off the children and the beauti-ful women.   594

"On hearing of such evil, Meleager's spirit relented. He clothed his flesh with armor that gleamed all over. Energized, he warded off the fateful day for the Aetolians, though the prom-ised gifts did not yet materialize. Even so, he did it. But you should consider those things in your heart: do not let some evil spirit turn you around, my friend. It would be more trouble to save the ships if they are already on fire, so go for the gifts. The Acheans honor you like a god. If you were to enter bat-tle, which destroys men, without any gifts, it would be alto-gether for the honor that you would win protecting them instead."   605

Fleet-footed Achilles answered him, saying: "Phoenix, noble-born old papa, it isn't necessary for me to have those honors. I think Zeus has granted me enough honor as is my fate. He will keep me beside the beaked ships, for as long as breath stays in my chest and my knees move agreeably. But I will tell you something else, and get it fixed in your mind. You should not confuse my afflicted heart in doing a favor for the hero son of Atreus. There is no need for you to love him, so that I would cease despising him. It is a worthy thing that you heap abuse on someone who provokes me, as you are a king equal to me and you rule with me, sharing equally in half the honor. These men will deliver the message. You stay here and sleep on a soft bed. With the revelation of Dawn, we will think about whether we ought to return to our business at home or stay." 619

And he silently raised his eyebrows to Patroclus as a signal to spread out a thick bed for Phoenix, so that the delegation would give thought right away to leaving the hut and returning. But Aias, the godlike son of Telamon, had his say: "Noble-born, ever-cunning Odysseus Laertesson, let's be off. It doesn't appear to me that our aim is to be accomplished here. We should immediately report the situation to the Danaans, even though it will disappoint. They are probably sitting, waiting for the news. Achilles has firmly fixed a brutish, haughty spirit in his chest. This is disgraceful! And he will not be turned away from that by the most beloved of his comrades, who here among the ships held him in the highest esteem. He is pitiless. Even for the murder of a brother or the death of a child one receives compensation, and the killer remains in the same district, after paying a large ransom. In that way a man's anger is curbed. But his will not be. Achilles, the gods have fixed an inflexible, evil spirit in your breast on account of one girl. But, we are here now with an offer of seven who are unquestionably superior, and there are others to be had. You should have a peaceful mind. But, we must respect your house as we are your guests who are from the ordinary Danaans. We want more than anything to be the most

caring and most loving, since so many of the Acheans feel the
same way."   642

Fleet-footed Achilles replied: "Noble-born Aias Telamonson,
Leader of the Troops, everything you seem to say is reasonable,
but my heart swells up in anger whenever I remember how unjustly Agamemnon treated me among the Argives. He treated
me as if I were a shiftless wanderer. But, go and tell him this
message: 'I have no interest in bloody fighting until warlike
Hector, noble son of Priam, arrives at the huts and the ships of
the Myrmidons, after killing the Argives and destroying the
ships with fire. I think Hector will be stopped near my hut and
my black ship, though he is most eager to do battle.' "   655

So, Achilles spoke, and each one of them took a two-handled
cup and poured a libation. They went back along the ships with
Odysseus in the lead. Patroclus ordered his companions and
servants to spread out the thick bed for Phoenix. And, they
obeyed, spreading it out with utmost speed, as he ordered:
fleeces, and a pillow, and thin sheets of the finest linen. There
the old man slept and waited for radiant Dawn.   662

But, Achilles slept in the innermost chamber of the well-built
hut. A woman, pretty-cheeked Diomede, daughter of Phorban-
tus, slept beside him. He had brought her from Lesbos. On the
other side Patroclus slept, and beside him was the buxom Iphis.
Noble Achilles gave her to him when he took lofty Scyrus, a
small city in Enyeus, the Northern Sporades.   668

When the delegation made it to the huts of the son of Atreus,
the sons of the Acheans received them with golden cups. They
stood up here and there asking how things went. The Supreme
Commander Agamemnon was the first to ask: "Well now, tell
me, O illustrious Odysseus, great glory of the Acheans, does
he want to protect the ships from the burning fire, or did he
refuse, and hold on to his haughty resentment?"   675

Noble Odysseus answered him: "Most glorious Supreme
Commander Agamemnon Atreusson, that man has no desire
to quench his anger, he is instead still completely filled with

rage. He refuses you and your gifts. He instructs you to consider the situation among the Argives, as to just how the ships and the troops of the Acheans might be saved. He threatens that he himself will be leaving with the opening of dawn, pulling his well-benched ships, which have rowers on both sides, to the sea. And, he declares to the rest of you that you consider sailing off homeward, since you will not figure out a resolution to lofty Troy. Zeus holds it fast under his arms, having given valor to its troops. That is what he said. Those who went with me now, Aias, and two heralds are entirely trustworthy. The old man Phoenix slept there as Achilles told him to, so that he could accompany Achilles back to his homeland in the morning, if Phoenix wants to go. Achilles will not take him under duress."   693

So Odysseus spoke, and everyone grew silent, aghast at what he said. It was especially harsh. For a long time, the sons of the Acheans were sorrowful and did not speak. After a time, Diomedes, of the shrill war cry, spoke up: "Most glorious Supreme Commander Agamemnon Atreusson, I wish that you had not given many gifts and that you had not pled with the exceptional son of Peleus. He is arrogant even so. Now you have inspired him to more arrogance. Make certain of it, we will leave him alone, whether he might go or stay! And then, if some god rouses him and orders the spirit in his breast, he will again fight. But, come, do as I tell you. Let everybody obey. You should now sleep, as we have delighted our hearts with bread and wine. In them is strength and valor. When the lovely, rose-fingered Dawn, reveals herself, we will quickly rise and form up the troops and horses in front of the ships. And you yourself, Agamemnon, will be in the forefront of the fighting."   693

So he spoke, and all of the kings concurred with him. They were surprised that the noble horseman Diomedes could make such a speech. Then they poured their libations and went, each to his hut. And there they laid themselves down and chose the gift of sleep.   713

Book 10

The other chiefs of all the Acheans lay, tamed by sleep, the whole night long beside the ships. But sweet sleep did not hold the Shepherd of the Troops, Agamemnon Atreusson, whose mind was churning around uneasily.

It was as when the husband of lovely-haired Hera causes a great, driving thunderstorm with a flash of lightning, or a hail-storm, or a snowstorm, when the fallen snow whitens the fields, or some place along the huge front of a putrid war. In such a way did a groaning Agamemnon anguish from the depths of the heart in his breast. His mind vibrated in his head.   10

Indeed, when he looked out over the Trojan plain, he was amazed by the many fires burning in front of Troy, and by the sounds of the pipes, and the shouts and the din of humanity. When he looked toward the ships and troops of the Acheans, he pulled many hairs from his head out by the roots, pleading with lofty Zeus, and groaning loudly from his glorious heart.   16

And then a first-rate idea was revealed to him, to go to Nestor Neleusson, foremost of warriors, to make together with that exceptional counselor some devising that would protect all of the Danaans from evil. He stood up and slid his tunic around his chest. He bound his handsome sandals under his oiled feet. Then, he draped a reddish lion's skin around himself, which was glossy and so huge that it reached down to his feet, and picked out a spear.   25

And in the same way, a trembling fear took hold of Menelaus, and sleep did not sit upon his eyelids either. He was concerned that the Argives might suffer, since it was on his account that they came over the vast, wet expanse of sea to Troy, urged on by him, into this reckless war. First, he covered his wide back with the skin of a spotted leopard. Next, he held up a bronze helmet and placed it on his head. Then, he grabbed a spear in his beefy hand and went to his brother who was already awake. It was, after all, his brother who ruled over all of them, his brother who was venerated like a god in their country. Menelaus found Agamemnon as he was placing his beautiful armor around his shoulders beside the stern of his ship. He was welcomed as he came over.   35

Menelaus, good at the war cry, was first to speak: "Why, sir, did you arm yourself in this way? Or, do you mean to alert some of the comrades to the possibility of a spy for the Trojans? I am very concerned that no one will undertake this assignment for you, and someone of the enemy might come alone to spy in the balmy night, especially one of stout heart."   41

Prince Agamemnon, answered him, saying: "Both you and I have need of a plan that is effective, noble-born Menelaus, a plan that would protect and save the Argives and the ships, since Zeus has changed his mind. He no doubt changed his mind because of Hector's sacrifices. I have never known, nor heard tell of one man capable of such mischief as Hector has done to the sons of the Acheans in one day by himself, even though he is not the son of a goddess or a god. I think what he has done to the Argives will be a concern for a long time afterward. But go now, running hurriedly beside the ships to summon Aias and Idomeneus. I myself am going to noble Nestor to rouse him, in hopes that he might want to go to the close-knit band of sentries and tell them what to do. They are very trusting of him. His son and Idomeneus's friend Meriones command the outposts. We depend completely on them."   59

Menelaus, of the shrill war cry, replied: "Just what is it that you are ordering me to do? Am I to stay here among the chiefs waiting until you come back? Or, am I to run back after you, when I have explained your orders carefully?"   63

The Supreme Commander Agamemnon answered him: "Stay here so that both of us don't somehow miss each other wandering about at night. There are many paths through the

camp. Speak up wherever you go ordering the men to be watchful and vigilant, calling each of them and their fathers by name
and tribe, praising them all. But don't be arrogant. Let us work
harder than anyone. Maybe Zeus sent this evil to us when we
were born."   71

So saying, Agamemnon sent off his brother, well instructed.
Next, he went off after Nestor, Shepherd of the Troops. Agamemnon found Nestor in a soft bed beside his hut and his black ship.
Lying beside him were his many-colored arms, his shield, and
two spears, and his gleaming helmet with its three plumes. Beside the helmet was his girdle, embroidered in bright colors. The
old man wrapped it around himself as he put on his armor when
leading the troops in war, which wastes away men. Indeed, he
was not turned away from war by the misery of old age.   79

Nestor rose up, propping his head up on his elbow. He spoke
to Agamemnon, asking: "Who is it that goes alone among the
ships and through the camp in this way in the dark of night,
when other mortals are asleep? Are you looking for one of the
guards or are you hunting for a comrade? Speak up! Don't come
near me without talking. What do you want?"   85

Then, the Supreme Commander Agamemnon answered
him: "O Nestor Neleusson, great glory of the Acheans, know
that I am Agamemnon Atreusson, the one to whom Zeus sends
so many troubles that pierce him through completely, though
he keeps the breath in my chest and urges me along on my own
knees. I am wandering around like this because sweet sleep did
not sit on my eyes. Instead, my mind is focused on war and
concern for the Acheans. I have a dreadful fear for the Danaans
and my heart is not fixed in its determination. I am very anxious
that it might just jump out of my chest and my usually jaunty
limbs shake underneath me. But, maybe you might think of
something, since sleep did not come to you. Perhaps, we might
go from here out to the sentries and check on them to be sure
they aren't worn down from fatigue and lying asleep, having
completely forgotten to stay watchful. The enemy sits close by,

and we have no idea whether they might hit on the idea of
fighting even through the night."   101

The Geranian horseman Nestor then replied: "Most glorious
Supreme Commander Agamemnon Atreusson, Zeus, the counselor, most assuredly does not mean to fulfill all of his designs
with Hector, though Hector now might very much wish it.
Instead, I think he will toil with grief aplenty, at such time as
Achilles turns his heart from its unmanageable anger. But, I
will certainly go with you. And then we will roust out the others who are near to us: Tydeusson, famed for the spear, and Odysseus, and the swift lesser Aias, and the valiant son of Phyleus.
Perhaps somebody could go around doing the same, calling
out godlike Telamonian Aias and Lord Idomeneus, whose ships
are farther out. And I will chastise glorious Menelaus, threatening that I will tell everyone if he lies abed. Though he is dear
to me, he would do the same to me. I think he will come out to
work for you. Now, I hope that all of the chiefs will toil when
asked. This direst urgency has come upon us."   118

And the Supreme Commander Agamemnon answered him:
"Old man, some other time I would have ordered you to scold
Menelaus. Often he has held back and lacked the desire for the
work. And it was not that he was lazy or because he didn't know
what he was doing. Rather, he was watching me and waiting
for me to take the lead. This time though, he rose out of bed
and got going much earlier than I did and came to me. I sent
him on to call out the men you asked about. So, let's get going.
We'll catch up with him in front of the gates among the sentries, so I can warn them as they are gathered together."   127

The Geranian horseman Nestor answered Agamemnon:
"Well now, this time there is no reason for anybody among the
Acheans to scold him or disobey him, since Menelaus got out
and started giving directions."   131

So speaking, he placed his tunic around his chest and bound
his fine sandals under his oiled feet. Around him, he put a long
crimson robe of two thicknesses, which was held by a belt with

a clasp. The soft nap of the wool fluffed out all over it. He chose
a strong spear tipped with sharp bronze and set out among
the ships of the brazen-shirted Acheans. First, the Geranian
horseman Nestor woke up Odysseus, equal to Zeus in counsel,
with the resonance of his voice. At Nestor's shout, the sleep immediately left Odysseus's mind. He came out of his hut and
spoke to them: "Why are you wandering around the ships by
yourselves in the balmy night? What is so urgent that it brings
you here?"   142

And, to that, Nestor, the Geranian horseman, responded:
"Noble-born, ever-cunning Odysseus Laertesson, don't protest,
for a great hardship has been laid on the Acheans. Instead, get
busy and follow along so that we may rouse up the others and
make a suitable plan, whether we are escaping or whether we
are to fight."   147

Thus, Nestor spoke. Ever-cunning Odysseus went into his
hut and set his many-colored shield about his shoulders, and
went off with the others. They came to Diomedes Tydeusson
and found him outside of his hut with his arms. Around him
were his comrades sleeping. They had shields underneath their
heads, while their spears stood upright with the iron fittings on
the butt ends driven into the ground. The bronze tip of each
gleamed like the lightning of father Zeus. The hero slept, and
underneath him was spread out the hide of one of the oxen
that sleep in the fields. A bright rug covered him, stretching up
under his head. Nestor, the Geranian horseman, stood beside
Diomedes, shook the heel of his foot, and roused him from
sleep. He stood in front of him, chastening: "Get up, son of
Tydeus! Why do you spend all night sleeping? Are you unaware
that Trojans sit on a rise in the plain close to the ships, and that
there is little to hold them back from our position?"   161

So Nestor spoke, and Diomedes instantly awoke from his
sleep and spoke with winged words: "You are relentless, old
man! You never let go of toil. But now, should you not let others of the sons of the Acheans who are younger go around all

over rousting out each of the kings? Old man, you are absolutely tireless!" 167

The Geranian horseman Nestor responded back: "Yes, my friend, all those things you say are true. I have fabulous sons and there are many troops. One of them could go around summoning. But it is necessary that I prevent the Acheans from being overpowered. At this point all of them are poised on a razor's edge: either a miserable end comes to the Acheans, or they live. So, if you would take pity on me, go now to roust out the swift lesser Aias and the son of Phyleus, since you are younger." 176

So Nestor spoke. Diomedes placed about his shoulders the glistening skin of a huge lion. It reached down to his feet. He selected a spear and set out to go among the heroes, ordering them to get up. 179

And when Agamemnon and Nestor caught up with the sentries who were gathered together, they found none of the leaders of the guards asleep. Instead, all of them sat with their arms at ready. They were like dogs keeping anxious watch over sheep in a fold, listening out for the fierce wild beast that comes out from a forest in the mountains. There is a lot of noise from men and of dogs around the beast. Their sleep is wiped away. In the same way is the sweet sleep wiped off the eyelids of sentries keeping watch through the evil night. They were constantly turning toward the plain to get a sense of whatever was going on among the Trojans. The old man was overjoyed on seeing them and his spirit was fired up. He spoke to them with winged words: "Keep watch this way, my beloved children, so that sleep doesn't take hold of somebody. We would not wish to bring joy to the enemy." 193

So speaking, Nestor moved through the trench. The Argive kings who had been summoned to council followed with him. With them were Meriones and the glorious son of Nestor as lookouts. They themselves were summoned to give counsel. They came away from the trench and sat down in a clean place

where they could see all around the corpses of those who fell,
where mighty Hector turned back from slaughtering Acheans
as night closed in. They sat and talked with one another.   202

Nestor, the Geranian horseman, was first to speak: "Oh, my
friends, I wonder if there is not a man with sufficient self-
confidence that he would dare to go among the greathearted
Trojans. If he might capture some straggler from the fighting,
or even somehow learn some rumor of what the Trojans have
in mind to do. He might learn whether they are intent on remaining here in front of the ships, or on pulling back to the city,
now that they have subdued the Acheans. Such a man might
learn all of these things, and come back to us safely. Great would
be his reputation among all the peoples under the heavens. And
there would be worthy gifts for him. As many as there are the
chiefs of the bravest, from each would come the gift of a black
ewe nursing a lamb, and if not that, then some similar gift.
And ever after, he will be present at banquets and feasts."   217

So Nestor spoke, and all grew silent at what he had said.
Diomedes, good at the war cry, then said: "Nestor, my heart
urges me to enter the camp of the Trojan enemy close by. But,
if another man were to go along with me there would be the
energy and boldness of warm comradeship, and I would be
more likely to succeed. It would be more profitable for two
than one observer. With one, the mind is slower and the report
trifling."   226

So, he spoke. And many wanted to go along with Diomedes.
The two Aiantes, attendants of Ares, wanted to; Meriones
wanted to; the son of Nestor especially wanted to; Menelaus
Atreusson, famed for the spear, wanted to; and daring Odysseus wanted to go down into the throng of the Trojans. The Supreme Commander Agamemnon spoke to them: "Diomedes
Tydeusson, you have brought joy to my heart. You should choose
your companion, whomever you want, since the best appear
eager to go. But do not, out of respect for rank, leave behind a
better man for fighting and take with you a lesser man because

you looked at someone's nobility of birth and chose him because of his higher royal rank."   239

So Agamemnon spoke, woefully afraid for red-haired Menelaus. But Diomedes, good at the war cry, spoke among them:
"If you order me to choose my companion myself, how then
could I overlook godlike Odysseus. There is not anyone with a
stronger mind or stouter heart in all maneuvers. Pallas Athena
loves him. If I were to accompany him, we would likely return
together even from a blazing fire, since he knows more about
everything than anybody."   247

Noble, ever-cunning Odysseus answered Diomedes back:
"Son of Tydeus, you ought not to praise me, nor speak ill of me
either, since you are talking among the Argives who know those
things. Instead, let us get going. The night quickly runs its course
and dawn draws near. The stars have clearly moved along.
More than two stages in the constellations' progress across the
night sky have passed and only the third still remains."   253

So Odysseus spoke and both put on their terrifying armor.
Intrepid Thrasymedes gave the son of Tydeus his double-edged
knife and his buckler that he had left around his ship. Thrasymedes placed a helmet around Diomedes's head made of bull's
hide. It had neither crest, nor plume. It was called a casque, and
was for protecting the head of vigorous youths. Meriones gave
Odysseus his bow and quiver, and his great sword. He placed
around Odysseus's head a helmet made of ox hide, fastened
tightly all around with strands of leather. Off from the helmet
stood the teeth of a wild boar, densely packed here and there,
very skillfully arranged. Inside the helmet was fastened a felt
lining. The helmet was taken from Eleon when Autolycus ran-
sacked the impregnable palace of Amyntor Ormenusson.
Autolycus then gave it to Amphidamas at Cythera to take to
Scandeia. Amphidamas gave it to Molos as a guest-friend gift
and Molos gave it to his son Meriones to wear. With this, Meriones covered Odysseus's head and fastened it all around.   271

And when both of them were fitted out in their dreadful

armaments, they set out, leaving all the heads of the troops in that place. Pallas Athena sent an orange-crowned black night heron on their right side, close to their route. They were unable to see it on account of the darkness of night, but they heard its barking quawk of a cry as it passed. Odysseus was delighted by the bird's omen, and prayed to Athena: "Hear me, child of aegis-bearing Zeus, you who have always stood by me in all my exploits, and do not forget me as I go along. Grant especially, dear Athena, that I may return again to the ships, having done a great deed that will trouble the Trojans."   282

And next after Odysseus, Diomedes, good at the war cry, prayed to her: "Hear me, too, indomitable child of Zeus. Go with me the same way you went with my father, noble Tydeus, to Thebes, when he was going as a messenger ahead of the Acheans. He left the brazen-shirted Acheans behind at Aesopus, so that he could bear a polite greeting to the Cadmeans there in Thebes. But on his return, he devised especially difficult tasks of war with you, divine goddess, when you stood beside him as his friend. In the same way now, may you wish to stand beside me and protect me. I will sacrifice to you an untamed yearling heifer with a wide forehead, which has not in any way been led under a man's yoke. I shall have her horns gilded for you."   294

So they spoke in prayer, and Pallas Athena heard them both. And after they prayed to the daughter of great Zeus, they went off like two lions through the dark night, along the gore of the carnage, by the corpses and through the armor and the black blood.   298

But Hector did not permit the brave Trojans to sleep at all. Instead, all of the best of them talked together, as many as there were chiefs and counselors of the Trojans. Hector called them together to frame a prudent plan: "Is there somebody who would promise to do this for me, for a magnificent gift? The reward for him would be adequate for the task. I will give both a chariot and two horses, with proud necks; they are the best that are beside the ships of the Acheans. I would give them to the one who would dare to undertake this task. They would earn fame for the one who would go close to the swift-sailing ships to learn there whether they intend to guard the swift ships and remain there, or whether they plan flight because they have been so battered under our hands. He could learn whether they have been so dreadfully beaten down that they don't want to maintain sentries through the night." 312

So Hector spoke, and all became silent. But, there was among the Trojans, a certain Dolon. He was the son of the godlike herald Eumedes, who was rich in gold and bronze. Dolon was the only son, among five sisters. To be sure, he was ugly to look at, but he was fast on his feet. At that moment, he spoke up to Hector and the Trojans: "Hector, my heart rouses me to go close to the swift-sailing ships and learn what you want to know. But, come now, raise up your scepter and swear to me that you will give me the horses and the chariot of multicolored bronze that bear the exceptional son of Peleus. I don't lack discernment and will not be an incompetent spy for you. I am going straight through the camp until I reach the ship of Agamemnon. There, the best of them are likely to be about making a plan for whether they will flee or fight." 327

So Dolon spoke. Hector took his scepter in his hands and swore to Dolon: "Let loud-thundering Zeus, the very husband of Hera, know now that no other man of the Trojans is to be charioteer to those horses—they are to be yours. I declare that you will be distinguished beyond all others." 331

So Hector spoke, swearing a false oath, urging Dolon on. Dolon quickly wrapped himself in the skin of a gray wolf, and tossed his curved bow around his shoulders. He placed a mink helmet on his head and grabbed a sharp javelin, and set off from the camp toward the ships. But, he was not going to return again carrying back word to Hector about the ships. 337

Instead, when he left behind the horses and men of the throng, he went eagerly along the road. Odysseus, born of Zeus, observed Dolon as he went along, and said to Diomedes: "Check out this guy who is going away from the camp, Diomedes. I don't know whether he is going to spy on our ships, or to strip some things off the corpses of the dead. Whichever the case, let's first let him go along a little ways into the plain, and then we can rush him and seize him quickly, and if he should outstrip us on foot we can get him with a spear as he goes from the camp to the ships. That way he cannot escape back to the city no matter what." 348

So the two of them talked and they ducked down by the roadside among the corpses. Dolon ran swiftly along, unawares. But, when he had got along about as far as the distance of the furrows made by mules—which are better than oxen at pulling a plow the first time through the deep, compacted soil—the two of them ran after him. He heard the pounding of their feet and stopped, hoping in his heart that they were his comrades of the Trojans come to turn him back, because Hector was ordering a withdrawal. But when they reached the distance of a spear cast away or even less, he realized that they were hostile warriors. He set his agile limbs in motion and took off. 359

But the two men quickly charged on in pursuit. It was like when two dogs, snarling with teeth bared, spot their quarry in some place in the forest, be it an antelope or a rabbit. They stay constantly after it, and outrun it as it groans in pain. In such a way did the son of Tydeus and Odysseus, the sacker of cities, cut Dolon off from his troops, staying in constant pursuit. 364

But when Dolon was about to blend in with the Achean sentries as he fled toward the ships, Athena inspired courage in the son of Tydeus, so that none of the brazen-shirted Acheans might boast that he had first got off a shot at Dolon and that the son of Tydeus came in second. Mighty Diomedes raised up his spear and shouted: "Hold still or I will overtake you with my spear, and I swear that you will not long escape a horrid death at my hands." 371

Diomedes hurled his spear, but he deliberately missed the

man. The polished shaft passed over Dolon's right shoulder and
its point fixed in the ground. Dolon froze in terror, shaking in
fear, white with fright. A grinding sound came out from the
gnashing of his teeth. The two men overtook him, breathless
from running, and grabbed his arms. Weeping, he spoke: "Take
me alive! I will ransom myself. In my house there is bronze, and
gold, and well-wrought iron. If my father learns that I am alive
by the ships of the Acheans he will reward you with a huge
ransom."   381

And the ever-cunning Odysseus answered him, saying:
"Take courage. There should be no thought of death in your
mind. But, come on, tell me this truthfully: why were you out
alone going from the camp toward the ships in the dark of night
when other mortals are asleep? Was it to strip the corpses of
those who have been killed? Or, did Hector send you to spy all
over the place around the hollow ships? Or, did you go off out
your own volition?"   389

And Dolon answered him, even as his limbs trembled under
him: "Hector enticed me away from good sense with many de-
lusions. He agreed to give me the solid-hoofed horses of the
noble son of Peleus, and his chariot of multicolored bronze, as
well. He told me to go out through the fearful, black night to
get close to the enemy, so that I might learn whether they were
guarding the swift ships so as to remain in place, or whether
they planned to take flight in the ships, having been beaten
down by us. He intended for me to learn whether they were so
terribly worn down that they no longer wanted to guard the
ships through the night."   399

The ever-cunning Odysseus smiled at him and said: "Well
now, those would be some grand gifts, indeed! Your heart's desire was to drive the horses of the warlike grandson of Aeacus.
Those horses are bad news for mortal men who try to subdue
and drive them other than Achilles, who is the son of an immor-
tal mother.   404

"But, come now, tell me this truthfully. Where did you leave

Hector, Shepherd of the Troops, before coming here? Where
does their armor lie and where are the horses, and where, I'd
like to know, are the sentries, and the other Trojans and where
are their quarters? What are they planning among themselves
and are they intent on remaining a distance off, but near the
ships? Or do they intend to give up their position and go back
to the city, having trounced the Acheans?"   411

Dolon, son of Eumedes, answered: "I will tell you those
things truthfully. Hector, along with those of wise counsel,
makes careful plans near the grave mound of godlike Ilus, away
from the commotion, but far off from Troy. Those you might
call guards, hero, have not been selected for anything and neither protect the camp nor take positions as sentries. As many
as there are Trojans fire grates, that many remain wakeful
under orders. They guard and tell each other what to do. But,
the allies, assembled from many places, do sleep. They trust the
Trojans to protect them. But their children are not living close
to them, nor their wives."   422

And the ever-cunning Odysseus replied to him, saying: "Are
the allies quartered separately, or mixed in with the Trojans,
noble horsemen? Tell me so that I might know."   425

And then, Dolon, son of Eumedes, answered: "I will tell you
about them, and very truthfully, you may be sure. On the seaside are the Carians, and the Paeonians, who have curved bows,
and the Leleges, and the noble Caucones, and the Pelasgi.
Facing the Thymbra, the channel, are those chosen by lot,
the Lycians, and the illustrious Mysians, and the Phrygians, who
fight from chariots, and the Maeonians, mounted warriors.
But, why would you ask me specifically about each of these? If
you are interested in entering the throng of the Trojans, I know
that the newly arrived Thracians are from farther off than the
others. Among them is their king Rhesus, son of Eïoneus. His
are the biggest and most beautiful horses I have ever seen.
They are whiter than snow and they run like the winds. His
chariot is of gold and silver, beautifully fashioned. The arms he

brought are of gold and huge, an amazing sight to see. They
are not like the ones mortal men might wear, but such as
would be fit for the immortal gods.   441

"But, now take me to the ships, or leave me here in cruel
bonds. That way you could go and test whether I have spoken the
truth to you or not."   445

Scowling at Dolon, mighty Diomedes said: "Do not get it
into your head, Dolon, to get away from me, even though what
you reported has been useful since you came into our hands. If
we let you loose, you would afterward go around the swift ships
of the Acheans, either spying or fighting against us. But if I
subdue you with my hands, taking your life, then you would
no longer be any problem for the Argives."   453

Dolon was about to plead with him, grasping Diomedes's
chin, when Diomedes rushed at him and struck, slicing clean
through both tendons of his neck with a sword. Dolon cried out,
but by then his head mingled with the dust. They took the mink
helmet from the head, and the wolf skin, the bent bow, and the
long spear. Odysseus took them and raised them up to Athena,
goddess of booty, and prayed: "Cheers, goddess, these are yours.
We praise you as first on Olympus of all the immortals. But send
us back to the horses and beds of the Thracian warriors."   464

So Odysseus spoke, and he raised up Dolon's effects and put
them up into a tamarisk bush. He made an obvious marker with
reeds and thick foliage of the tamarisk that he gathered up, so
they would not overlook the spot as they went running back
through the black night. And the two of them went forward
through the armaments and dark blood. They went along and
quickly got to the company of Thracian warriors. Completely
worn out, the Thracians slept with their beautiful arms beside
them, propped up on the ground. They were arranged neatly
in three rows. Along each of them were their double-yoked
chariots and horses. Rhesus slept in the middle and beside him
were his swift horses. Their reins were tied to the bottom of the
chariot's front. Odysseus, seeing all those around him, showed

Rhesus to Diomedes: "This is your man, Diomedes, and these are your horses. Dolon told us about them when we killed him. So, come on, let's see that irresistible power. And don't worry about the arms that are around, but instead, loose the horses. Better yet, you kill the men and I'll deal with the horses."   481

So Odysseus spoke, and Athena, with lovely eyes, breathed might into Diomedes. He spun one way and the other, killing everywhere. As he hacked and slashed with his sword, there rose up a horrid groaning, and the earth turned red with blood. It was like when a lion comes upon unguarded livestock, he charges the goats and sheep with his evil intent. So it was when the son of Tydeus went through the Thracian warriors until he killed twelve of them. And ever-cunning Odysseus stood beside the son of Tydeus and when he struck one of the Thracians, Odysseus grabbed the foot from behind and pulled the body back out of the way so Diomedes could move on to the next man.   490

Odysseus was considering how he might easily make off with the horses with the beautiful manes. He worried that they might startle going over the corpses, since the horses were not used to them. But when the son of Tydeus reached the Thracian king, he took away the sweet breath of his life, making him number thirteen. A bad dream of the son of Oeneusson stood over the king's head that night, a plan of Athena.   497

Meanwhile, patient Odysseus loosed the solid-hoofed horses and with their reins he drove them from the throng. He struck them with his bow, since he did not see the shining whip to take to hand. Whistling, he caught the attention of noble Diomedes. But he pondered in his mind as he stood there what might be the most outrageous thing he might do, or whether to grab the chariot where it lay, raise it up the pole, and with his arms pull it or carry it off. As those things passed through his mind, Athena stood close by and said: "Greathearted son of Tydeus, be mindful of your return to the hollow ships, so that you do not get there being chased, if another god were to spur on the Trojans."   511

So she spoke, and Diomedes recognized the sound of the goddess's voice. Immediately, he mounted the horses. Odysseus cracked his bow and they flew off toward the swift ships of the Acheans.   514

And, indeed, all this did not escape the notice of Apollo of the silver bow, because he saw Athena going along with the son of Tydeus. Annoyed at her, Apollo entered into the great throng of the Trojans and roused Hippocoon, a counselor of the Thracians and a worthy relative of Rhesus. Hippocoon arose from his sleep so that he saw the vacant space where the swift horses had stood, and the men, gasping in the wretched voices of the agony of death. Then he went about calling the name of his beloved cousin. Shouting, he roused up a huge hubbub among the Trojans who became enraged together. They looked about with amazement as they pondered the deeds done by the men who were going to the hollow ships.   525

And when they arrived at the place where they had killed Hector's spy, Odysseus, beloved of Zeus, reined in the horses. Diomedes leapt to the ground, and retrieving the gory spoils taken from the corpse, placed them in Odysseus's hand, and mounted the horses. Odysseus spurred them on and both horses flew without reluctance.   530

Nestor was the first to hear the sound of the horses' hooves. He said: "O my beloved chiefs and counselors of the Argives, am I mistaken or do I speak the truth? My heart orders me to speak. The sound of the hooves of fleet-footed horses beats on both my ears. Maybe Odysseus, or both he and mighty Diomedes, could drive solid-hoofed horses of the Trojans in this way. I had a terrible fear in my mind that something befell those men, the best of the Argives, underneath the ruckus of the Trojans."   536

But he had not spoken all of his words when the men themselves arrived. And they descended to the ground to meet joy and proper welcoming and pleasant words. Nestor, the Geranian horseman, was first to question them: "Most illustrious

Odysseus, great pride of the Acheans, tell me how the two of you got into the host of the Trojans and grabbed horses like these—or did some god meet you and give them to you? They are awesome, like the rays of the sun! We have been engaged with the Trojans for a long time, and maybe I have stayed back by the ships because I was too old for fighting, but I swear that I never saw or imagined any such horses. I suspected you two probably made offerings to some god who gave you the horses. Both Zeus the cloud-gatherer and Athena, the beautiful-eyed daughter of aegis-bearing Zeus, love both of you."   553

And the ever-cunning Odysseus answered Nestor, saying: "O Nestor Neleusson, great glory of the Acheans, it is easy for a god who wishes to give even better horses and to know how to do it, because the gods are so much more powerful. Old man, these horses you ask about were newly arrived with the Thracians. Diomedes killed their king, and twelve others beside him who were of the best. And we seized the thirteenth, a spy close by the ships. Hector and the other illustrious Trojans sent him out from their camp to scout us out."   563

So speaking, Odysseus drove the solid-hoofed horses through the ditch with noisy rejoicing. The others of the Acheans cheered as they went. When they arrived at the well-built hut of the son of Tydeus, they tied up the horses with their beautifully wrought reins in the stables where Diomedes's horses were kept. There, the fleet-footed horses stood munching delicious grain. Odysseus put the gory spoils from Dolon in the stern of his ship, so that they would be ready for sacrifice to Athena.   571

They went into the shining sea up to the shin, and, splashing themselves about their necks and thighs, washed themselves off with lots of water, ridding themselves of so much sweat that it delighted their dear hearts. And then they went into their well-polished baths for bathing. When both had bathed and been anointed with olive oil, they sat down to supper. They drew sweet wine from the full mixing bowl and poured libations to Athena.   579

Book 11

Dawn rose up from her sleep beside illustrious Tithonus so that she might bring light to the gods and to mortal men. But Zeus sent troublesome Strife to the swift ships of the Acheans with an omen of war in her hands. She stood beside the enormous black ship of Odysseus, in the middle of the ships' formation, so she could shout in both directions: in one way to the hut of Telamonian Aias, and in the other direction to that of Achilles. Theirs were the ships farthest from the rest, as Aias and Achilles relied on their own manliness and the might of their hands for their defense. There stood the goddess Strife, and shouting in a loud voice, she gave forth a great and terrifying cry of war. It inspired in each of the Acheans great determination for might in battle and unending fighting. For them then, the thought of war became sweeter than returning to their beloved homeland in their hollow ships.   14

The son of Atreus gave the war cry and ordered the Argives to put on armor. He dressed himself in dazzling bronze. First, he put around his shins beautiful greaves fitted with silver ankle guards. Next, he placed his breastplate around his chest. It was a gift from the time he was a guest-friend of Cinyrus, who learned in Cyprus the great news that the Acheans were about to sail for Troy. Because of that, Cinyrus gave it as a favor to the king.   23

On the breastplate, there were exactly ten dark, cyan-blue stripes, and twelve of gold and twenty of tin. On each side, there were three cyan-blue snakes striking toward their necks that looked like the rainbow that the son of Cronus props against a cloud as a sign to humans with the power of his speech. Around both shoulders he tossed his sword. In it were golden rivets that gleamed all around. Around the sword was its silver scabbard fitted with golden chains. He took up his beautiful, warlike shield that gleamed brilliantly and protected its owner from all sides. Around it ran ten circles of bronze that had twenty bosses of white tin and in the middle was one of dark cyan blue. On the front of that boss appeared the horrible face of Gorgon that was terrible to look at. Around her were Fear and Rout. The shield's strap was of silver and around it coiled a cyan-blue snake. It had three heads coming up from one neck. On his head Agamemnon placed a helmet that shone all around. It had a crest of horsehair, and its plume was terrifying when it bobbed from the top. He grabbed two sturdy spears, tipped with sharp bronze. From far off the bronze gleamed like the heavens, where Athena and Hera thundered to honor the king of Mycene, rich in gold.   46

Then, each man gave directions to his charioteer to pull his horses into close formation at a place beside the ditch, while they themselves went on foot, armed with their breastplates, and rushed violently forward. Just at dawn, there arose an unquench-able war cry. They advanced a little ahead of the horses, and a little bit behind them were the charioteers drawn up near the ditch. The son of Cronus made mischief in the hubbub, send-ing down on them dew from above that had a faint tint of blood, as a sign that he was about to hurl many valiant heads down to Hades.   55

The Trojans were off apart from them on a ridge in the plain. Among them were great Hector and the exceptional Polydamas, and Aeneas, whom the Trojans honored as a god, and the three sons of Antenor: Polybus, and the noble Agenor, and the youth Acamas, equal of the immortals. Hector was in the first ranks carrying his shield, which was balanced all around. Just as the ominous dog star Sirius rises up from the clouds to be revealed shining brightly, but at another time enters back into the clouds, so it was when Hector was revealed among the front ranks at one moment, but at another he was seen in the farthest back giv-ing directions. Always, he appeared in his bronze that gleamed like the lightning of father Zeus, who bears the aegis.   66

They were like reapers positioned opposite one another as they mow a swath of wheat or barley in the field of a man blessed in the harvest; the bundles of grain fall rapidly. So the Trojans and the Acheans leapt upon and ravaged one another. And neither side had a concern for dreaded fear, as both concentrated their minds on fighting. They were like raging wolves. Watching over them Strife, agent of pain and misery, rejoiced, for she alone of the gods was to be found in the melee. None of the others were present. Instead, they sat quietly in the halls of the palaces that had been elegantly built for each among the folds of Olympus. All were peeved at the son of Cronus, the source of darkening storm clouds, because he planned to grant glory to the Trojans. But their father spared not a thought for them. Instead, he sat apart from the others, enjoying his own glory, as he watched over the city of the Trojans and the ships of the Acheans, and the lightning flash of bronze, and those destroying and those being destroyed.   83

For as long as it was dawn and the sacred day waxed, both sides were struck by darts, and the troops fell. There is a time though, when a logger of oaks in the glades of the mountains prepares his meal. When his arms have tired from cutting long branches and he feels he has done enough, an appetite rises in his mind for sweet bread. At that time the Danaans with their bravery smashed through the ranks of men, calling to support their comrades along the formations. In the front, Agamemnon urged his men on. He took the warrior Bienor, himself a Shepherd of the Troops, and then Bienor's comrade Oïleus who drove his horses. I tell you, Oïleus got down from the chariot and stood opposite Agamemnon, who rushed straight at him and with his sharp spear instantly punctured Oïleus's forehead. The thick bronze helmet did not hold it back. Instead, the spear went through the helmet and the bone and smashed up all of his brains inside. The eagerness of the charioteer was thus vanquished.   98

And, the Supreme Commander Agamemnon stripped off their tunics, and left them there with their chests all shiny and exposed. Then, he went off and killed Isus and Antiphus, two of the sons of Priam, one a bastard and the other legitimate, together in the same chariot. The bastard son was the charioteer and illustrious Antiphus rode alongside him. At some time before, they had been seeking pasture for their sheep on the ridges of Mount Ida when Achilles captured them. He trussed them up with the flexible young twigs of a willow tree, and released them for a ransom. Agamemnon recognized them, as he had seen them back beside the swift ships when fleet-footed Achilles brought them from Ida. But this time Atreusson, the eminent Prince Agamemnon, hit Isus with his spear in the chest above the nipple, and also drove his sword into Antiphus beside his ear and hurled them from the chariot. Moving quickly, he stripped them of their beautiful armor.   112

He was like a lion that easily crushes the suckling fawn of a swift doe, seizing it with his powerful teeth and taking it to his den. He rips away its tender spirit. Even though the doe is very close by when the lion strikes, she is unable to save it, for she is seized with dreadful fear and trembling. Instantly, she dashes off through the oak thicket and the forest. She goes hurriedly, sweating as she goes, because of the attack of the powerful beast. And so it was for those of the Trojans, since none was able to prevent the deaths of Isus and Antiphus because they themselves were put to rout by the Argives.   121

Next, Agamemnon chased after both Pisander and Hippolochus, solid in the martial arts. They were the sons of canny Antimachus who had especially expected much gold from Alexander for persuading the Trojans not to allow Helen to be given back to redheaded Menelaus. The Prince Agamemnon though, captured Antimachus's two sons who were in one chariot with the same swift horses. The glittering reins slipped out of their hands and the horses were thrown into confusion, and the men unable to respond. Like a lion, the son of Atreus charged over against them. At that, both got down from the chariot, pleading: "Take us alive, son of Atreus, and you will receive a worthy ransom. Much treasure lies in the house of Antimachus: bronze, and gold and well-wrought iron. Our father would reward you with a huge ransom if he were to learn that both of us are alive by the ships of the Acheans." 135

In such a way did the two of them address the king with soft words, and they wept. But what they heard was a hard, callous voice: "Are you two indeed the sons of canny Antimachus, who was the leader of the Trojan assembly when Menelaus went there with godlike Odysseus? He ordered that they be killed then and there so that they wouldn't be able to return to the Acheans and fight against the Trojans. Now, count on it, you shall pay for his outrageous disgrace." 142

Agamemnon got down from his chariot and thrust Pisander to the ground and rammed his spear through his chest so that he was staked faceup into the ground. Hippolochus jumped down and Agamemnon slew him on the ground, too. Agamemnon cut off Hippolochus's arms with his sword and sliced off his head, and sent the trunk rolling like a stone mortar through the throng of the melee. Agamemnon left them there and rushed to the place where most of the ranks of men were shouting, with the rest of the well-armed Acheans. 149

The foot soldiers killed those fleeing on foot because of necessity. The mounted warriors killed those who were mounted. Underneath them rose a cloud of dust from the plain, increased by the pounding of the hooves of the horses, and the chariots dazzled like fire with their bronze. Lord Agamemnon was constantly urging the Argives who accompanied him on, constantly leading them in the killing. It was as when a burning fire rages in a forest that has not been logged: The circling wind carries it everywhere and the lower shrubs fall, uprooted by the force of the fire as it accelerates. In the same way the heads of the Trojans who fled fell under the hand of Agamemnon Atreusson. There were many proud-necked horses with empty chariots

jangling along the field of war, longing for their valiant charioteers. Those lay on the earth, loved much more by vultures than
by their wives.   162

But Zeus led Hector away from the dust, and from the slaughtering of men, and from the blood, and the hubbub. The son of
Atreus rushed in furious pursuit, giving orders to the Danaans.
The Trojans rushed from beside the standard of the ancient son
of Dardanus and from near the fig tree in the middle of the plain
as they scrambled for the city. The son of Atreus was in steady
pursuit shouting, his invincible hands stained with gore. But
when they reached the Scaean Gate and the oak, the armies
stopped and stood their ground, poised at one another. Those
who were still down in the middle of the plain were routed like
cattle that have been chased by a lion happening upon them in
the dead of night. He pursues them all but on one he visits terrible destruction, taking it by the neck and crushing it with his
powerful teeth at first, and then greedily gobbling down the
blood and all of the entrails. In such a way did the Lord Agamemnon Atreusson pursue them, steadily killing those farthest behind, and they were terrified. There were many who had fallen
from their chariots lying facedown and faceup, killed by the
hands of the son of Atreus as he raged with his spear in front of
him. But just as he was about to get to the wall under the high
city, then, I tell you, the father of both men and gods came down
from heaven and sat among the peaks of Ida, where there are
many springs, with thunder and lightning in his hands.   184

Zeus roused golden-winged Iris to be his messenger: "Go
speedily, Iris, tell this to Hector: For as long as he sees Agamemnon, Shepherd of the Troops, raging in the front lines, slaughtering ranks of warriors, he should hold back, and order the rest
of his troops to wage fiery combat with a mighty clash of arms
against Agamemnon. But when Agamemnon is struck by a
spear or hit by an arrow and leaps into his chariot, then I shall
grant Hector the might to kill until he arrives at the well-
benched ships as the sun is setting and sacred dusk arrives."   194

So spoke Zeus, and Iris, swift as the wind, did not disobey. She went speedily down from the mountains of Ida to sacred Troy. Iris found noble, warlike Hector Priamson standing in his framed-wood chariot with his horses. She stood close to him and said: "Hector, son of Priam, equal of Zeus in counsel, Zeus sent me here to tell you this: For as long as you see Agamemnon, Shepherd of the Troops, raging in the front lines of battle, hold back. Order the rest of the troops to wage a fiery combat with a mighty clash of arms against him. When Agamemnon is struck by a spear or hit by an arrow, and leaps into his chariot, then Zeus will grant you the might to kill until you reach the well-benched ships, and the sun is setting and sacred dusk arrives." 209

She spoke thus, and Iris, fleet of foot, went away. Hector jumped down from his chariot in his armor. Brandishing a sharp spear, he went around urging all to fight and roused up a furious ruckus. The Trojans turned around and stood their ground opposite the Acheans. The Argives stiffened up their own ranks. Fixed in position, they stood facing each other. Agamemnon was the first to attack, because he wanted always to be in the first assault. 217

Tell now, Muses who dwell on Olympus, which one was the first to go against Agamemnon: Was it one of the Trojans themselves, or was it one of their illustrious allies? 220

It was Iphidamas Antenorson, one great and good. The child of pretty-cheeked Theano, he was brought up in Thrace, which has rich soil and is the mother of fruit. Cisses, his maternal grandfather, reared Iphidamas in his house when he was but a little thing. He was most illustrious and took charge of his own affairs when he reached the age of manhood. Cisses tried to restrain him by giving him his daughter in marriage, but Iphidamas came directly from his marriage bed when news reached him of the coming of the Acheans. He arrived in Percote with twelve beaked ships. He left his balanced ships there and, along with those who accompanied him, he came on foot to Troy. 230

Now, he came against Agamemnon Atreusson, and when they had come close to one another, the son of Atreus missed. His spear was turned aside, but Iphidamas struck him below the belt of Agamemnon's breastplate. Even though Iphidamas believed that he had driven the spear with great force of his arm, it did not pierce Agamemnon's many-colored girdle; before that happened, the spear point collided with silver, and was deflected like lead. The eminent Prince Agamemnon grabbed the spear with his hands and dragged it with the ferocity of a lion. He pulled it from Iphidamas's hand and stabbed him in the neck with his sword, loosening his limbs. In such a way Iphidamas fell there to bed down with bronze, poor wretch, far away from his wife. He was aiding the inhabitants of the city, but of his wife, he knew no pleasure. He had given much as her bride price, a hundred oxen, and promised a vast herd in addition: a thousand goats and the same number of sheep. Then, to be sure, Agamemnon Atreusson stripped the corpse and left carrying Iphidamas's beautiful armor along the throng.   247

Coon, very outstanding among men, took note of what had happened. He was an older son of Antenor. A deep sorrow closed in on his eyes as he watched his brother by the same father fall. Coon was standing over to the side with his spear, unnoticed by noble Agamemnon. He struck Agamemnon in the middle of his arm, below the elbow, and the tip of the shining shaft passed clean through. At that, Agamemnon shuddered, but he didn't stop fighting and warring on account of it. Instead, he charged at Coon with his wind-fed spear and stabbed him with his polished, brazen weapon, loosening his limbs. Savagely, Agamemnon grabbed him by the foot, and shouting to all of the best, dragged Coon away from the throng. He positioned the body over that of Iphidamas and cut off his head. In that place the sons of Antenor met their destinies and entered into the House of Hades due to the exploits of a king, the son of Atreus.   263

After that, Agamemnon wiped out others among the ranks

of warriors with his spear, and his huge dagger, and by hurling
rocks, until the warm blood gushed from the place where he had
been struck. When he had stanched the wound, the bleeding stopped, but sharp pain came over the son of Atreus. It was
like when a woman is hit by the sharp pang of childbirth, sent
by the Eilithyas, daughters of Hera, who traffics in intense pain.
In such a way did sharp soreness come to the spirit of the son of
Atreus. He rushed up into his chariot, and ordered his charioteer to drive to the hollow ships, because of his heartache. He
shouted to the Danaans in a loud, piercing voice: "O friends,
chiefs, and counselors of the Argives, it is up to you now to
protect the ships that sail the sea in arduous combat, since Zeus,
the counselor, will not allow me to fight against the Trojans all
day long."   279

So yelled Agamemnon, and his charioteer cracked his whip
over the horses, with beautiful manes. Not at all reluctantly,
they both flew toward the hollow ships. There was foam on
their chests and they were spattered with dust underneath
as they carried their suffering king away from the fight.   283

And Hector took notice as Agamemnon went away from
them, and called to the Trojans and the Lycians in a loud voice:
"Trojans, and Lycians, and Dardanians, who fight close in, you
warriors who are my friends, keep in mind your furious valor.
The best man has left. Zeus Cronusson grants me great honor.
Drive the solid-hoofed horses straight on toward the stout
Danaans, so that you can win still greater honor."   290

So speaking, he roused the strength and spirit of each man.
It was like when a hunter sets snarling dogs, their white teeth
exposed, on a feral pig, or a lion. So Hector Priamson, man-
killer, equal of Ares, set the greathearted Trojans on the Acheans. He moved into the front lines with great confidence, and
fell on those in the melee like the downpour of a thunderstorm
that plunges down, churning up the waves of the dark blue deep.

And, you ask: "Who were the first and who the last that Hector slew, when Zeus gave him glory?" Well, Asaeus was first,

and Autonous, and Opites, and Dolops Klutusson, and Opheltius, and Agelaus, and Orus, and Hipponous, solid in martial arts. Hector took those chiefs of the Danaans and then charged on the common soldiers. It was like when the clouds of West Wind smack against the white clouds of South Wind, striking up an intense cyclone. Many swelling waves are roiled up, and foam is scattered all over by gusts of wandering wind. So many were the heads of the troops Hector took down.   309

Then there was death, and so Hector's invincible exploits began. Even then might he have fallen on the ships as the Acheans fled, had not Odysseus called out to Diomedes Tydeusson: "Son of Tydeus, what's happening, have we forgotten our furious valor? Come here, my friend. Stand beside me. For surely it will be a disgrace if Hector, he of the helmet with the waving plume, takes the ships."   315

And, mighty Diomedes answered him, saying: "Count on it, I'll make a stand, and a bold one, too! But there will be but little profit in it for us, seeing that Zeus the cloud-gatherer plans to give might to the Trojans. Even though he favored us earlier, he doesn't now."   319

Well, whatever it might be, Diomedes shoved Thumbraeus from his chariot onto the ground and Odysseus hurled his spear at Molion, the godlike attendant of his king, hitting him on the left nipple. Then they left them, since they were out of the fighting. The two men prowled through the hubbub of the throng, like two wild boars falling ferociously on hunting dogs. In such a way did the two visit destruction back on the Trojans, and welcome they were to those resting after fleeing from noble Hector.   327

There, the two captured both a chariot and two of the most distinguished men of the district, the two sons of Merops of Percote, who was known as the best of all at oracular divination. He did not permit his sons to muster for war, that destroyer of men, but they did not obey him at all, for fates of black death were leading them on. Diomedes Tydeusson, famed for his spear, took away their breath and spirits, seizing their famous armor, and Odysseus stripped that armor from Hippodamas and Hypeirochus. 335

The son of Cronus, watching over them from Ida, extended the equal fight, and they continued killing each other. The son of Tydeus struck Agastrophus Paeonson on the hip with his spear, but his chariot was not close by, so he could not escape. He had sent his attendant away so that he could rage along through the front lines on foot. Agastrophus was miserable as his own spirit perished. 342

Hector took keen notice along the formations, and, shouted to them, rousing up the ranks of the Trojans and they followed with him. Seeing him, Diomedes, good at the war cry, shuddered. Quickly he shouted to Odysseus, who was close by: "Violent Hector is turning around our fate with this. But come on anyway, let us stop and by making a stand we will ward him off." 348

Maybe not, but he raised up in his hand his spear that cast a long shadow, hurled it, and hit Hector. The cast was not off the mark of the head that was his target. The spear hit on the top of the helmet, with bronze smashing against bronze. But it did not reach Hector's lovely flesh, because the three-layered helmet, with its visor and plume that Phoebus Apollo had provided for him, protected him. Hector immediately drove back a long way and blended into the throng. He collapsed to his knees, and propped himself up off the ground with his beefy hands. The black of night closed in around his eyes. 356

The son of Tydeus went after the spear he had cast. Searching for the place where it landed, he came closer to Hector, who got back on his chariot and drove into the horde of common soldiers to ward off black fate. Retrieving his spear, mighty Diomedes called to him: "Yet again, you escape from death, dog! For sure, you came close to harm, but once again Phoebus Apollo has spared you. You ought to be praying to him as you go through the spear casts in the melee. For, most definitely,

I will get you when I come on you in the future, if there is one god who will jump in to help me, as Apollo did you. For now, I will go after the others, such as I meet." And with that, he began stripping the armor off the son of Paeon, famed for the spear.   368

Alexander, husband of beautiful-haired Helen, drew his bow on the son of Tydeus, Shepherd of the Troops. Paris was leaning against the stele on the tumulus of Ilus Dardanusson, the ancient founder of the dynasty of Trojan rulers. At that moment, Diomedes was taking the breastplate and the many-colored shield of powerful Agastrophus away from his chest and shoulders, as well as his heavy helmet. Paris pulled back the middle of the bow and fired off a shot, and the dart that took flight from his hands was not wasted. It hit the wide part of Diomedes's right foot, and the arrow went through and fixed itself into the earth. Paris giggled gleefully as he bounded out from his hiding place and said boastfully: "You were not hit by a dart that flew for nothing, though it would have been better if it had struck the lowest part of your belly. Then it would have taken away your life. That way the Trojans could get respite from your mischief. They shudder with fear of you, like bleating goats do of a lion."   383

Unafraid, mighty Diomedes replied to him: "Archer, pervert, with your pretty curls, you are just an ogler of little girls! If you were to prove yourself with serious arms, your bow and sheaf of arrows would not save you. Now, having scratched the wide part of my foot, you boast so. But I will not stop. It is as if a woman or a stupid child had hit me. It is the dull dart of a man who is inept and worthless. How different it is for a dart from my hand, even on a light hit. For my weapon is sharp and renders its target lifeless. Such a man's wife tears the flesh of her checks in grief; his children are orphaned, while he reddens the earth with his blood and rots. There are more birds around him than women."   395

So spoke Diomedes. Odysseus, famed for the spear, went

over and stopped in front of him. Diomedes sat down behind him and Odysseus pulled out the sharp arrow from his foot. Agonizing pain traveled through his flesh. He mounted his chariot and gave the order to his charioteer to drive to the hollow ships. His heart ached.   400

Odysseus, famed for his spear, found himself alone with no other Argive nearby; fear had seized them all. Upset, he spoke to his great heart: "What is really happening to me? I'm afraid that some horrific evil might come on me and I would be absolutely terrified. It would be more frightening to be captured alone. The son of Cronus has put fear into the other Danaans. But, why am I debating those things with my own heart? I certainly know that cowards walk away from war, but that someone of special might has to make his stand bravely, and either he is struck down, or he strikes down somebody else." These things he cycled back and forth in his mind.   411

In the meantime, the ranks of Trojan shield bearers advanced, surrounding Odysseus in their middle, and their fate settled down on them. It was like when dogs and energetic youths rush in to surround a boar in the depths of a forest, as he is whetting his white teeth in his curved jaws. The sound of the tusks comes out from below and the youths hold their positions even though it is terrifying. So it was when the Trojans rushed in to surround Odysseus, beloved of Zeus. First off, he struck Deiopites from above in the shoulder, jumping at him with his sharp spear. Next, he killed Thoon and Ennomus. Then he took Chersidamantes as he was rushing down from his chariot, with a thrust under his bossed shield against his navel. As he fell into the dust, Chersidamentes grasped the earth in his hand. Odysseus left them and struck Charops Hippasson with his spear. He was the brother of prosperous Socus. A man equal to a god, Socus rushed to aid his brother. He came and, standing very close to Odysseus, said: "O Odysseus, you are much celebrated for your treacheries and doing terrible things. Today, either you boast that you took two sons of Hippas, killing both men and

carrying off their armor or you will be struck by my spear and
your life will be taken from you."   433

Having so spoken, Socus cast against Odysseus's shield,
which was balanced all around. The shining, powerful spear
passed through the shield and the highly polished and fitted
breastplate and sliced off all the skin on the side of his chest.
Pallas Athena did not allow the spear to enter the man's viscera.
Odysseus realized that his life had not come to an end. Immediately, he backed off and said to Socus: "You scum! Now, a
horrible death has tracked you down. To be sure, you have
stopped me from fighting against the Trojans. But, I tell you
that death and a black, bloody fate is yours for that. You will be
taken down by my spear and give me glory. Your soul is going to
Hades, who is famed for horsemanship."   446

Then Socus quickly wheeled around and took off in flight.
But, as he turned, Odysseus made a cast, fixing his spear in
Socus's back, midway between his shoulders. He fell with a
thud. Noble Odysseus boasted: "O Socus, son of warlike Hippas, noble horseman, I told you that the end of death had found
you, and you did not escape it. Trash that you are, your father
and revered mother will not pull down your eyelids, even in
death. Instead, birds that eat raw flesh will drag them out.
They will fly over you in dense flocks. But if I die, the noble
Acheans will hold funeral rites for me."   455

So he spoke. He pulled out the great spear of warlike Socus
from his flesh and from his bossed shield. Blood gushed out,
spattering all around, and his heart was pained. The greathearted Trojans, seeing how Odysseus bled, called out, and all
came charging from the throng toward him. He retreated
back from them and shouted to his comrades. Three times he
shouted, as loud as the voice of a man can shout, while he pulled
back. And three times Menelaus, beloved of Ares, heard his
shouting. Immediately, he spoke to Aias, who was close by:
"Aias, noble-born son of Telamon, leader of the troops, the
shouts around me come from patient Odysseus. It seems like he

may be overpowered and alone. The Trojans have cut him off in the furious fighting. Let's go against the horde. It is better that we rescue him. I am afraid for him alone among the Trojans, even though he is brave. That would bring great regret to the Danaans."

471

So saying, he set off, and the man equal to a god followed with him. They found Odysseus, beloved of Zeus, and around him were gathered the Trojans. It was as if bloodthirsty jackals were attacking an antlered stag that some hunter shot with an arrow, but the animal got away, fleeing on its hooves for as long as its blood was warm and its limbs moved. But when, in the end, the sharp arrow conquers it, the jackals gobble it down raw in a shady glen in the mountains. When chance brings a destructive lion to it, the jackals turn away and the lion devours it. So it was when the Trojans, many and valiant, closed in around warlike, wily Odysseus. But that hero rushed them with his spear, averting the day of pitiless destruction. Aias came in close, carrying his shield that was like a fortified tower, and stood beside him. The Trojans scattered hither and thither while warlike Menelaus led Odysseus by the hand from the throng. Menelaus's attendant drove his chariot in closer.

488

Aias jumped on the Trojans and took out Doruclus, a bastard son of Priam. Next, he struck Pandocus, and he struck Lysandrus, and Pyrasus, and Pylartes. It was like when a river swollen by winter ice melt rushes down onto a plain from the mountains in the driving rains that Zeus provides. It carries with it many dried oaks and many pines, sweeping mud and debris into the sea. So it was when glorious Aias made confusion on the plain, igniting a fiery conflict of war on both horses and men.

497

But Hector still knew nothing of it, since he was on the left side of all the fighting, beside the banks of the river Scamander. On his account many men in the front were falling. He roused up an unquenchable pandemonium of war around great Nestor and warlike Idomeneus. Hector was doing terrible harm among

those in the throng with his spear and with his horsemanship,
wiping out whole ranks of youths. But the noble Acheans
would never have backed off their course, if Alexander, husband
of beautiful-haired Helen, had not stopped one of the best in
fighting, Machaon, Shepherd of the Troops. Paris hit him on
the right shoulder with a three-barbed arrow. The Acheans
were frantic that somehow he might be taken in a reversal in
the fighting. Immediately, Idomeneus called out to noble Nestor:
"O Nestor Neleusson, great glory of the Acheans, come on,
mount up on your chariot and have Machaon get up beside
you. He is a healer, a man who is worth more than all of the
others, since he cuts out arrows and applies soothing herbs.
Once you collect him, drive Machaon speedily to the ships
with your solid-hoofed horses."   515

So Idomeneus spoke, and Nestor, the Geranian horseman,
did not disobey. Right away, he mounted his chariot and the
healer, the son of the exceptional Asclepius, got up beside him.
When Machaon was on board, Nestor cracked his whip over his
horses and without hesitation they flew to the hollow ships,
where they were happy to be.   520

Cebriones, realizing that the Trojans were struggling, went
over beside Hector and said this to him: "Hector, the two of us
are here fighting at the outermost fringe of the terrifying din
of battle. But, for sure, the other Trojans are struggling in confusion, both the horses and the men themselves. Telamonian
Aias is wreaking havoc on them. I recognize him easily with
his wide shield around his shoulders. Instead of fighting here,
let us go straight there with horses and chariot, since there they
are being thrown into evil strife, both horsemen and foot soldiers. They are perishing together as he raises an unquenchable
fury of fighting."   530

So speaking, he lashed his horses, with their beautiful manes,
with a sharp crack of his whip. Hearing the snap, they raced
along, pulling the swift chariot into the midst of the Trojans
and the Acheans. As they went, they trampled both corpses

and shields. The axle was splattered with blood underneath, and the sides around the upper part of the chariot as well. The hooves of the horses drove out a cloud of dust, and so did the iron tires around the wheel rims. Rushing in, Hector dashed furiously into the throng. In the commotion, he brought evil to the Danaans. He gave his spear but little rest. He wiped out ranks of warriors on the other side with his spear, and his dagger, and with huge rocks. But he kept away from Aias Telamonson there in the fight. 542

Father Zeus, who weighs human affairs on high, roused fear in Aias. Aias stood frozen in astonishment behind his shield of seven layers of hide as the fear hit him. He trembled like a wild animal as he looked out cautiously at the throng. He turned as he retreated back a little bit, shifting from limb to limb. He was like a fiery lion that watches dogs and men of the countryside as they drive cattle out from a courtyard. They do not allow him to seize a fat one of the herd. They remain vigilant all night long. Craving flesh, the lion goes straight for them, but to no avail. He is unwilling to rush on the cattle when they are densely packed together and the men go about bravely with burning torches in their hands. Though the lion moves in on them, he is afraid. At dawn, he goes away from them with a dejected heart. It was that way that Aias turned away from the Trojans, very much against his will, sad at heart. He feared for the ships of the Acheans. 557

It was like when a donkey going along beside a field overpowers young boys. It is a stupid one on which many rods have been broken. Because it went in and devoured an entire field of corn, the boys thrash it with clubs, but their effort is foolish. They send him scurrying off in a hurry, but only after he has already had his fill. So it was when the haughty Trojans and their allies, gathered from all around, followed after Aias, the great son of Telamon. They constantly hit the middle of his shield with their polished shafts. Once, he remembered his ardent courage and turned back around to hold off ranks of the Trojans, those noble horsemen. But again he turned himself to escape. He barged his way toward the swift ships, keeping off everybody in his path. He positioned himself midway between the Trojans and the Acheans and went on a rampage. The Trojans hurled a rain of spears from their hands, but many rushed at the huge shield only to be fixed in front of it. Many went to the side, before pale skin could stop them. The spears stood fixed in the earth, yearning for their fill of flesh.   574

Eurypylus, the magnificent son of Euaemon, saw Aias being overpowered by the thicket of missiles. He went and stood beside Aias and cast his shining spear. He hit Apisaon Phausiusson, Shepherd of the Troops, in the liver under his diaphragm. Immediately, were his knees loosened under him. Eurypylus rushed over to strip his armor from his shoulders. Just as he was taking the armor off Apisaon, godlike Alexander took notice and drew his bow on Eurypylus, hitting him on his right thigh. The arrow splintered, but it whacked his thigh smartly. Right away, Eurypylus retreated back into his band of soldiers, avoiding his fate. But he shouted in a loud, clear voice to the Danaans who heard him all around: "O my friends, leaders and counselors of the Argives, turn back around and stand to protect Aias from a pitiless day. He is being overwhelmed with lances, and I am sure that he will not escape from the terrifying din of fighting. Let us position ourselves in the very front around Aias, the great son of Telamon."   591

So spoke the wounded Eurypylus, and they came and stood close to each other with their shields leaning off their shoulders and their spears raised up. Aias came opposite them and turned around to make a stand, since his band of comrades had arrived. And so it was that their fighting took on the appearance of a blazing fire.   596

The horses ferried Nestor Neleusson from the fighting, sweating as they carried the commander Machaon, Shepherd of the Troops, as well. Fleet-footed Achilles recognized them when he saw them. He was standing on the stern of his huge ship looking out over the deep distress and din of war, which brings tears. Quickly, he called out to his companion Patroclus from the ship. Equal of Ares, he heard Achilles from inside the hut and came out. This was the beginning of calamity for him.   604

The brave son of Menoetius was the first to speak: "Why have you called me, Achilles? Do you need anything from me?" And Achilles, fleet of foot, responded: "Noble son of Menoetius, you who have brought bliss to my heart, I think now that the Acheans will be grasping my knees and pleading with me, as unbearable need has come on them. But go now, Patroclus, beloved of Zeus, and ask Nestor who it is that he brought wounded from the fighting. For I saw them from behind, and it looked like Machaon, son of Asclepius. But it was impossible to see the man's face, as the spirited horses passed by in front of me so quickly."   615

So spoke Achilles, and Patroclus obeyed his beloved companion. He went running along the huts and the ships of the Acheans.   618

When Nestor and his companion arrived at his hut, the two men stepped down onto the fertile ground. Eurymedon, the attendant of the old man, unhitched the horses from the chariot. The two stood in their tunics, cooling down by drying their sweat in the sea breeze by the beach. Then they went into the hut and sat down on couches. Fair-haired Hecamede prepared a refreshment made of barley, goat cheese, and Pramnian wine. The old man had taken her from Tenedos when Achilles sacked it. She was the daughter of greathearted Arsinous, and the Acheans had chosen her for him because he excelled over everyone else in counsel. She first set before them a beautiful, highly polished table with cyan-blue feet. Then she set on it a brazen basket, with an onion in it as a condiment for their drink, and white sugar. Beside those, she set the sacred barley and a beautiful goblet, brought from home by the old man. There were golden studs set in its side. It had four handles and two doves feeding around it, fashioned of gold, and there were two more golden doves feeding on the bases of the cup. Anyone else could scarcely move the vessel to the table because it was full, but old Nestor lifted it with no difficulty. In that cup the woman, who resembled the goddesses, mixed the wine. Against a bronze scraper she grated the goat cheese, which she sprinkled, along with white barley, over the mixing bowl. Then she bid them drink up, as she had prepared the refreshment. At that, the two of them drank and put aside their parched thirst. They were exchanging pleasantries with each other when Patroclus, a man equal to a god, stopped at the door. Seeing him, the old man rose from his brilliantly shining throne. He went and took Patroclus by the hand and led him in and told him to sit down. But Patroclus refused, saying: "No sitting, illustrious old man, and you will not persuade me. The revered one who has been wronged sent me to find out whom it was that you brought back wounded. However, I know that anyway, since I see Machaon, Shepherd of the Troops. Now that I've asked my question, I must get back to Achilles with the answer. As you well know, he is a distraught man and he was easily upset, even without cause."   654

Then, Nestor, the Geranian horseman, responded to Patroclus: "Why is it that Achilles is so concerned about the sons of the Acheans and how many there are that have been wounded by missiles? He knows nothing of the suffering. The best men lie in their ships, struck down and wounded. Mighty Diomedes Tydeusson was wounded. Odysseus, famed for the spear, was struck, and Agamemnon was wounded, and even Eurypylus was hit by an arrow in the thigh. This man I have most recently fetched from the fighting; he was wounded by an arrow. Though Achilles is esteemed among the Danaans, he has neither concern nor pity for them. Will he hang back without doing anything until the ships of the Acheans are consumed by raging fire and we ourselves are killed off one by one?

"Not that there is anything I could do in my bent-over frame. Oh, how I wish that I might be the young, virile man I was, firm in my strength. I wish I were as I was when a brawl broke out between the Eleans and us over cattle rustling. It was when I killed Itymoneus, the brave son of Hypeirochus, who lived in Elis, as I was driving off cattle taken in reprisal. He was defending his cattle in the front lines when he was hit by a cast from my hand, and fell. The peasants who were his troops scattered in fear.

"I drove off collected spoils of the greatest abundance. There were fifty herds of cattle, as many flocks of sheep, as many herds of swine, as many herds of flatland goats, and a hundred and fifty horses with blond manes. All of those were mares, and there were foals underneath many of them. We drove them all night to Neleian Pylos, in front of the city itself. Neleus was delighted that such good fortune was mine in war, even though I was young.

"At the moment when Dawn revealed herself, the heralds announced in distinct voices that those who were owed debts in sacred Elis were to go to the assembly and the chief men of Pylos were to divide up the spoils. There were debts owed to many by the Epeans. Though we in Pylos were less numerous, we had been disadvantaged by them. In earlier times, the mighty Heracles came and did us harm, killing off many of the best men. There were twelve sons of illustrious Neleus, but of them, I alone was left; all the rest perished. Because of those things the insolent, brazen-shirted Epeans arrogantly devised a treacherous plot against us. Neleus sent horses and a chariot to Elis as they were about to run a race for a tripod as prize.

"But Augeas, Supreme Commander of the Epeans, detained them, and sent the driver of the horses away brokenhearted. Old Neleus was furious over both Augeas's words and actions because he had taken away such a huge amount of property. Old Neleus picked out thirty herds of cattle and thirty flocks of sheep at pasture, as settlement for the large debt owed him in sacred Elis. It was recompense for the four horses and their

684

chariot that went to the race. The other things I took, Neleus
divided up and gave them to those living around the district so
that none would go away having been cheated of his fair share.   704

"We were administering these matters, and around the city
we performed our sacred duties. Three days later, all of the
Epeans came together to our city with their solid-hoofed horses
going full speed. The two Moliones had suited up in their armor and came with them, though they were just boys and did
not yet know the ways of furious valor. There is a certain city
Thryessa on a high spire a long way away on the Alpheius, on
the farthest outskirts of sandy Pylos.

"All of the Epeans were eager to lay siege to the city and destroy it. But when they had come together on the plain, Athena
came to us as a messenger from Olympus, telling us to arm ourselves during the night. And there was no reluctance among
the Pylian troops she raised up to go into battle. They were
keen to charge into the fray. But Neleus did not allow me to
take up arms; he hid my horses. He claimed that I did not yet
know the deeds of war at all. Even so, I excelled our troops in
horsemanship, though I was on foot, since Athena was then
leading on the brawl.   721

"There is a certain river Minyeius that falls into the sea near
Arene. There we waited for sacred Dawn, the Pylian horsemen
and scads of foot soldiers running all around. We left and
went all out with full armor and at noon arrived at the sacred
stream of Alpheus, and made beautiful sacrifices to almighty
Zeus, a bull to Alpheus, a bull to Poseidon, and finally a cow of
the herd to beautiful-eyed Athena. Afterward, we took our
meal and set up our camp. We bedded down, but with each
man in his armor, beside the currents of the river.   732

"The greathearted Epeans took up a position around the city,
determined to completely destroy it. But before they could, a
great deed of Ares was revealed to them. When the sun shone
from its place over the earth, we prayed to Zeus and Athena,
and we were brought together with the Epeans in battle. You

may be sure that when the ruckus between the Pylians and the Epeans commenced, I was the first to take out a man, and I took over his horses. He was the warrior Mulius, a son-in-law of Augeus. Mulius was married to the eldest of Augeus's daughters, the strawberry-blond Agamede. She knew as much about herbs as anybody in the wide world who grows them. Going in front of Mulius, I hit him with my bronze-tipped spear, and he fell in the dust. I climbed up into his chariot and easily positioned it in the front lines of the fight. At that, the greathearted Epeans turned, some this way, some that, when they saw the Commander of the Horsemen fall, the most skilled of them in fighting. I charged against them like a dark cyclone and took fifty chariots. Two men in each bit the dirt, vanquished by my spear. 749

"At that point I might have ravaged the two Moliones, sons of Actor, had not their actual father—Poseidon, the widely reigning earth-shaker—saved them by enclosing them in a dense mist. Then did Zeus grant great might to the Pylians. We chased the Epeans across the wide plain, both killing them and collecting their beautiful armor. We drove our horses toward Buprasium, with fields full of grain, and the Olenian headland, and a hill called Alesium. Athena turned the troops back there, after I had killed the last man and left him. Then the Pylians drove their swift horses back from Buprasium to Pylos. Everyone praised Zeus among the gods and Nestor among the men. 762

"It was then that I was, if at any time I have ever been, in the company of warriors. But Achilles will take no pleasure in his bravery by himself. I surely think he will lament with many tears the troops who perish on his account. Oh, my dear boy, how Menoetius instructed you, his son, on that day when he sent you from Phthia to Agamemnon. Two of us were there in his great hall, myself and noble Odysseus, and we heard everything he told you. We had arrived at the happily occupied palace of Peleus while recruiting troops across Achaia, with its rich soil. There at the same time, we found inside the hero

Menoetius and you. You were at the side of Achilles. The old noble horseman Peleus was in the courtyard burning fat thighs of an ox to Zeus, who delights in thunder. Peleus held a golden cup in his hand as he poured libations of wine the color of burning coals onto the burning sacrifices. You and Achilles were preparing the flesh of the ox when we stood in the entrance hall. With astonishment, Achilles rose up and came to take us by the hand, led us in, and bid us to sit down. He offered us excellent guest-friendship, as is the custom to offer strangers. After we enjoyed food and drink, I began my pitch, urging the two of you to come along with us. Both of you were keen to do it. But, your fathers had much to tell both of you in preparation. Peleus instructed his son Achilles that he must always be the bravest in fighting and that he should be preeminent over all others.

784

"Menoetius, son of Actor, instructed you in this way: 'My child, Achilles is superior to you in birth and rank. You are older, though he has much more strength. But you must speak to him in carefully considered words and advise him, and explain things to him so that he will be persuaded to the most virtuous course.' That is what Menoetius told you, but you have forgotten. Even now, you should speak to warlike Achilles in such a way. Maybe he will be convinced. Who knows whether you might rouse his heart with the help of some god? The advice of a friend is valuable. If he is avoiding some oracle or a prophecy of Zeus that his revered mother put into his mind, he should send you instead. The rest of the troops of the Myrmidons ought to follow. It is to be hoped that you would become a shining light to the Danaans. And, he ought to give you his beautiful armor to wear into battle. We would hope the Trojans see you wearing it, for you will look just like him in the fight, and they will pull back, and give the warlike sons of the Acheans respite. Now they are worn down and resting from the fight, but few will rest from the fighting when they hear the shouts of

warriors easily smiting men. Perhaps you could push the Trojans back toward the city and away from the ships and the huts." 803

So spoke Nestor, and he roused up spirit in the chest of Patroclus, who went off running beside the ships to Achilles,
grandson of Aecus. But as Patroclus came running he came
alongside the ships of godlike Odysseus, where their place of assembly and justice was, and where they had set up the altars of
the gods. There, the wounded Eurypylus, noble-born son of
Euaemon, met him. Eurypylus had been hit in the thigh with
an arrow and withdrawn from the fighting. Sweat poured down
his back and shoulders and from his head. From the nasty wound
dripped dark blood. But his mind, at least, was steady. 813

Seeing Eurypylus, the valiant son of Menoetius took pity
on him, and, choking back tears, spoke to him with winged
words: "Oh you miserable commanders and counselors of the
Danaans, how dreadful it is that you are about to gorge the
swift dogs with your white fat so far from your friends and your
fatherland! But come now, noble-born Eurypylus, you are a hero,
so tell me this. Will the Acheans yet somehow hold off huge
Hector, or will they be wasted, being beaten down under his
spear?" 820

And the wounded Eurypylus answered him: "Patroclus,
born of Zeus, there will no longer be a barrier for the Acheans, for they are in the ships, having fallen in the field. All the
best lie there either struck or speared by the Trojans, whose
might is steadily increasing. Please save me and take me to my
black ship. Cut the arrow out of my thigh, and then wash away
the dark blood with warm water and put a healing poultice of
soothing herbs on it. They say that Achilles taught you in the
past the things he learned from Chiron, the most just of the Centaurs. Of the healers Podaleirius and Machaon, one of them I
think has been wounded himself and lies in a hut in need of a
worthy healer. The other is on the plain holding off the fierce
Ares of the Trojans." 836

The valiant son of Menoetius answered: "How could that happen? What are we doing, hero Eurypylus? I was on my way to Achilles so that I could tell him what the Geranian Nestor, guardian of the Acheans, instructed me to. But there is no way that I can go away now, when you are suffering so."   841

And you may be sure, he grabbed Eurypylus, Shepherd of the Troops, under the chest and took him to his hut. When his attendant saw them, he spread out ox hides. There Patroclus stretched Eurypylus out and cut the sharp dart from the thigh with a knife. It was very painful. He washed away the dark blood with warm water, and he put on a bitter, analgesic root that he rubbed in carefully with his hands to relieve the pain. The wound dried up and the bleeding was stopped.   848

Book 12

The valiant son of Menoetius worked in the huts, healing the wounded Eurypylus, while the others, Argives and Trojans, fought in companies. But the trench was no longer going to protect the Danaans, nor the thick wall above it that they built around the ships. They did not give the gods extravagant offerings so that the gods would protect the swift ships with their great treasure. What the Argives had built without the blessing of the immortals still stood firm, but not for very long. For the time being, Hector still lived and Achilles remained angry. The city of King Priam remained unharmed, and even the great wall of the Acheans solidly stood.

But, at some point, according Zeus's plan, the best of the Trojans would die, and many Argives would be vanquished. Those surviving Argives would sack the city in the tenth year. They would return in their ships to their beloved homeland. Then, you may be sure, Poseidon and Apollo planned to destroy the wall and have the power of a river overwhelm it. The power of as many rivers as flow from the mountain peaks of Ida to the sea: the Rhesus, and the Heptaporus, and the Caresus, and the Rhodius, and the Granicus, and even the Aesepus, and the noble Scamander, and the Simois where many ox hide shields and plumed helmets and even a race of demigods had fallen down into the dust. Phoebus Apollo turned all the rivers to form a single mouth and the son of Zeus, having gathered them together, set them to flow over the wall for nine days. So that the wall might be inundated faster, the earth-shaker himself, with trident in hand, heaved up all the foundations of the waves into a tsunami and drove it over the timbers and the stones that were smoothed by the rushing currents of the Hellespont. They were the very stones the Acheans had toiled at setting into place. The

wall was demolished and the sands again enclosed it in a great
reef. Apollo then turned the rivers back into their own channels, back where the gently rippling waters flowed before.   33

Such things, you may be sure, Poseidon and Apollo were going to accomplish eventually. But for now, the shouts of war
raged all about the carefully built wall. The rafters of its fortified towers rang with the sound of the bombardment. The Argives, whipped by the scourge of Zeus, holed up in the hollow
ships, cooped up from fear of Hector, master of stampede. He
fought before the ships like a storm. It was like when a wild boar
or a lion turns on dogs and hunters, as he is delighting in his
own might. The hunters fall into formations and stand opposite him casting their spears from their hands in a dense barrage.
But there is no fear nor thought of flight in his stout heart, and
his bravery kills him. Often, he turns and takes on whole formations of men, and where he rages forward the formations of
men back off. So it was with Hector, as he proceeded through
the throng, turning around his comrades, urging them to cross
over the trench. But his solid-hoofed horses had not the daring.
Instead they stood at the high cusp of the trench, neighing. They
were afraid that they could not leap over it, and when they got
closer to it they didn't try. They stood bunched together at its
steep edge, looking down at the sharply fashioned palisade. The
sons of the Acheans placed it there to make a safe spot for men
under attack. It would not be easy for the horses to pull their
chariots with their fine wheels over it. Seeing that, the foot soldiers were keen to cross the palisade.   59

At that moment, Polydamas stood beside valiant Hector and
said: "Hector and you other chiefs of the Trojans and our allies,
it would be absurd for us to drive the swift horses across the
trench, and very hard going. The palings of the palisade set in it
are sharp, and there is the Acheans' wall ahead of that. Fighting
from chariots, there is no way we can go against that. It is a tight
space where I think the horses would be hurt. If loud-thundering
Zeus is minded to bring destruction and all manner of evil on

them, he will send aid to the Trojans. If he does, I would want to begin right away on the ignominious destruction of the Acheans here, far from Argos. But if they turn around and begin a sally back from the ships, they might trap us in the trench. If the Acheans turn and roll over the top of us, I don't think even a messenger would survive to trace his steps back to the city. But, come now, let's everybody do as I say. Let the attendants draw the chariots back from the trench and we will follow Hector on foot close together with our panoply of arms. The Acheans will not be able to hold us off if the ropes of destruction are tied on them."   79

So spoke Polydamas, and his proposal pleased Hector, who immediately jumped down from his chariot with his armor. And the other Trojans did not stay with their chariots either; when they saw what Hector was doing they all dismounted, and each of them instructed his charioteer to carefully draw back his horses from the trench. The men formed themselves into five groups to follow their commanders.   87

The men who went with Hector and illustrious Polydamas were the strongest and bravest; they were especially eager to rush headlong into battle beside the hollow ships. And Cebriones went as the third commander of the group, since Hector left behind another man with his chariot who was less able than Cebriones. Paris, Alcathous, and Agenor led the next group. In the third were Helenus and godlike Deïphobus, two sons of Priam. Also in the third was the hero Asius. Asius was the son of Hyrtacus. Dazzling horses brought him from Arisbe beside the river Selleis. Aeneas, the upright son of Anchises, commanded the fourth group, and with him were the two sons of Antenor, Archelochus and Acamas, both very knowledgeable in all aspects of fighting. Sarpedon commanded the renowned allies, as he excelled among all. He chose Glaucus and warlike Asteropaeus as his lieutenants because they seemed to Sarpedon to be the best among the others. They went straight on toward the Danaans, especially eager with their fitted shields, advancing hurriedly to fall on the black ships.   107

There the other Trojans and their widely famed allies
followed the plan of exceptional Polydamas. All but the squad
leader Asius Hyrtacusson, who did not intend to leave either his
horses or his charioteer and attendant there. Instead, with his
horses, he closed in on the swift ships. What a fool he was. He
was not going to escape bad fortune and return from the ships
to windy Troy, rejoicing with his horses and chariot. Unlucky
fate was about to zero in on him with a spear held by Idomeneus Deucalionson. Asius went along the left of the ships, where
the Acheans were accustomed to come driving in from the
plain. There the wide gate was not locked, nor was the long bar
drawn. The men kept it open so that their comrades escaping
the fighting might find safety among the ships. Asius confidantly
drove his horses and chariot through. His men followed, shouting loudly, for they thought that they would no longer be kept
back by the Acheans; instead, they set about falling on the black
ships. What fools they were!   127

Inside the gates they found two of the bravest warriors, stout-
hearted sons of spearmen of the Lapithae. They were Polypoetes, mighty son of Perithous, and Leonteus, a man-killer equal
to Ares. The two of them stood before the lofty gate like oaks
with high crowns in the mountains that stand against winds and
rain every day, and with roots that spread out forever. So they
stood, trusting in their arms and their courage, waiting on great
Asius without fear. They stood directly in front of the well-built
wall, calling their loud war whoops, and roused up Ialmenus,
and Orestes, and Asiades, and Adamas, Thoon, and Oenomaus
among those there to surround King Asius so that they might
protect the ships. When they realized that the Trojans were slip-
ping inside the wall, there arose a cry of fright.   144

The two Lapiths rushed in front of the gate to fight like a pair
of wild boar in the mountains who wait as the noise of men and
dogs rises as they approach, rushing across an area where the
boar smashed the forest flat, cutting off tree roots. The noise of
the whetting of their tusks becomes audible until someone

strikes them and takes away their lives. And so it was that the sound rose from the shining bronze on their chests hitting against itself as they turned to meet the enemy. They fought very powerfully, confident of the troops above on the wall and their own might. The men hurled rocks down from the fortified towers to save themselves, their huts, and their swift-sailing ships. The rocks were like snowflakes falling on the ground that pour thickly down from darkening clouds driven along by a furious wind—so it was with the missiles streaming from the hands of both the Acheans and from the Trojans. Shouts were heard all around as the round stones struck against helmets and bossed shields. And at that point Asius Hyrtacusson cried out in pain as he was struck in both his thighs, and bellowed: "Father Zeus, it would seem now that even you have made yourself, altogether and completely, a lover of liars. I certainly did not think any Achean heroes would withstand our strength and overpowering hands. But they are like wasps, with differing colors in the middle, or bees that make their homes in craggy rocks beside roadways. They do not leave their hollow home, except for defense of their young against hunters. Like them, these men, even though there are just two of them, do not wish to retreat from the gate until they kill or are killed."   172

So spoke Asius. But Zeus paid no mind to what he said. It was his plan to grant courage and glory to Hector.

The others fought each other fiercely at the gates, and it would be hard for me to tell everything about the fighting as though I were a god. Everywhere along the stone wall there arose a consuming fire. The Argives were suffering of nesessity to protect their ships. The gods were grieved at heart, since all would rush to the aid of the Danaans in the fight. Together, the Lapiths lunged into the fighting and fury.   181

There, Polypoetes, mighty son of Perithous, hit Damasus on the bronze cheek-piece of his helmet, but the bronze did not hold back the brazen point. Rather, the bronze spear went completely through, crushing the bone and scrambling the brains inside his head. Damasus's eager spirit was subdued. Next, Polypoetes slew Pylon and Ormenus. Leonteus, scion of Ares, hit Hippomachus, son of Antimachus, with a spear in his fitted girdle. Next Leonteus pulled out his sharp sword from its scabbard and rushed through the throng to whack Antiphates first in close combat. He fell faceup on the ground. Then, he sent Medon, and Ialmenus, and Orestes, one after the other down to the fertile earth.

194

At that time the Lapiths were stripping the shining armor from the corpses of those they slew. In the meantime the youths followed Polydamas and Hector and they were many and they were brave, and especially eager to break through the wall and set fire to the ships. Pondering that, they stood beside the trench, when a bird crossed over their heads. It was an eagle flying high on the left to avoid the troops, carrying a bloodied snake in its talons. The snake was huge, and though alive, was gasping for breath. But it did not forget its combative instincts. It whipped back around and stung the bird that held it on its breast, beside the neck. The eagle, pained by the bite, let go of the snake and it fell to the ground. The bird itself uttered a high-pitched scream and flew off on a draft of the wind. The Trojans trembled with fear as they looked at the variegated serpent lying in their midst, an omen of Zeus, who bears the aegis.

209

At that, Polydamas spoke to valiant Hector as he stood beside him: "Hector, you are forever disparaging me in assemblies when I speak out after careful consideration. Inasmuch as it is not seemly that a man in the community contradict you, I don't. You should always increase your power. But I will tell you now, again, what seems best to me. I am deeply concerned about our fighting with the Danaans around the ships. This is how I think it would turn out. The bird that passed over the Trojans was an eagle coming from the left and avoiding the troops. It was carrying a bloodied snake in its talons that was huge and alive. The eagle surely was taking food home to its own nest, but it did not finish getting it to its chicks. So it will be for us. If somehow we batter our way through the gates and the wall with great force, the Acheans will pull back. But there is not enough room beside the ships for us to go along in formation. We will leave behind many Trojans, whom the Acheans will slaughter, fighting furiously with bronze to protect their ships. This is what an augur of birds would divine, one who is wise of heart, and understands signs, and who is trusted by the troops." 229

Hector, of the helmet with the waving plume, scowled at him and said: "Polydamas, what you say is no longer acceptable to me. Even you know better than to talk like that. If you are really serious about what you were saying now, the gods themselves must have wiped out your brains. You are telling me to forget the plans spoken by loud-thundering Zeus, which he promised me and nodded in agreement. You say we should trust in birds, with outstretched wings, but I don't care at all which way they turn. It doesn't matter to me if the bird goes to the right toward the dawn and the sun, or to the left toward the dusky darkness. We should trust the counsel of great Zeus, who rules over all of the mortals and the immortals. The best omen is the one that protects those around our homeland! 243

"Why would you be afraid of war and deadly conflict? If all of the rest of us are killed beside the ships of the Acheans, you have no reason for concern that you would perish. Because you don't have the stomach for mortal combat and fighting. But, if you abstain from fighting, or if you turn any of the others away from it with your deceptive talk, I will immediately strike you with my spear and your breath will be taken away." 250

So speaking, he went off, and you may be sure that the others followed with a hearty shout. And Zeus, who delights in thunder, raised up a wind storm on Mount Ida and sent it straight toward the ships, picking up dust as it went, which unnerved the Acheans and gave glory to the Trojans and Hector. Trusting in the omens that seemed clear and in their own might, they set about smashing the great wall of the Acheans. They yanked off the coping stones of the towers and tore down the battlements. With levers, they pried up the framing posts and pilings that the Acheans had first set in the ground as supports for the towers. Once pulled away, those were used as battering rams for smashing the Acheans' wall. But even so, the Danaans did not give any ground. Instead they defended the battlements holding their ox hide shields close together and throwing missiles from their wall down on their assailants.   264

Both of the Aiantes were giving orders on the towers. They went back and forth all over rousing the determination of the Acheans, the one by speaking gently, while the other harshly criticized anyone he saw shrink back from the fighting: "O friends of the Argives, some of you are outstanding, some average, and some less skilled, because there is no way that all warriors are of the same skill in war. But, for now, war is the work of everybody, so do what you yourselves know how to do. Do what you can, so that down the line we will not hear some braggart claim that we were turned back toward the ships. If thundering Zeus, the Olympian, grants it, we will push back this warring brawl and send them back to the city."   276

In such a way, with loud shouting, these two roused the Acheans in the fight. And from them, it was like snowflakes falling thickly on a winter day, when Zeus the counselor rouses himself to reveal to mankind the kind of missiles he throws in the falling snow. The wind is calmed, and the snowflakes pour thickly over the ground, so that they enclose the upper forests and jutting peaks of the mountains, and the lotus-covered marshes, and the fertile fields of men. The snow pours down upon the inlets and shores of the gray sea, but the sea's waves spread out to keep it off. The flakes come down from above whenever a heavy storm from Zeus weighs down on all. In such a way did stones fly thickly from both sides, the Trojans and the Acheans. A din rose up over the whole wall.   289

But not even then would the Trojans and glorious Hector have been able to break through the wall or the gates and the long bolt, had not counseling Zeus roused his son Sarpedon against the Argives. He was like a lion that wheels around on oxen. Sarpedon quickly held his shield in front of him. It was balanced all around and covered with beautiful bronze, and on the inside were ox hides sewn tightly together, and golden stitches ran around its perimeter. Holding the shield up before him and brandishing two spears, Sarpedon set out like a mountain-bred lion who has been a long time in want of meat. His heart commands him to go after sheep in their tightly secured fold, even though he finds their herders, with dogs and spears, keeping watch around them. He is not of a mind to run off without trying, but once he has leapt in, he either makes a kill or he is first hit by a cast from a ready hand. In such a way did the heart of godlike Sarpedon direct him to rush on the wall and smash through the battlements.   308

Right away, he spoke to Glaucus, son of Hippolochus: "Glaucus, why are we both the most honored men in Lycia with seats at their feasts and both meat and full cups? Why do all the Lycians look on us as gods, and why do we live on a plantation granted to us on the banks of the Xanthus, which has abundant orchards and fields? It is because now both of us must stand in the front lines of the Lycians and engage in fiery battle. Then one of the heavily armed Lycians might say: 'The kings who rule over Lycia are not without glory. They eat the fat sheep and drink the best of the sweet wine, but one may count on their might and valor when they fight in the front lines for the Lycians.'   321

"Oh, dear friend, if we were to live forever, ageless and immortal, by escaping from this war, I would not fight in the front lines myself nor would I be preparing you for the fighting that brings men glory. But now, ten thousand fates of death threaten us from every direction, and it is not possible to escape our mortality. Let us go ahead and strive for glory for one of us or another."   328

So Sarpedon spoke, and Glaucus neither turned away nor disobeyed him. The two of them went straight into the band of Lycians to lead them. Seeing them, the Athenian Menestheus, son of Peteus, shuddered in fear. He looked around the front of the tower for someone he knew who might lead the Acheans up on the tower against the Lycians bringing the worst trouble to his section of the wall. He hoped to find one to protect his comrades in the fight. Looking around, he recognized the two Aiantes, insatiable for war, standing there, and he saw Teucer coming from the huts close by. But there was no way he could call to them and be heard. The sound of the shouting reached up to the heavens, and the racket from the banging of shields and the plumed helmets and the gates was thunderous. The gates were completely locked, but there were men moving against them, trying to smash them by force and to gain entry. Right away, Menestheus dispatched the herald Thootes to the Aiantes: "Go, noble Thootes, run to summon the Aiantes, preferably both of them since they are by far the best of all. Very soon this will become a disastrous slaughter. The Lycian commanders will overpower us here, because they fight with greater violence than anyone else. If serious fighting has arisen where the Aiantes are now, at least have valiant Telamonian Aias come alone. But Teucer should come with him, since he is so skilled with his bow and arrows." 350

So, Menestheus spoke, and the herald, having heard him, obeyed instantly. Thootes set out running along the wall of the brazen-shirted Acheans. He went and stood beside the Aiantes, wasting no time before saying: "Aiantes, commanders of the brazen-shirted Acheans, noble-born son of Peteus bids you to come and meet up with him to fight, even for a little while. It would be better if both of you were to go, since you are by far the best of all men. His situation will soon become a disastrous slaughter. The Lycian commanders will likely overpower them there; they have fought in the past with greater violence than anyone else. But, if fighting is intense here, at least have valiant Telamonian Aias come alone. And Teucer should come with him, since he is so skilled with his bow and arrows." 363

So spoke the herald, and great Telamonian Aias did not disobey. Immediately, he said to the son of Oïleus in winged words: "Aias, both Teucer and I should go there and make a stand, rousing up the Danaans to a stout fight. You and mighty Lycomedes continue the fight here, and I will return as soon as I have protected the others well."   369

So speaking, Telamonian Aias went off and with him went Teucer, his half-brother by the same father. Pandion went along with them, carrying Teucer's curved bow. While they were going to the tower of greathearted Menestheus, the Lycians were storming the wall to enter it. Their overpowering commanders and counselors went after the battlements like a darkening storm as they drove the fight against the wall, raising shouts of war.   377

Telamonian Aias was the first to kill a man, greathearted Epicles, a comrade of Sarpedon, by throwing a jagged stone that was lying inside the wall beside the highest parapet. It was so large that no man or youth could easily manage it with both arms. Aias raised the stone up and hurled it down, shattering the helmet, which had a mount for four plumes. At the same time, it smashed to pieces the bones of his head. Like a diver, Epicles fell down from the height of the tower and his spirit abandoned his bones. Teucer hit mighty Glaucus, son of Hippolochus, striking him with an arrow from the high wall on an arm that Teucer could see was bare, stopping Glaucus's martial ardor. Glaucus jumped down from the wall and hid, so none of the Acheans might notice he was wounded and gloat over it. Grief rose up in Sarpedon as soon as he realized that Glaucus was leaving the earth, although he did not forget his warlike spirit. Instead, Sarpedon struck Alcmaon Thestorson dead with his spear, and as he pulled out the spear, the body followed along and fell facedown. His beautifully colored armor of bronze crashed around him. Sarpedon seized him with his beefy hand and dragged him through the throng, and then stripped the corpse naked. He made way for many coming behind him.   399

Aias and Teucer came at Sarpedon together. Teucer hit him

with an arrow on the gleaming strap of his whole-body shield, close to his chest. But Zeus protected his son from the fates, as it was not his destiny to be brought down beside the sterns of the ships. Aias, casting from his palm, struck the shield: the spear did not pass through, but the blow stupefied Sarpedon in its intensity. He backed off a bit from the battlements, but did not retreat altogether, since his heart longed to win glory.   407

He shouted to the godlike Lycians, as they were turning back: "O Lycians, why do you forsake your furious valor in this way? Think of how hard it is for me to be put in a position to break through a path to the ships by myself. Follow me. From more men there is better work."   412

So Sarpedon spoke, and the men, frightened by the threats on their king, rushed in fiercely around one who was both prince and counselor. The Argives strengthened their own ranks within the wall, and great was the struggle they saw. For neither did the courageous Lycians batter their way through the wall and come inside, nor did the Danaan warriors push the Lycians back from the wall after they first came close to it. Instead, it was like two men engaged in a boundary dispute. They meet in a field with measuring sticks in hand and quarrel over little bits of space, but things stay about the same. So it was with them as they struggled around the battlements. Those under them raged with ox hides around them, both shields that cover all around and light bucklers. Pitiless bronze wounded the flesh of whoever might turn to expose his unprotected back while fighting. And many spears went through shields, as well. And all about the towers and battlements was spattered the blood of Trojans and Acheans alike. But it was not as though fear had entered the Acheans. It was like an honest woman who spins thread for a living and so holds up a balance. She puts the weight on one side and the spun wool on the other until the height of both is the same, so that she can take her miserable wage for the sake of her children. So it was with the two sides held in the balance, equal in the fighting and warring. At least, that was the way it was before Zeus gave Hector Priamson, who first leapt up onto the wall of the Acheans, the upper hand. He gave a piercing cry that resounded all around: "Rise up, Trojans, noble horsemen! Batter down the wall of the Acheans and send the fire of the heavens into the ships!" 441

So shouted Hector in encouragement. And all who heard made straight for the wall in a dense formation and set on the battlements with their sharp spears. Hector carried a sharp stone he had seized from where it was fixed in the front of the solid foundation. It was a stone that two men from the district could not have pried up with a lever from the ground into a wagon. Now, made light by the son of crooked-dealing Cronus, it was lifted by just one man, who easily grasped it by himself. It was as when a shepherd easily carries the fleece of a ram along in his left hand: he lifts it with little effort. So Hector lifted the stone and carried it to the doors that were thick and sturdy, carefully fitted into the high gates, and twice locked. Two bars fitted into each other and interlocked; one key fit into them. Hector stood very close, braced himself, and threw it in the middle between the doors so that the hit would be effective. He broke the hinges on both sides and the weighty stone fell through the great, thick gate. The locking bars did not hold, and the planks of the doors split apart under the blow of the stone. 462

At that, glorious Hector leapt inside the gate. He had the look on his face of terrible, unending night. He glowed from the horrifying bronze that clothed his flesh, and his eyes burned with fire. He had two spears in his hands, and he was unsparing in the thrusting of them when he got down from the gates and yelled to the Trojans to turn back from the throng and climb over the wall. They eagerly obeyed. Quickly some climbed up and shouted as others entered the gates. The Danaans up on the hollow ships were terrified, and the clash of the boundless din was fearsome. 471

Book 13

After Zeus allowed the Trojans and Hector to get close to the ships and set them to struggle in unremitting misery there, he turned his own bright eyes away from them to return to his constant oversight of the horse-training Thracians, the Mysians, who fight in close, the distinguished Scythians, who drink mare's milk, and the Abians, who are the most just of men. His heart was fixed in his desire that none of the immortals go to the aid of either the Trojans or the Danaans.   9

But the lord earth-shaker did not turn a blind eye. He came up from the sea to sit among the highest of the forested peaks of Samothrace. From there, he looked out with amazement over all of Ida, and the city of Priam, and the ships of the Acheans. He was upset by the turbulence and fighting, and felt pity for the Acheans who were being beaten down by the Trojans, and he was mightily resentful of Zeus.   16

Immediately, he came down from the craggy mountain, moving with quick steps. He stretched forth his feet, stepping three times on his way, and the tall mountains and forest trembled under Poseidon's immortal feet as he went along. His fourth step brought him to his destination, Aegae. There was his famous palace in the depths of a secluded harbor. It was fashioned of shining gold, which is forever incorruptible. There, he harnessed his two horses to his chariot. Their swift hooves were shod with bronze and their flowing manes were golden. He decked himself in gold over his skin and took hold of his whip, worked carefully in gold. He mounted the chariot and drove it toward the waves. The creatures of the sea came out from their hiding places and frolicked around him, as they would not ignore their king. Joyfully, the sea parted to make way. The horses pranced as they flew, but the axle of bronze

underneath the chariot did not get wet. The high-stepping
horses brought Poseidon to the ships of the Acheans.   31

There is a wide cave deep below a harbor midway between
Tenedos and rocky Imbros. There Poseidon the earth-shaker
reined in his horses. He unhitched them from the chariot, and
tossed them ambrosial fodder to eat. He set golden hobbles
about their hooves that could not be loosed, so they would remain in place until their master returned, and he set out for the
Acheans' army.   38

The Trojans packed in together were like the flames of a fire-
storm as they followed Hector Priamson with unstoppable fervor, in a clamor of shouting. They hoped to capture the ships
of the Acheans and to kill all of the best of them beside the
ships. But Poseidon, earth-surrounder, earth-shaker, had come
up from the depths of the sea to encourage the Argives. He took
on the guise of Chalchas, his body, and his voice with its tireless resonance. He spoke to the Aiantes, charging up one first
and then the other: "You two Aiantes must save the Achean
troops. You must keep in mind your valor and not succumb to
chilling fear. There is no reason for me to fear the overpowering hands of the Trojans who have come from the throng and
over the great wall. The well-armed Acheans will hold off all
of them. But I have a terrible fear that we might suffer harm
because of that madman who leads them like someone on fire.
Hector claims that he is the son of almighty Zeus. But one of
the gods will place in both your minds what is needed to make
a stand and to lead the others and so push Hector back from the
swift ships, even if the Olympian inspired Hector."   58

At that, the earth-shaker struck both of them with his staff,
filling them with power. He made their limbs light in weight
and their feet and hands above. He himself was like a hawk, fleet
of wing, which is perched on a cliff so steep that it is inaccessible
even to goats and then rises up to make a stoop on another bird
down on a plain. In such a way did the earth-shaker Poseidon rush
off. But both recognized him: speedy Oïlean Aias was first, and

immediately said to Aias, son of Telamon, "That was not Calchas who makes prophecies from birds. We had one of the gods
who hold Olympus with us, in the guise of an oracle, telling
us to fight beside the ships. Those footsteps and the stride of
those limbs were so quick as he went off. They were surely divine. And because of him the spirit in my chest is all fired up to
fight and do battle. And my feet under me, and my hands at my
sides, are all ready for a fight."   75

And Telamonian Aias answered him, saying: "Now, on account of this I'm anxious to get my invincible hand around a
spear; my strength has been invigorated and it has affected both
my feet under me. My mind is focused only on zealous fighting, even alone, against Hector Priamson, who fights without
letup."   80

In such a way did the two men talk to each other, enjoying
the warlike fervor that the god had fixed in their minds. Meanwhile, the earth-surrounder roused up the Acheans in the rear.
They were cooling off, each resting beside the swift ships. Their
very limbs were tired and beaten down. They became sick at
heart as they looked on at the Trojans coming up from the
throng and going over the wall, and as they watched, tears
welled up underneath Achean brows. But even then, no one
spoke of a retreat from the evil.   89

The earth-shaker appeared among them and easily roused
them into powerful formations. First, he went to Teucer, then
he gave directions to Leïtus, and the hero Peneleos, and Thoas,
and Deïpyrus and Meriones, and even Antilochus, master of the
war cry. He roused them with winged words, saying: "Take
courage, Argive youths! I am convinced that you can save our
ships by fighting. But if you shrink back from the awful warring
now, it appears we will be trounced by the Trojans today. Oh,
my friends, what a terrible wonder is in front of my eyes! How
I swore that it would never happen! But the Trojans have come
to our ships, though in the past they were like skittish does. If
the does come down from the forest, they become prey for

jackals, and leopards, and wolves as they wander around aimlessly, and there is no fighting spirit in them. So it used to be, when the Trojans displayed no taste for standing up against the powerful hands of the Acheans. Now they fight beside the hollow ships, far from the city, yet our troops are listless because of the fault of our commander; they show no desire to protect the swift ships. Instead the Trojans are killing our men. So if there is truly one to blame for this, it is the hero Prince Agamemnon Atreusson, because he dishonored the fleet-footed son of Peleus.   113

"But that is no cause for us to give up the fight. Instead, we can fix this quickly, and mend your brave hearts. It is not yet the time when you should toss away your furious valor. You should all be the bravest in the vanguard of the army. I would not fight against men with anyone who avoids miserable war. Yet here we are quarreling among ourselves over our fates. Dear friends, make this evil lethargy here now into something better. Let each man fix in his mind courage and strength, and then there will be raised a huge brawl. For, I tell you, mighty Hector, good at the war cry, has smashed the gates and the long, locking bar, and fights beside our ships!"   124

The earth-surrounder stirred up the Acheans. The mighty formations came together around the two Aiantes. They were such that neither Ares nor Athena, salvation of troops, would speak lightly of them, were either to come among them. The men selected the best to stand against noble Hector and the Trojans, touching spear to spear, closing in buckler to buckler, overlapping shield with shield, helmet to helmet, man to man. The crested helmets glistened as their plumes nodded, lightly touching. So they stood, tightly packed in together, thrusting the spears they brandished in their hands. They were sound of mind and ready to go straight into battle.   135

The Trojans, led by Hector, pushed on forward in close formation, intent on going straight through. They rushed on like a rock that is broken off from the top of a massive rock formation by the raging river in the thaw of the winter snow melt. It is broken off by the torrents of rain from a giant boulder, and bounces around as it flies along. It is knocked about and smoothed as it goes through the forest. The river runs along gently when it arrives on the level plain, and the rock no longer tumbles, but comes to rest. So, it was with Hector, as he got closer to the sea. He went easily along the huts and ships of the Acheans, killing as he went. But when he encountered the close formations, he stopped. There, the sons of the Acheans struck with their swords and spears that were sharpened on both ends, pushing him away. Shaken, he pulled back. He shouted in a clear, loud voice to the Trojans: "Trojans, Lycians, and Dardanians, who fight in close, stay firm beside me. The Acheans will not hold me off for long, even though they have arranged themselves in these fortresslike formations. I think they will pull back from the threat of my spear instead, if the best of the gods, the thundering husband of Hera, has truly granted me his favor."   154

So Hector spoke, and roused strength and courage in each man. Deïphobus Priamson went toward the Acheans with great zeal, with his shield that was balanced all around. Nimbly, he stepped forward, being cautious under his shield as he went. Meriones cast his shining spear and hit Deïphobus's shield of bull's hide that was balanced all around. Though not miscast, the spear did not drive through the shield, but broke at the stem before it could penetrate. Deïphobus held his ox hide shield away from his body, but Meriones's spear had terrified him. The hero retreated back into the company of his comrades. Meriones was furious because his attempt at victory and his spear had broken at the same time. He set out along the huts and the ships of the Acheans to get a long spear from a hut in the rear.   168

But the rest of the troops fought on, raising up a war cry that could not be silenced. Teucer Telamonson was first to kill a man, the warrior Imbrius, son of Mentor, who had many horses.

He lived in Pedaeum before the sons of the Acheans came. He had taken Medesicasta, a bastard daughter of Priam, as a wife, and she then went with him to live near Pedeum. But when the Danaans came, they went back to live in Troy alongside Priam, who valued him equal to his sons. Imbrius was considered outstanding . . . But the son of Telamon now struck him under the ear with a long spear, then pulled it out. At that, Imbrius fell like an ash on a peak of the mountains, conspicuous from all sides. When cut by bronze, it falls with its soft leaves spread out on the ground. In such a way did Imbrius fall. His armor of variegated bronze crashed around him. Teucer was keen to spirit away the armor, but Hector rushed him, casting his gleaming spear. Teucer saw it coming just before the brazen spear arrived. Hector's spear then hit Amphimachus, son of Cteatus Actorson in the chest, as he arrived at the fighting. Amphimachus fell with a thud, and his armor crashed on top of him. Hector moved forward quickly to make a grab for the helmet fitted to Amphimachus's temples, but Aias sprang over to strike Hector with his gleaming spear. But the spear didn't see any flesh. Hector was completely covered with terrifying bronze, and the spear hit the boss of Hector's shield. But he was knocked back by the huge impact, and retreated from both of the bodies. The Acheans pulled them away. Noble Stichius, who together with Menestheus was a commander of the Athenian contingent, pulled back Amphimachus's body. The Aiantes, charged up with furious valor, pulled back that of Imbrius, in the manner of two lions that grab a goat from under snarling dogs and carry it over the ground in their mouths to a dense thicket. In such a way they took the bodies, holding them up high, and the two Aiantes stripped the heaped-up armor. The son of Oïleus cut the head of wretched Imbrius off his soft neck and heaved it, spiraling like a ball, through the throng. It landed in the dust at Hector's feet.

205

Then Poseidon was saddened over the fate of his grandson Imbrius, who fell in the awful heat of war. Even so, he set out along the huts and ships of the Acheans, rousing the Danaans and making trouble for the Trojans. He ran into Idomeneus, going along after checking on a comrade who had been wounded in the lower part of his hip by sharp bronze. The man's comrades had carried him out, and Idomeneus was urging the healers to help him. Yet he was of a mind to stay in the fighting. The lord earth-shaker spoke to him, taking the guise and voice of Thoas, son of Andraemon, who ruled the Aetolians in all of Pleuron and steep Calydon, and who was esteemed as a god in his community: "Idomeneus, counselor of the Cretans, where have the threats gone, with which the sons of the Acheans once menaced the Trojans?"   220

And Idomeneus, commander of the Cretans, spoke back to him: "O Thoas, no one man is to blame, so far as I know. Everybody knows how to fight and no god holds us by any bonds. Nor is anybody holding back out of reluctance or refusal to fight. Instead, it seems to be the pleasure of the almighty son of Cronus that the Acheans perish here in disgrace, far from Argos. But, Thoas, as you go alongside someone who is firm in the fight, encourage him, and if you see another hanging back, tell him that this is not the time to retreat. Speak to each man."   230

And then the earth-shaker Poseidon replied: "Idomeneus, that Trojan man, Hector, will never return home. On the day when Achilles comes willingly into the fight, Hector will run away and become the sport of dogs! Anyway, go grab your arms and come back here. Be quick, if the two of us are to profit. If we unite, it will instill bravery in the men, even those with many troubles. The two of us could show even the brave how to fight."   238

So he spoke, and the god returned to the men's struggle. When Idomeneus arrived at his well-built hut, he covered his skin with beautiful armor and reached for two spears. Then, he set out like a bolt of lightning with flashing rays, such as the son of Cronus takes into his hands and shakes from shining Olympus as a sign to mortal men. In such a way did the bronze gleam around Idomeneus's chest as he ran. Meriones, his attendant, ran into him when he was still close to his hut. Meriones was going to get a brazen spear. Mighty Idomeneus addressed him: "Meriones, fleet-footed son of Molus, most beloved by his comrades, why did you leave the battle and the heat of war and come here? Have you been wounded? Or have you come with a message for me? For sure, I don't relish hanging around inside a hut. Instead, I'd rather fight."   253

And thoughtful Meriones said back: "Idomeneus, counselor of the brazen-shirted Cretans, I have come so I could get a spear if one has been left behind in your hut. I threw the one I had, but it shattered, stopped by the shield of haughty Deïphobus."   258

And Idomeneus, commander of the Cretans, replied: "If it's spears you want, you'd probably find twenty if you find one on display in the vestibule of my hut. Gleaming Trojans' spears that I have brought back from those I killed. I brought not only spears of the enemy warriors back from where we faced off in battle, but bossed shields, and helmets, and breastplates polished 'til they glowed."   265

Thoughtful Meriones answered back: "In my hut and black ship are also many Trojan arms, but I have taken nowhere near so many as you. I have never forgotten how to be valiant, though. Instead, whenever anyone started a brawl, I have stood in the vanguard of the army where men earn glory. Somehow or other, many of the brazen-shirted Acheans seem to have forgotten that. But you know that yourself."   273

Idomeneus, the Cretan commander, replied: "I know that you are one who strives for valor. So why is it necessary for you to talk about these things? If now all of the best of us were to lie in ambush beside the ships, then would the valor of men be clearly revealed; there the wretch or the brave man would be seen for what he is. The complexion of the coward turns another shade, and he is unable to control the trembling of his breathing. Instead he crouches, shifting from one foot to another, and his swollen heart pounds in his chest, and as he thinks about his fate, his teeth begin to chatter. But the complexion of the brave man doesn't change color at all, and he has little fear. When he first comes to sit in ambush, he prays for a speedy engagement with awful conflict. And one would not speak lightly of such a man. If you, Meriones, were wounded in the fight, it would not be in the back of the neck or the spine. Rather, you would be hit in the chest or the belly, advancing in the front ranks among the best men. But come, let's not stand here talking like idiots. It is pointless to carp so. Instead, go to my hut and choose a huge spear." So spoke Idomeneus, and Meriones, with speed equal to Ares, went to the hut and selected a bronze spear. He set off with Idomeneus with an ardent desire for war.   300

Just as man-killing Ares goes into war with his own son, Fear, who is powerful and daring, and terrifies even someone confident in his skills as a warrior, in such a way did Idomeneus and Meriones, coming from Thrace, take up arms with the Corinthians or with the greathearted Phlegians. They claimed nothing for each other; they gave the glory to the others. In that way, Meriones and Idomeneus, leaders of men, armed in gleaming bronze, urged the men on to war. Meriones was first to speak: "Son of Deucalion, where did you have in mind for us to enter the throng, to the right of all of the army, up the middle, or to the left side? I hope there is nowhere that the long-haired Acheans don't have the fighting covered."   310

And Idomeneus, commander of the Cretans, replied: "There are others in the middle protecting the ships. The two Aiantes and Teucer are there. He is the best archer among the Acheans and good at hand-to-hand combat as well. They can push back Hector Priamson enough while he stays active in the fight, even if he is unusually strong. They are able to win against him even if he has the keenest desire to set fire to the ships, unless the son of Cronus throws a flaming torch at the ships himself. Great Aias Telamonson would never yield to a man who is mortal and eats the gifts of Demeter. Such a man will prove vulnerable to bronze, and fragile under huge rocks.

And neither would Achilles, who smashes whole ranks, give Hector any ground. There is no way Hector could win against those feet. So, let's the two of us stand with the left of the army, and we will soon see whether one of us wins glory." 327

So he spoke and Meriones, with speed equal to Ares, was first to set off, and so arrived alongside the army as he had been told. The Trojans who saw Idomeneus and his attendant thought they were like flames of fire in their dazzling armor, going all around the throng, calling out encouragement. There was a brawl taking place near the sterns of the ships, and they were in that same place. It was like when a tornado rushes on, driven by shrill winds. On a day when there is a lot of dust on both sides of the storm's path, it sucks it up and raises a huge cloud. So it was when Idomeneus and Meriones went into the fight together, stirring up each other for action. They raised up their sharp bronze against the throng, bristling with long spears that cut flesh in the fighting that withers men. Those who saw them were blinded by the glint from their brazen helmets, and the dazzling gleam from their freshly polished breastplates and shining bucklers, as they came on together. Anyone who might look on with pleasure, without cringing, would certainly be intrepid. 344

The two mighty sons of Cronus hit the heroes on both sides with miserable suffering. It was Zeus's plan to let Hector win, then give glory to fleet-footed Achilles. He did not wish that the troops of the Acheans perish before Troy, but rather to give glory to the brave-hearted son of Thetis. But Poseidon was upset at seeing them vanquished by the Trojans, and exceedingly angry with Zeus on that account, and he covertly came up from the gray sea and went around rousing the Argives. The two gods were both born to one father, but Zeus was born first and was entitled to greater respect. On that account, Poseidon avoided helping the Acheans openly and always went around rousing the army stealthily, taking the guise of a mortal man. But with both in the mighty struggle, there was a tug-of-war back and forth, each pulling toward an end. Their hold on the men was

unbreakable and ineluctable, and the limbs of many were loosed
in death.   360

Grizzled though he was, Idomeneus jumped in there and
gave orders to the Danaans, stirring up fear in the Trojans. He
killed Othryoneus who had come from Cabesus. He had come
recently to the war, and the rumor was that he asked for
the hand of Priam's daughter Cassandra, the most beautiful of
his daughters, and that he offered no bride price. Instead he
promised the great deed of driving the unwelcome sons of the
Acheans away from Troy. It was also rumored that old Priam
nodded in agreement and promised to give her to Othryoneus,
trusting in his promise to fight. Idomeneus cast his shining spear
at Othryoneus as he strutted along, and hit him. The bronze
breastplate he wore didn't hold the spear back. It struck him in
the middle of his stomach. He fell with a thud.   373

Idomeneus spoke to the corpse in boast: "Othryoneus, you
would have been truly the most praiseworthy of all mortal men
had you pulled off what you promised Priam Dardanusson. And
he promised you his daughter. Well, so much for that. These
are the things we promise to do. We would give you the best
looking of the daughters of Argos, who was taken from the son
of Atreus, to have as wife, if she will go with us after we sack the
teeming city of Troy. But, I'll tell you for sure, when we go, together with you as husband in our ships, which sail over the sea,
there is to be no bride price for you, seeing as how we are not
expecting it!"   382

So saying, the hero Idomeneus dragged the corpse by the feet
through the heavy fighting. Asius, who was the protector for
Othryoneus, came ahead of his horses on foot, as they both
panted from the constant lashing on their backs by their charioteer, Asius's attendant. He was keen to hit Idomeneus, but he
made his counter ahead of Asius, and hurled his spear into
Asius's neck below the chin. It drove through the bronze that
was in front of his neck. Asius fell, and it was like when an oak
falls, or a poplar or a tall pitch pine, in the mountains. Wood-

cutters fell it with axes they have just sharpened so that it can
be fashioned into a ship. In such a way Asius lay stretched out
in front of his horses and chariot. Gnashing his teeth, he grasped
the bloody dust. His charioteer reeled as the shock took away
the focus of mind he previously had, and he didn't dare turn
back his horses from the burning conflict to escape his enemies'
hands. As he stood there, Antilochus, firm in valor, hit him in
the middle of the clasp of his armor with a spear. The bronze
breastplate he wore didn't protect him: the spear smashed into
the middle of his stomach. Gasping, the charioteer fell from
his well-wrought chariot. Antilochus, the son of greathearted
Nestor, drove the horses away from the Trojans and back among
the well-armed Acheans.   401

Deïphobus, upset over the loss of Asius, moved in close to
Idomeneus and cast his gleaming spear. But Idomeneus saw the
brazen spear coming ahead of time and covered himself with
his well-balanced shield, avoiding the spear. The shield was
round, fashioned of ox hides and gleaming bronze and fitted
with two handles. Idomeneus crouched down so that he was under it completely, and the shield made a dry, scraping noise as
the spear glanced off it. But the throw from Deïphobus's heavy
hand was not harmless: the spear hit Hypsenor Hippasusson,
Shepherd of the Troops, in the liver under the diaphragm. Immediately his limbs collapsed under him.   412

Deïphobus boasted in a loud voice: "Asius certainly does not
lie unavenged. Instead, I think that even though he is going to
Hades, of the mighty gates closed tight, he should be glad at
heart, since I furnished him a guide."   416

So he spoke, and his boasting aggrieved the Argives. It especially aroused the warlike spirit of Antilochus, but, even though
he was upset by it, he did not neglect his comrade. He ran over
and covered the body with his buckler and then two especially
brave comrades, Mecisteus, son of Echius, and noble Alastor,
went in and bore it back to the hollow ships, groaning griev-
ously as they went.   423

Idomeneus did not let up on his rampage. He strove constantly either to wrap some Trojans up in dusky night or to fall
himself while protecting the Acheans from ruin. He bagged
there the hero Alcathous, the beloved son of noble-born Aisy-
etes. Alcathous was the son-in-law of Anchises, and was married to Hippodamea, his eldest daughter. She was dearest to the
hearts of her father and revered mother in their halls, and surpassed all others of her own age in beauty, and needlecraft, and
brains. On that account she married Alcathous, the best warrior in vast Troy.   433

Poseidon subdued him on behalf of Idomeneus, casting a
spell on Alcathous with his dazzling eyes and binding his glorious limbs. He was able neither to turn and run, nor to hold off
Idomeneus. Instead, he was like a post or a tree with a lofty
crown of leaves, standing stock-still when the hero Idomeneus
struck him with his spear in the middle of his chest. The bronze
that covered him was supposed to hold off destruction of his
flesh, but when it should have done so, there was a dry, scratching noise as the spear smashed through and tore apart the brazen tunic that he wore. Alcathous fell with a thud, the spear
fixed in his heart. For a time, the heart still beat and the butt
end of the spear oscillated back and forth from the heart's con-
tractions. Then, the spirit of impetuous Ares darted off, leaving
him still.   444

It was Idomeneus's turn for extravagant boasting, and he did
it in a loud voice: "Deïphobus, is there any way that we could
compare the worth of three kills as opposed to one, since it was
you who boasted so? Instead, braggart, you ought to stand opposite me yourself, so you might know that such a one as I, a
seed of Zeus, has come here. Zeus first sired Minos, a Cretan
prince, and Minos sired the exceptional Deucalion, a king over
many men in sprawling Crete, and he sired me. Now men from
our ships wrangle in this place to trouble you, and your father,
and the rest of the Trojans."   454

So he spoke. Deïphobus considered two possibilities that he

turned over in his mind. Either he could withdraw quickly and some of the greathearted Trojans might come to help him, or he could take on Idomeneus by himself. A crafty resolution came to him. He went off in search of Aeneas and found him standing at the throng's outer edge. Aeneas was always bitter toward noble Priam, because he didn't prize Aeneas highly enough, even though he was worthy among the warriors. Deïphobus stood close to Aeneas and spoke to him with winged words: "Aeneas, counselor of the Trojans, Idomeneus, famed for the spear, killed Alcathous. You absolutely must avenge your brother-in-law, if you care at all for him! Before he became your brother-in-law he raised you as a little thing in his halls. Follow me and we will avenge him." 467

So Deïphobus spoke, and roused up spirit in Aeneas's breast, and he went off most eager to do battle with great Idomeneus. But fear didn't seize Idomeneus as it would one who was timorous. Instead, it was like when a boar in the mountains is convinced of his bravery as he stands against the clamor of many men approaching the place where he lives alone. The ridge on his back bristles up and his eyes glow with fire. Next, he whets his tusks, for he is keen to ward off both dogs and men. In such a way did Idomeneus, famed for the spear, hold his ground, as Aeneas advanced, assisting Deïphobus. Idomeneus looked around and shouted to his comrades Ascalaphus, and Aphereus, and Deïpyrus, and Meriones, and even Antilochus, masters of the war cry. He roused them with winged words: "Here, men. You need to help me because I'm by myself. I'm dreadfully afraid of Aeneas, who comes quickly at me. He's adept at killing mortals. He's in the bloom of youth, when his strength is at its peak. If we were the same age with the courage we have, either he would carry off a trophy quickly, or I would." 486

So Idomeneus spoke, and they all were as one with courage in their breasts, standing close together with their shields leaning against their shoulders. Aeneas, from the other side, looked around and called out to his comrades, Deïphobus, and Paris,

and noble Agenor, Trojan commanders, and after them the
troops followed. It was as when the sheep follow the ram away
from a pasture to drink; it delights the mind of the shepherd.
So was there delight in the heart of Aeneas's breast at seeing the
company of troops following after him.   495

And around Alcathous there was close combat with long
spears with polished shafts. There was a terrifying clanging
from the bronze around their chests as they prepared to go
against the throng in turn. Aeneas and Idomeneus, both men
equal to Ares and the best by far over the rest, each hurled pitiless bronze to cut the other's flesh. Aeneas first cast at Idomeneus, but he saw it before it reached him and ducked. Aeneas's
spear flew over and stuck in the ground, oscillating. It rushed
off from Aeneas's mighty hands, but his cast was wasted.
Idomeneus hit Oenomaus in the middle of the belly, smashing
through a dimple in his breastplate. The bronze went through
and his guts spilled out. Oenomaus fell in the dust and grabbed
the earth with the palm of his hand. Idomeneus pulled his spear,
which made a long shadow, from the corpse. But he was not able
to take the beautiful armor off its shoulders because of the missiles coming at him. He could neither rush on with his weapon
nor avert the missiles, since his feet and limbs were no longer
charging forward. His feet were fixed where they were, averting the day of destruction, but not yet trembling so that they
might skip lightly away from the fighting.   515

Deïphobus was one who was always angry at Idomeneus. He
backed off step by step and made a cast at Idomeneus with his
shining spear. He missed, but the spear hit Ascalaphus, son of
Enyalius. The mighty point went through the shoulder, and Ascalaphus fell in the dust, grabbing the earth in the palm of his
hand. But the powerful, loud-shouting Ares knew nothing about
how his son had fallen in the fierce fighting. He was on high
Olympus under golden clouds. He sat cooped up with the other
immortal gods according to Zeus's plan, avoiding the fighting.   525

There was hand-to-hand combat around Ascalaphus. Deïphobus grabbed the gleaming helmet away from the body. Meriones, with speed equal to Ares, rushed at Deïphobus and thrust a spear at him. He jabbed Deïphobus in his shoulder. The shining, plumed helmet fell from Deïphobus's hand to the ground with a crashing sound. Like a vulture, Meriones again took hold of the huge spear and pulled it out of Deïphobus's shoulder blade, retreating back into his own group. Deïphobus's own brother Polites put his arm around his waist to lead him from the clamorous fighting until they reached his swift horses where they were standing with their charioteer and variegated chariot. The horses bore weary Deïphobus toward the city, groaning deeply. Blood ran down his newly wounded arm. 539

The others fought on, raising up the unquenchable cry of war. There Aeneas rushed toward Aphareus Caletorson as he turned, striking him in the neck that was cut altogether through by the sharp bronze. The head leaned to one side, together with the shield and helmet. Death, which shatters the spirit, poured around him. Antilochus was keeping an eye out for Thoon and as he turned around, rushed him and struck. The spear sheared a vein that ran up his back all the way to the neck, and sheared completely through the neck, too. Thoon fell faceup in the dust, and his arms were stretched out on both sides to his beloved comrades. Antilochus rushed over and, cautiously looking around him, took the armor from the shoulders. The other Trojans who were standing around him struck his wide shield with its many colors, but they were unable to get in to scratch Antilochus's tender flesh with their cruel bronze because the earth-shaker Poseidon had extended his protection around the son of Nestor, even amid the many missiles coming in. And he was never distant from the fiery struggle. He turned them away from Antilochus. And nobody could hold his spear steady, since Poseidon rushed in and shook it every time. He rattled anyone preparing to cast a spear or close in on Antilochus. 559

And Adamas Asiusson assuredly did not escape his notice when he was preparing to rush from the throng and strike the

middle of Antilochus's shield at close range with sharp bronze.
But the black-bearded Poseidon weakened the spear point with
his great might and held it away. It was like a wooden stake
hardened by fire against Antilochus's shield. It fell to the ground,
broken in half. Adamas retreated back to the company of his
comrades to avoid his fate, but as he did, Meriones was watching and went after him. He hit Adamas with the spear midway
between his navel and his genitals, where Ares causes the most
pain for tormented men. There, the spear fixed in him. He went
along struggling around the spear. It was like when an ox in the
mountains struggles against a rope around his neck when the
herders are leading him, because he doesn't want to be bound
tightly. So it was with Adamas: though he was wounded, he
struggled a little while, but not for very long. Then the hero
Meriones came over close and pulled out his spear from Adamas's flesh, and darkness enveloped his eyes.   575

   Helenus came in close to Deïpyrus and drove his great Thracian sword down on his helmet. It smashed the plumed helmet
to pieces. Deïpyrus staggered around a bit and fell to the ground.
One of the Acheans who was fighting saw the helmet rolling
around his feet and picked it up. The duskiness of night closed
in on Deïpyrus's eyes.   580

   A deep sadness seized Menelaus Atreusson, of the shrill war
cry, and he went over and brandished his sharp spear to threaten
Helenus, the hero king. And Helenus drew back the middle of
his bow. At the same moment, one made a cast with his sharp
spear while the other shot off an arrow from his bowstring.
Helenus fired the arrow at Menelaus's chest, at a dimple in his
breastplate. Off the bitter arrow flew. It was like when black
beans or the dark brown seeds of a vetch bounce off the great,
wide fanner-basket against the threshing floor because of a shrill
gust of wind and the thresher's toss. In such a way did the bitter
arrow fly against glorious Menelaus's breastplate, bounce off,
and wander far away. But, Menelaus Atreusson, good at the war
cry, hit the arm that held the highly polished bow. The brazen

spear drove straight through Helenus's arm. Helenus retreated back into the company of his comrades to avoid his fate with his arm dangling, and the ashen shaft dragged after him. Great-hearted Agenor pulled the spear from his arm and bound it well around with a bandage of the finest worsted sheep's wool, which his attendant had for the Shepherd of the Troops. 600

Pesandrus went straight for glorious Menelaus. But an evil fate of death was leading him to you, Menelaus. His end was to be taken down by you in the fiery conflict. When the two came close in together, the son of Atreus cast at Pesandrus and missed: the spear was turned aside. So Pesandrus struck the shield of glorious Menelaus, but the wide shield held firm, and Pesandrus was unable to drive the bronze through. The shaft of the spear snapped off. Yet Pesandrus still hoped in his heart and mind for victory. The son of Atreus pulled out his silver-studded sword and leapt at Pesandrus. From under his shield Menelaus grabbed his fine battle-ax. It had a long handle of polished olive wood and a double head of stout bronze. He had it with him when the two came together. For sure, he drove the ax onto the crest of Pesandrus's helmet, the crest that the horsehair plume was fitted into. Pesandrus was advancing when he was hit and so the ax continued on through his forehead and down to the tip of his nose. It crashed through the bone and both bloody orbs of his eyes fell down to the ground beside his feet in the dust. Pesandrus writhed as he collapsed. 618

Menelaus went over, put his heel on Pesandrus's chest, and stripped the corpse of its armor. He said, boasting: "You arrogant Trojans, who have an insatiable appetite for horrible war, this is how you must leave the swift-sailing ships of the Danaans, at some point. You don't lack any disgrace or shame. You evil dogs, you violated her and harmed me. You have no fear in your hearts for the stern anger of thundering Zeus, who protects the guest-friendship, who will someday destroy your high city. You senselessly led off my young wife, taking her and her property back home with you after she showed you her

friendship. And now, you are determined to toss ruinous fire
into our seagoing ships and to kill Achean heroes. But at some
point you will be stopped, even though Ares is urging you on.   630

"Father Zeus, they say that you keep track of the affairs of
men and the other gods, and that all things come from you. So,
then it must please you to give this to these arrogant Trojans
whose instincts are always criminal and who are unable to satisfy their craving for war that is equally destructive for all. The
fulfillment of desire for everyone comes from sleep, and lovemaking, and sweet singing, and elegant dancing. Surely though,
a man would rather make love than to be away fighting. But not
the Trojans: they have an insatiable desire for war."   640

So speaking, the exceptional Menelaus gave the bloody arms
he had stripped from the corpse to his comrades, and he himself went back and joined in the front lines of the fighting.   642

There, Harpalian, son of King Pylaemenes, leapt at Menelaus. He came with his beloved father to Troy for the fighting,
but he would not return back to the land of his fathers. When
he closed in on the son of Atreus, he struck the middle of his
shield with a spear, but was unable to drive it through. He retreated back into the company of his comrades to avoid his
fate, looking cautiously around for fear that somebody might
strike his flesh with bronze. Meriones shot a bronze-tipped arrow and hit the prince in the right hip. The arrow penetrated
clean through under the bone and into the bladder. The prince
sagged down into the arms of his beloved comrades, gasping for
breath. He lay stretched out on the ground like a worm, and
dark blood trickled out of him, dampening the earth. The
greathearted Pamphlagonians surrounded him and lifted him
up into a chariot and took him back to sacred Troy, grieving as
they went. His father went among his men gushing tears;
nothing can lessen the pain the death of a son brings.   659

Paris's heart was very troubled over that death, because he
had been a guest-friend when he was among the many Pamphlagonians. In his anger he shot off a bronze-tipped arrow. There

was a certain Euchenor, who was the son of the prophet Polyidus, who was a rich and worthy man living on an estate in Corinth. He knew well what his miserable fate was to be when he set out in his ship. The upright old Polyidus had told Euchenor many times that either he would wither away from a miserable plague alone in his halls or be brought down by the Trojans among the ships of the Acheans. Considering both possibilities, he went with the Acheans so as to avoid their harsh penalty for not participating, and to avoid the suffering and pain of lingering disease. It was Euchenor that Paris hit. The arrow passed underneath the jawbone and the ear. Swiftly his spirit departed from his limbs, and then hateful darkness seized him.   672

And so they fought on like a blazing fire. And soon glory would come to the Acheans, since the earth-shaker, the gatherer of the earth, had so empowered the Argives, and protected them with his own might. But Hector, beloved of Zeus, had not heard, and he had no idea of the firefight by the Achean troops on the left of the ships. Instead, he remained where he first broke the gates and leapt over the wall against the dense ranks of the shield-bearing Danaans. There, the ships of Aias and Protesilaus were drawn up from the gray sea onto the beach, and the wall had been toppled down the furthest. It was in that place that the fight took on a special violence, both for the men themselves and for the horses.   684

There were the Boeotians, and the long-shirted Ionians, and the Locrians, and Phthians, and the glorious Epeans. They held the ships and they rushed forward with speed, but the select Athenian troops were unable to push noble Hector back away from them. He was like the flames of a fire. Menestheus, son of Peteus, was the Athenians' commander. Those who came with him were Pheidas, and Stichius, and right-thinking Bias. Then came Meges Phyleusson of the Epeans, and Amphion, and Dracius. In front of the Phthians came Medon, and Podarces, firm in the fight. Indeed, Medon was the bastard son of godlike Oïleus and brother to Aias. He lived in Phylace away from the land of his father, because he had killed a kinsman of his stepmother Eriopis, Oïleus's wife. Podarces was the son of Iphiclus and he was the son of Phylacus. Those of the great-hearted Phthians were well armed and fought before the ships, along with the Boeotians, to protect them.   700

Aias, the swift son of Oïleus, no longer stood distant from Telamonian Aias. Instead, it was like when a young, dark red ox is hitched to a firm plow with another of equal heart, and around the base of both their horns pours sweat. Both work under the same well-polished yoke, going along the furrows. The plow cuts to the end of the field. So it was with Aias and Aias— the Aiantes. They stood very close together. And you may be sure that the son of Telamon was the leader of many and certainly the best of his comrades among the troops. They would hold his shield for him whenever he was tired or when sweat came to his limbs. But the greathearted Locrians did not follow their leader, the son of Oïleus, into battle, nor did they stand solidly with him in the front. They had no brazen helmets with horsehair plumes, nor had they carefully curved shields, nor ashen spears. Instead though, they had well-curved bows with well-twisted lamb's wool bowstrings, and arrows, and with them they were better than anybody. They were believed to be so by all who came to Troy. They shot off arrows with a frequency that allowed them to shatter whole formations of Trojans. I tell you for sure, while there were those in the front line with their gleaming arms fighting with the Trojans and brazen-helmeted Hector, there were others behind them, hiding under their protection as they fired off their missiles. And the Trojans couldn't concentrate at all on the fight because the arrows put them in such a state of confusion.   722

There might the Trojans in their misery have withdrawn from the ships and the huts back to windy Troy, had not Polydamas come beside bold Hector and spoken: "Hector, it is difficult to persuade you with words, since it was a god who gave you the power to do exceedingly great feats of war, so it seems that you insist that you are better informed at counsel than others. It doesn't seem possible for you to choose someone else for that. To one man a god gave the power of great feats of war, but to another he gives skill in dancing, and to another in singing and playing his lyre. Loud-thundering Zeus placed wisdom in the breast of yet another. There are many men who take advantage of his gift, and he saves many that way. You must surely realize that yourself. But I will tell you myself what seems best to me. The circle of war burns when all are around you. The greathearted Trojans have gone over against the wall and they just stand there with their arms. Few of them are fighting, more are scattered among the ships. Instead, the order should be given to pull back all the best to this place and you should advise them of a first-rate plan. Otherwise, we will fall near the well-benched ships. But if a god wishes to give us might, we could pass along the ships unharmed. For, I tell you, I fear that the Acheans might just pay back yesterday's debt, if a man insatiable of war—Achilles—should make a stand beside the ships. I think he will no longer hold back from the fighting." 747

So spoke Polydamas, and what he said pleased Hector. Instantly, he jumped from his chariot to the ground with his arms and replied, saying with winged words: "Polydamas, you should rein in all of the bravest men here. As you advised, I am going there to meet with the men who are fighting, and I shall return immediately, as soon as I give them careful orders." 753

And so he did. Hector pressed forward, sticking out from the crowd like a snowcapped mountain, shouting as he flew through the Trojans and their allies. They all rushed over to manly Polydamas Panthousson as soon as they heard Hector's voice. Still, he wandered around asking where he might find Deïphobus, and mighty King Helenus, and Adamas Asiusson, and Asius, son of Hyrtacus. He had yet to find any of them, either unhurt or dead. Some lay beside the sterns of the ships, killed at the hands of the Argives, while others near the wall were wounded or hit. Soon, on the left side of the fighting, which brings tears to men, he came upon noble Alexander, husband of fair-haired Helen. He was encouraging his comrades and rousing them to fight. Hector stood close and spoke harshly to him: "Worthless Paris, your face is at its best in the seduction of women. Where are Deïphobus, and mighty King Helenus, and Adamas Asiusson, and Asius, son of Hyrtacus? Where, indeed is Othryoneus? Now all perish in the high city and heinous ruin is certain indeed."

773

And Alexander, with a face like a god, spoke back: "Hector, your heart accuses an innocent man. Some other time I would have been ready to quit fighting, but not this time, since my mother did not bear me to be a coward. Because you gathered those of our comrades for the fight beside the ships, we have been here constantly wrangling with the Danaans. The comrades you asked about are dead. Only two of them, Deïphobus and mighty King Helenus, left, and both of them had been hit in the arm by long spears. The son of Cronus protected them from death. Now, head off for wherever your spirit directs you. We will eagerly follow you, and I swear that there is no want of valor here. What we are able to do, we will do. Though, more than we are able, we cannot, even in the rush of fighting."

787

So saying, the hero convinced his brother. They set off for the place where the fighting and the noise of conflict were most intense, around Cebriones, and exceptional Polydamas, and Phalces, and Orthaeus, and the godlike Polyphetes, and Palmys, and Ascanius, and Morys, son of Hippotion. They had come as auxiliaries from fertile Ascania the previous day. Now Zeus urged them to fight. They went like a storm of harsh winds that goes to the plain under the lightning of Zeus. With a huge commotion it mingles with the sea. Many waves crash with the rumbling of the humps of the foam-covered sea, which go this way and that. So it was with the Trojans. Some went forth in close formation, while others followed their leaders, glittering with bronze. Hector Priamson, equal to man-killing Ares, took the lead. He went forward with his shield of thick hides that was balanced all around, and covered over with much bronze. Around his temples, the plumes of his gleaming helmet shook. All around the formations inched forward, trying to find some way to rush forward under the cover of their shields.   803

But he had not overwhelmed the courage in the breasts of the Acheans. Having gone forward with his long stride, Aias was the first to call out: "Come closer, ghoul! Why this attempt to terrify the Argives? We are not at all ignorant of warfare. Rather, we were beat down by the evil scourge of Zeus. For some reason your heart longs to plunder the ships, but they are safe, protected by our hands. Long before you could get to them we will have taken your well-populated city with our hands and sacked it. I swear to you that I will close in so that you will run off, and that as you flee, you will pray to Zeus and the other gods for horses, that have beautiful manes, and would be faster than hawks to carry you back to the city, covered with dust."   820

As Aias spoke, a bird flew over on the right, a high-flying eagle. At that the troops of the Acheans cheered, emboldened by the omen of the bird. But glorious Hector replied: "Aias, you hulk, what nonsense you say! If I were a son of aegis-bearing Zeus, who has existed forever, and had been born of revered Hera, I would be esteemed as Athena and Apollo are. So now this day brings a great catastrophe on all the Argives. On account of what you have said, if you are so bold as to stand against my long spear, it will tear your lilylike flesh to pieces. You will satisfy the hunger of the dogs and birds in the region of the Trojans with your fattened flesh when you fall beside the Acheans' ships."   832

So saying, Hector took the lead. And with a tremendous shout they followed with him and he shouted to the troops in the rear. And the Argives shouted from the other side. They did not hide their valor. Instead, the best of them went forward and took a stand against the Trojans. The clamor from both went up into the ether and to the eyes of Zeus.   837

Book 14

Though he was occupied with drinking, the shouting didn't escape the notice of Nestor. He spoke to the son of Asclepius in winged words: "Tell me, noble Machaon, how these doings will turn out. The war cry is stronger from the vigorous young men near the ships. You sit there now and drink the dark red wine until fair-haired Hecamede heats up your warm bath, and then she will wash off the bloody mess. But I am going in short order to a vantage spot to have a look around."   8

So saying, he grabbed the well-fashioned buckler of his son the noble horseman Thrasymedes that was lying in the hut. The son had his father's shield. He selected a sturdy spear with a point of sharp bronze. He stood outside the hut and quickly surveyed the shameful struggle as the men rushed on. The haughty Trojans advanced from behind, shouting as they broke through the Acheans' wall. It was like watching violent gusts of shrill wind on a purple, silent wave in the great open sea. It doesn't turn one way or the other until a wind of Zeus selects a direction for it. In such a manner was the old man's mind distracted with two possibilities. Either he could go into the throng of the Danaans, with their swift horses, or he could go to Agamemnon Atreusson, Shepherd of the Troops. And so when he decided which would be the better choice, he went to Agamemnon, while the others fought each other in the slaughter, and tireless bronze creaked around their flesh with the thrusting of both swords and sharp-pointed spears.   26

The highborn kings met Nestor. Odysseus, Diomedes Tydeusson, and Agamemnon Atreusson were coming up along the ships because they had been wounded by bronze. The ships had been drawn up onto the beach of the gray sea a considerable distance away from the fighting. Theirs were the first drawn up on the plain and then they built the wall in front of the sterns of the ships. They were unable to leave a wide space between the sterns and the wall so there was little room for retreat of the troops in the narrow strip along the beach. They had been drawn up in rows, one ship behind another on the beach, and they filled the wide mouth of the beach's inlet enclosed within such space as lay within the heights that surrounded them.   36

The kings looked out, trying to learn about the commotion and the fighting, as they went along in a group, each with his scepter. They were grieved at heart. And old Nestor joined them. He was one who inspired awe into the breasts and hearts of the Acheans. The Lord Agamemnon spoke to him in his resonant voice: "O Nestor Neleusson, great glory of the Acheans, why have you left the fighting, which wastes men, to come here? I fear that burly Hector might bring an end of me as he said in his speech to the Trojans when they gathered by the ships earlier. He claimed that he would set fire to the ships and kill the men before returning to Troy. And now it all seems to be coming to pass. Even the other well-armed Acheans have fixed in their mind the same hatred of me that Achilles has and don't want to fight beside the sterns of the ships."   51

At that, Nestor, the Geranian horseman, answered him: "The things that are to be will be, according to plan. Not even almighty Zeus himself determines otherwise. What is so is that Hector has broken through the wall that we built and that we trusted to be a bulwark for the ships and ourselves. His men fight furiously and relentlessly beside the swift ships. But what you do not yet know from looking around from here is whether the Acheans on the other side are rushing forward and slashing here and there, killing those they meet as they engage the Trojans. The din rises up to the heavens. We ought to consider how things will come out and whether there's anything we might do. I say that we ought not to enter the fighting, since there is no benefit in having the wounded fight."   63

And the Supreme Commander Agamemnon answered him:

"Nestor, since they fight near the sterns of the ships, the wall offers no protection. And, as it happens, neither does the trench that the Danaans endured much to build in front of the ships, hoping that it would serve as a bulwark, too. Thus, it would seem that the pleasure for almighty Zeus is to ordain that the Acheans perish ignominiously, far from Argos. Once I was convinced that he was minded to protect the Danaans, but now I know with equal assurance that Hector is given glory by the blessed gods, while our hands are tied. So, come now, I say that we should all be persuaded of this. We should push the ships that we first pulled up, back close to the sea, drag them all into the sea again, and anchor them at a safe harborage. We should go at night, when no man is out, and even the Trojans hold off from fighting. It is not a bad thing to flee from a disaster that is divinely ordained, nor to do it in the night. Which is better, one who runs away from evil, or one who is captured by it?" 81

Looking at Agamemnon, the ever-cunning Odysseus scowled and spoke: "Son of Atreus, what words escape the barricade of your teeth! You wreck! Oh, how I wish you were a commander of some other wretched army, since you definitely are not acting like a king over this one. Zeus gave it to us when it was most youthful and has wound it around into old age in this harsh war, and each of us has been withered by it. Why are you so determined to leave the city of the Trojans, with its wide streets? On its account we have suffered many difficulties. At least keep quiet, lest some other of the Acheans hear this idea. No one who fully comprehends the situation would say what I heard just now. But you are a scepter-bearing king saying such things. You are trusted by the troops, you who rule among the Argives. Now that I have carped at you, I still can't believe what you said! What you would order, gathering the men from the fighting and the ruckus, to pull the ships to the sea—that would fulfill the greatest hopes of the Trojans and give them total victory. For us it portends a complete disaster. The Acheans cannot hold off the Trojans while pulling the ships to the sea.

Instead, they would be peering around cautiously while doing it, abandoning their courage. And there, your plan will mislead us!" 102

At that the Supreme Commander Agamemnon, responded: "O Odysseus, your harsh scolding crushes my heart! I am not about to order the sons of the Acheans to drag their well-benched ships to the sea against their will. So now, tell me, all of you, what would be a better plan, it could come either from someone young, or from one who is old. I would be delighted to hear something." 108

And Diomedes, good at the war cry, spoke to them: "Our man is close by; we will not be searching for him long. That is, if you will trust me, and do not be all upset with me because I am the youngest among us. Even though I am youngest, I do claim to have been born of a worthy father, Tydeus. The earth now surrounds him beneath a mound in Thebes. Three illustrious sons were born to Porthus. Living in Pleuron and steep Calydon were Agrius and Melus, and a third the horseman Oeneus, the father of my father. He exceeded all who lived in virtue. While Oeneus remained where he was, my father wandered and made his dwelling in Argos, as it pleased Zeus and the other gods. He married one of the daughters of Adrastus and lived in his palace and was rich and powerful. There were an abundance of fields that produced grain. There were many vineyards and orchards around and he had many sheep in his folds. He excelled over all of the Acheans in his skill with his spear. And we have heard of the things he was obliged to do, since they are true. Both of you know that my tribe is neither cowardly nor unskilled, and you would not take lightly what I have said, because I say what is good. So come! Let's go to war! Even though we are wounded, it is necessary. We will stay back from the heated fighting, avoiding the missiles, so that no one should raise a wound on top of a wound. We will send the others rushing forward, those who previously were carrying resentment and didn't care to fight." 132

So spoke Diomedes. The others listened to him with great

care and were persuaded. They set off for the fight, and the Supreme Commander Agamemnon led them.   134

The famed earth-shaker was not one to have the eyes of a blind man. Instead, he went among them in the guise of an aged man. He took Agamemnon Atreusson by the hand and spoke to him with winged words: "Now the agonized heart of Achilles rejoices in his breast when he looks on at the slaughter of the Acheans as they run away to escape danger, since they have neither the courage nor the vigor that he has. But in such a way will he perish; a god will mangle him. But the blessed gods are not at all annoyed with you. You will see for yourself when the commanders and counselors of the Trojans run away from the ships and huts back across the dusty plain to the city."   146

And so saying, he rushed onto the plain with a great shout that was as loud as the shouts of nine or ten thousand men. It was such that the voice of the lord earth-shaker came from his breast to the men fighting together in the strife of Ares. It fixed strength in the heart of each of the Acheans for relentless war and fighting.   152

And Hera, of the golden throne, looked on as she stood on a peak of Olympus. Immediately she recognized her very own brother and the brother of her husband busying himself with the war, which wins glory for men, and she rejoiced in her heart. She looked also at Zeus sitting on the highest peak of Ida, which has many springs. He was miserable at heart.   158

Then the lovely-eyed, revered Hera pondered how she might trick the mind of aegis-bearing Zeus. And, to be sure, the best of plans was revealed in her heart. It was to go to Ida with herself well fitted out and somehow entice him to an ardent desire for carnal lovemaking and afterward to pour onto his eyelids and his serious mind a harmless and pleasant sleep. She set out and went to her chamber, made for her by her beloved son Hephaestus. She worked her secret key in the heavy entrance doors that none of the other gods could open. Once she entered the handsomely made doors, she first purged her ravishing flesh of all impurities with ambrosia. Next, she anointed herself with sweet ambrosial olive oil, which was made exceedingly fragrant. If shaken on the brazen, solid foundation of Zeus its redolence would radiate from there to arrive at both earth and heavens. She anointed her lovely flesh and combed her hair, twisting tresses of curls that glowed with ambrosial beauty around her immortal head. She draped herself with a soft ambrosial gown, which Athena had skillfully woven for her. In it she was dazzling. The gown was clasped at her breast with gold broaches. She placed around her waist a girdle fitted with a hundred fringed tassels, and put into her pierced lobes earrings with three drops of exquisitely cut gems. Their glow was most charming. The noblest of goddesses covered herself with a veil that was lovely and newly made, white like the sun. Underneath her oiled feet she bound her beautiful sandals. And when she had set all about her flesh in careful order, she left her chamber. She called out to Aphrodite, who was apart from the other gods. Hera went to her and said: "Dear child, would you do as I ask, or would you refuse me because you resent that I go to help the Danaans while you aid the Trojans?"   192

Aphrodite, daughter of Zeus, answered her then: "Hera, elder goddess, daughter of great Cronus, say what is on your mind. My heart orders me to bring it to pass, if I am able to do it and if it is possible to do."   196

Dissembling, the revered Hera said to her: "Give me now the gift of lovemaking and desire with which you captivate all men, mortal as well as immortal. I am going to the ends of the bountiful earth to see Ocean, origin of the gods, and Tethys. When loud-thundering Zeus cast Cronus down beneath the earth and the barren sea, Ocean and Tethys took me from Rhea and tended after me and brought me up carefully in their palace. I am going to see them and I shall bring an end to a quarrel between them that has already kept them from sleeping together and making love to each other for a long time, because anger rendered their hearts intransigent. If I can persuade both of them

with words from a loving heart to bed down and make love together, they will describe me ever after as dear and venerable." 210

And Aphrodite answered her back: "There is no way that I
could refuse a request like yours. After all, you spend your nights
in the arms of Zeus, who is supreme." 213

Then, she loosed from her chest her embroidered girdle of
charms. Woven into it were all the devices that make enchant-
ment. In it was the charm for lovemaking. In it was desire. In it
was sweet talk fixed, the sweet talk that those who woo use to
entice others, which steals reason, even from those who usually
have sound judgment. She thrust it into Hera's hand and said
to her: "Fasten this variegated belt underneath your bosom. Into
it have been woven spells, and I think that you will not return
without accomplishing your mission. With this you create an
urgent desire in their beings." 221

So Aphrodite spoke, and lovely-eyed Hera giggled a little.
Next, she fastened it under her bosom, smiling as she did it. 223

Aphrodite, daughter of Zeus went off toward her palace.
Hera rushed off, leaving the ridge of Olympus behind. She hurried past Pieria and lovely Emathia over the snowcapped highest peaks of the mountains of the horse-training Thracians. She
rushed so quickly that her feet didn't touch the ground. From
Athos she went over the surging deep and arrived at Lemnos,
the city of the divine Thoas. There she met up with Sleep, the
brother of Death. She took him by the hand and spoke to him,
addressing him by his name: "Sleep, lord over all gods and all
mankind, if ever there was a time that you heard my petition,
be persuaded by one even now. For I would know your favor
always. I want to put the bright eyes and brow of Zeus to sleep
immediately after I lie beside him entwined in lovemaking. And
I shall give you gifts, a beautiful chair of gold that is incorruptible forever. My son Hephaestus, lame in both legs, is most accomplished and he will make it. And to go under the chair there
will be a footstool, and it will support your oiled feet while you
are feasting." 241

And sweet Sleep replied to her in his resonant voice: "Hera, elder goddess, daughter of great Cronus, I could easily put to sleep another of the everlasting gods, even rippling Ocean, who is the origin of all. But I would not draw close to Zeus, nor would I put him to sleep unless he ordered me to do it himself. I'll tell you surely, he laid on me a heavy threat some time ago. It was the day when that greathearted son of Zeus—Heracles—set sail from the city of the Trojans after plundering it. I put Zeus's mind to rest with sweetness all around him, because you had mischief planned for Heracles. You raised up gales of harsh wind over the deep that carried Zeus's son to teeming Kos, far from all his friends. When Zeus woke up, he was furious and went tearing around the palace of the gods. But it was me more than anyone else he was hunting for. Had I not found Night, tamer of both gods and men, who threw a dense, invisible cover over me to save me, Zeus would have found me. I escaped that time. Zeus held off even though he was furious, because he has respect for Night and he feared that she might do unthinkable things. And now again, you're telling me to pull off another scheme that is doomed to failure."   262

The revered Hera, of lovely eyes, spoke back to him: "Sleep, why would you talk like that? Do you really believe that Zeus's helping the Trojans is the same as his furious anger over his son Heracles? So come. I'll give you Pasithea, one of the younger Graces, for your mutual pleasure and you can call her your wife. You have always lusted after her."   269

So Hera spoke and Sleep was overjoyed. He replied: "Come, swear by the boundless water of the Styx. With one hand grab the bountiful earth and the other the shining sea, so that all are witnesses for both of us. There are as many witnesses as there are gods around Cronus down below. Swear that you will give me one of the younger Graces, Pasithea. I have always longed to have her for myself."   276

So spoke Sleep, and the white-armed goddess Hera did not fail to comply. She swore as he asked; she swore by all the gods

under Tartarus who are called Titans. And when she had made
her inviolable oath, they set out from Lemnos and left behind
the city of Imbrus. In the dusky light that precedes dawn they
sped along their way, prancing as they went.   282

It was at Cape Lecton that the two first left the sea and went
up on dry land. They arrived at Ida, mother of beasts, and source
of many springs. They raced up to the forested heights on foot.
Sleep went up into a very tall pine tree, the kind one finds on
Ida, on which the highest crown of branches reaches up through
the dusky mist. He sat in the thicket of piney branches taking
on the likeness of a sweet-sounding songbird, the kind of bird
found in the mountains that the gods call *chalcis* but men call
cymidis. There Sleep waited before going to see the eyes of
Zeus.   291

Hera proceeded on swiftly to the Gargarus peak in the high
forests of Ida, and cloud-gathering Zeus caught sight of her. On
seeing her as she was, love closed in on his shrewd mind from
all directions. It was like when they first mingled in lovemaking, going often to bed, but concealing it from their loving
parents. He stood in front of her and spoke, calling her by
name: "Hera, how is it that you have come down so eagerly
from Olympus? Your horses and chariot that would usually
bring you are not with you."   299

The revered Hera, dissembling, answered him: "I am going
to the ends of the bountiful earth to see both Ocean, origin of the
gods, and mother Tethys. They raised me carefully and
tended after me in their palace. I am going to see them and I
shall bring an end to a quarrel between them that has already
kept them from sleeping together and making love to each other
for a long time, because anger rendered their hearts intransigent. My horses are standing at the feet of Ida, source of many
springs. They will carry me over both dry and wet. At this time
they have brought me here, down from Olympus. And so, I have
come, lest you be upset afterward, that I kept quiet about going
to the palace of deep-running Ocean."   310

And cloud-gathering Zeus answered her: "Hera, you belong
there and should get going after a while. But come, let's the two
of us lie down and enjoy some lovemaking. Never before have
I been so smitten by love for goddesses any more than now for
my wife. Love pours out in torrents onto the heart in my breast.
This didn't even happen when I made love to the wife of Ixion,
who gave birth to Perithous, strategist equal to the gods. Nor
was it so with Arcrisius's daughter Danae, with lovely ankles.
She bore Perseus, most striking in looks of all men. It never happened with the daughter of widely renowned Phoenix. She
bore to me both Minos and godlike Rhadymanthys. And it didn't
happen with Semele, nor with Alcmene in Thebes. To her was
born the intrepid child Heracles. Nothing like this happened
when Semele gave birth to Dionysus, charmer of mortal men.
It was never so with the Princess Demeter, of beautiful hair, and
never with Leto. Not even with you yourself have I ever been
so taken with sweet desire to make love to you as I am now."

And pretending, the revered Hera responded: "Shame on
you, son of Cronus, such words you say! If you are so urgently
wishing to go and make love now on the peaks of Ida, it would
be seen by everyone. What would happen if one of the everlasting gods caught sight of us? There would be talk among all of
them about it. I would not like to get up from here and return
to your palace to face them; that would not be a good idea. Instead, if you wish and have your heart set on love, let it be in
your chamber built by your son Hephaestus. He has put up thick
doors in their frames. There, we can go and lie down, since it
pleases you to make love."   340

And Zeus, the cloud-gatherer, replied: "Don't worry about
any of the gods or men looking on. I will wrap around us a
golden cloud and not even Sun will see us through it, though
he has sharpest vision to look over all."   345

At that the son of Cronus embraced his wife in his arms. On
the ground beneath them fresh blooms sprouted through the
grass, lotus covered with droplets of moisture, crocus and

hyacinth, piled thick and soft that protected them from the bare ground. They lay in that and a lovely, golden mist settled on them, and a shimmering translucent dew fell.   351

And so the father slept without moving, worn out by lovemaking and Sleep, and he held his wife in his arms. But sweet Sleep went running to the Acheans' ships with a message for the earth-shaker, who holds the earth. He stood close to him and spoke with winged words: "Now, Poseidon, you may be ready to protect the Danaans and grant them glory, at least for a little while, for Zeus is sleeping. I enveloped him in a soft state of total quiet. Hera enticed him into bedding down and making love."   360

So spoke Sleep, and he went about among the famed tribes of men, but Poseidon was especially energized to still save the Danaans. Immediately he made a great leap to the front and demanded of them: "Argives, are we again to cede the victory to Hector Priamson, so that he can seize the ships and gain glory? This is what he says and how he boasts, because Achilles remains among the hollow ships with an angry heart. He will not have any serious desire to help, but if the rest of us rise up we can protect each other. So come everybody, let's do as I say. Let's take up the shields that are the best and largest in the camp, and let's hide our heads under brilliantly shining helmets, and we'll choose the longest spears and we'll go with them in our hands. I will take the lead, and I think that Hector will not yet prevail, no matter how zealous he is. He is a courageous warrior, but he has a small buckler on his shoulder. It makes a man inferior to one who picks up a better shield."   376

So Poseidon spoke, and those who heard him readily obeyed. The kings themselves drew the men into formation, even those who were wounded, the son of Tydeus, Odysseus, and Agamemnon Atreusson. They went around exchanging their martial arms; they put the best on the best and gave the worn to those worse. And when they had clothed their flesh in gleaming bronze, they set off. Poseidon, the earth-shaker, led them, with a terrible sword stretched out in his hefty hand that looked like a lightning bolt. Custom forbids challenging him in the miserable heat of battle, but the fear he inspires keeps men in check.   387

Glorious Hector again formed up the Trojans on the other side. And then, you may be sure, black-bearded Poseidon and glorious Hector lengthened the most terrifying struggle of war, the one helping the Trojans, the other the Argives. Being set free, the sea moved toward the huts and ships of the Argives. The men came together with a huge war cry. The roar of a wave of the sea driven by a calamitous gust of the North Wind that rises up from the deep and crashes on the dry land is not so great. Nor is the sound of a fire glowing in the glades of the mountains as it rushes along burning the forest. Nor was the cracking sound of the crowns of the tallest of oaks when greatly agitated by loud thunder. So great was the dreadful sound of the shouting as they rushed toward one another.   401

First off, glorious Hector made a cast with his spear at Aias when he turned to go straight for Hector. It wasn't altogether a miss. He hit the two straps around Aias's chest, first the strap of his buckler and then the baldric of his silver-studded sword. But the two straps kept the spear away from his tender flesh. Hector was furious that his sharp missile flew unsuccessfully from his hand. He retreated back into a group of his comrades to avoid fate. When he did, the great Telamonian Aias went off in search of a stone. There were lots of them around the stays for the swift ships, and they set them to rolling around with their feet as they were fighting. Aias raised up one of them and hurled it so it passed above the rim of Hector's buckler and hit him in the chest near his neck. The blow hit Hector with such force that he was sent spinning around like a top. It was like when an oak tree hit by a lightning bolt of father Zeus is ripped up by the roots, and an awful smell of burning sulfur comes out from it. Even one who knew the tree was sound, on witnessing the event, would see how destructive the lightning of great Zeus is. And so it was with mighty Hector, who immediately fell down into the dust. His spear fell from his hand, and he and his shield fell together. Even his helmet fell off. His variegated armor with its bronze plates crashed around him.   420

With loud shouting, the sons of the Acheans ran toward Hector, hoping to drag him off. They hurled dense volleys of spear points, but no one was able to hit or wound the Shepherd of the Troops. Before they could, the best of the Trojans gathered around him, Polydamas, and Aeneas, and noble Agenor, and Sarpedon, commander of the Lycians, and exceptional Glaucus. None was at all careless of Hector. Instead, they encircled him closely with shields. His comrades raised him up in their arms and carried him from the action so that they could get to his swift horses that stood back at the rear of the battle and the fighting, along with Hector's charioteer and his variegated chariot. They bore him back toward the city, groaning deeply.   432

But when they arrived at the bed of the wide-flowing, swirling Xanthus, which Zeus gave birth to, they took Hector from his chariot and placed him on the ground, and poured water on him. Panting for breath, he looked up, kneeled, and vomited blood the color of dark purple storm clouds. Then he fell back flat on the ground and the blackness of night closed in on both his eyes. At last, the stone's blow had brought down his spirit.   439

Seeing that Hector was departing, the Argives leapt on the Trojans with increased vigor, remembering their martial ardor. There, the very first to act was swift Oïlean Aias. He jumped forward and struck Satnius Enopsson with a sharp spear. Satnius was born to Enops by an excellent one of the fountain nymphs near the banks of the river Satnioeis where Enops was pasturing cattle. The son of Oïleus hit Satnius in the abdomen and he fell prostrate on the ground. Around him the Trojans and the Danaans gathered in intense fighting. Violent Polydamas Panthousson went over to Satnius as his protector. He hit Prothoenor, son of Areïlycus, in the right shoulder. The mighty spear passed through the shoulder and Prothoenor fell in the dust, clutching at the ground. Polydamas made an extravagant boast in a loud voice: "I don't think that the son of Panthoüs can jump up and miss a cast from his stout arm—instead, the flesh of some Argive receives it. And I think that one, even though he is leaning propped up by the spear, is going down to the House of Hades."   457

So Polydamas spoke and his boasting gave rise to grief for the Argives. It especially roused up the demon in the heart of Aias Telamonson, since Prothoenor was very close by him when he fell. Aias went off quickly and made a cast with his shining spear. Polydamas jumped to the side and avoided the spear himself, but Archelochus, son of Antenor, took the spear. The gods were planning peril for him. It hit him in the head and the neck at the juncture of the neck and the spine. The spear sheared through both tendons. His head, mouth, and nose came close to the ground sooner than his shins and knees as Archelochus fell to the ground.   478

Aias shouted back to exceptional Polydamas: "Think about it, Polydamas, and tell me the truth. Is this man not what you might say to be the equal of Prothoenor in value? It doesn't seem to me that he is some peasant. Instead, he's the brother of the noble horseman Antenor, or his son, or some other of his close kin, since he looks most like Antenor."   474

As Aias well knew, the hearts of the Trojans were grief-stricken. At that point Acamas struck Promachus the Boeotian with his spear as he was standing over his brother. Promachus was trying to drag the corpse back by the feet. At that Acamas boasted with a vengeance: "You Argives who kill with arrows, who can't stop anyone with your threats, do you think we would be a long time in misery without doing something about it? Instead, we go about killing this way. Consider how we brought down Promachus, who sleeps because of my spear. We did this so that the compensation due for the loss of a brother would not be unavenged for long. And a man might pray that war left both as protectors for their families in their palaces."   485

So he spoke, and his boasting created grief among the

Argives. It especially roused a frenzy of ire in Peneleos. He charged at Acamas, but Acamas did not make a stand against the assault of Lord Peneleos. Instead, Peneleos struck Ilioneus, the son of Forbas, who had many sheep. Hermes had a special fondness for Forbas and provided him with many possessions, but Ilioneus was his mother's only child. Peneleos struck his skull under the brow ridge. The spear went first through the back of the head and the base of the eye socket, pushing out the orb. Ilioneus sat down with his arms outstretched. Pulling out his sharp sword, Peneleos drove it into the middle of Ilioneus's neck, cutting off his head, which fell to the ground with the helmet. Even then the mighty spear still had the orb of the eye on it, holding it up like the head of a poppy. Peneleos pointed it out and then boasted to the Trojans with these words: "Tell me, Trojans, about worthy Ilioneus; tell his beloved father and mother to moan in anguish in their halls. And the wife of Promachus Alegenorson is not to take pleasures with her man when he comes either, whenever we youths of the Acheans return from Troy in our ships."   505

So Peneleos spoke, and the limbs of all were seized with trembling. Each of them looked around anxiously for a way to escape a horrible end.

Tell me now, you Muses who dwell in the mansions of Olympus, who was the first of the Acheans to take gory spoils of war when the famed earth-shaker turned the battle? First off, Telamonian Aias hit Hyrtius Gyrtiusson, greathearted commander of the Mysians. Antilochus slew Phalces and Mermerus. Meriones killed both Morus and Hippotion. Teucer took out Prothoön and Periphetes. And then the son of Atreus hit Hyperenor, Shepherd of the Troops, in the abdomen. The bronze sliced through, spilling his guts out. His spirit rushed out from the wound when he was hit, and dusky darkness enveloped his eyes. But Aias, the swift son of Oïleus, killed the most. There was no one found among the trembling men to be his equal on his feet when Zeus raised up fear in them.   522

Book 15

A fter that the Trojans fled through the palisade and the trench, and many were vanquished under the hands of the Danaans. Some were restrained by their chariots and made a stand, but they were white with fear and terrified.   4

Zeus arose from sleep on the peaks of Ida beside Hera, of the golden throne. He looked out over the Trojans and the Acheans, and saw the Trojans being routed and the Acheans shouting in chase behind them, and among the Acheans was the Lord Poseidon. He saw Hector lying on the plain with his comrades seated around him. His breathing was labored, his spirit completely exhausted, and he was vomiting blood, since it was not the weakest of the Acheans who hit him. On seeing him, the father of both men and gods, felt pity for him. With a terrifying scowl, he spoke to Hera: "Your sinister plot has made a mess of things. It stopped noble Hector from fighting, and put fear into the troops. You ought to be the first to reap the harvest from this reckless mischief, and I will flog you until you are striped with welts! Do you not remember when I hung you from high up and stretched an anvil from each of your feet, and put a golden chain around your hands that could not be released? You were up high in the air and the clouds. Those down on high Olympus were very upset about it, but they were not able to come close and free you. Anyone who tried, I'd grab, shake up, and toss from my threshold down to earth where he'd arrive fainting. Also, have you forgotten the relentless pain you caused me to endure over divine Heracles? You cooked up an evil scheme and persuaded North Wind to join you in sending storms over the barren deep. You carried Heracles to teeming Coos. I protected him there and led him back to Argos, where they raise horses, though he went through many travails. I will

remember those deceits so that I can crush you if I learn that
you used the lovemaking and our embraces in the bed as your
part of a deception to help one of the gods by keeping me away
from the action."   33

So spoke Zeus, and the revered, lovely-eyed Hera shivered
in fear, and spoke to him with winged words: "Now, let it be
known thus by the earth and the wide heavens and by the
water that pours down from the Styx underneath that I make
the most solemn oath to the blessed gods, to your sacred head,
and our bed of which you are my lawful husband. And I would
never swear rashly. It was not on account of my designs that
Poseidon, the earth-shaker, harmed the Trojans and Hector.
He warded them off, but it was on his own volition that he
roused the Acheans and gave them orders. He saw them being
beaten down around the ships and took pity on them. I encourage you and him, too. I would advise him to go wherever you,
of dark clouds, might direct."   46

So Hera spoke and the father of both men and gods smiled.
And then he replied to her with winged words: "So then, revered
Hera, with lovely eyes, it is so that you sit as my equal among
the immortals, my equal in intellect, both you and Poseidon.
But even if it happens that he has a plan that is thoroughly different from mine, he should quickly change his mind to accord
with my heart. But, if indeed, what you say is the truth, go
among the tiers of the gods, and there call out Iris and Apollo,
famed for the bow, to go forth and when they have come among
the troops of the brazen-shirted Acheans, they can tell the Lord
Poseidon to stop fighting and return to his palace. And Phoebus Apollo may rouse up Hector to fight, breathing into him
renewed strength, that he may forget the woes that now weigh
on his mind. Then, he can turn back the Acheans, who will
be helpless. They will be sent into a total rout as they flee. Hector will fall upon the many-oared ships that belong to Achilles
Peleusson. When that happens, Achilles will send out his companion Patroclus, whom glorious Hector will kill with his spear.

He will do that before Troy after Patroclus has slain many other youths, including my son Sarpedon. Angry over the loss of Patroclus, divine Achilles will force a retreat back from the ships and then slay Hector. Throughout all this, I will be constantly preparing the Acheans to take the high city of Troy, according to Athena's plan. But, until this comes to pass I am not stopping my anger, and neither will I allow any of the other immortals to give aid to the Danaans, until I have fulfilled a wish for the son of Peleus, that he should stand up high above all. I gave a nod of my head and promised to do it that day when the goddess Thetis clasped my knees and pleaded with me to honor Achilles, sacker of cities."   77

So he spoke and Hera, the white-armed goddess, did not disobey. She went from the peaks of Ida to high Olympus. It was like when the mind of a man who has come into much property prudently realizes that he should rush around here and there, being gracious about everything. So it was with revered Hera. When she arrived at the height of Olympus, she flew right away to the immortal gods who were assembled in the palace of Zeus. Seeing her they all rushed over, offering her their cups in welcome. She passed by the others, but received a cup from pretty-cheeked Custom, who was first to come near and stand in front of the goddess and speak to her with winged words: "Hera, why have you come? You look frightened. Has your husband the son of Cronus made you fearful?"   91

Hera, the white-armed goddess, answered: "O goddess Custom, do not ask me about such things! Even you know yourself how arrogant and cruel his heart is. Instead host the proper feast for the gods in the palace. The evil things he threatens are heard by all of the immortals. But I say nothing at all of either mortals or gods alike while we enjoy ourselves. There is still time now for feasting in good spirits."   99

As she spoke in this way, the revered Hera sat down. The gods were troubled in the palace of Zeus. Hera laughed with her lips, but her dark scowl remained fixed. She chided them all saying: "What fools we are to be exasperated with Zeus. We are crazy. But still we want to go closer in and control him because he is powerful. But he doesn't care. He sits apart, and doesn't give a damn. He says that among the gods he is the best at displaying power and making plans. With both of those he has sent trouble to each one of you. And now he hopes to land a painful blow on Ares. His son Ascalaphus, the most beloved of men, perished in the fighting. Mighty Ares says he was his own son."   112

So she spoke. At that, Ares slapped his muscled thigh with the palm of his hand, and cried out in a rage: "Those who dwell on Olympus cannot be angry at me for going to the ships of the Acheans to avenge the death of my son, even if my fate comes with a lightning bolt from Zeus so that I lie like the corpses in the blood and the dust."   118

So he spoke, and he ordered Fear and Rout to hitch up his horses. He dressed himself in gleaming armor, and there would have been more and harsher troubles fashioned by Zeus in his wrath, had not Athena left the throne she had been sitting on and rushed through the vestibule. She took the helmet from Ares's head and the buckler from around his shoulders, and the stout brazen spear from his hand, and confronted violent Ares: "Your rage has completely wiped out your mind. Now, you have ears for hearing, but you are destroying your reason and respect. Are things not always as Hera, the white-armed goddess, says they are? Are they as she says, even now that she has come from the side of Olympian Zeus? If you wish to make big trouble for yourself he will come back to Olympus angry that he had to return, and you will sow the seeds of trouble for the rest of us. He will leave the greathearted Trojans and the Acheans immediately, and make a ruckus for us on Olympus, seizing first the one who is to blame and then the one who is not. I urge you to give up your resentment over your son. At some time or other, one who is stronger or more dexterous than he has been slain, or will be eventually. It is hard to save all men, especially a descendent or a child."   141

So she spoke, and Athena made furious Ares sit down on his throne. Hera summoned Apollo out from the palace and Iris, the messenger between the immortal gods, as well. She spoke to them with winged words: "Zeus has ordered you two to Ida as soon as possible. When you get there, look on the countenance of Zeus, and do what he tells you to."   148

Having so spoken, the revered Hera went back and sat on her throne. Both Apollo and Iris rushed on their wings and arrived at Ida, mother of beasts, with many springs. They found loud-thundering Zeus sitting up on the Gargarus peak. Around him circled a fragrant cloud. The two went and stood in front of Zeus the cloud-gatherer, and when he looked at them he was not angry, because he realized they were there in obedience to his beloved wife to quickly obey whatever commands he might have for them. He spoke first to Iris with winged words: "Go quickly, Iris, to the Lord Poseidon and tell him everything I say, lest he think it a false report. Order him to stop fighting and go to the tiers of the gods or into the shining sea. If he does not obey the command, I will consider going against him. He would not endure standing against me even though he is mighty, because I declare clearly that I am much mightier than he, and I was born before him. His own heart feels no shame in claiming that he is equal to me, though others dread my might."   167

So Zeus spoke, and Iris, swift as the wind, went down from Ida to sacred Troy. It was like when snowflakes and hailstones fly from clouds chilled by a blast of North Wind, which produces cold weather. So quickly and eagerly did swift Iris fly. She stood close to the famed earth-shaker: "I have come here from beside Zeus, who bears the aegis, bearing an important message for you, who holds the earth, black beard. He orders you to stop fighting and either to go to the tiers of the gods or into the shining sea. If you do not obey, he threatens to come here and face you in combat. He orders you to escape his hands, since he is mightier, and was born before you. Though your

own heart feels no shame in claiming that you are equal to
him, others dread his might." 183

Greatly vexed, the famed earth-shaker said: "As worthy at
arms as he says he is, the same degree of limitless power has
been settled on me as well! There are three of us brothers born
by Rhea from Cronus. Zeus and I, and the third is Hades, who
rules over the dead. Everything was divided into three parts
and each of us has a portion of the universe. Indeed, after the
toss, my lot was dwelling always in the gray sea. To Hades fell
the lot for the dusky darkness and to Zeus the lot of the wide
heavens, the sky and the clouds. Yet, the whole earth is common to us all, and the peak of Olympus. I go about my life and
it is none of Zeus's business. Instead, such matters that are
peaceful and those concerning power are fixed into three separate divisions. I do not fear his hands at all. It would be better
for him to chide his own children when he hears what they've
done, because they have to listen to him. I don't." 199

And then Iris, swift as the wind, answered him: "One who
holds the earth, black beard, am I to carry this fierce, vehement
message to him or would you prefer to change it? A change of
mind is a good and worthy thing. You know that the Vengeances
obey those who are older." 204

And the earth-shaker Poseidon replied: "Iris, goddess, what
you have said is certainly proper, and a worthy thing it is that a
messenger knows what is correct. But this destruction of the
Acheans has touched my heart and soul with terrible grief. It
was done by one who is equal to me in rank and shares the same
fate, and even then wishes to reproach me harshly. But now,
even though I am indignant, I will yield. But let me tell you
something else, and I'll make a threat from my heart: If then
I am to stay away and so should Athena, goddess of spoils of war,
and Hera, and Hermes, and the Lord Hephaestus; if Zeus spares
the high city of Troy, unwilling that it be sacked, unwilling to
give great might to the Acheans, let it be known that there will
be wrath between us that cannot abate." So saying, the earth-

shaker left the troops of the Acheans, and entered the sea. The
Achean heroes felt his absence.   219

And then Zeus, the cloud-gatherer, spoke to Apollo: "Go
now, dear Phoebus, to Hector, of the brazen helmet. Already,
you may be sure, the one who holds the earth, earth-shaker, has
gone back into the shining sea, thus avoiding our great anger.
Surely the other gods would know this and the others of the
lower gods who are around Cronus. I am much more powerful
than they are and than he is, too. On that account, even when
he is filled with resentment, he will yield to my hands. And that
is a good thing, too, since a quarrel between us could not be
resolved without serious trouble for me.   228

"You who shoot from afar, go into the fighting, making glorious Hector your main concern. Until you raise up in him great
strength, the Acheans will not flee to the ships and the Hellespont. Then take the tasseled aegis in your hands, shake it
hard, and so press the Achean heroes into a rout. At that point,
I myself will consider how to work it out so that even the Acheans can rest from the fighting."   235

So he spoke and Apollo did what he heard his father say. He
went down from the mountains of Ida like a hawk. He was like
a peregrine falcon that kills pigeons; the peregrine is the fastest
of flying creatures. He found the warlike Hector Priamson sitting. He had just recently revived his spirit, and was no longer
lying down. He recognized his comrades around him. The panting and sweating had stopped when the mind of Zeus, who
bears the aegis, roused him.   242

Apollo, who works from afar, stood close to him and spoke:
"Hector, son of Priam, why are you sitting apart from the others in such pathetic condition? Have you sustained some sort of
injury?" Hector, of the helmet with a waving plume, responded
weakly: "Which one of the best of the gods are you who stand
in front of me and ask such a thing? Did you not hear what happened around the sterns of the Achean ships? Aias, of the shrill
the war cry, wiped out my comrades and hit me in the chest

with a rock, bringing an end to my furious valor. And for certain, I thought in my own heart that the day had come when I was to find myself among the dead, arriving at the House of Hades."   252

But the Lord Apollo, who works from afar, answered: "Take courage now. An aide to the son of Cronus has been sent from Ida to stand beside you and protect you. I am Phoebus Apollo, of the golden quiver, who will be there beside you to keep harm away. I am the one who in the past gave equal protection to you and the high city. So come now! Rouse up many chariots. I will go ahead of you and smooth the way for them, and we will drive the swift horses to the hollow ships. I shall turn back the Achean heroes."   261

So spoke Apollo, and he breathed a great might into the Shepherd of the Troops. It was like when a horse who is fat and well fed breaks loose from its tether, and runs speeding joyfully from its stable across the plain, where it is accustomed to bathing in a wide-running river. The horse holds its head high and its mane streams across its shoulders. It seems to trust in its own magnificence as it prances with knees up high, as is the habit and nature of horses. In such a way did Hector rouse the chariots on his agile feet and churning knees, when he heard the voice of the god.   270

The Acheans were like a buck with antlers or a wild goat that dogs and men of the countryside pursue. It ascends to a rock accessible only to the sun or enters a dense forest, and they are not destined to get to it. But along the way, a thickly bearded lion makes its presence known by its roar. Immediately, he turns them all around and they beat a hasty retreat. So it was with the Danaans who were constantly driving forward in the throng with their swords and spears banging against their limbs. That is, until they caught sight of Hector among the ranks of men. They stood in shocked amazement, and the hearts of all fell to their feet.   281

And Thoas, the son of Andraemon, spoke to them. He was

the best by far of the Aetolians at casting a spear, and good at standing in close combat. Very few of the Acheans could best him in debate before the assembly. He carefully analyzed the situation and spoke to them: "What a surprise this is for our eyes that Hector escaped his fates, and is back in the lines again! We all hoped that he was dead at the hands of Aias Telamonson. But, one of the gods has saved Hector and brought him back. He loosed the knees of many Danaans before and I think he will again now. He would not be standing in the front unless it were the wish of loud-thundering Zeus. But, come now and do what I tell you. We'll order the bulk of the men to return to the ships. And we ourselves, who claim to be the best in the army, will make a stand. If we first stand against those advancing with our spears held up, I think we may restrain the panic that has so readily entered the hearts of the Danaans in the throng." 299

So Thoas spoke. They heard what he said and purposely obeyed him. They called out those around the Aiantes, and the Lord Idomeneus, and Teucer, and Meriones, and Meges, the equal of Ares, to come up and stand against Hector and the Trojans. Behind them, the bulk of the men went back to the ships of the Acheans. 305

Led by Hector, the Trojans slashed their way forward in a dense mass. In front of him went Phoebus Apollo, cloaked in a cloud on both shoulders. And Apollo held the furious aegis that bristled with terror all around. Exceptionally well crafted, it was fashioned of bronze. Hephaestus gave it to Zeus to bear so that he could strike fear in men, and Apollo had it in his hands as he led the troops. 311

The Argives stood their ground tightly packed in together. A sharp cry rose up from both sides. Arrows jumped off bowstrings, and many spears leapt from bold hands. Some pierced the flesh of the war-minded youths, but others stopped midway in front of the white skin, and fixed in the ground, longing for enough flesh to satisfy them. As long as Phoebus Apollo shook the aegis from his hand, the missiles hit on both sides, and the

troops fell. But when the Danaans, who have swift horses, saw
Apollo's countenance as they rushed, and as he shouted in a very
loud voice, he cast a spell on the spirits in their chests, and they
forgot their furious valor. They were like a herd of cattle or a
flock of sheep that two roaring wild beasts come upon suddenly
in the dead of dark night when there is no herder around. In
such a way were the helpless Acheans frightened. Apollo put
the urge to rout in them, and granted glory to the Trojans and
Hector.   327

There, man took man in fighting, which dismembers men.
Hector slew both Stichius and Arcesilaus. Stichius was the commander of the brazen-shirted Boeotians, and Arcesilaus was a
faithful comrade of greathearted Menestheus. Aeneas killed
Medon and Jason. Medon was the bastard son of godlike Oïleus,
and the brother of Aias. He lived in Phylace, apart from the land
of his father, because he had killed a kinsman of his stepmother
Eriopis, Oïleus's wife. Jason had been designated commander
of the Athenians. He was the son of Sphelus, son of Bucolos.
Polydamas took Mecisteus, and Polites took Exius, in the front
ranks of the fighting. Noble Agenor took Clonius. Paris hit
Deiochus in the lowest part of the shoulder from behind as he
was fleeing from the front lines. The arrow drove clean through
the bronze that covered his skin.   342

While the Acheans were in rout around the trench they had
dug and the palisade they had erected, the Trojans were stripping the arms from the dead here and there. The Acheans went
back through the wall because they had to. But Hector called
to the Trojans in a loud voice, ordering them: "Rush on the ships
and leave the gory spoils of war. If I catch anybody staying back
some distance from the ships, I will deal out death to him then
and there. And his brothers and sisters will not now serve him
his share of the funeral pyre. Instead, dogs will pull him to pieces
in front of our city."   351

So Hector spoke. With a crack of the whip, he drove his
horses into the fracas, shouting to the Trojans to get into for-

mations. With an apocalyptic shout, they were with him, all
yelling together, driving their horses that pulled chariots. In
the forefront was Phoebus Apollo. He easily stomped down the
bank of the deep trench, and tossed down the palisade in the
middle, making a path for the formations of men that was long
and wide. It was about what is known as a spear cast, the distance a fit man can hurl a spear in practice. Through the opening poured the ranks, and in front of them was Apollo with the
much-honored aegis. He stomped the wall down with the greatest of ease. It was like when a child plays in the sand close to
the sea. Whatever he has made of sand in his play, the sea quickly
pours back over it, and he plays in the wreck with his hands and
feet. In such a way, Phoebus, skilled archer, you rendered useless what the Argives made with much work and trouble when
you rushed on them and drove them to rout.   366

So the Acheans withdrew and holed up around the ships,
yelling to each other and to all the gods. Each of them raised
his arms in intense prayer. And, again it was Nestor the Geranian who was the rock of the Acheans. With his arms outstretched, he prayed to the starry heavens: "Father Zeus, if ever
there were for you in Argos, with abundant grain, fat thighs of
either ox or sheep burning over many fires, promise and nod in
agreement to remember them, Olympian, and preserve us from
this cruel day. Do not allow the Trojans to wipe out the Acheans in this way."   376

So Nestor prayed, and great Zeus, the counselor, thundered
when he heard the prayers of the old son of Neleus.   378

When the Trojans heard the thundering of Zeus, who bears
the aegis, they jumped on the Argives with greater relish, remembering their warlike ardor. They were like a great wave in
the wide pathways of the sea that sweeps over the sides of a ship.
Whenever the wind pushes equally on both sides, the wind increases the waves substantially. So it was with the Trojans. With
a huge shout they went against the wall. They drove their chariots through it to the sterns of the ships. There they fought

close in with spears sharpened on both ends. The Acheans who went from there up high in the black ships fought with long boarding pikes that lay in their ships. They were crafted for marine warfare, framed of wood, with tips sheathed in bronze.　389

While the Acheans and the Trojans were fighting around the wall, but away from the ships, Patroclus was sitting in the hut of the gentlemanly Eurypylus, soothing him with words while he spread herbs over his painful wound to heal it, and to relieve his severe aches. But, he realized that the Trojans were breeching the Danaans' wall, and heard the shout rise up and the rout. He groaned and slapped both his thighs with the palms of his hands, and sobbed as he said: "Eurypylus, I cannot stay here with you any longer, even though you still need help. There is trouble brewing. In my place, your attendant can provide you with soothing care. But I have to rush off to Achilles so that I can urge him to fight. Who knows if I might persuade him with the help of some god? Nevertheless, excellent is the advice of a friend." So he spoke and Patroclus's feet carried him away.　405

The Acheans stood firm against the advancing Trojans. But because there were fewer of them, they were unable to drive them away from around the ships. Neither were the Trojans able to break the formations of the Acheans and mix it up around the huts and the ships. Instead, it was as though a skilled shipwright scribed a straight line with a spear held in his hand, one very knowledgeable of the precepts of Athena. So equal were they in the setting of the fight. Some fought each other here and others there beside the ships. Hector went against famed Aias. The two of them engaged in a duel around one ship. Hector was unable to drive Aias away so that he could set the ship afire, but Aias was not able to push Hector back away from it, since there was a god present.　418

Glorious Aias hit Caletor, the son of Clytius, in the chest with a spear as he was carrying the fire to the ship. Caletor fell with a thud, and the torch dropped from his hand. Hector realized on seeing with his eyes that his cousin had just fallen in the dust in front of the black ship. He called out in a loud voice: "Trojans, and Lycians, and Dardanians, who fight hand to hand, do not give any ground in the fighting in this narrow place. Instead, save the son of Clytius, so that they will not strip his armor, as he has fallen in the contest for the ships." 428

So Hector spoke, and then made a cast at Aias with his shining spear. Hector missed him, and instead hit Lycophron, the son of Mastor. He was the Cytheran attendant of Aias, who lived beside Aias ever since he killed a man among the holy Cytherans. Hector hit him in the head with sharp bronze under the ear as he stood close to Aias. He fell from the stern of the ship to the ground and landed faceup in the dust, loosening his limbs. Aias shuddered, and called out to his brother: "Dear Teucer, a true friend to us both has been killed, the son of Mastor. He came from Cythera to live with us in our halls where he was held in equal honor with our kin. Greathearted Hector has killed him. Where, now are your arrows of swift death and the bow that Phoebus Apollo provided for you?" 441

So Aias spoke, and Teucer met up with him. He ran over and stood close to Aias with his curved bow in his hand and the quiver that dispenses arrows. He let fly a swift dart at the Trojans and hit Cletus, the glorious son of Peseinor, comrade of Polydamas, worthy son of Panthous, as Cletus held the reins in his hand. He was busying himself with the horses in the place where most of the formations were being thrown into disorder, as a favor to Hector and the Trojans of all the men in the ranks. Even though they rushed in, no one could protect him and misfortune quickly came his way. The deadly arrow hit the back of his neck and he fell from the chariot. The horses swerved to the side and the empty chariot went clanging along. The Lord Polydamas realized instantly what had happened and was the first to go after the horses. He gave them to Astynous, the son of Protiaon, and strenuously urged him to get close and hold onto them. He returned to join in the front ranks in the fighting himself. 457

Teucer notched another arrow intended for brazen-helmeted
Hector. It was his intent to hit the best and take away his spirit,
so that the fighting might cease beside the Acheans' ships. But
his wish did not escape the diligent notice of Zeus, who was
guarding Hector. He snatched that hope from Teucer Telamonson. At the draw of Teucer's celebrated bow, Zeus snapped the
well-twisted bowstring. The bronze-tipped arrow skittered off,
and the bow fell from his hand. Teucer shuddered and said to
his brother: "Would you look at that! Some god has shorn the
hair off from our plan, leaving us helpless. He knocked my bow
out of my hand and broke my newly-twisted bowstring. I tied it
in just this morning so that it could withstand the repeated
firing of arrows."   470

And great Telamonian Aias answered him: "Brother! Well,
leave the bow and sheaves of arrows lying, since a god is leaning heavily on us Danaans. In their place, grab a long spear in
your hand and put a buckler on your shoulders and fight against
the Trojans and rouse the other troops. If we are careless we will
be beaten down and the well-benched ships may be taken. Instead, let us keep our warring spirit in mind."   477

So Aias spoke, and Teucer put the bow in his hut and then
set a four-ply buckler around his shoulders. On his valiant head
he placed a carefully fashioned helmet with a horsehair crest.
The plume nodded dreadfully from the top of it. He selected a
worthy spear, tipped with sharp bronze, and set off running fast
to stand beside Aias.   483

When Hector saw Teucer deprived of his arrows, he called
out to the Trojans and the Lycians in a loud voice: "Trojans, and
Lycians, and Dardanians, who fight hand to hand, you men who
are my friends, remember your furious valor up on the hollow
ships. I saw with my own eyes the best of Achean warriors deprived of his arrows by Zeus. It is well known that from Zeus
valor comes to warriors. He would grant higher glory to our
missiles, and he could diminish those he might not wish to protect. In such a way does he lessen the might of the Argives while

he helps us. So, fight in tight formation around the ships. Any
of us who might be wounded or struck down, and might meet
his fate and death, let him die. It is not unworthy for him to die
for the sake of his family in a valiant manner, because his wife
and children will be safe in the future. His home will stand secure and his land will be undivided if the Acheans return in
their ships to their beloved homeland." So Hector spoke and he
roused the might and spirit of each man.   500

On the other side, Aias again called to his comrades: "For
shame, Argives! Now it is certain that we either perish or we
are saved and push disaster away from the ships. If Hector, of
the helmet with a waving plume, takes the ships as he intends
to, does each of us expect to get back to his homeland on foot?
Did you not hear Hector when he was rousing his troops, rav-
ing that he wants to set the ships on fire? Be serious, he did not
come here to call a dance, but to fight! For us now, there is no
one with a better mind or a better plan than to fight in close
combat using our hands and our might. It is better to perish at
once than to survive for a long time in fiery conflict, wasting
away a little at a time, under the hands of inferior men!" So
spoke Aias, and he roused the strength and spirit of each man.   514

Then, Hector took Schedius, the son of Perimedes and chief
of the Phocians. And Aias took Laodamas, commander of the
foot soldiers, glorious son of Antenor. Polydamas killed Otus of
Cyllene, comrade of Phyleus's son, and chief of the greathearted
Epeans. Meges caught sight of that and charged toward him. But
Polydamas lurched from underneath as he made his cast and he
missed him, because Apollo would not allow the son of Panthous
to be brought down in the front ranks. Next, Meges hit Croes-
mos in the middle of his chest with a spear. He fell with a thud,
and Meges stripped the armor from his shoulders. At that, Dolops rushed at Meges. Dolops, widely known for the spear, was
the most excellent son of Lampus, well known for his furious
valor, who was the son of Laomedon. Dolops hit the middle of
the buckler of the son of Phyleus, as he rushed in at close range.

The thick breastplate he wore was fitted with hollows that warded off the spear. Once Phyleus brought the breastplate from Ephyre, away from the river Seleïs. Euphetes, king of the men of Ephyre, gave it to him as a guest-friend gift to wear as protection from hostile men. And now it warded off destruction from his son's flesh.   533

But Meges whacked Dolops on the top of his head with his sharp spear, on the crest of the bronze helmet with its horsehair plume. The horsehair crest broke completely off and fell to the ground, newly polished with its red color in the dust. In spite of that, Dolops remained in the fighting, hoping even yet for victory. And so he did until the warlike Menelaus came as protector for Meges. He stood at an angle with his spear hidden, and hit Dolops behind the shoulder. The spear went readily through his breastbone and he tumbled over, facedown. Menelaus and Meges both went over and stripped the bronze armor from his shoulders.   545

Hector called out urgently to all his relatives. But first, he scolded brave Melanippus Hicetaonson, who had been living apart from Troy because he was on poor terms with his family. He herded cloven-hoofed cattle in Percote. But when the Danaans' ships, curved on both sides, came to Troy, he immediately returned and lived near Priam, who valued him equally to his children. He was a standout among the Trojans. Hector upbraided him, addressing him by name: "Are we to give up in this way, Melanippus? Are you not now turning away from your own dead relative? Can you not see that they are stripping Dolops's armor? Instead, follow along! And don't stay back from fighting against the Argives, until either we kill them or they take the high city of Troy and kill its citizens." So Hector spoke and he led off. And Melanippus, a man equal to a god, followed after him.   559

Great Telamonian Aias roused the Argives: "O friends, be warriors, and respect the things that are sacred in your hearts. Hold each other in honor in the furious fighting. Of those who

have honor, more are saved than are killed. But, neither fame
nor valor comes to one who runs away." 564

So Aias spoke and both he and they were eager to ward off
the Trojans. They fixed his words firmly in their hearts and
were determined to protect the ships with a bulwark of bronze.
But, Zeus held up his balance for the Trojans. 567

But Menelaus, good at the war cry, urged on Antilochus:
"Antilochus, no other Achean is younger than you, but none is
faster on his feet nor is any braver than you in the fight. Could
you not somehow jump out and cast against some Trojan
warrior?" So Menelaus spoke and drove off again.

And what he said excited Antilochus, who jumped out from
the front lines, and, cautiously looking around, made a cast with
his gleaming spear. The Trojans pulled back from the man casting, but the flight of the missile was not wasted. The spear hit
Melanippus, son of Hicetaon, as he was returning to the fighting. He was struck in the chest beside a nipple, and fell with a
thud. Darkness closed in on his eyes. Antilochus rushed forward
like dogs who rush on a wounded fawn shot by a hunter as it
left its lair. Quickly its limbs are loosed. So Antilochus, firm in
his martial ardor, jumped on you, Melanippus, stripping off your
armor. But this did not escape the notice of Hector, who went
running over opposite him from the heat of the fighting. Swift
Antilochus did not make a stand, though he was a warrior. Instead, he trembled like a wild beast who has done his mischief,
one who has killed a dog or a herder among cattle. He runs away
before making a stand before a densely crowded throng of men.
In such a way did the son of Nestor tremble when the Trojans
and Hector, with an otherworldly noise, rained down on him
grief-giving darts. Then he turned around and returned to the
squadrons of his comrades. 591

The Trojans rushed on the ships like lions that eat raw flesh,
bringing to completion the directive of Zeus. He was constantly raising great strength in them, and diminishing the glory

of the Acheans while exciting the Trojans. His heart planned to grant glory to Hector, so that he might throw unquenchable fire at the tops of the ships. Then he planned to grant the wish of Thetis to raise her son up above all. From the mind of counseling Zeus, the flaming ships were to be a sign shown to the eyes of all. After that he intended for the Trojans to retreat from the ships, and he would grant glory to the Danaans. With those intentions, he raised up in Hector an intense eagerness, especially intense even for him. He went on a rampage that was like when spear-brandishing Ares rages or a perilous fire rages deep in the thickets of forests of the mountains. He began to foam at the mouth. His eyes glowed beneath a dreadful scowl. The temple-pieces on both sides of his helmet shook fearfully. So it was as Hector went to warring. And from the ethereal regions, Zeus was his protector, who gave a surfeit of honor and fame to him alone among men. But his was to be but a brief life. Yes indeed, Pallas Athena would drive him to his day of doom under the might of the son of Peleus. Hector wanted to smash formations of men in the contest wherever he saw the best of arms as he looked out over the mass of the throng assembled. It was impossible to smash much, even though he desired it greatly. The Acheans held like a well-made fortress tower, like a great rock formation close to the gray sea that batters it repeatedly. It stands against violent gusts of shrill winds and swelling waves that slam against it. So the Danaans stood firm against the Trojans, without fear. But Hector leapt into the throng with glowing fire and rushed on like when a wave falls violently into a swift ship underneath clouds driven by the wind. It is altogether hidden in the foam and a fearsome wind smacks against the sail with a loud noise, terrifying the trembling sailors, who under it are borne away from death for a little while. So, too, were the hearts in the breasts of the Acheans battered. 629

Hector was like a lion that goes among cattle, bent on destruction, as countless numbers of them are grazing in a large marshy meadow. The herder who is with them clearly has no idea how to fight against a wild beast and neither do the curved-horned cows, as they are slaughtered from all around. The herder always tends to the first and the last of the herd, but the lion rushes into the middle and eats a cow. All the rest stand trembling. So it was when Hector and father Zeus put an amazing fear into all the Acheans.   638

But only one of them was killed, the Mycenaean Periphetes, the beloved son of Copreus, who abandoned mighty Heracles because of a message from King Eurystheus. Periphetes was by far the better son of an inferior father who sired him, with respect to all virtues, being better on his feet, better at fighting, as well as smarter. He was considered among the foremost of the Mycenaeans, and at the time was granted greater fame than Hector. He was brandishing the shield that he carried. It covered him down to his ankles, a bulwark against a spear cast. But as he turned back around he tripped on the shield's rim. Wounded, he fell faceup, and around his helmet there was a terrible crashing sound as the temple-pieces fell. Hector took keen notice of what happened and ran to stand close to Periphetes and fixed a spear in his chest. He died with his comrades close by. Though they were grief stricken, they were unable to help their friend, as they were themselves afraid of noble Hector.   652

Those on the opposite side came to the high ships that were in the same place where they first pulled them up, and the enemy rushed on them. The Argives withdrew back to the ships at the outer limits because they had to. There they remained closely packed in around the huts, but they were not swept through the camp. Respect for the gods and fear held them. They shouted and called back and forth to each other.

Nestor the Geranian was again the rock of the Acheans. He pleaded with them, clasping the knees of each man: "O friends, be steadfast as warriors and make certain that you are held in respect in the minds of other men. It is imperative that you remember, each of you, your children and your wives, your property and your parents. They exist no matter whether they are

among the living or among the dead. I beg you not to turn away,
but to make a stand in a powerful way. Do not turn from here
to rout!" So spoke Nestor, and he roused strength and courage
in each man.   667

Athena pushed away the dark cloud covering their eyes in
her divine way. That made everything bright around the ships
and the same around the fighting. The Acheans kept Hector,
good at the war cry, and his comrades fenced in. He was back
at the rear and away from the fighting and there were as many
at the rear as there were those who fought in around the swift
ships.   673

And it did not please the spirit of greathearted Aias to stand
in the fight at that time, though others of the sons of the Acheans did so. Instead, he went about on the decks of the ships,
taking long strides, brandishing a boarding pike suitable for
marine fighting in his fists. It was joined with metal bands and
was twenty-two cubits long, about twenty-eight feet. It was like
when a man who is accomplished at jumping from one horse
to another while riding goes from a city through a plain
along the military road, driving four horses hitched together
back toward the city. When he does, many men and women
stand watching in amazement as he jumps from one horse to
another, always landing safely as the horses fly along. So it was
with Aias as he jumped from one ship's deck to another among
the many swift ships. The sound of his voice went up into the
air, as he encouraged the Danaans with his terrifying shouts to
protect both the ships and the huts.   688

But Hector did not remain in the densely crowded knot of
armed Trojans. He was like a golden eagle that rushes on a flock
of high-flying birds that are feeding beside a river—geese, or
cranes, or long-necked swans. In such a way did Hector rush
straight on against the black-prowed ships. And Zeus shoved
him from behind with his huge hands, rousing the troops to follow with him.   695

Again there was bitter fighting among the ships. You might

suppose that there were untiring warriors or fresh troops as they set themselves against each other in the fighting, such was the intensity of it. Their minds were set on fighting in this way. To be sure, the Acheans did not talk of escaping because of cowardice, but of perishing. The Trojans hoped in the heart of each to set fire to the ships and kill the Achean heroes. With their minds set in this way they stood against each other. Hector grabbed on to the stern of one of the ships that goes over the deep waters, one that was beautiful and swift through the sea. It bore Protesilaus to Troy, but it would not take him back to his homeland. It was around his ship that both the Acheans and the Trojans were fighting in close combat with one another. But, you may be sure there were not any bows and arrows, and no casting of spears in this fighting. They stood too close to each other for that. They used sharp axes instead, and they fought with long-handled poleaxes and huge swords, and spears sharpened on both ends. There were many swords with beautiful black scabbards and hilts. Some fell to the ground from hands, others from shoulders of men fighting. The dark earth ran with blood.   715

When Hector reached the crest of the stern, he did not let go, but held on to it, and called to the Trojans: "Bring fire. Zeus now brings to us all our day of reckoning: we will take the ships that came here against the will of the gods. They caused many misdeeds and many spells to be put on us. I myself wanted to fight around the sterns of the ships, but the cowardly elders kept me back there, restraining the troops. But, if back then, thundering Zeus was hindering our resolve, he now urges me on himself, and gives me orders."   725

So Hector spoke and the Trojans rushed on the Argives with a vengeance. Aias no longer remained where he had been. He was overpowered with missiles coming at him. Instead, he pulled back a little bit, realizing that he might be killed. He left the decks of the balanced ship and went down about seven feet to a rower's bench. There he took his place, with his spear constantly protecting the ships from the Trojans. He kept a watchful eye out for anyone who might bring unquenchable fire. He repeatedly called out to the Danaans in his terrifying yell: "O friends, Danaan heroes, attendants of Ares, be warriors, my friends! Remember your furious valor! We will claim down the line that some things helped. Would a better defense wall have protected the men from misery? But there is no city close by with a well-built tower that would protect us who are in a different country from our own. We are situated in the Trojan plain lying close to the deep sea, and there is a dense hoard of heavily armed Trojans around. We are a long way off from our homeland. Seize the light of hope in both your hands! There is nothing sweet in war!"   741

So, eagerly he took his sharp spear. Whichever of the Trojans might approach the hollow ships with burning fire to please Hector, that one was greeted by Aias, who struck him with his long spear. And twelve men were thus struck down before the ships in that close combat.   746

Book 16

And so they fought around the well-benched ships.
Patroclus stood beside Achilles, Shepherd of the Troops, gushing warm tears like a dark-water spring that pours murky water down a cliff so high that even goats can't get to it. Seeing him, noble Achilles, fleet of foot, felt pity for him, and said with winged words: "Why are you crying, Patroclus? You look like a little girl who comes running to her mother, asking to be picked up. She tugs at her mother's robe, then pulls on it harder, bursting out in tears until she is picked up. You look like her, Patroclus, as you drip soft tears. Is there anything you have to say to the Myrmidons, or concerning me, or have you alone heard something in a message from Phthia? Do they say that Menoetius, son of Actor, still lives, and is Peleus Aeacusson still alive among the Myrmidons? Both of us would be greatly saddened by the death of either of them. Or do you weep in grief for the Acheans who perish near the hollow ships on account of their arrogance? Out with it! Hide nothing that is on your mind, so that we both may know what it is."   19

And, with deep groaning, you said to him, Patroclus, sir: "O Achilles, son of Peleus, most worthy in might of the Acheans, do not be angry that I grieve because the Acheans have been overpowered. They all have been, even the best of them. They lie nearby in their huts, struck by blows and wounded. Mighty Diomedes Tydeusson was wounded, and Odysseus, famed for the spear, was struck, and so was Agamemnon. Even Eurypylus was wounded by an arrow in his thigh. The healers are busy with medicinal herbs relieving the wounds. But you are implacable, Achilles.   29

"The anger that you nurse so relentlessly would not hold on to me in the same way. What curses will someone yet born say

of you, if you would not protect the Argives from dreadful peril?
You are pitiless. The noble horseman Peleus was not cruel to
you, nor was your mother Thetis, who bore you in the azure
sea and tended you on cliffs so high that only the sun can reach.
Whatever cruelty there is in your nature did not come from
them. If you are trying to avoid what the oracle has in mind for
you, and the things your revered mother has discussed with
Zeus, send me instead. The other troops of the Myrmidons will
follow, and in that way become a light of hope to the Danaans.
Give me your armor and dress both my shoulders with your
breastplate. If the Trojans think that I am you, they will draw
back from the fighting and the worn-out sons of the Acheans
can rest. As it is now, there is little rest from the fighting. It will
be easy, with just a shout, for the fresh Myrmidon troops to push
the weary Trojan warriors toward the city and away from the
ships and the huts."   45

So pleaded the fool. He was close to begging for both his own
miserable death and his fates. Annoyed, fleet-footed Achilles
replied: "Oh my, noble-born Patroclus, what in the world are
you saying! I don't care a thing for what I know of oracles, nor
do I care about anything my revered mother cooked up for me
beside Zeus. However, there is terrible grief in my heart and
spirit that came when that man—Agamemnon—chose to divide things up like he did, and take my prize from me. He went
beyond his authority. On that account I have a dreadful grief
and have since experienced heartache. I had piled up much
treasure sacking a well-fortified city, and the sons of the Acheans chose the girl as a prize for me. The Lord Agamemnon
Atreusson unscrupulously snatched her back from my hands, as
if I were some menial without rights. There is no way that he
didn't forsee that such treatment would earn my quick and
lasting anger. Very quickly might the storehouses have been
filled with corpses, had the Lord Agamemnon recognized me
in a kind way, but now the camp is surrounded with fighting.

But we will leave all that alone. As you know, I have been saying that I will not stop the wrath altogether until the shouting
and fighting come to my own ships. Diomedes Tydeusson is
not protecting the Danaans from destruction, raging with a
spear in his hand, and no longer does anyone hear shouting
from the hateful face of the son of Atreus. Instead, the sound of
man-killing Hector's commands resonates, as the Trojans pour
out all over the plain with their war cry, trampling down the
Acheans. But come, clothe your shoulders in my famous armor
and lead the war-loving Myrmidons to battle. If the black cloud
of the Trojans settles in a powerful way on the ships, they will
be turned from the headlands of the sea, that small space still
fated to be held by the Acheans. They will be pressed back altogether to the city of the Trojans. But they will not see my
countenance in the shining helmet.   79

"And so, Patroclus, fall on the Trojans with force to protect
the ships so that they do not torch the ships and destroy them
with fire. That would rob us of our own return home. Trust
what I tell you and keep your mind focused on the goal.
That way I would win great honor and fame before all Danaans.
They will bring back the pretty girl and parade before me magnificent gifts, so that I will drive the Trojans back away from
the ships. If you do your part, the thundering husband of Hera
will give you glory, too. But, you ought not to crave fighting
apart from me against the war-loving Trojans, as you would
make me less honored. And we should be careful not to take
any pleasure from killing them in the fighting as we lead them
to Troy, since one of the everlasting gods from Olympus may
have come into the fighting. Apollo, who works from afar, loves
the Trojans passionately. Turn back after you place a light of
hope among the ships, and let others do the wrangling across
the plain. Oh, how I wish by father Zeus, and Athena, and
Apollo that none of the Trojans, even as many as there are,
would escape death, and that none of the Acheans, and not the

two of us, would perish. And when we are by ourselves alone, then we might loose the sacred battlements of Troy." In this way Patroclus and Achilles talked between themselves.   101

Aias could no longer hold his position. He was overwhelmed by the arrows. The mind of Zeus and the worthy Trojans beat him down with their shooting. Dreadful was the sound of the arrows flying in around the shining temple-pieces of his helmet. They rained in constantly on the boss that protected his forehead. His left shoulder tired under the weight of his variegated shield. Even with the bristling of arrows all around, they were unable to push him back. But he was constantly breathing hard. Lots of sweat poured out of his limbs all over his body. But he could take no rest in his situation. From all directions, trouble stacked up on trouble.   111

Tell me now, you Muses who dwell on Olympus, how the first fire fell into the ships of the Acheans.   112

Hector went and stood close to the ashen spear of Aias. With his great sword he struck it along its shaft, behind the spearhead. The sword slashed all the way through. Aias looked at the damaged shaft in his hand and rotated it, and the bronze head fell from the end to the ground with a thump. Aias shuddered as he realized this to be the work of gods. His exceptional mind knew how to recognize when one of the gods was emasculating him in the fight. Loud-thundering Zeus was about to slice completely through everything in the fighting. He planned victory for the Trojans. And Aias withdrew from the fighting.   122

Now it was at this point that the Trojans threw the destructive fire into the swift ship. Immediately, unquenchable flames poured around it, as the fire hit the stern. At that, Achilles slapped both his thighs and said to Patroclus: "Get up, noble-born Patroclus, charioteer! I see fire burning among the ships. Don't let it take the ships yet. Dress in the armor now! I will alert the troops."   129

So Achilles spoke, and Patroclus armed himself in gleaming bronze. First, he put the beautiful greaves around his shins.

They had handsomely wrought silver ankle plates. Next, he put around his chest the breastplate of the fleet-footed grandson of Aeacus. It was of several colors, decorated with stars. Around his shoulders he tossed the silver-studded bronze sword. And then he put on his shoulders the buckler that was big and stout. On his noble head he placed the helmet with its horsehair crest. Terrifying was the sight of its plume as it nodded. Then he selected two worthy spears that fit well in his hand, though he did not choose the huge, stout spear that only the exceptional grandson of Aeacus could handle. None of the other Acheans could hold on to it. Achilles Peleusson alone could handle the ashen spear that Chiron gave to his beloved father on the heights of Pelion, so that he could visit death upon heroes.   144

Patroclus ordered Automedon to hitch up the swift horses. Automedon was greatly esteemed, next only to Achilles, who smashed whole ranks of men himself. He could be counted on to remain solidly firm in the din of battle. At that, Automedon lifted up the yoke over the swift horses Xanthus and Balias. The two of them could fly like the wind. The harpy Podarge bore them to West Wind when she was grazing in a meadow beside the currents of Ocean. Automedon hitched up the celebrated Pedasus as the outside horse. Achilles led him away when he took Eetion's city of Thebes. He was mortal, but followed along with the immortal horses.   154

Achilles went around the Myrmidons' huts getting them armed. They were like wolves who eat flesh raw, who have boundless courage in their minds. Having taken down a huge buck with large antlers in the mountains, they gorge on it, and the cheeks of all are red with blood. And in groups they go from the spring where they drank the dark water, slobbering with their spongy tongues. In the end, they vomit out the bloody gore. But the spirit in their chest is firm, though their stomachs are distended. So it was with the chiefs and counselors of the Myrmidons as they gathered around the attendant of the fleet-footed grandson of Aeacus. Warlike Achilles stood

among them urging along both the horses and shield-bearing
men.   167

There were fifty swift ships that Achilles, beloved of Zeus,
led to Troy. In each were fifty men at opposite oarlocks. There
were five commanders whom he trusted to give directions,
while he himself was overlord. Menestheus, with his variegated
breastplate, led the first company. He was the son of the river
Spercheus, which pours from Zeus. Polydora, the lovely daughter
of Peleus, bore him after the girl slept with the ever-flowing
god Spercheus. The incident was a disgrace for Boreus, son of
Perieres, who openly provided a huge bride price for her.   178

Warlike Eudorus commanded the second company. He was
the son of an unwed mother. The beautiful Polymele of the cho-
rus bore him. The powerful Argiphontes was enamored of her
when he saw her among those singing and dancing in the cho-
rus of Artemis, whose arrows have golden shafts. Immediately,
Hermes, who does no harm, went up to the upper chamber
where the women sleep and lay beside her in secret. She gave
him a magnificent son, Eudorus, who excelled at running and
fighting. And when the Eilethyia, who preside over childbirth,
led Eudorus into the light and the rays of the sun, the powerful
Echecles Actorson took Polymele to his palace, after providing
a vast bride price. The old man Phylas took in Eudorus and
brought him up. He loved the boy extravagantly, as if he were
his own son.   192

Warlike Pisandrus Memalisson commanded the third company. He was a standout among all the Myrmidons in fighting with the spear, next after the son of Peleus. The old noble
horseman Phoenix commanded the fourth company, and Alcimedon, the exceptional son of Laerces, the fifth.   197

After he gathered the men into proper formation with their
commanders, Achilles laid on them a stern order: "Myrmidons,
none of you should hide his annoyance with me since the Trojans
threaten the swift ships, altogether on account of my wrath.
And each of you ought to blame me, saying: 'You miserable son

of Peleus, your mother raised you in anger. You are cruel and heartless, who would keep back your comrades around the ships, even though we didn't want to be kept away. Let's go home in our ships, which sail over the sea, since your heart is locked in such destructive anger.' Those things you would have been talking about over and over. But now a huge cry of conflict has appeared. In the past, you were fond of fighting. Now, fight the Trojans as would one with a valiant heart!" 209

So speaking, he roused the strength and spirit of each man. The companies were truly energized on hearing their king. It was like when a mason fits thick stones together into a wall of a lofty palace to protect it from the power of winds. In such a way did their helmets and bossed shields fit together. Shield fitted in close to shield, helmet to helmet and man to man. The helmets, with their long horsehair crests touching, their gleaming plumes nodding, as they stood close to each other. And in front of them all were two armed men with one spirit to fight in front of the Myrmidons—Patroclus and Automedon. 220

Then, Achilles left and went into his hut. And he lifted the lid of the beautiful, polished chest that silver-footed Thetis placed in his ship for the voyage well filled with tunics, and robes, and shaggy carpets to keep off the wind. There she placed for him a well-made cup. No other man had ever drunk dark red wine from it, and none had poured libations to any god other than to father Zeus. Achilles took it from the chest and first purified it with brimstone. Next, he washed it with water from beautifully flowing currents. He washed his own hands, and filled the cup with dark red wine. Then he prayed, standing in the middle of the courtyard. He held up the wine and raised his eyes to the heavens and said: "Zeus above, you who are Dodonian and Pelasgian, dwelling far from here in Dodona, with its severe winter storms, and making counsel there. Around Dodona live your diviners, the Sellai, who go with their feet unwashed and sleep on the ground. Now, hear my prayer. You have honored me and done great harm to the troops of the

Acheans, and yet again, now fulfill my petition. I remain myself, among the ships during the contest, but I am sending another among the warring Myrmidons to fight. Send him glory
while he is with them, loud-thundering Zeus. Send courage to
his heart and mind, so that even if Hector sees him and Patroclus should chance to stand alone in the fight against him, he
will have invincible hands, as though I were going into the dance
of Ares. And when he has sent the noisy fighting away from the
ships, may he come back unharmed to the swift ships, with all
his arms and his comrades who fight close in."   248

So spoke Achilles in prayer, and counseling Zeus heard him.
The father granted the one request, while lifting his brow in refusal to the other. He granted that the ships be preserved from
the war and fighting, but he refused that Patroclus should return home safe from the battle. So, I tell you, after pouring the
libation and making his prayer to father Zeus, Achilles went
back into his hut and put the cup back into the chest. He went
and stood in front of the hut, still intent on looking out over the
Trojans and the Acheans in the dire struggle.   256

Those greathearted men with Patroclus, formed into ranks
and heavily armed, with great confidence, charged in among the
Trojans. Suddenly, they were like ground wasps pouring out,
having been repeatedly taunted by boys who foolishly cut into
their nests in the road where they live. This brings shared harm
to many, for if some man should come along the road and un-
wittingly stir them up, they all fly out with valiant hearts to
protect their young. In such a manner did the Myrmidons pour
out from among the ships, with might and spirit. They raised an
unstoppable war cry. Patroclus cried out to his comrades: "Myrmidons and comrades of Achilles Peleusson, you are my friends.
Remember your furious valor so that we might bring honor to
Achilles, who is far and away the best man around the ships of the
Argives and their attendants, who fight close in. Do it so that even
the eminent Prince Agamemnon Atreusson might realize his disastrous blindness in failing to value the best of the Acheans."   274

Thus he roused the strength and spirit of each man and their dense formation fell on the Trojans. Around the ships there was a terrifying, resounding noise from the shouts of the Acheans. And so the Trojans, seeing the valiant son of Menoetius and his attendant in their gleaming armor, the spirits of all were troubled, rattling their ranks, for they thought the fleet-footed son of Peleus had dropped his wrath around the ships and chosen friendship. Each of the Trojans cautiously peered out, looking around for a place where he might escape utter destruction. 283

And Patroclus made the first cast with his shining spear. He hurled straight into the middle where most of the wrangling was, alongside the stern of greathearted Protesilaus's ship. And he hit Pyraechmes, who commanded the Paeonians, mounted warriors, from Amydon, along the wide, rippling Axius. Patroclus hit Pyraechmes in the right shoulder, and he fell down faceup in the dust with a groan. The other Paeonians around him were terrified. The urge to run entered them all when Patroclus killed their commander. He drove them away from the ships and stamped down the brightly burning fire until it was extinguished. He left the half-burned ship where it was, but because of him the Trojans fled from the dire conflict. The Danaans poured out from among the hollow ships, fighting furiously. It was like when Zeus, who gathers lightning bolts, pushes along a dense cloud. As it passes, all lookouts, and prominent peaks, and valleys are revealed and from the heavens upward, a limitless sky opens. In such a way the Danaans saved the ships from burning fire. They rested for a little while, but this was not the beginning of a big retreat. In no way did the warlike Trojans turn tail and run from the black ships on account of the Acheans, beloved of Ares. Instead they persisted, after retreating from the ships because they had to. 304

There, man took man among the commanders in the intense fighting, which smashes men to pieces. As he turned, the valiant son of Menoetius was first to hit Areïlycus's thigh with his sharp spear. The bronze drove through the front, and the spear shattered the bone. Areïlycus fell facedown in the dirt. Next, warlike Menelaus struck Thoas in the sternum that was exposed beside his shield. It loosed his limbs. The son of Phyleus hunkered down to wait for Amphiclus as he charged and struck Amphiclus before he reached him in the thigh. It is there that the thickest muscles of a man are found. The point of the spear went through and slashed the tendons. Darkness enveloped Amphiclus's eyes.   317

And, Antilochus, one of the sons of Nestor, struck Antymnius with his sharp-pointed shaft, and drove the brazen spear through the abdomen. Antymnius pitched forward as he fell. Maris was close by and rushed on Antilochus with his spear, as he was angry over his brother. He stood in front of his brother's corpse. But godlike Thrasymedes rushed in instantly and whacked Maris on the shoulder before he could strike his brother Antilochus. Thrasymedes did not waste his effort. The point of his spear slashed through the base of the arm all the way to the bone, severing the muscles. Maris fell down with a thud, and darkness enclosed his eyes.   325

And so it was that both of the two brothers were brought down, and they both went to Erebus. They were brave comrades of Sarpedon, and spear-wielding sons of Amisodarus, who reared the Chimaera, a monstrous evil for many men. Oïlean Aias rushed in and whacked Cleoboulus on the buttocks, taking him alive, but disabled among the throng. But, Aias quickly took his spirit, when he struck his neck with his sword hilt. The whole sword was slightly warmed by the blood. Cleoboulus fell down, and purple death seized his eyes. Peneleos and Lycon ran toward the same place, both intent on casting their spears at each other. Both missed, so again they ran toward each other, this time with swords. There Lycon drove his sword onto Peneleos's helmet, with its horsehair plume. Near the hilt, the sword shattered. Peneleos sliced Lycon in the neck, under the ear. The sword sunk all the way in, leaving only skin. Lycon's head drooped over to the side and his limbs collapsed beneath him. Speedy Meriones caught up with Acamas as he was mounting his chariot. Meriones hit him in the right shoulder and he fell from the chariot. Darkness poured down onto his eyes. Idomeneus hit Erymantes in the mouth with his pitiless bronze. The brazen spear penetrated him completely below the brain, slicing through the white bone. His teeth rattled with it, and both eyes filled with blood, and gore spurted up from his mouth and nose as he gaped upward. He fell and a dark cloud of death closed in all around.   350

In these ways did each of the commanders of the Danaans take himself a man. They were like she-wolves, who forage furiously on young prey. They charge on lambs or kids in the mountains, ones that a shepherd has foolishly let wander from the herd. When the wolves see them, they immediately bring down the ones with weak spirits. So it was with the Danaans as they charged on the Trojans, who set their minds on rout, which makes a shameful noise, and forgot their furious valor.   356

Great Aias was after Hector, of the bronze helmet, seeking to make a spear cast at him. Aias was skilled in the things of war and with his shield of laminated bull hides on his wide shoulders kept off the whizzing arrows and thudding spear casts. He well understood the change of the tide of victory in battle, but he remained firm. He must save his much loved comrades.   363

It was like when a cloud comes from Olympus to the heavens, pushed from the sky, when Zeus stretches forth his arm to create a tempest. So it was when there arose from the ships both a loud racket and a rout. And the Trojans' return was not in proper order. Hector's swift-hoofed horses carried off him with his armor, leaving behind the Trojan troops whom he pulled back to the ditch, even though they protested. In the ditch were many fast, chariot-pulling horses, going along at the ends of the poles of the chariots of their kings as they left. Patroclus, sensing the cowardice of the Trojans, followed furiously, ordering the Danaans along. On account of the din and the rout, all

the roads were full when the Trojans cut and ran. High above
rose a storm of dust into the clouds. Down below, the solid-
hoofed Trojan horses retraced their steps back to the city, away
from the ships and the huts.   376

Patroclus understood where most of the troops were rushing, and he drove there, shouting. Underneath the axle were
men who had fallen facedown from their chariots, when chariots flipped and crashed. The immortal horses leapt completely
over the trench to the opposite side. Those were a magnificent
gift the gods gave to Peleus. As they shot forward, Patroclus's
heart urged him on toward Hector, as he was sent to drive Hector away. But Hector's fast horses carried him away. It was like
being under a storm on a day in early fall that overpowers the
dark earth, when Zeus dumps water on the greediest of men.
And when he is angry at those who use their might in councils
to make twisted judgments, because they don't care about what
is right or whether the gods might take vengeance. All the rivers overflow, and then cleave out steep banks and canyons as
they rush, roaring headlong toward the great purple sea from
the mountains, and the fields of men are devastated. In such a
way did the Achean chariots push back the Trojans with much
groaning.   393

Patroclus then cut off the front of the formations to prevent
their falling back on the ships, but neither did he allow their
return to the city. Instead he rushed on them midway between
the river and the lofty wall and killed them, exacting a penalty
for the many they had slain. There he first hit Pronous in the
sternum with his shining spear, exposed beside his shield. It
loosed his limbs, and he fell with a thud. Next he rushed on
Thestor, son of Enops, who sat hunched over in his chariot, from
being hit in the diaphragm, the reins fallen from his hands.
Patroclus came alongside and stuck him with his spear in the
right cheek. The spear pierced through his teeth and Patroclus
grabbed hold of the shaft and pulled Thestor up over the chariot's rail. It was like when a man sitting on a rocky promontory

draws up a big fish from the deep on his line and shining bronze hook. In the same way the spear pushed down on the mouth and Thestor was pulled from his chariot gaping wide with gleaming bronze in his mouth. He fell and his spirit left him. Next Erylaus rushed on Patroclus, who hit him with a rock in the middle of his head. His head was completely cleaved in two inside the stout helmet. Erylaus fell facedown on the ground, and death, which destroys the spirit, poured over him. After that Patroclus killed Erymantes, and Amphoterus, and Epaltes, and Tlepolemus, and Echius Damastorson, and Pyris, and Iphees, and Euippus, and Polymelus Argesson. He rushed on all of them and delivered them one after the other to the bountiful earth.   418

Sarpedon saw how many of his comrades, who wore tunics without belts, were felled under the hands of Patroclus Menoetiusson. He felt the urge to address the Lycians: "O Lycians, how shameful is this? Where can you escape? Now is the time you should be brave! I shall meet with this man so that I can learn who it is with the might to do so much harm to the Trojans; he has loosed the limbs of many valiant men."   425

He jumped down onto the ground in his armor. On the other side, Patroclus saw to leap from his chariot. They were like vultures with curved talons and bent beaks that make a great clamor as they fight on a high cliff. So the two men shouted at each other as they charged. Seeing them, the son of crooked-dealing Cronus felt pity, and said to his sister and wife Hera: "I am distressed! I love Sarpedon most of all men, but it is his fate to be brought down by the hands of Patroclus Menoetiusson. It is for me a dilemma in my heart and in my mind: am I going to snatch him up alive from the fighting, which brings tears, and place him in the wealthy district of the Lycians, or do I allow him to be brought down at the hand of the son of Menoetius?"   438

The revered Hera, with lovely eyes, replied: "Dreaded son of Cronus, what are you saying? Death has been the man's fate for a long time. Do you want to take that fate back and free him from death, which brings great pain? If so, do it. But all of us

other gods will not agree with you in it. And I will tell you something else, and fix it clearly in your mind. If you send Sarpedon
alive to his palace, you will send the gods into terrible anger.
Understand that the rest of the gods would also want to send
their sons away from the dreadful conflict. There are many sons
of the immortals fighting around the city of great Priam. But,
if you love him and your heart is full of sorrow over this, I tell
you—allow him to be taken down by the hands of Patroclus
Menoetiusson in furious fighting. Then send Death and sweet
Sleep to carry him even in death until they arrive in the widespread district of the Lycians. There, his brothers and his kin
can give him funeral rites and erect both a mound and a column. That is the reward of mortals."   457

So Hera spoke, and the father of both men and gods did as
she said. He was honoring his beloved son who was about to
pour bloody droplets onto the ground as Patroclus wasted him
in Troy with its bountiful soil, far away from his homeland of
Lycia.   460

When they were close and moved in on one another there,
Patroclus hit the renowned Thrasymelus. He was the upright
attendant of King Sarpedon. Patroclus hit him in the lower part
of his stomach and loosed his limbs. Then Sarpedon rushed on
Patroclus but missed with his shining spear, instead striking the
horse Pedasus in the right shoulder. The hit winded him, and
with a scream he fell down in the dust, whinnying in pain. His
spirit flew away. The pair of horses stood beside him and their
yoke creaked. He had been harnessed together with them and
now lay beside them in the dust. But Automedon, famed for the
spear, found a solution. He pulled out the heavy sword that hung
from his thigh and moved in to cut the harness for the third
horse, and he did not fail. Both horses straightened up and their
bridles grew taut. And the two men were back together in the
dire conflict.   476

Then Sarpedon made a miscast with his shining spear. Its
point went over Patroclus's left shoulder, but did not hit him.

Patroclus, at last, rushed with his bronze, and the missile did not take flight from his hand in a wasted effort. The hit was where the diaphragm compresses the pulsating heart. Sarpedon fell and it was like when an oak, or a tulip poplar, or a tall pine falls in the mountains—such a one as wood cutters might fell with their newly sharpened axes to become timber for a ship. In such a way Sarpedon fell in front of his horses and chariot and lay stretched out, bellowing in pain and grasping the bloody dust. He was like a greathearted, gleaming bull killed by a lion that goes into a herd of cloven-hoofed cattle. He perishes, groaning, under the jaws of the lion. So the leader of the shield-bearing Lycians was killed by Patroclus as he raged in battle. He called the name of his beloved companion: "Dear Glaucus, it is now especially necessary that you be first in battle among the warriors, the bravest spearman in the fight. Now you must take over the evil war. First you must go among all of the Lycians' commanders and encourage them to fight close in for Sarpedon, and then you yourself must fight for my arms. I tell you for sure that I will be angry forever if the Acheans strip my arms and make trophies of them in their ships. Instead, stand firm, rouse all the troops!"   501

So speaking, death closed in on his eyes and nose. Glaucus went and put his heel on Sarpedon's chest to pull the spear from his flesh. As he pulled out the spearhead Sarpedon's breath escaped and his spirit along with it. The Myrmidons held Glaucus's snorting horses, which were eager, since the Lycians had abandoned their king's chariot.   507

When Glaucus heard the terrible sound of Sarpedon's voice, grief arose in his heart, because he had not been able to protect Sarpedon. Worn down from his own wound, he grasped his arm tightly with his free hand. He had been in pain since Teucer rushed over and hit him with an arrow from the top of the wall, as he was protecting the van of his comrades in the charge against the high wall. He prayed to far-shooting Apollo: "Hear me, lord, you who are able to hear men in distress both in the wealthy district of Lycia or in Troy, do it now, as trouble has caught up with me. I have a serious wound that drives sharp pain around my arm, and I am unable to staunch the blood. The arm weighs heavily on my shoulders, since I cannot hold a spear firmly, nor can I go fight against the enemy. The very best of men has perished—Sarpedon, a son of Zeus, who did not protect his child. Please lessen the pain and heal this terrible wound, lord. Give me strength so I can rise up and call out to my Lycian comrades. Then they and I myself can fight around the corpse."   526

So spoke Glaucus in prayer, and Phoebus Apollo heard him. Immediately Apollo dried the dark blood from the serious wound and stopped the pain, and strengthened Glaucus's resolve. Glaucus understood and his heart rejoiced that the great god heard his prayer so quickly and responded. First off, he went around rousing all the commanders and the warriors of the Lycians to fight around Sarpedon. Next he went, taking long strides, among the Trojans: to Polydamas Panthousson, and noble Agenor, and he went to Aeneas, and even to Hector, of the brazen helmet. Glaucus stood close to him and spoke in winged words: "Hector, it is clear now that you are completely overlooking the allies who are withering in spirit far from their homeland on your account. You do not wish to protect them. Sarpedon, leader of the Lycians, now lies dead. He preserved Lycia both justly and forcefully. Ares brought him down with a brazen spear at the hand of Patroclus. His friends are standing around him, worried that the Myrmidons might take away his armor. They are angry because we killed so many with our spears near the Acheans' swift ships and they might desecrate the corpse in revenge."   547

So Glaucus spoke, and those among the Trojans were seized by a huge heartache since Sarpedon had been a rock of support for their city, even though he was a foreigner. And many troops came along with him who were some of the very best fighters,

like himself. Hell-bent, they went straight for the Danaans, and
Hector, angered by the loss of Sarpedon, led them.   553

Patroclus Menoetiusson had the heart of a shaggy beast, and
it stirred up the Acheans. He spoke first to the two Aiantes with
a great ferocity that both of them felt: "Aiantes, you two should
avenge a friend, such as those whom you used to have. Sarpedon, who was the first to drive over the wall of the Acheans
and kill many, now lies dead. If we desecrate the body by taking the armor off its shoulders and slay his comrades who would
protect him with pitiless bronze, we might avenge what he has
done to us."   561

So Patroclus spoke, and they were ready to help him. Then,
those on both sides strengthened their formations. The Trojans,
and Lycians, and the Myrmidons, and the Acheans came together around the corpse in deadly fighting, with terrifying
shouts. Great was the sound of the men's armor clashing. Zeus
stretched noxious dark of night over the mighty conflict, so that
what happened around his beloved son would be murderous.   568

At first, the Trojans pushed back the bright-eyed Acheans,
and struck a man who was not at all the worst among the
Myrmidons. Noble Epegeus, son of greathearted King Agacles,
who used to live in wide Boudeun. But when Epegeus killed a
worthy kinsman, he left home and came to Peleus and silver-
footed Thetis seeking sanctuary. They sent him with Achilles,
sacker of cities, to Troy, which produces fine horses, to fight
against the Trojans. Glorious Hector hit Epegeus in the head
with a rock as he was touching the corpse. The rock cleaved his
head in two inside the stout helmet. Epegeus fell facedown on
the body, and death, which strikes the heart, poured around
him. A great grief rose up in Patroclus over the death of his
comrade, and he moved through the front lines like a swift
hawk frightening jays and starlings. So Patroclus, charioteer,
you charged straight at the Lycians and the Trojans, your heart
furious over your comrade. And Patroclus hit Sthenelaus, the

beloved son of Ithaemenes, in the neck with a rock that crushed his tendons. Those in the front lines gave ground, even glorious Hector. They pulled back about the length of the cast of a long javelin made by an athlete competing in a contest or a warrior in that fiery conflict that destroys the spirit. That distance the Trojans pulled back as the Acheans pushed forward. Glaucus was the first leader of the shield-bearing Lycians to turn back. He killed greathearted Bathycles, the beloved son of Chalcon. Bathycles lived in a palace in Hellas with possessions and wealth, and was prominent among the Myrmidons. Glaucus turned around and struck him in the chest with a spear when Bathycles caught up with him in pursuit. Bathycles fell with a thud. A dense sadness took hold of the Acheans that such a worthy man had fallen, while the Trojans were greatly delighted. They went and stood closely packed around him. But the Acheans didn't forget their valor; they went straight over and stormed on the Trojans. 602

There again Meriones took a helmeted Trojan warrior, Laogonus, brave son of Onetor. He had been made a priest of sacred Zeus of Ida and was esteemed as a god in his district. Meriones hit Laogonus below the jaw and ear. Swiftly does the spirit depart from those in misery; the darkness of death seized him. Aeneas came at Meriones with a bronze-tipped shaft, hoping to strike him as he advanced with his shield in place. But Meriones caught sight of Aeneas before he threw the brazen spear, and ducked forward. The long spear fixed itself in the ground behind Meriones, where mighty Ares hurled it. The spear tip left Aeneas only to be firmly set in the earth, rushing from his powerful arm in vain. Angry in spirit, Aeneas shouted: "Meriones, even if you had been dancing, your life would have been extinguished by my spear, if I had hit you." 618

And Meriones, famed for the spear, answered: "Even though you are mighty, it is hard to quench the strength of all the men who come against you and protect themselves. Even you were made mortal, and if I can hit you in the middle with my sharp spear, you will quickly give me glory. You are mighty and trust in your hands, but your soul would be on its way to Hades, that famous horseman."   625

So Meriones spoke, and the valiant son of Menoetius rebuked him: "Meriones, is it worthy for you to talk like this? O dear friend, the Trojans will not retreat from the corpse because of your shameful words. The earth will hold some of them before they back off. Talking is for planning; in your hands is the end of the fighting. Of the two, it is not necessary to increase the talking, but rather the fighting."   631

Having said that, Patroclus led off, and the other, a man who was like a god, followed along with him. From them there rose up a tremendous noise, like that of men felling oaks in the glades of the mountains. The noise is recognized when it is heard coming from far-off places. So rose the sound of pounding from the broad expanse of ground, the pounding of bronze, of leather, and of well-made shields. Also rose the sound of the striking of both swords and spears fashioned with points on both ends. Even one who might have known noble Sarpedon well would no longer recognize him, since he was covered from head to toe with missiles, and blood and dust. They warred constantly around his corpse. It was like when on a farm in the spring, buzzing flies swarm around when the jars are filled from the milking pails full of milk. Such was the swarm around the corpse.   644

But Zeus never turned his shining eyes away from the terrible conflict. Instead, he was concentrating intently on the death of Patroclus. Should glorious Hector kill him in furious fighting around the godlike Sarpedon and take the armor from Patroclus's shoulders or should he increase even more the awful toil for everyone? After some thought, he settled on a plan that suited him. In it, the upright attendant of Achilles Peleusson would push the Trojans and bronze-helmeted Hector back toward the city and the spirit from many would be taken in the fighting there.   655

First, Zeus sent weakness into Hector's spirit. He recognized
the shifting of the sacred balance of Zeus and mounted his chariot to turn in flight. He ordered the other Trojans to retreat.
Even the stout Lycians did not remain; all were in full rout, since
they had seen their king wounded and lying in a heap of corpses.
Many fell down around him during the time Cronus's son extended the intense conflict.   662

The Acheans took the dazzling bronze armor from Sarpedon's shoulders. The valiant son of Menoetius gave it to his
comrades to carry back to the hollow ships.   665

And then, Zeus the cloud-gatherer spoke to Apollo: "Come
now, dear Phoebus, go and remove Sarpedon from the hail of
arrows and spears, and clean away the dark clotted blood from
his body. Carry him far away and wash him in the currents of
a river. Anoint him with ambrosia and wrap him in a sacred
shroud. Send him to be ferried by the speedy twin guides, Sleep
and Death. They will place him quickly in the broad, wealthy
land of the Lycians. There his brothers and his kin will give him
funeral rites and erect a burial mound and a column. Such is
the reward of mortal men."   675

So Zeus spoke, and Apollo did not wait for his father to re-
peat what he had said. He went from the mountains of Ida into
the terrible din, and quickly lifted noble Sarpedon up from the
hail of arrows and spears. He carried him far away to the currents of a river where he bathed him, and anointed him with
ambrosia, and encased him in a sacred shroud. He sent Sarpedon with the twins Sleep and Death, who swiftly carried him
with them and set him down in the broad, rich land of the
Lycians.   688

Patroclus was ordering Automedon and the horses to go
among the Trojans and the Lycians, about to do himself great
harm, the fool! If he had heeded the advice of the son of Peleus
in protecting him, he would have escaped the dark, evil fate of
death. But the mind of Zeus is more powerful than that of men.
He easily puts even valiant warriors to rout, or grants victory

when he rouses them in the fight. Even then, it was he who put
the spirit in Patroclus's breast. 691

Patroclus, who were the first and who the last that you killed,
when the gods decreed your death? Adrastus was the first, and
Autonous, and Echeclus, and Perimus Megasson, and Epistor,
and Melanippus, and Elasus and Mulius, and Pylartes. Them,
he slew. Everyone else was minded to escape. 697

At that point might the sons of the Acheans have taken Troy,
with its lofty gate, led by Patroclus as he rushed forward with
his spear, had not Phoebus Apollo been standing on the well-
built wall, considering Patroclus's destruction and giving aid to
the Trojans. Three times Patroclus charged at an angle in the
lofty wall, and three times Apollo stunned him by striking his
shining shield with his immortal hands. But when he rushed
like a madman on the fourth attempt, Apollo shouted in a terrifying voice with winged words: "Pull back, noble-born Patroclus! It is not destined that the city of the haughty Trojans be
sacked under your spear, nor that of Achilles, who is far better
than you!" 709

So Apollo shouted. And Patroclus pulled way back to avoid
the wrath of far-shooting Apollo. 710

Hector had his solid-hoofed horses in the Scaean Gate thinking about whether he should drive back into the fray to fight or
whether he ought to call out to the troops to hole up in the city.
As he considered those things, Phoebus Apollo stood beside
him, taking the guise of Asius, son of Dymas, Hector's uncle,
and his mother Hecuba's own brother. Asius lived in Phrygia
along the currents of the Sangarius. Apollo, son of Zeus, said:
"Hector, why have you quit fighting? There is no way you should
do this. Since I am weaker, you should be much stronger. It
would soon be a sad state of affairs if you hold off from the fighting. But, come. Meet Patroclus, driving the horses with the
powerful hooves. If you could take him, Apollo might yet give
you glory!" 725

So the god spoke and he went back into the warriors' struggle.

Glorious Hector ordered warlike Cebriones to put the goad to
the horses and drive into the fighting. As Apollo went about
through the throng, he brought trouble for the Acheans in the
clamor, and gave glory to the Trojans and Hector. But, he did
not allow Hector to kill any other Danaans. Instead, he drove
the horses, with their powerful hooves, to meet Patroclus.   732

Opposite Hector, Patroclus hopped down from his chariot
onto the ground with a spear in his left hand. In the other was
a rock he picked up. It was jagged with gleaming crystals. His
hand wrapped around it. Patroclus pulled back as though to
steady himself, but neither did the man pull back for long, nor
did he waste his throw. He hit Hector's charioteer Cebriones, a
bastard son of renowned Priam. The sharp stone hit Cebriones
in the forehead as he held the reins of the horses. The rock
smashed in both sides of the brow and the bone didn't hold it
off. His eyes fell into the dust on the ground while he pitched
over his feet, falling down from the beautifully wrought chariot like a diver. His spirit abandoned his bones. And you, Patroclus, charioteer, said awful things to him: "Look at that! What
an agile man is this! If he were ever in the fishy deep, he could
be like a diver who looks for oysters after leaping from a ship.
He could do it even if the sea were stormy. In the same way he
now dives gracefully from his chariot here into the plain. For
sure, there are divers among the Trojans!" So Patroclus charged
at Cebriones, Patroclus, who was a hero with the heart of a lion
who had been struck while prowling about a farm and is
wounded in the chest. His valor perishes. And so did you eagerly
leap on Cebriones, Patroclus!   754

At that, Hector, on the other side, jumped down from his
chariot onto the ground. The two fought around Cebriones as
two lions fight around a killed doe on the peaks of the mountains. Both are hungry, and they fight with great ferocity. In
such a way did the two masters of the war cry, Patroclus Menoetiusson and glorious Hector, attack each other, aiming to slice
flesh with pitiless bronze. Hector grabbed Cebriones's head and

would not let go, while Patroclus at the other end held the feet. The other Trojans and Acheans joined in the mighty conflict. 764

In the same way as East Wind and South Wind fight against each other in the defiles of the mountains on the tops of the trees in the forest where the beech, and ash, and smooth-barked cornel tree are found—they hit each other's long branches with an ungodly sound, and their cracking raises a commotion—so it was as the Trojans and the Acheans leapt at each other in the fiery conflict. But neither side had ruinous rout in mind. Sharp spears wounded many around Cebriones, and arrows jumped to flight from bow strings, and huge rocks collided with shields as they fought around him. But he lay in a whirlwind of dust in the great open space, unconscious of his skill as a horseman. 776

For as long as Sun rested in the middle of the heavens, they struck with missiles on both sides, and the troops fell. After that, Sun moved on to evening when oxen are unyoked. Then were the Acheans ascendant in destiny and thus better off. They protected the heroes from the Trojans' missiles in the din of the fight, and took the armor from Cebriones's shoulders. 782

Patroclus set on the Trojans with the intent to do harm. Three times he charged them, one after the next, with speed the equal of Ares. Three times he killed nine men. On the fourth try he rushed in like a madman, but there, Patroclus, was the end of your prowess revealed. Terrible Phoebus met you in the desperate fighting. He had come down into the noise and confusion, but Patroclus didn't realize it, since Apollo dropped a pall of darkness that enclosed everything. He stood behind Patroclus and smacked him on the back, between his broad shoulders, with the palm of his hand. The impact sent his eyes spinning around. Phoebus Apollo knocked the helmet off his head. It crashed and rolled under the horses' feet. The hair on the crest of the visored helmet was stained with blood and dust. Never before had the gods allowed that helmet with its horsehair plume to be stained with dust, since it protected the divine head and handsome face of Achilles. But, now Zeus gave it to

Hector to wear on his head, since his destruction was coming
closer.   800

Everything that Patroclus had in his hands, the long spear,
the shield that reached to his ankles with its straps, fell to the
ground. Phoebus Apollo loosened the breastplate and enclosed
his mind in blindness, weakening his glorious limbs. Patroclus
stood in a daze. A Dardanian man came up from behind and
hit Patroclus midway between the shoulders with a sharp spear
at close range. He was Euphorbus Panthousson, who excelled
over those his age for hurling the spear, driving horses, and
being fast on his feet. He had taken twenty warriors in his
first time in warfare. Wouldn't you know, Patroclus, charioteer,
that the first one to hit you, didn't take you down? Euphorbus
snatched the spear from the flesh and ran back to blend in with
the throng. He didn't make a stand, even though Patroclus was
unarmed in the heated conflict. Struck by the god and weakened
by the spear, Patroclus withdrew back into the squadrons of
his comrades to avoid his fate.   817

When Hector saw greathearted Patroclus, wounded by a
spear, retreating, he came from among the formations and
struck him in the lower abdomen with his spear, driving it
through. Patroclus fell with a thud. And great was the grief in the
troops of the Acheans.   822

It was like when a lion attacks a warlike boar with overwhelming force. The two of them in the peaks of the mountains fight ferociously over a meager spring. They both want to
drink. There is much gasping from the one that is brought
down. So it was with the valiant son of Menoetius as he died.
Hector Priamson came close to finish Patroclus with his spear,
boasting with winged words: "Patroclus, once you claimed
you would plow over our city and take off with our Trojan
women. Though they are free, you claimed you would take
them in your ships to your beloved homeland. You fool! You
longed to fight for the women in front of the fast horses of
Hector, even though you were on foot. With my spear, I am

foremost among the war-loving Trojans. Afterward, I protect them because I have to. But the buzzards there will eat you. Scoundrel, Achilles is brave but he did not come to your aid, he who ordered you to come here and make a stand against me: 'Do not return to the hollow ships, Patroclus, charioteer, not until you have sliced man-killing Hector's tunic to pieces and leave it bloody around his chest.' This is what he said. You were stupid to let him persuade you." 842

And Patroclus, charioteer, you answered him in your waning gasps: "Now Hector, you make a grandiose boast. Zeus Cronusson and Apollo gave you a victory. They brought me down easily. They themselves took away my armor. If as many as twenty men were like you, I would have taken all down under my spear. Instead, it was my fate that the son of Leto was to kill me, and of men it was Euphorbus who struck the blow. You were third in line to strike me. And something else I will tell you, and fix it in your mind. You yourself will not live long. For I tell you surely that death stands nearby, and a terrible end awaits you at the hands of Achilles, the exceptional grandson of Aeacus."

Having so spoken, the end of death closed in around him. His soul took flight from his limbs and set off for Hades, leaving behind his manhood and youth, and moaning because of that. And glorious Hector said to him, even as he was dying: "Patroclus, why now do you prophesy destruction for me? Who knows if Achilles, son of Thetis, with her beautiful hair, might be first to perish, struck by my spear?" 861

So Hector spoke. Then he stuck out his heel and pulled his brazen spear from the wound, and pushed the body faceup with the shaft. Immediately, he set off with the spear after Automedon, the godlike attendant of the fleet-footed grandson of Aeacus. Hector was keen to hit him. But the fast horses carried Automedon away, the ones that the gods gave to Peleus as a magnificent gift. 867

Book 17

I t did not escape the notice of Menelaus, war-loving son of Atreus, that Patroclus was taken down by the Trojans in the fiery conflict. Armed in gleaming bronze he went through the front lines to him. He went as would a mother cow on hearing the cries of her firstborn calf, when she recognizes that the cry is from her own child. In that way red-haired Menelaus went over to Patroclus. He stood with his spear and his shield, which was balanced all around, in front of the corpse, eager to kill anybody who came against him.

8

And neither did Euphorbus, the spearman son of Panthous, miss the fact that the exceptional Patroclus had fallen. He stood close to him and spoke to war-loving Menelaus: "Go away, noble-born Menelaus Atreusson, Commander of the Troops. Back off, and leave the corpse, and the gory trophy armor. Since I am the one of the Trojans and their famous allies who first hit Patroclus with my spear in the furious fighting, Hector will not be alone in winning fame. This will allow me to do so as well; it is a worthy thing for us both to win glory. So, back off, or I will make a cast on you, and take away your sweet spirit."

17

Exceedingly angry at that, red-haired Menelaus replied: "Father Zeus, it is not a pretty thing to boast in such an insolent manner! Especially since the man has not so much courage as a leopard, or a lion, or a destructive wild boar, who has the greatest spirit in his chest and delights in his strength. The spearmen sons of Panthous are not so spirited! Nor have they the might of the noble horseman Hyperenor who easily achieved his manhood when he rushed on me and made his challenge, claiming that I was the sorriest of the Danaan warriors. But I'll tell you this: he did not go home on his feet to give pleasure to his loving wife and joy to his noble parents. Euphorbus, if you make a stand against me, I will certainly loosen your spirit in the same way. Instead, I order you to pull back and go into the throng before you suffer some terrible harm because you came against me. I know you to be a fool!"   32

So Menelaus spoke, but Euphorbus did not obey. He answered: "Now, noble-born Menelaus, we both know that you will pay the penalty for killing my brother. You talked about it, boasting about making a widow of his wife in the recess of his new chamber, and of bringing sadness to his parents. But I will bring an end to their misery and wailing if I hit your head and carry both it and your armor to Panthous and noble Frontis. It will not be long that this deed is untested for either valor or cowardice."   42

So, Euphorbus spoke, and he struck Menelaus's shield that was balanced all around, but his bronze did not break through; the spear point bent in the mighty shield. Menelaus Atreusson next rushed with his bronze, making a prayer to father Zeus. As Euphorbus was pulling back the spear Menelaus struck him in the base of the mouth. The bronze sped forward, obedient to the heavy hand that sent it, and the point went completely through Euphorbus's soft palate and the neck. He fell with a thud, and his armor crashed around him.   50

His hair was drenched with blood. Like the curls of the Graces, it was cinched up with gold and silver. It was as when a gardener tends the sprout of a luxuriant olive tree in a remote place. When it has absorbed enough water it produces beautiful foliage. The breezes of all the Winds rustle the leaves, and it produces white flowers. But high winds come with many storms and pull it from its hole, spreading it out on the earth. It was like that when Menelaus Atreusson killed the son of Panthous, the spearman Euphorbus, and stripped off his armor.   60

It was like when a mountain-bred lion, obedient to its valiant nature, snatches one of the best cows in a grazing herd. First off, the lion grabs her by the neck and crushes it with his powerful teeth. Next, he feasts by gorging on the blood and entrails.

There are dogs around him and herdsmen shrieking in front of him, but none wishes to take him on. Instead, pale white fear seizes them. So it was that none of those around the fallen Euphorbus had the guts to stand against glorious Menelaus.   69

There might the son of Atreus easily have carried off the celebrated arms of Panthous's son, had not Phoebus Apollo eyed him with annoyance. He rushed over to Hector, equal of Ares, taking on the guise of a man, the Ciconian commander Mentes, and spoke to Hector with winged words: "Hector, you could now run in pursuit of the invincible horses belonging to the warlike grandson of Aeacus, but they have proven calamitous to mortal men who sought to subdue and drive them other than Achilles, who was born of an immortal mother. In the meantime, though, Menelaus, warlike son of Atreus, has come beside Patroclus and killed one of the best of the Trojans, Euphorbus Panthousson, bringing an end to his furious valor."   81

After saying this, the god went back into the struggle of men. Sharp grief completely overloaded the dark mind of Hector. He cautiously peered out from the ranks of men, and immediately recognized Euphorbus's beautiful armor that was being taken away while he lay on the ground, blood flowing from the wound where he was struck. Hector set out through the front lines, armed in glowing red bronze that clanged sharply as he went along. His armor was like the unquenchable flames of Hephaestus.   89

He did not escape the notice of the son of Atreus as Hector gave a shrill war cry. Upset, Menelaus spoke to his own greathearted spirit: "What now? If I leave Patroclus, who lies here because of my honor, and the beautiful armor he wears, none of the Danaans would respect me for it; they would be angry with me, even though if I stay I will be fighting Hector and the Trojans by myself. It is not just one coming toward me, but many—Hector is leading all of them here. But why am I debating these things in my own mind? Whenever a warrior chooses to fight in front of a crazed man a god has honored, he is quickly swept up into a huge disaster! No one who saw both my and Hector's advance would be upset with me, since he fights with a god alongside him. But if I could find Aias, good at the war cry, we can both come back and remember our warring spirit, even if there is a demon in front of us. We might somehow save the corpse for Achilles Peleusson. That would make the best of a bad situation." 105

Those things rushed around in his mind until the ranks of Trojans advanced on him, with Hector leading them. Then he pulled back, leaving the corpse behind. He lingered just a bit before turning around, like a lion with a full mane that both dogs and men are chasing from a country house with spears and the sound of shouting. His valiant heart thickens in his chest, but he goes away from the courtyard grudgingly. That was how red-haired Menelaus left Patroclus. 113

He stood briefly before turning when he arrived at the companies of his comrades, peering about cautiously for a glimpse of Aias, the huge son of Telamon. He quickly caught sight of him on the left of all the fighting, encouraging his comrades, since Phoebus Apollo hurled an immense fear into them. Menelaus set off at a run and soon stood beside Aias: "Aias, my friend, let us hurry to dead Patroclus so that we can carry his body back to Achilles, even though it has been stripped. Hector, of the helmet with the waving plume, already has the armor." 122

So Menelaus spoke, and he roused the spirit in warlike Aias. He went through the front lines with red-haired Menelaus. After Hector got hold of the famous armor, he dragged Patroclus, so that he might cut the head from the shoulders with sharp bronze, keeping the corpse for the Trojan dogs. Aias closed in carrying his shield that was like a siege tower. Hector quickly pulled back, went into the throng of his comrades, and mounted his chariot. He gave the beautiful armor to the

Trojans to carry back to the city as his great trophy. Aias enclosed the son of Menoetius under his wide shield, standing like a lion would around its cubs, lest hunters come upon them while they are going through a forest. He rejoices in his might, pulling down his brow to surround the eyes in a scowl. So it was that Aias approached the hero Patroclus. Standing close by was war-loving Menelaus Atreusson. A huge grief swelled inside his breast.   139

Glaucus, son of Hippolochus, commander of the Lycian warriors, scowled at Hector and laid harsh words on him: "Hector, you lack the character required to be the best man in a fight. Yet again, you get yourself a fine trophy while being a cowardly woman! I think that now, you should somehow save the city and the surrounding area with only your troops who are native to Troy. None of the Lycians will be fighting against the Danaans around the city. It was no pleasure fighting furiously against warriors without ceasing. You are a disgrace; you would save an inferior man from those in the throng, yet Sarpedon, who was at the same time a guest-friend and a comrade, you left behind to become prey and spoils for the Argives. When he was alive, he was helpful both to the city and to you yourself. But even so, you didn't dare protect him from dogs. If there are one or two of the Lycian warriors who obey me, we are going home now.   155

"If we do, there will be horrific death and destruction for Troy. Would that some who were courageous send unflinching strength into the Trojans, such as these Lycians brought, sent by their fathers to make war against the enemies. Then we would immediately drag Patroclus back to Troy. If we did, even though he is dead, the Argives might, with equal speed, release Sarpedon's beautiful armor. They could then take possession of the corpse in an exchange, since he was the attendant of a man who is by far the best of the Argives and their attendants, who fight in close beside the ships. But you did not have the courage to make a stand against greathearted Aias, who looked down

at you with burning eyes and shouted. And you did not dare to
go straight at him, because he is better than you!"   168

Frowning, Hector, of the helmet with the waving plume, replied: "Glaucus, why are you talking so arrogantly? I would
certainly have sworn that you had the best mind of all those living in fertile Lycia. But now, I am insulted by everything you
say. So you claim that I would not make a stand against the giant Aias. But be assured that I never tremble in battle or from
the pounding of horses' hooves. But always, the mind of Zeus,
who bears the aegis, is better. He easily sends the brave man to
rout or chooses for him victory, when he himself rouses the man
to fight.   178

"But, come here, dear friend. Stand beside me and look at
what is going on, or else I will be cowardly all day long, as
you were saying. Although some of the Danaans will be
charged with valor, I will keep them away from dead Patroclus." 182

So Hector spoke. He called out to the Trojans in a loud voice:
"Trojans, and Lycians, and Dardanians, who fight in close; warriors, my friends, remember your furious valor, while I put on
the beautiful armor of exceptional Achilles. I stripped it off
Patroclus after killing him with my might."   187

So shouted Hector, of the helmet with the waving plume.
And he left the raging conflict and set off running fast after his
comrades, who had not yet gone very far on their swift feet,
carrying the famous armor of Peleus back to the city. Hector
stood apart from that fighting, which brings tears to men, to
change his armor. You may be sure, he gave his to the war-
loving Trojans to be carried back to sacred Troy, and he donned
the immortal armor of Achilles Peleusson that the heavenly
gods provided for his dear father. In his old age he had passed it
along to his son; but the son was not to grow old in the armor
of his father.   197

Zeus the cloud-gatherer watched from far off as Hector
dressed himself in the armor of the divine son of Peleus. He
shook his head and thought to himself: "Oh, you wretch! You

have no thought of death, though it will certainly come closer. You would put on the immortal armor of the best man, when others tremble before him. You killed his companion who was both mighty and kind. In defiance of custom you took the armor from Patroclus's head and shoulders. Well, for now I will grant you great power. The penalty for your transgression is that nothing of yours is to return home from the fighting. Andromache will not receive the famous armor of Peleus."   208

And the son of Cronus nodded his black eyebrows at Hector as he cinched the armor around his flesh, and the terrible warlike Ares, Enyalius, entered him. And as it filled him, it increased his strength and valor within. He set out, shouting loudly among the famous allies, appearing before all of them in the gleaming armor of the greathearted son of Peleus. He went about rousing the spirit of each one: Mesthles, and Glaucus, and Medon, and Thersilochus, and Asteropaeus, and Deisenor, and Hippothous, and Phorcys, and Chromius, and even Ennomus, the bird augur. He roused them with winged words: "Listen, you countless ranks of allies, who are our neighbors. I am not talking to the masses, nor am I hosting a festival, which has roused each to come from your homes to our city. I am mindful that it is to protect the Trojan wives and young children from the warlike Acheans. I am exhausted from making gifts and feeding the troops just to secure their goodwill, but I will rouse the spirit in each one of you. There are just two things that are true for one who turns back from flight to advance on the enemy, either he perishes or is saved. But that is the sweet secret of war. Whoever might make Aias yield, and then pull dead Patroclus toward the Trojan horsemen, with him I will divide the spoils of armor so that half is his, and I will take half for myself. His glory will be the same as mine."   232

So Hector spoke, and they charged straight at the Danaans with spears raised up and bristling. They hoped devoutly in their hearts to pull the corpse from under Aias Telamonson. What

fools they were! Aias took away the breath of many who were
so minded. 236

Aias said to Menelaus, good at the war cry: "O dear friend,
noble-born Menelaus, I no longer have hope that we ourselves
will return home from the war. As much as I feared that the
corpse of Patroclus would soon satisfy the hunger of dogs and
birds, so fearful am I for my head and what it might suffer, and
yours, too, when Hector encloses us all in a cloud of war. When
that happens, utter destruction is to be revealed to us. But come
now, call out to the best of the Danaans. Maybe one might
hear." 245

So Aias spoke, and Menelaus, of the shrill war cry, complied.
He shouted to the Danaans with a sound that traveled a long
way: "O friends, chiefs, and counselors of the Argives, who drink
at public expense beside Agamemnon and Menelaus, sons of
Atreus. Each of you directs troops, and has received honor and
glory from Zeus. It is hard for me to see every one of you, because the struggle of war is kindled so intensely. But every one
of you should come with me—you will blame yourselves if
Patroclus becomes the sport of Trojan dogs." 255

So Menelaus shouted. And swift Aias Oïleusson heard him
clearly, and was first to come running back through the flaming conflict. With him came Idomeneus and his companion
Meriones, equal of man-killing Enyalius. Who could say from
his own mind the names of so many of the others of the Acheans who were roused from the rear of the fighting?

The Trojans slashed their way forward in a dense formation
with Hector in the lead. It was like when a great wave in the
flood of a river, fed by the water Zeus sends, roars as the current carries it forward, and resounds all around as the headlands
spew it out onto the sea. So great was the shouting of the Trojans as they went along. On the other hand, the Acheans stood
around the son of Menoetius unified in spirit, forming a palisade with their bucklers overlaid with bronze. Around them the

son of Cronus poured a dense, gleaming shimmer. He had never despised the son of Menoetius while he lived and was the attendant of the grandson of Aeacus, and he would hate for him to become the prey of the Trojan dogs because of their hostility. And so Zeus roused Patroclus's comrades to protect him. 273

At first, the Trojans pushed toward the bright-eyed Acheans and they shrank back with fear, abandoning the corpse. But the haughty Trojans didn't slay even one of the Acheans, though they eagerly hurled their spears. Instead, they pulled the corpse back a little bit while the Acheans were pulling back. Then Aias quickly wheeled around on them. He was the best looking and had the best fighting technique of all of them, next to the exceptional son of Peleus. Aias charged through the front lines with valor like that of a wild boar that wheels around in the defiles of the mountains, easily scattering dogs and vigorous youths. In such a way did glorious Aias, son of illustrious Telamon, charge the Trojan ranks, and scatter those gathered around Patroclus, keen to drag him back to their city and gain glory. 287

For sure, Hippothous, the glorious son of Lathus the Pelasgian, took Patroclus by the foot during the intense fighting and tied a belt around the tendons near the ankle of both his feet. This delighted Hector and the Trojans. But evil came swiftly on him, and those who sent him could not prevent it, though they wished they could have. Aias came though the throng and charged Hippothous. He smashed the helmet with its bronze cheek-pieces. Aias's beefy hand drove the point of a huge spear through the helmet and the horsehair crest. Bloody brains oozed out from the wound around the spear's socket. There his strength was loosed, and Patroclus's foot dropped from his hands to the ground, and lay there. Being close, Hippothous fell facedown on top of the corpse, far from the very fertile Larisa. Hippothous had not yet returned to his beloved parents the customary compensation of his upbringing and education. For his

was but a short life, brought down by the spear of greathearted
Aias.   303

Hector made a cast back at Aias with his shining spear, but
Aias saw it coming and avoided it by a hair. The spear hit Schedius, the greathearted son of Iphitus. Schedius was the best by
far of the Phoceans. He dwelt in the palace in famous Panopeus
and ruled over many men. The spear hit him squarely underneath his collarbone. The tip of the bronze spearhead lodged in
the base of his shoulder. He fell with a thud, and his armor
crashed on top of him.   311

Aias went around Hippothous and struck Phorcys, the warlike son of Phaenops, in the stomach. The bronze smashed a
hole in his breastplate and through it gushed his entrails. He fell
in the dust and grabbed the dirt in the palm of his hand. Under
Aias's assault, both the Trojan front lines and glorious Hector
pulled back. The Acheans gave a great shout. They dragged off
the corpses of Hippothous and Phorcys, and loosed their armor from their shoulders.   318

At that point might the Trojans have gone helplessly back up
to Troy, trounced by the war-loving Acheans. The Argives
would have taken glory, even though that was contrary to the
plan of Zeus. However, Apollo himself roused Aeneas, taking a
form like that of the herald Periphas Epytesson. Himself a herald, Epytes had grown old being a herald in the house of his old
father, Anchises. Periphas was known to have valuable counsel
in his mind. In his guise, Apollo, son of Zeus, said: "Aeneas, how
can you preserve Troy like this, even if a god is against you? I
have seen how other men held on to the district, trusting in
their might, and strength, and manliness, and their enlisted men.
I have seen other men even beyond having fear! Zeus favors
victory for us over the Acheans, but you yourselves tremble
constantly and do not fight."   332

So he spoke, and Aeneas realized that he was looking
at Apollo, who shoots from afar. He shouted a loud war cry to

Hector and the other commanders of the Trojans and their allies: "It would be a disgrace for us to go back up to Troy now as
helpless cowards, whipped by the war-loving Acheans! One of
the gods has stood close beside me and told me that Zeus, the
greatest master of fighting, is going to run to our aid. We
should go straight at the Danaans, so they can't transport the
dead Patroclus to the ships unmolested."   341

So spoke Aeneas, and he jumped out and stood well in front
of the front lines, and so turned them around to make a stand
against the Acheans. Aeneas struck Leocritus with a spear. Leocritus was the son of Arisbas and the worthy friend of Lycomedes, who was aggrieved at his fall. Lycomedes went and stood
close by and cast his shining spear, and he hit Apisaon Hippasusson, Shepherd of the Troops, in the liver, under his diaphragm. Immediately, his knees were loosed beneath him. He
had come from Paeonia, with its rich soil, and was beside Asteropaeus, a brilliant fighter.   351

Warlike Asteropaeus was deeply grieved when Apisaon fell,
and he went straight at the Danaans, determined to beat them
off. But there wasn't to be any headway yet. They stood with
their shields completely locked around Patroclus, with their
spears in front of them. Aias went around everywhere vigorously giving orders. He gave the order that none should retreat
back from the corpse, nor should any stand out from the other
Acheans in the front lines to fight. Rather, they were to stand
close together to fight hand to hand around the corpse. That was
what giant Aias ordered, and the ground was soaked with crimson blood. Those who were closest fell in the same place. The
corpses of the haughty Trojans and their allies were in the same
pile as the Danaans. For those who fight, it is never bloodless.
The armies waste away to much fewer men. But, to be sure,
they always remembered to protect each other from terrible
death.   365

So they fought in the likeness of a fire, and you could not say
whether the sun was dimmed, or the moon either, so great was

the darkness that enclosed the best men as they made their stand around the dead son of Menoetius. The rest of the Trojans and well-armed Acheans were at ease fighting under the open sky: the brilliant rays of the sun fluttered down, and there was no cloud to be seen anywhere on earth, even in the mountains. They took breaks in fighting, avoiding each other's misery-causing missiles, since many were thrown. But those in the middle suffered the pain and darkness of war, so worn down by the pitiless bronze were the best men. 377

Elsewhere, there were two men who did not know that exceptional Patroclus was dead, the illustrious warriors Thrasymedes and Antilochus. They still thought he was alive, fighting in the forefront of the Trojan horde. Both watched the death and rout of their comrades as they themselves fought some distance away, having been ordered by their father Nestor to drive the war away from the ships. 383

All day long there rose for those around the corpse an intense struggle. There was no letup for them; they were constantly tired and sweaty. The knees, and shins, and feet of each tired and dripped with sweat. Their hands and eyes were spattered with filth as they fought around the brave attendant of the fleet-footed grandson of Aeacus. 388

It was like when a man sets out to make a shield from the hide of a great bull, he delivers it saturated with oil to a group of men standing around in a circle. Once all are in place, they receive it and pull on it. Immediately, the moisture goes, and with much pulling the oil is absorbed. In the same way were those in that tiny space pulling on the corpse from opposite sides. The Trojans wanted very much in their hearts to pull it to Troy, and the Acheans desiring equally to take it to the hollow ships. Around the corpse there arose a savage tug-of-war. Watching it, neither Ares, who rouses the troops to battle, nor Athena condemned it, but it angered them. Such was the evil struggle of men and horses harsh when Zeus extended the fighting over Patroclus on account of his fury. 401

But where he was, noble Achilles knew nothing about Patroclus's death. He thought Patroclus was far away from the ships fighting under the Trojans' wall. Never, in his heart, had he expected Patroclus to die; he had wished for Patroclus to return home alive after getting close to the Trojan gates. Achilles never imagined Patroclus would try sacking the city without him, nor with him, either. He had learned from listening to his mother when they were alone many times as she told him about the plan of great Zeus. But his mother never told him he would be hit by such evil, that his friend whom he loved most, more by far than anyone, would perish.   411

They stood around the corpse and constantly fought each other with sharp spears. There was no letup. So might one of the brazen-shirted Acheans have said: "O friends, we are not going to return to the hollow ships with more glory. Instead, the black earth in this place may gape open for all of us. It will be better for us immediately if we yield this one to those noble horsemen, the Trojans, and they drag the corpse back to their city and win glory."   419

And so might one of the greathearted Trojans have responded: "O friends, if it is fate that all alike be brought down beside this warrior in this way, no one can ever stop the fighting." So he might have spoken and have roused strength in each one. So they fought on. The din of iron went up to the heavens of bronze through the lifeless upper air.   425

The horses of the grandson of Aeacus were away from the fighting, weeping. They had been weeping since first learning that their charioteer had fallen in the dust under the hand of man-killing Hector. Automedon, the valiant son of Diores, cracked his whip many times to get them running fast, tried many gentle words, and many threats. But the two of them desired neither to go back to the ships on the flat Hellespont, nor into battle with the Acheans. Instead, they stood stock-still like a column erected beside the mound of a man or woman who has died. So they stood motionless with their variegated chariot, their heads bowed down to the ground. Hot tears poured from their eyes down onto the earth as they wept, longing for their charioteer. Their handsome manes were stained by the tears dropping off the under-harness from their yoke on both sides. 440

Watching them weep, the son of Cronus felt pity for them. He shook his head, and said to himself: "Oh you miserable pair, why, oh why, did we give you to King Peleus who was mortal, when you both are ageless and immortal? Did I do it so that you would have pain among unlucky men? There is nothing anywhere more miserable than man, of all the things that breathe or crawl upon the earth. But Hector Priamson is not to drive you or ride on your dazzling chariot. I will not allow it. Is it not enough that he both has the armor and boasts the way he does? I shall fix strength firmly in the knees and hearts of you both, so that you can save Automedon from the fighting and take him to the hollow ships. I will grant the Trojans glory to kill a while longer, until they arrive at the well-benched ships as the sun sets and sacred dusk comes." 455

So saying, Zeus breathed healthy strength into the horses. Both of their manes shot up from the dust and they pranced along, pulling their chariot quickly among the Trojans and the Acheans. Automedon fought behind them, though he grieved for his comrade. He rushed with the horses like a buzzard after geese. It was easy for him to put the Trojans to flight from the mass of men underneath him. But since he was alone in the sacred chariot, it wasn't possible to attack with a spear and drive the swift horses at the same time, so he couldn't kill any men as he rushed back. But after some time, a comrade caught sight of him: Alcimedon, son of Laerces Haemonson. He stood behind the chariot and spoke to Automedon: "Automedon, which of the gods put such an unprofitable idea in your head, and robbed you of your worthy mind? You are here alone in

front of the Trojans, at the forefront of the throng. Yet your
comrade is dead and Hector delights in wearing the armor of
Aeacus's grandson on his shoulders."   473

Automedon, the son of Diores, answered: "Alcimedon, who
else of the Acheans could drive the immortal horses with skill
in handling and strength equal to Patroclus, a master equal to
a god when he was alive? Now though, death and fate have come
for him. But you take the whip and the shining reins. I'll get
down so that I can fight."   480

So Automedon spoke and Alcimedon, helping out, hopped
quickly up into the chariot and grabbed the whip and reins in
his hands. Automedon jumped down, and glorious Hector saw
it immediately, and said to Aeneas who was close by: "Aeneas,
counselor of the brazen-shirted Trojans, I recognize the two
horses there that belong to the fleet-footed grandson of Aeacus.
They have appeared in the fighting with incompetent charioteers. I'd like to snatch them away, if you're game, since nobody
would dare make a stand against the two of us in the fighting
of Ares."   490

So Hector spoke and the illustrious son of Anchises agreed.
Both of them went straight off, shouting and taking their
bull's-hide shields, which had much bronze cladding, on their
shoulders. With them on both sides were Chromius and
godlike Aretus. They intensely desired to kill both Automedon and Alcimedon and to drive away the horses with the
beautiful necks. What fools they were! They were not going to
return bloodless from an encounter with Automedon.   498

Automedon prayed to father Zeus, and the somber con-
sciousness within him was filled with valor and strength. He
said to his loyal comrade: "Alcimedon, do not keep the horses
far off from me. Instead they should be breathing hard on my
back, for I do not think I can hold out for long against mighty
Hector Priamson, before he kills both of us and drives off with
the horses, with the beautiful manes. That might incite rout
among the ranks of the Achean warriors, but then again,

maybe he will be the one killed in the forefront of the Trojans."   506

So speaking, he called out to the Aiantes and to Menelaus: "Aiantes and Menelaus, you commanders of the Argives, surely you should turn away from the corpse. You, the best around it who came to protect it, ought to protect the two of us from a dreadful fate, while we are still alive. Hector and Aeneas, the best of the Trojans, are pressing down here the weight of war, which causes men to weep. I for sure will send these matters to lie on the knees of the gods, the concerns of Zeus."   515

That done, Automedon shifted a long spear about in his palm and threw it. He hit the shield of Aretus that was balanced all around. But the shield did not hold off the bronze that went straight through, and drove through the armored belt into the stomach at the base of the belly. It was like when a young man cuts behind the horns of an ox from the fields with a sharp ax. It cuts all the way through, but the animal lunges forward as it falls. In the same way Aretus lunged forward as he fell faceup. The sharp spear in his belly shook violently as his limbs were loosed.   524

Hector made a cast on Automedon with his shining spear. But Automedon saw it and ducked, averting it. The long spear was fixed in the ground behind him and the butt end of the spear was set into oscillation, thrown there with the force of powerful Ares.   529

And at that point might Automedon and Alcimedon have been overwhelmed in close combat with swords, had not the Aiantes promptly split themselves away from those around the corpse. They came through the throng, summoned by their friend. So terrified were they that Hector, Aeneas, and the godlike Chromius drew back again. They left Aretus lying down there with his pierced heart. Automedon, with speed equal to Ares, stripped him of his armor and boasted: "Certainly, this takes away a tiny bit of the grief from my heart over the death of the son of Menoetius, though this was a worse man I killed."   539

So saying, he took the gory armor and put it in the chariot. As he himself went off, his feet and hands above were bloody, like a lion that has taken down a bull and eaten it.   542

Back beside Patroclus was set a fierce fight, a hard thing it was and it brought many tears. Loud-thundering Zeus had changed his mind, and sent Athena to rouse the Danaans. She raised up the struggle as she went down from the heavens. She was like the violet rainbow that Zeus extends from heaven to be a sign of war or of chilly winter, which gives men a rest from work in the fields and from caring for sheep. In the same way she came down in a dense violet cloud on the tribe of the Acheans and roused each man. First she spoke to the son of Atreus, powerful Menelaus, to encourage him. Taking the likeness of Phoenix, both his form and his tireless voice, she came close and said: "Menelaus, there will be disgrace and reproof for you if the swift dogs tear the loyal friend of the illustrious Achilles to pieces under the Trojans' wall. Instead, be brave! Rouse the troops!"

Menelaus, good at the war cry, answered her: "Phoenix, Father, old man, born long ago, I would do as you say if Athena would give me courage, and would hold off the casts of missiles. If both she and I were there, I could stand beside Patroclus and protect him. But I have a profound foreboding of death in my heart—Zeus gives Hector glory and the might of a dreadful fire; he cannot be stopped with bronze."   566

So Menelaus spoke, and sharp-eyed Athena was overjoyed that he prayed to her first among all the gods. She put might in his shoulders and knees, and into his chest she put the courage of a stable fly, because the fly works tirelessly, even though it is restrained from biting the skin of a man. To it, a man's blood is sweet to the taste. With such courage she filled Menelaus's somber mind. He went over to Patroclus and made a cast with his shining spear.   574

There was among the Trojans one Podes, a son of Eetion, both rich and worthy. Hector held Podes in great esteem in the district, and he was a favorite among the revelers at Hector's feasts. Red-haired Menelaus hit Podes when he rushed forward trying to rout Menelaus. He hit him in his armored belt, and the bronze drove straight through. Podes fell with a thud. Afterward, Menelaus Atreusson dragged the corpse along the ranks of his comrades.　　　581

　　Apollo stood close to Hector and roused him, taking on the guise of Phaenops Asiusson, who was the best loved of the guest-friends. He lived in a palace in Abydos. Looking like Phaenops, Apollo, who works from afar, said: "Hector, who is there left of the Acheans who doesn't frighten you? You tremble so from fear of Menelaus, who was such a weakling in the past. But now, by himself, he lifts a corpse from under the Trojans and carries it off. He killed your loyal and honorable comrade Podes, son of Eetion, in the front lines." So Apollo spoke, and a black cloud of grief enveloped Hector, and he went off through the front lines armed in glowing red bronze.　　　592

　　And, at that point, Zeus took the tasseled aegis and shook it. Ida was covered by clouds and Zeus hurled huge thunderbolts as he shook the aegis. He gave victory to the Trojans, and to the Acheans, rout.　　　596

Peneleos the Boeotian was the first to run away. He was hit in the shoulder with a spear as he turned to flee from the enemy. The point grazed him and the spear point of Polydamas scratched its way close to the bone, since he had hit Peneleos at close range as he passed. There, Hector struck Leïtus, son of the greathearted Alectryon, on the hand near the wrist, bringing his martial ardor to an end. He trembled as he looked cautiously around, since he could no longer fight the Trojans with a spear in that hand. Idomeneus was fighting beside Leïtus, and hit Hector in his breastplate, on his chest beside the nipple. But the shaft of the long spear broke. At that, the Trojans shouted, and Hector made a cast on Idomeneus Deucalionson, as he stood in his chariot. Hector was at a distance and so missed by a little.

Nevertheless, he did hit Coeranus, the attendant and charioteer of Meriones. Coeranus had accompanied Idomeneus from crowded Lyttus. They came by foot after leaving their ships, which had rowers on both sides. And it would have given the Trojans much glory, if Coeranus had not driven the swift-hoofed horses fast. He protected the Acheans from doomsday, but his own spirit perished at the hand of man-killing Hector. He was hit in the jaw, under the ear. The spear pushed from the base of the teeth, and cut through the middle of his tongue. Coeranus was torn from the chariot, and the reins poured down onto the ground. Meriones stooped over and took them from the plain with his own hands and said to Idomeneus: "Lay on the lash until you arrive at the swift ships. You know that might is no longer on the Acheans' side." So Meriones spoke and Idomeneus cracked the whip over the horses, with their beautiful manes, and drove them to the hollow ships, since fear had taken hold of his spirit.   625

But it did not escape the notice of greathearted Aias and Menelaus that Zeus had turned the tide of battle to the Trojans. Between them, Telamonian Aias was first to speak: "By now even a total idiot would know that father Zeus himself is helping the Trojans. Somebody is hit by every one of the weapons they've thrown, whether the one casting is skilled or not. It is always Zeus who aims it, always! Meanwhile our casts fall to the ground, wasted. But come, no matter what, let's think about what the best plan is for dragging away Patroclus's corpse and, by returning it, bringing joy to our beloved comrades and ourselves, too. They are no doubt concerned about what they see going on, and they are saying that since man-killing Hector has strength and invincible hands, he will fall on the black ships. I wish there were some comrade who could quickly take a message to the son of Peleus. I don't think he has learned the horrible news that his beloved friend has perished. But I can't see any of the Acheans anyway, because a mist has settled on us and the horses alike. Father Zeus, protect the sons of the Acheans from

the mist; make it clear. Grant that I may see, even if I perish because the sun shines, since certainly it pleases you thus." 647

So Aias spoke and the father was filled with grief for him,
and his eye welled a tear. Immediately, a cloud pushed it away,
and the mist was scattered. The sun shone and all the fighting
was revealed to Aias. He then spoke to Menelaus, good at the
war cry: "Look around now, noble-born Menelaus, and see if
Antilochus, son of greathearted Nestor, is still alive. If he is, we
should dispatch him right away to tell warlike Achilles that the
friend he loved above all others has perished." 655

So Aias spoke, and Menelaus, of the shrill war cry, complied,
and he set off like a lion that is worn down from provoking both
dogs and men who would not allow it to take a one of the fat
cows. They were on guard all night, and the lion, desirous of
meat, made straight for it. The men resisted and sent a barrage
of spears, rushing the lion and brandishing flaming torches from
their hands. At dawn, though still eager, the lion retreats with
a longing in its heart. In the same way Menelaus, of the shrill
war cry, left Patroclus. He was going, but very much did not
want to do it. He had a ghastly fear that the Acheans might not
hold their position around him and, in the face of a hard rout,
Patroclus might be left prey for those who were hostile. 667

He gave stern orders to both Meriones and the Aiantes:
"Aiantes and Meriones, commanders, one should remember
that miserable Patroclus was kind. He was consistently sweet-
tempered with everybody while he was alive. Now, however,
death and fate have come." 672

So saying, red-haired Menelaus set off. He looked cautiously
all around, like an eagle, which they say has the keenest sight
of all the things that fly under the heavens, and even those that
have swift feet beneath. A rabbit hiding under the thick foliage
of a shrub does not escape his notice. Instead, he stoops on it
and swiftly grabs it, taking away its breath. In the same way you,
noble-born Menelaus, turned your shining eyes all around over
the groups of your comrades in the fighting to see whether

Nestor's son was still alive. He quickly recognized Antilochus
on the left of all the fighting, encouraging his comrades. Red-
haired Menelaus went over and said: "Antilochus, come closer
to hear some sad news that I wish I was not the source of. I think
now that as you look around you understand that a god has
turned fate toward the Danaans, and victory to the Trojans. Patroclus, the very best of the Acheans, is dead. It is a huge loss
for the Danaans. Run quickly to the ships of the Acheans and
tell Achilles. Maybe he could save the corpse and get it to his
ship the quickest. It is already stripped: Hector, of the helmet
with the waving plume, has the special armor."   693

So Menelaus spoke, and Antilochus was stunned. For a long
time dumbness robbed him of words. His eyes filled with tears
and his robust voice was stilled. Even so, he did not disregard
Menelaus's order. He gave his fine armor to his exceptional
comrade Laodocus, who was close by tending his solid-hoofed
horses for him, and Antilochus set off running.   699

Even as he wept, his feet carried him away from the fighting to deliver the horrible news to Achilles Peleusson. But you,
noble-born Menelaus, were concerned with protecting the
others who were tired. You did not realize that when Antilochus left, it would create apprehension among the Pylians,
now bereft of a leader. When Menelaus realized this, he sent
noble Thrasymedes to them, and he himself went running back
to the heroes near Patroclus, and stood beside the Aiantes. He
said: "I sent Antilochus off quickly on his way to the swift
ships and Achilles. But now I don't think that Achilles will be
coming at all, even though he will be angry at noble Hector.
There is no way that he could fight the Trojans naked and
unarmed. We should consider what the best plan is for us, just
what we can do to protect the corpse, and how we can escape
from this din and the Trojans."   715

Great Telamonian Aias replied: "Everything you said is correct, Menelaus! Now, you and Meriones slip under quickly and
lift the corpse and carry it from the struggle, while the two of

us behind take on the Trojans and noble Hector. We have the same heart, just as we have the same name! In the past we have stood beside one another in the hard fighting of Ares."   721

So spoke Aias. And they took the corpse into their arms and hoisted it up high with a great deal of effort. The Trojan troops behind them shouted as they watched the Acheans lifting the corpse. They made straight for it like dogs rushing on a wounded boar in front of youthful hunters. They are impetuous and run to destroy it, but when it turns on them, trusting in its own valor, they immediately back off, and turning away trembling, go off this way and that. So it was for the Trojans who followed steadily in groups, brandishing both swords and spears sharpened on both ends. But when the Aiantes turned around and made a stand against them, the Trojans' skin blanched, and there was not a single one who dared rushed forward to wrangle over the corpse.   734

Menelaus and Meriones were ardently carrying it from the fighting to the hollow ships. Around them was kindled a fight that was like a wildfire, which rushes on a city of men. Suddenly the flames rise up and houses are consumed in a great conflagration, and the force of the wind roars. So it was for the horses and warriors in the never ending din of those coming and going. Menelaus and Meriones were like mules clothed in powerful force, dragging a roof beam or a ship's timber along a steep pathway from a mountain. Their hearts are tired and worn down, and even sweaty, as they proceed. So it was for those who ardently carried the corpse.   746

At the same time, the Aiantes behind them held back the throng, like a promontory on a wooded plain holds back water that has been driven from a long way, making calamitous currents of mighty rivers. When the plain becomes flat they suddenly rush forward, but the currents do not have the strength to break through the promontory. In such a way did the Aiantes hold off the Trojans in the rear. But the Trojans followed on them, nonetheless, and two were especially prominent: Aeneas

Anchisesson and glorious Hector. It was like when a multitude of starlings or jays arrive, making a great discordance of rasping noise. A falcon sees them from afar and comes, bringing death to the small birds. So it was for Achean youths under the assault of Aeneas and Hector; they cried out in the same way, and forgot their warlike spirit. Much beautiful armor fell near and around the trench as the Danaans fled. But this was not the beginning of retreat from war.　　　　　761

Book 18

And so their combat took on the appearance of an incandescent fire.

Antilochus went on his speedy feet as messenger to Achilles, and found him in front of the ships, with their elevated sterns. Achilles was pondering in his heart how things were to play out. He was upset and said to himself: "Why in the world have the long-haired Acheans retreated from the plain back to the ships making such noise? Unless this is what my mother once told me about: the best of the Myrmidons still living would leave the light of the sun under the hands of the Trojans, and the gods are creating a crisis for me. It must be that the valiant son of Menoetius is dead. Horrible! I told him to return to the ships after saving them from the burning fire, and not to fight against mighty Hector." 14

Such thoughts raged in his mind, until the son of illustrious Nestor came close to deliver his distressing news, his eyes welling up with hot tears. "O dear son of warlike Peleus, you will learn something especially wrenching from this message. How I wish I were not the source of it. Patroclus lies dead, and there is intense fighting around his naked body. Hector, of the helmet with the waving plume, has already claimed the armor." 21

Antilochus spoke, and a dark cloud of grief enveloped Achilles. He took ashes with both hands and poured them on his head, and gently dusted his eyebrows. The black ash settled on his sweet-smelling tunic. He stretched out his own great body, lying in the dust, tearing out pieces of his hair with his own hands, disfiguring his head. The slaves that Achilles and Patroclus had taken as booty from their conquests screamed in horror and ran from the door over to warlike Achilles beating their breasts; their limbs collapsed underneath them. On the other

side, Antilochus wept bitterly as he took hold of Achilles's hands
and held them. Achilles's valiant heart was so strained that Antilochus was afraid he might slit his own throat with an iron
weapon. His groans were so agonizing that his revered mother
heard them from the depths of the sea. The many daughters of
Nereus were all gathered around him in the depths of the sea.
Those present were Glauce, and Thaleia, and Cymodoce, and
Nesaea, and Speo, and Thoe, and lovely-eyed Halia, and
Cymothoe, and Actaeë, and Limnoria, and Melite, and Iaera,
and Amphithoe, and Agave, and Doto, and Proto, and Pherousa,
and Dynamene, and Dexamene, and Amphinome, and Callin-
eira, Doris, and Panope, and renowned Galatia, and Nemertes,
and Apseudes, and Callianassa. And there was Clymene, and
Janira, and Janassa, and Maera, and Oreithyia, and Amathia, with
beautiful hair. These and other daughters of Nereus resided in
the depths of the sea, where a white cave had been fashioned
for them. Thetis was beside her old father, and wailed with
loud sobs when she heard her son. And they all beat their
breasts together when Thetis began her lamentation: "Listen,
sisters, daughters of Nereus, I speak so that you all may know
well the concerns of my heart. Oh, what a miserable soul I am!
I have a child, a most elegant, but ill-fated child. He is a son most
illustrious and mighty beyond the best of heroes. He was like
a sprout that shoots up in a fertile orchard. And I tended him as
he grew, and sent him in the beaked ships to Troy so that he
might fight against the Trojans. He will not return home to
Peleus's palace, but while he still lives and can see the light of
the sun, he is my concern, though I am not able to defend him.
But I am going, so that I might see my son, and hear what sadness has befallen him while he stays away from the campaign
of the war."   64

   So Thetis spoke, and left the cave. The sea nymphs went with
her, crying as much as she was. A wave of the sea split open
around them when they reached the fertile Trojan coast. They

came forward one by one where the ships of the Myrmidons were drawn up together in rows around Achilles. His revered mother stood beside him as he groaned deeply. She sobbed as she touched her son's head. Filled with grief, she spoke to him with winged words: "Child, why are you crying? What sadness has come to you? Out with it, hide nothing! Tell me what things have come to pass for you from Zeus, since earlier you were praying with arms extended that for want of you all the sons of the Acheans would shrink back to the sterns of the ships, and that they would suffer excruciating toil." 77

Groaning deeply, fleet-footed Achilles replied: "My mother, you ask what has come to pass for me from the Olympian. But there is no pleasure in it, since Patroclus, my sweet, loving friend, has perished. I prized him more highly than all of my companions. I valued him the same as myself. He is gone, and Hector looks like a monster as he ravages, dressed in the beautiful armor that the gods gave Peleus as a magnificent gift on the day when they tossed you into the bed of that mortal man. If only you had stayed in the company of immortals, and Peleus had taken a mortal wife. Now there is sorrow for you beyond counting because your child withers away. He will not remain alive to return home. But Hector is going to be struck by my spear and his spirit destroyed; he will pay the penalty owed for Patroclus Menoetiusson." 93

Thetis replied to him, through her tears: "Mine is a harsh fate, as you say. But the first fate is at hand and comes from you to Hector." 96

Greatly annoyed, fleet-footed Achilles answered: "Patroclus was destroyed far from his father, in need of me as his protector in war. Now, since I will not again dwell in my own homeland, and I was not a light of help for Patroclus, nor for his comrades, or any of the others, I ought to die immediately, since I did not protect my dead comrade. Noble Hector snuffed them all out. Yet here I am sitting in a field beside the ships, nursing a pointless grief. None of the brazen-shirted Acheans is my equal in the fighting, though there are others who are more worthy in counsel. Strife and anger destroy that which is within, both of gods and of men. One who is prudent lets go of strife and anger, even if provoked. It is preferable to have sweet honey dripping into the minds of men than smoke. Well, the Lord Agamemnon, the Supreme Commander, still angers me, but we will set that aside and go forward in the fight, suppressing our own feelings out of necessity. I am leaving now so that I can catch up with Hector, the murderer of my own head. And then I shall receive whatever fate Zeus might indeed wish to cause, and the other gods, as well. Nobody, not even mighty Heracles, escapes fate. He was one most loved by the Lord Zeus Cronusson, though the harsh anger of Hera crushed even him.

"And so I, if the same fate is fashioned for me, then I shall lie dead. But now I seek to gain valiant glory, and some of the Trojan and buxom Dardanian women will wipe tears from their soft cheeks and give in to ceaseless groaning. They know that I stopped fighting for a long time. Don't hold me back from the fighting; even though you love me, you won't persuade me." 126

And the goddess Thetis, of the silver feet, answered: "Yes indeed, my faithful child, those things are true. It is not wrong to protect your tired comrades from utter destruction! But your beautiful brazen armor is in the hands of the Trojans. Hector, of the helmet with the waving plume, delights in that armor that he wears on his own shoulders, but I think that he will not gloat for long, since death is close by. But you should not enter the fray of Ares until you see me come here again. I will return with the rising of the sun, bringing beautiful armor from the Lord Hephaestus." 137

So Thetis spoke and turned back from her son, and she turned to her sisters of the sea and said: "It is time now that you enter the wide bosom of the sea and return to our father's palace to check on the old mariner Nereus. Tell him everything. I am off to high Olympus, to see the famed craftsman Hepha-

estus and learn whether he might wish to give my son glorious, gleaming armor."   144

So she spoke, and they immediately went down under a wave
of the sea, while silver-footed Thetis headed back to Olympus to
secure glorious armor for her beloved son, and accordingly her
feet carried her there.   148

Meanwhile, the Acheans, with demonic shouting, reached
the ships and the Hellespont, having fled from man-killing Hector. Though the well-armed Acheans made it, they had not
dragged the corpse of Patroclus, attendant of Achilles, from under the missiles. The Trojan troops and horses reached him
again, and Hector, son of Priam, had valor like flames of a fire.
Three times glorious Hector grabbed the feet from behind, pulling feverishly, shouting loudly to the Trojans. And three times
the two Aiantes, with matchless valor, smacked him back from
the corpse. But he stood firm, trusting in his valor, rushing at
one time through the wrangling, at another making a stand,
shouting loudly. And he gave no ground. Just as rustic shepherds
are not able to drive away a lion the color of glowing coals from
a body when it is ravenously hungry, in the same way the two
warrior Aiantes were not able to frighten Hector Priamson off
the corpse of Patroclus.   164

At that point might Hector have dragged it away and won
endless glory, had not swift Iris, with her winged feet, come running from Olympus to the son of Peleus with a message to arm
himself. This was kept secret from Zeus and the other gods,
since it was Hera who sent Iris forth. She stood close to him and
said with winged words: "Rise up, son of Peleus, most magnificent of men, to protect Patroclus. There is dreadful fighting
in front of the ships on his account. They are killing each other
around the corpse, both those trying to protect it and the Trojans who would drag it to windy Troy. The fighting is violent,
since glorious Hector is determined to drag it off. He intends to
cut the head from the soft neck and cram it onto a stake. Get
up! Do not lie around any longer. It would come as a shock to

you if Patroclus becomes sport for Trojan dogs. If the corpse were to be desecrated in any way, it would be a disgrace to you." 180

Noble Achilles, fleet of foot, answered: "Iris, goddess, which one of the gods sent you with this message?" 183

Swift Iris, of the winged feet, replied: "Hera sent me, the illustrious wife of Zeus. Zeus, who weighs human affairs on high, knows nothing of it, nor do any of the other immortals who dwell around snowcapped Olympus." 186

Achilles, fleet of foot, replied: "How am I to go into battle? The Trojans have my armor. My beloved mother is not allowing me to arm myself before I see her come. She promised that she will bring beautiful armor from Hephaestus. I don't know whether I should put on someone else's glorious armor, or whose it would be. If not, maybe the shield of Aias Telamonson might work. But I would hope that he himself would be in the forefront of those fighting in the conflagration around dead Patroclus." 195

And swift Iris, of the winged feet, said back to him: "We are certainly aware that they have your famous armor. But you should go to the trench and be seen just as you are. The Trojans are frightened of you, and they might shrink back in the fighting, allowing the sons of the Acheans, who are worn down from the warring, to catch their breath. They might rest from the fight just a little." 201

So she spoke and Iris, fleet of foot, went away. At that Achilles, beloved of Zeus, was roused. He went and stood by the trench, away from the wall. Around his powerful shoulders Athena tossed the tasseled aegis, and the exceptional goddess crowned his head with a golden cloud, and from him burned flames, gleaming all around. It was like when smoke going up from a city on a remote island, where they have been waging the deadly warfare of Ares all day long for the sake of their home, reaches the height of the sky. When the sun goes down, the citizens set closely spaced fires, and the rays of the flames rise up to be seen by those living around the island.

When they realize that they are being summoned, they come on their ships to give assistance in war. In the same way, the light from the head of Achilles reached the height of the sky. Respectful of his mother's wise direction, he did not mix with the Acheans who were fighting. He stood there shouting, and a ways off. Pallas Athena yelled. At this there arose in the Trojans an indescribable terror. It was like when a clear voice sounds along with a trumpet when a city is surrounded by murderous enemies. So it was when the clear voice of the grandson of Aeacus began to be heard. The sound of his voice was like the sound of bronze to those who heard it, and it disturbed the spirit in everybody. The horses, with their beautiful manes, turned back their chariots, so great was the pain in their spirits. Their charioteers were astounded when they saw terrible, uncontrollable fire burning above the head of the greathearted son of Peleus, stoked by Athena, the lovely-eyed goddess. Noble Achilles shouted above the trench three times, and three times the Trojans and their famed allies were thrown into confusion. Twelve of their best men perished then and there as their own chariots and spears were turned on them.   231

After that the Acheans gladly pulled Patroclus out from under the missiles and placed him down on a reposing couch. His living comrades stood around him melting into tears, and with them was Achilles, fleet of foot, his eyes welling hot tears when he saw his loyal friend lying pierced through by sharp bronze. Achilles had sent him off to war with his horses and chariot, but Achilles was not to receive Patroclus back home.   238

Revered Hera, with lovely eyes, sent untiring Sun home to the currents of Ocean, against his will. On the one side the noble Acheans stopped both the loud whooping and that fighting that is a danger to all.   242

On the other side, the Trojans pulled back from the mighty conflict and loosed their speedy horses from under their chariots. They gathered in assembly before giving thought to their supper. They stood upright—not one dared to sit, as all were trembling from Achilles's appearance, a man who had held off from the calamitous fight for such a long time. Wise Polydamas Panthousson was the first to speak, as he alone could see what had been and what was to be. He was a comrade of Hector's, and they were both born on the same night. Though Polydamas was skilled with words, Hector was the one who had beaten down many with a spear. He addressed them thoughtfully and said: "Consider very carefully, my friends! I tell you that we should go now to the city. We should not remain on the plain near the ships until the shining dawn. We should be far away from their wall. While this man was furious with noble Agamemnon, the Acheans were easier to fight against. I was happy to spend the night near the swift ships, in hopes that we might seize them. But now, I am filled with dread of the fleet-footed son of Peleus. He has such might that he will not want to remain on the plain where the Trojans and the Acheans are divided on both sides by the might of Ares. Instead, his main objective in the fighting will be the city and the women. We should definitely be going to the city, trust me. That's how it is! For now, ambrosial night has checked the fleet-footed son of Peleus. If we are here when he comes out at dawn, rushing in his armor to catch up with us, surely everybody can see what will happen. Whoever might escape will be glad to get to sacred Troy, but the dogs and the buzzards will eat many of the Trojans who don't make it. This will happen if we remain, from what I have been told. If we are persuaded by my words, which come from the greatest concern, we will go vigorously forward tonight from the council, and then at the first light of dawn we will hold the high towers of the city, and the doors of the gates, fashioned of well-worked planks, will be drawn tightly closed. We will gird ourselves with armor, standing on the towers. The greatest pain will await the one who comes from the ships to fight against us on the wall. He will return to the ships, when he is disgusted from wandering around here and there, running his horses, with their proud necks, under the walls of city. The spirit within will not allow him to charge against the wall, nor will he completely destroy it. Before he does, the swift dogs will eat him."

283

Scowling at him, Hector, of the helmet with the waving plume, said: "Polydamas, you no longer please me, saying that the men should shrink back and return to the city. Have you not had enough of being cooped up inside a wall? In the past, all those with the power of speech talked about how much gold and how much bronze there was in Priam's city. But now all the beautiful things from the palaces have been wasted. All the goods have gone to Phrygia and lovely Maeonia to be sold. Then great Zeus was angry. But now, when the son of crooked-dealing Cronus grants me glory around the ships, I can hem the Acheans in by the sea. You idiot! You are never to reveal such prophecies in the district, nor is any of the Trojans to obey them! I will not have it! But, come, do as I say. We should all conciliate. Take your supper now, by units, in the camp. And post sentries, and each should stay wakeful. Let the Trojan who frets overly much about possessions know that I will give those goods as though from the public purse and give them to the troops as a group. It is better that they have the use of them than the Acheans. At dawn we will put on our armor and raise the sharp war of Ares among the hollow ships. If it is true that noble Achilles is standing beside the ships, his will be the worst pain. I will not run away from him; instead, I will stand against him. Either he will bring might or I will. Together with Ares, Enyalius, either I will kill or be killed."

309

So Hector told them, and they gave the loudest shout imaginable. What fools they were! Pallas Athena snatched their minds from them so that they embraced the bad planning of Hector, rather than the carefully thought out counsel of Polydamas. After that, they took their supper in the camp.

314

Meanwhile, the Acheans stood around all night moaning in grief over Patroclus. Among them the son of Peleus led with

the most frequent groans, placing his man-killing hands on Patroclus's chest. He was like a full-maned lion whose cubs some
deer hunter has snatched from a dense forest. In grief he returns
after it has happened. He goes through many defiles searching
for the man's tracks, earnestly hoping to find them. He is seized
with bitter anger. So, groaning deeply, Achilles raised his voice
to the Myrmidons: "How worthless was that notion I tossed out
that day when I was encouraging the hero Menoetius in his
halls! I claimed that I would lead his famous son back to Opoeis,
with his customary share of the booty after I sacked Troy. But
it is not for men to know how Zeus brings to completion the
products of his mind. We were both destined to dampen the
same ground with blood here in Troy. And consequently, it is
not for me to return to the halls of the old horseman Peleus, nor
to Thetis, my mother. Instead, it is for me to go down into the
ground here. Therefore, Patroclus, I am going under the earth
after you, but I will not give you funeral rites before the armor
and spirited head of Hector is brought here to pay for your murder. I will behead twelve magnificent offspring of the Trojans
before the pyre in anger over your killing. Until then, you will
lie here beside the beaked ships, and Trojan and buxom Dardanian women will weep day and night, pouring out tears for
those the two of us have brought down with our long, mighty
spears, when we wreaked havoc on prosperous cities of men."   342
    So saying, noble Achilles ordered his comrades to set a great
tripod around the fire, so that they might most quickly wash
the bloody gore off Patroclus. They positioned the bathing tripod over a wood fire and placed a basin on it. They poured water
into the basin and placed more kindling on the fire. The water
heated up, and when the water was bubbling in the gleaming
bronze cauldron, they washed the body and anointed it with
olive oil. They filled the wounds with an unguent that was nine
years old, and wrapped the body in windings of soft linen from
feet to head, and placed a white shroud over that, and set it on
a reposing couch. Then the Myrmidons stood around both Pa-

troclus and fleet-footed Achilles groaning in grief the whole
night.   355

And Zeus said to Hera, his sister and wife: "You've gone
and done it now, revered Hera, with lovely eyes! You raised up
Achilles, fleet of foot. That makes it clear that the long-haired
Acheans must surely have been born of you."   359

Then lovely-eyed, revered Hera replied to him: "You are terrible, son of Cronus. What nonsense! For sure, some mortal
somewhere is about to finish off another man, though no mortal has a clue as to his plans. So how is it that I myself, whom I
think to be best among the goddesses, both because of my birth
and because I have claimed you, who rules over all immortals,
how would it be possible that I wouldn't want to contrive evil
for the Trojans, since I'm annoyed with them?" So they talked
to each other.   378

Thetis, with the silver feet, arrived at the palace of Hephaestus. It was prominent among the palaces of the immortals,
fashioned in incorruptible, starry bronze, which the lame god
made himself. She found him bustling around hurriedly, dripping with sweat. Twenty tripods he was making were placed
close to the wall in the palace. He had fitted golden wheels onto
their bases so that they ran on their own power on a track to
the front of the palace and returned on their own. It was wondrous to see. And, to be sure, this all came to a stop, for no
gleaming handles had yet been applied to any of them. He had
already crafted the handles, at that moment he was beating the
rivets to hold them on. He worked at that skillfully until
Thetis, the goddess with silver feet, came near. Beautiful Charis, of the gleaming veil, saw her coming. She was married to
the famous god, lame in both feet. Charis took Thetis's hand
and spoke to her, calling her by name: "Thetis, of the long
gown, why have you come to our home, venerable and dear
friend? In the past you have not visited often. But first, follow
me, so that I may provide hospitality for you." So speaking, the

illustrious goddess led her forward. She seated Thetis on a beautiful, gleaming silver-studded throne; underneath it was a footstool. Then she called out to the famed craftsman: "Come in
here, Thetis wants something from you now." The famous
god, lame in both legs, replied: "Indeed, a goddess who is both
feared and revered is now in my home. She saved me when I
arrived, pained from a long fall instigated by my quarrelsome
mother, who wanted to conceal me because of my lameness.
Then I would have suffered, had not both Eurymone and Thetis received me into their bosom. Eurymone is the daughter of
ever-flowing Ocean. For nine years I worked bronze beside
them in a hollow cave around which the currents of Ocean
constantly sloshed and swirled along. There I fashioned dazzling things, curved buckles, curved metal flowers, and neck-
laces. But no one else knew, neither god nor mortal, except
Thetis and Eurymone; they saved me. Now that she has come
to our palace, it is necessary for both of us, but especially me,
to do everything possible for Thetis, of the long gown, as recompense for saving me. Set before her pleasant hospitality
while I put away the bellows and all the tools."   409

And the bellows monster stood up, limping, from his anvil
block. Underneath him his shins loosened and went into motion. He moved the pair of bellows away from the fire. All of
the tools he had made were collected in a silver chest. He wiped
off his face and hands with a sponge, and his stout neck and
hairy chest. He put on a tunic, then took hold of a sturdy crutch
and went limping through the door. Underneath their lord
danced mechanical golden maidens who seemed lifelike. They
were conscious of mind and had voice, and they knew the skills
of handwork that are gifts of the immortal gods. And they scut-
tled around underneath their lord, holding him aloft as they
went. They drew him close to where Thetis was and he sat on
a gleaming throne. Hephaestus took her hand in his, and called
her by name, saying: "Why have you come, Thetis? You are revered and loved by both of us, but you do not often visit. Say

what is on your mind. Order me to fulfill your wish. If it is possible for me to bring it off, it will be done."   427

And then Thetis answered him, while gushing tears: "Hephaestus, is there really any, of all the goddesses on Olympus,
who must bear up under such terrible grief as Zeus Cronusson
has given me? He crushes me more than the other aimless goddesses, because I dared sleep with a mortal man, Peleus Aeacusson, even though I very much didn't wish it. Peleus is now old
and in a miserable state in his halls, worn down from the effects
of age. But at that time he gave me a son to bear and rear. He is
now the most excellent of heroes. The boy shot up like the
sprout of a tree, and I tended him as though he were a plant in
a fertile orchard. I sent him off in the beaked ships to Troy to
fight against the Trojans. But it is not his destiny to return home
to the palace of Peleus and I will not receive him back. For as
long as he lives and can see the light of the sun, he is a grief for
me, since there is nothing I can do to help him. The sons of the
Acheans selected a girl to be his prize, but the Lord Agamemnon took her back from his arms. You may be certain that sent
grief over her into his mind. Next thing, Trojans hemmed the
Acheans in around the sterns of their ships, and they were not
able to get out of their gate. The Argive elders pled with my
son, and even specified many extravagant gifts. But he refused
to protect them there because of his anger. Next though, he
put his own armor on Patroclus and sent him to fight, and
he drove the Trojans far back. For an entire day Patroclus
made war around the Scaean Gate, and that very day he would
have sacked the city, had not Apollo struck down the valiant
son of Menoetius. Apollo killed him in the front lines and gave
the glory for that to Hector. That is why I have come now to
your knees, to learn whether you might wish to give my son,
who is destined to a short life, a shield, and a plumed helmet,
and beautiful greaves with fitted ankle guards, and a breastplate, so that he might savage the Trojans who destroyed his
loyal friend. My son lies on the ground grieving for him."   461

The famed one, who was lame in both feet, replied: "Do not trouble your mind over this. While I certainly may not be able to hide him far from death, which brings men grief, at least when it arrives, he will be wearing the most beautiful armor possible. I think he will be an amazement to many men when he is seen in it."   467

So he spoke to her, and left her to go to his bellows. He stoked the fire and ordered them to get to work. There were twenty bellows blowing into twenty furnaces and all were exhaling gusts of wind. He went about hurriedly first to one, then back to another. This is how Hephaestus went about creating what Thetis wanted to take back with her. He tossed tireless bronze on the fire, and tin, and precious gold, and silver. Next then, he put a huge anvil on the anvil block, and seized in one hand a mighty smith's hammer, and in the other fire tongs.   477

First he made the shield, big and stout, gleaming all around. He hammered a rim around it with three folds that was brilliant and gleaming. From it, there was a silver strap. The shield had five layers there, and he made brilliantly gleaming devices for it, as he knew so well how to do. On it he fashioned the earth, and the heavens, and the sea, and the inextinguishable sun, and the full moon, and on it were all the stars that the heavens crown. There were the Pleiades, and the Hyades, and powerful Orion, and Arctus, the Great Bear, which they call by the nickname Wagon. It turns where it is and keeps watch on Orion alone, with no concern for the baths of Ocean.   489

On the shield, Hephaestus fashioned two cities of men, who speak in words. In one there were wedding feasts. Nymphs led a procession from the gleaming chamber under torchlight up to the city, with much singing. Dancing youths feasted, and among them there were pipes and lyres accompanying their voices. Young women stood in rapt amazement in the entryways of all the houses. The troops stood at attention in the assembly, where a brawl was imminent. Two men were arguing over the penalty payment for the death of a man. The one prayed to all in the district to accept the payment he offered, but the other was angry and did not take it. Both were anxious for an arbiter to choose a final judgment. Troops of assistants stood around both men shouting encouragement, but heralds at least restrained the troops. The elders sat on their polished stones in the sacred circle, and there the question was raised to them, and they spoke their judgments in turn. In their midst lay two golden talents, to be given to the one who might make the most straightforward proposition.

508

Around the other city sat two camps of troops in gleaming arms. There was a dilemma as to which plan pleased them, either to sack the city, or to divide into two parts all the property such as was enclosed within the lovely city as a ransom. Those under siege could not agree at all, and armed to lie in ambush. The loving wives and small children were protecting a wall they stood on. Among them were the old men. The warriors went out, and leading them were Ares and Pallas Athena, both in gold, and they wore beautiful, golden garments and they had huge weapons. The two gods were made so as to stand out with the greatest clarity, while the troops were less conspicuous. And when they were lying in wait like an ambush on the river, the spot was a watering place for all kinds of animals. There they sat gleaming in wine-colored bronze. Apart from the troops sat two scouts, keeping an eye out for sheep or cattle with curved horns. And soon they came forward, followed by two shepherds amusing themselves with pipes, who did not anticipate the trap at all. Those waiting ran forward and quickly cut off the herds of cattle and the beautiful flocks of white sheep, killing the herders, too. Those besieging learned what was happening from the great ruckus of the cattle roaring as they were sitting in assembly. Immediately they charged with their prancing horses; arriving quickly, they made a stand and fought a battle on the riverbank. They hurled brazen spears at one another. Strife and Tumult joined the horde, and ruthless Fate. There was one man recently wounded, and another unhurt. Fate pulled another dead from the fracas by his feet. The tunic around her shoulders was stained with the purple blood of humankind. They were engaging in conflict in the way that living mortals do, making war. They were pulling each other's corpses as they were slain.   541

And Hephaestus placed there a soft, fecund field, wide and plowed three times. There were many plowmen in it, the pairs of oxen treading along as they were driven here and there. And whenever they reached the end of the field, they turned. And in time, they held cups of sweet wine that a man gave them to drink. As the plow shot along a recently deepened furrow it arrived at the limit of the field, and the earth behind the plowshare was darkened, like it is when really plowing, though it actually was of gold. So unbelievably wondrous was the craftsmanship.   549

And Hephaestus placed on the shield a royal plantation. There mowers bent over with sharp scythes in their hands. And along the swath, a profusion of grain fell to the ground, and the bundlers bound them into sheaves. Three bundlers stood close by. And behind them were groups of boys carrying bundles cradled in their arms, going along steadily. Among them the king stood silently in the swath with his scepter in the hand, happy at heart. His heralds were some distance off under an oak tree preparing a feast with a great ox they had sacrificed. The women were sprinkling a lot of white barley for the mowers' supper.   561

Hephaestus placed there a fertile vineyard with vines worked in lovely gold. The bunches of grapes on top of the vines were dark. The stakes the vines grow on were all round and fashioned of silver. Around the vineyard there was a dark drainage ditch, and Hephaestus hammered on a dyke of tin. Only one path went to the vineyard. Bearers proceeded along it as they cropped the vineyard. Young girls and youths of tender age carried the sweet fruit in woven baskets. In their midst was a boy with high-pitched pipes, who plucked a lyre sweetly. He sang in a subtle voice while plucking the beautiful string he holds down below.

The young people clapped, keeping time together. And they sang and danced, and whistled, as they skipped along following him.   572

Hephaestus also fashioned a herd of straight-horned cattle. The cows were crafted of gold and tin. They low as they move from a dung heap to a pasture close by a gurgling river, and along wavering reeds. There are four golden herders with the cows that are proceeding one by one. Nine fleet-footed dogs follow them. Two terrifying lions hold a loud-bellowing bull in the forefront of the cows. He is being dragged while protesting in loud shrieks. Dogs and youths are in pursuit. The two lions tear into the hide of the huge bovine, gobbling down its entrails and dark blood. The herders pursue the lions, urging on the swift dogs. To be sure, they torment the lions as they turn about, but even though they stand close in and bark, the lions escape.   586

And the famed one who was lame in both feet put on the shield a multicolored dance floor like one that Daedalus once worked on in wide Knossos for Ariadne, with beautiful hair. There were youths and highly desirable young maidens dancing with each other, with wrists held in hands. The girls among them had soft veils, and the youths wore finely woven tunics that had a slight rubbing of olive oil for sheen. The girls had lovely crowns, and the boys wore golden daggers that hung from silver baldrics. And whenever the boys ran, they came to a stop quite easily, just as when the seated potter stops the wheel with his hand. The girls look on with admiration. In another place, the boys run with each other in formations. A big crowd stands on the sacred dance floor, and many are enjoying themselves, and among them is a divine singer, singing and dancing as he plays his lyre. There are two tumblers down from them. They lead off the singing and dancing, as they whirl around in the middle of the crowd. Hephaestus placed the great, mighty river of Ocean as the sturdy, outermost border of the shield.   607

After he made the shield, which was both big and robust, he then made a breastplate that was shinier than the gleam of a fire,

and he made for Achilles a strong helmet fitted with temple-
pieces that was beautiful and shining. On it he set a golden
crest. And he made for him greaves of tin that were comfortable to wear.   613

After he had done with all the arms, the famed one who was
lame in both legs placed them in front of the mother of Achilles. She rose up like a hawk and swooped down from snowy
Olympus with the gleaming armor she had received from Hephaestus.   617

Book 19

Gowned in purple, Dawn rose from the currents of Ocean so that she might bring light to the immortals and to living mortals. Thetis arrived at the ships bearing the gifts from the god, and she found her beloved son lying close to Patroclus, weeping bitterly. Many of his comrades were around him dissolved in tears. And she, most illustrious of goddesses, stood beside them, and took her son's hands in her own, called him by name, and spoke: "My child, though all are grieving we will allow this one to lie here, since it was first the command of the gods that he be smitten. Receive your glorious armor from Hephaestus. It is beautiful. No other man has ever worn such as this on his shoulders."

So spoke the goddess, and she set down the armor in front of Achilles. It crashed as it fell, and the radiance was dazzling. The brilliance seized all the Myrmidons with trembling fear, turning their heads, and none dared look at it. Achilles, as he was clothed in special wrath, was the same. But it was something terrible in his eyes. Under his eyelids, it was as if a blaze of the sun were shining. Holding in his hands the god's magnificent gifts, he was pleased. And he rejoiced in his mind over the dazzling whiteness. Immediately he spoke to his mother with winged words: "Mother of mine, these arms the god has provided are like work fit for an immortal, not what is made for a mortal man. Now, for sure, I shall put on this armor. However, I am very terribly afraid to do it until I deal with the valiant son of Menoetius; I am concerned that flies will go down into the wounds, inflicted by bronze, and produce maggots that will corrupt the corpse. If I take up arms, it will have been a long time since his death, and the flesh will be completely rotten." 27

At that, Thetis, the silver-footed goddess, answered: "My

child, you should not let such a matter distract you. I'll try to
enervate the wild type of flies, those that invade men who die
in battle. And his flesh will remain firm, or even better, though
he might lie for a long time, even a year. Instead, you call the
Achean heroes to the assembly, renounce your wrath against
Agamemnon, Shepherd of the Troops, and get very quickly
into arms for the fight. Clothe yourself with valor!"   36

So saying, she sent him courageous might. She went back to
Patroclus and put drops of ambrosia and red nectar down his
nostrils, so that his flesh would remain firm.   39

After that, noble Achilles went along the beach, with the
most terrible yelling, to rouse the Achean heroes. And those
who before had remained by the ships while the contest went
on—the pilots, and the helmsmen, and the servants who were
the dispensers of bread near the ships—even they came to the
assembly, because Achilles appeared. It had been a long time
since he had withdrawn from the calamitous fighting. Two of
the attendants of Ares came along limping, the son of Tydeus,
firm in the fight, and noble Odysseus. They both leaned on
spears, as their wounds were still painful. They went and sat in
the front of the assembly. After them came the Supreme Commander Agamemnon, with his wound. Even he had been struck
in the intense fighting by Coon Antenorson with his brazen
spear.   53

After all the Acheans were crowded in together, Achilles,
fleet of foot, stood up and addressed them: "Why is it that we
two are so angry with one another and keep this conflict between us that destroys souls, and over a girl? We should hope
somehow to make things better between you and me. How I
wish Artemis had killed her with an arrow that day when I chose
her after the sack of Lyrnessus. Then so many Acheans would
not have bitten the dust at the enemies' hands, had I not been
so awfully angry. It was a huge number of them. I think that it
has been more profitable to Hector the Trojans than for the
Acheans that you and I have kept this wrangle going so long.

Instead, even though we are angry, we should suppress that
out of necessity, and put a loving spirit in our hearts. Now, you
may be sure, I am stopping the anger. It is not necessary for me
to maintain this wrath that has no end. But come, I am rousing the long-haired Acheans to war right away, and I will still
try to go against the Trojans for as long as they are keen to
spend the night near the ships. But, I think some of them will
welcome the chance to bend their knees, as animals do when
resting, especially ones who might escape from the furious
warring under my spear."   73

So he spoke, and the well-armed Acheans were overjoyed
that the greathearted son of Peleus renounced his wrath.
And the Supreme Commander Agamemnon addressed them
from the place where he sat, not standing in their midst: "O beloved Danaan heroes, attendants of Ares, it would be proper if
I stood to reply so you could hear, not like this. But it is hard for
me to stand. Is there anyone in the big crowd who cannot hear
me? Wounded though your speaker is, he will speak in a shrill,
piercing manner. I offer my reply to the son of Peleus, and indeed to the others of the Argives here gathered. Each of you has
made your thoughts well known to me. Many times the
Acheans have talked about it, and you have fussed at me often.
But, I am not to blame for this! Instead the fault lies with Zeus,
and Fate and the airborne Furies. They hurled a beastly blindness into my mind on that day in the assembly when I took
away Achilles's prize for myself. Otherwise, why would I do
such a thing? It was on account of some god that it happened.
Ate is the eldest daughter of Zeus. It is she who blinds everybody, out of sheer meanness. She has cushiony soft feet, and
they don't get close to the ground. Instead they come down on
the heads of men as she goes around. She wounds one man,
and then she goes and steps down on another. Even Zeus was
blinded once, even though they say he is the best of men and of
gods. But Hera treacherously seduced him with her feminine

wiles on the day when Alcmene was about to give birth to mighty Heracles in well-fortified Thebes. Indeed, she boasted about it, telling all the gods: 'Hear me, all gods, and goddesses, so that I can tell you what the heart in my breast orders me to. The Elethyia presided over the birth of a man who saw light and will rule over all his neighbors. He was of the men who are of the tribe of men who are from my blood.' But revered Hera, you deceived Zeus in your treachery, and the end didn't come out as you thought.   107

"What she said was: 'Come on now, Olympian, swear a mighty oath to me that one who would rule over all his neighbors, who today would fall between the feet of a woman, and he is of the same clan of men from your blood.' That's what she said. And Zeus, had no clue of her treachery. Instead, he swore the great oath, and afterward was totally blinded. Hera rose up and left the peak of Olympus, and quickly arrived in Achean Argos, and there was the illustrious wife of Sthenelus Perseusson. She was pregnant with her own son, whom she had carried seven months. Hera led him forward into the light so that he was born prematurely. She had the Elethyia hold back the birthing labor of Alcmene. She went herself with the news, saying to Zeus Cronusson: 'Zeus, Father, wielder of bright lightning, fix this idea in your mind. For certain, a virtuous man will grow old ruling the Argives, Eurystheus, son of Sthenelus Perseusson, your kin. And he is not unworthy to rule the Argives.' So she spoke, and a sharp anger struck deep in Zeus's mind. Immediately, he seized Ate by her head, with its oiled hair. He was furious at her, and swore a stronger oath that she could never return again to Olympus and the starry heavens. After swearing that, he hurled her away from there, and soon she arrived among the affairs of men. Zeus was perpetually angry that his own son— Heracles—would toil unjustly under Eurystheus's trials.   133

"And so it was with me. When Hector, of the helmet with the waving plume, was wiping out Argives around the sterns of the ships, I was unaware that Ate had earlier blinded me. And when she did it, Zeus snatched away my mind. But I want to make amends, and give you, Achilles, a huge compensation for injury I've done you. Charge into war and rouse the other troops. I will have the gifts transported to you that noble Odysseus promised to you yesterday in your hut. Or, if you want, hold off on the work of Ares, so that my attendants can carry the gifts from my ships, so that you can see whether what I shall give is suitable." 144

Achilles, fleet of foot, answered him: "Most glorious Supreme Commander Agamemnon Atreusson, if you wish to transport gifts such as are suitable you may, or we could fetch them from your stores. But right now, we must immediately remember our valor. It is not necessary to hang around here talking or debating. There is still much toil that both of us must avert. So Hector will see Achilles back in the front lines wiping out whole formations of Trojans with his brazen spear. In such a way will one of ours remember how to fight against a warrior." 153

And the ever-cunning Odysseus had his say: "Though this is worthy, godlike Achilles, you ought not to rouse the sons of the Acheans to war, advancing on Troy when they haven't eaten today. Once begun, there is such a little bit of time before the fighting, whenever the troops assemble into formations and some god breathes his spirit into both sides. Instead, order that the Acheans be provisioned with bread and wine beside the swift ships, as that would improve strength and valor. A man who is hungry but has had no bread before he fights is not able to fight the whole day 'til the setting of the sun. Even though he is eager to fight in his heart, his limbs are worn down without his awareness. Both thirst and hunger come on him, and his knees hurt as he goes along. But the warrior who is satiated with wine and food can fight against enemy warriors all day long. His limbs are not weary before everyone rushes into war, and there is courage in his mind. So come, order the troops to disperse and get about preparing their meal. 172

"Supreme Commander Agamemnon, you should bring the

gifts to the middle of the assembly so that you may delight his mind, and so all the Acheans can see them for themselves. You should swear an oath to him and before the Acheans standing around that you have never rolled into bed and copulated with the girl, though that is, O king, the custom of men and women. With that you should placate the spirit of his mind. Afterward you should conciliate matters with a lavish feast in your hut, so that this thing wants for nothing that is just. In the future, son of Atreus, none of us may scold a king who has placated a man who was formerly angry, since you are better in dispensing judgment than anyone else."

183

And the Supreme Commander Agamemnon replied to Odysseus: "I like the speech I have heard. As you explain it, you say what is altogether just. And I do wish to swear those things, as my heart moves me. And, I will not break an oath sworn before a god. Accordingly, Achilles should remain here until he charges into the affairs of Ares. All of the others should remain assembled so that the gifts might come from my hut and we make our solemn vow. I lay it on you yourself to select the choicest young men of all the Acheans to bring my gifts from the ships, those you promised to Achilles yesterday. You are to lead the women. Talthybius should quickly go down to the wide camp of the Acheans to prepare a boar for me to sacrifice to Zeus and Sun."

197

But, Achilles, fleet of foot, said to him in answer: "Most glorious Supreme Commander Agamemnon Atreusson, some other time when a lull occurs in the fighting, and there is not such strength in my breast, you should increase those things that are wanting. But, those taken down by Hector Priamson when Zeus gave him glory are lying there, cut to pieces, and you are now urging us to eat. To be sure, I would order the sons of the Acheans into the fight hungry and after fasting, and after we avenge the insult to make a huge meal with the setting of the sun. Before that I would send neither drink nor food down my own throat on account of my dead friend, who is in my hut, slain by sharp bronze. He lies pierced through with his feet turned toward the vestibule, and around him our comrades weep. Those other things are of no consequence to me, but I am keen for death, and blood and the harsh groaning of dying men." 214

The ever-cunning Odysseus answered him: "O Achilles, great son of Peleus, bravest of the Acheans. Even though you are braver than I, and better, not by a little bit, with a spear than I am, I can toss out many more ideas than you can. That is because I was born earlier, and because I know more. On both accounts, you have to listen to what I say. Going immediately into battle is an arrogance of humanity. Certainly, the bronze scatters the most grain around, but for the smallest harvest. When the weights make the balance turn, it is Zeus, master of men and of war, who makes it happen. 224

"Acheans never grieve for the dead with their stomachs. Having eaten and drunk, many can stand without trembling, even for a whole day. When is there any break from a struggle? It comes because it is necessary to bury one who has died with a savage spirit in a day of weeping. For that one takes leave of cruel fighting, to remember the dead with drink and food, so that they are even more vigorous in the fight against the enemy, whose flesh is overcome by tireless bronze. So, you see, it would be a bad thing to leave the ships and rouse the Acheans now. Instead, the whole lot of us will charge against the Trojans, noble horsemen, in the sharp war of Ares." 237

And Odysseus was followed by the sons of glorious Nestor, and the son of Phyleus, and Thoas the Megarian, and Meriones, and Lycomedeon Creonson, and Melanippus. They set off for the hut of Agamemnon Atreusson. After weighing out all ten talents of gold, Odysseus led and the rest of the young warriors of the Acheans were with him bearing gifts. From Agamemnon's huts they carried the seven tripods that were promised to Achilles, and twenty gleaming cauldrons. They drove twelve horses from there and escorted seven women with incomparable skill at handwork. After them, the eighth was Briseis, with pretty cheeks.   248

And, they placed the gifts in the middle of the assembly. Agamemnon stood up. And Talthybius, whose voice had the resonance of a god, stood beside the Shepherd of the Troops with a boar in his hands. The son of Atreus pulled out a dagger that always hung beside him in the scabbard of his great sword. He began by cutting off some hairs of the boar. Then he raised up his arms in prayer to Zeus. All the Acheans sat apart from him silently listening to their king, as was customary. Agamemnon looked to the wide heavens and prayed saying: "Let it be known now, Zeus, first of the gods, highest and best, and Earth, and Sun, and the Furies, who dwell under the earth who punish men who break oaths, that I did not put my hands on the girl Briseis, nor was she in my bed on terms of physical intimacy or anything else. Rather, she was untouched by me in my hut. If this be a false statement let the gods give me the most awful pain, such as they would give to anyone who sins against them in false swearing."   265

Then, he cut across the throat of the boar with his pitiless bronze. Talthybius wheeled it around and threw it into the great depths of the gray sea to be food for fish. After that Achilles stood up and spoke among the war-loving Argives: "Father Zeus, you give huge blindness to men. The son of Atreus would never have thoroughly enraged the heart in my chest, nor would he have led the girl from me against my will. I was unable to do anything about it. None of this would have happened had not Zeus somehow wished to bring death to many Acheans. Now, lead us to the meal, so that we can marshal together with Ares."   275

So he spoke and quickly broke up the assembly. The others dispersed, each to his ship, but the greathearted Myrmidons busied themselves with the gifts of the godlike Achilles, taking

them and placing them in his hut. They sat the women down
and the illustrious attendants drove the horses to the herd.   281

Briseis at that point looked like a golden Aphrodite, but when
she saw Patroclus, slain by sharp bronze, she went near him and
spilled tears and made a sharp wailing sound, scratching and
tearing her breast, her soft neck, and her face with her hands.
As she wept, this woman who was like a goddess said: "Patroclus, I am so miserable! You brought the most joy to my heart
when you were living, as you were when I left the hut to go
away. But, now I return to find you a dead officer of the troops.
I have always received evil from evil. They gave me that when
I saw my husband, my father, my revered mother pierced
through by sharp bronze. And I had three sisters slain, too. They
were born of the same mother as I was, and were all caring
people. And they all met their day of destruction. But you did
not allow me to weep when swift Achilles killed my husband
at the sack of divine Myna. Instead, you assured me that you
would make me the lawful wife of godlike Achilles, that you
would take me in the ships to Phthia for a wedding feast among
the Myrmidons. So, I weep unceasingly over your death. You
were always sweet to me."   300

So Briseis spoke, weeping as she did. The women raised up
the greatest wailing from their grief, for each of them had her
own reason to care for Patroclus. The elders of the Acheans
gathered around Achilles, pleading with him to eat breakfast.
But he refused, in his grieving: "I beg you, if there is any of my
beloved comrades who believes me, do not ask me to satiate my
own heart with food and drink, since such a terrible grief has
come upon me. I will wait for sundown and I will dare to stand
firm."   309

So he spoke, and the other kings dispersed. But the two sons
of Atreus stayed, along with noble Odysseus, Idomeneus,
Nestor, and the old horseman Phoenix, trying to console him

in his deep grief. But his heart was not to be consoled, and nothing was to pass his mouth before the bloody fighting. He reminisced as they clustered around; the sound of his voice was carried up: "Yes, you ill-fated man, most beloved of my friends, now and then you yourself put a pleasant breakfast beside me in the hut, quickly and efficiently, whenever the Acheans charged off to carry the work of Ares, which brings many tears, to the Trojans, noble horsemen. But now you lie slain, and because of that my heart fasts from drink and food longing for you, though they are available. I could not suffer anything else worse, unless it were that I might learn of the demise of my father, if somehow he is still alive in Phthia. He would be feeble and would shed tears over the lack of a son like me in a foreign country, while I am fighting against the Trojans on account of that worthless harridan Helen. Or the one reared by me on Scyrus, my own son godlike Neoptolemus, if he is still alive. Before, it had been my hope only that both of you would return home to Phthia when I perished here in Troy, away from horse-raising Argos. That hope was that you might gather him up from Scyrus and lead my son with you in the black ships and show him every piece of my property, my servants and the big palace, with the high ceilings. And maybe you might introduce him to Peleus, though I think he might be down among all those who have died. Or, perhaps, he has a little longer yet to live grieving, savaged by old age and from constantly awaiting the sad message, when he learns that I have perished." 337

So Achilles spoke, crying as he did so. The elders around him groaned from grief, as each one remembered those they left behind in their great halls. And upon seeing them melt into tears, the son of Cronus took pity on them. Immediately he spoke to Athena with winged words: "My child, for sure you have completely abandoned your warrior. Is Achilles now no longer at all a concern of your mind? He is in front of the ships, with raised sterns, and sits grieving for his beloved friend, while the others have left and tended to their breakfasts. But he has not eaten and is fasting. Go to him and drizzle nectar and lovely ambrosia on his breast, so that no hunger may come upon him." 348

So Zeus spoke and roused Athena, who had already been fervent. In the likeness of a peregrine with stretched-out wings and shrill call, she vaulted from the heavens, through the upper atmosphere. Meanwhile the Acheans quickly armed themselves in the camp. But Athena drizzled nectar and lovely ambrosia on the chest of Achilles, so that hunger would not come upon him and bring discomfort to his knees. She departed and returned to the sturdy palace of her father, mighty in a struggle, while the Acheans poured out away from the swift ships. 356

It was like when the dense multitude of snowflakes pours down from Zeus, chilled by the blasts of North Wind, the source of crisp frigid air. So it was when the dense multitude of helmets shone in a glow as they were borne from the ships, and the bossed shields, and the breastplates with their dimples that made them stronger, and the ashen spears. The gleam reached the heavens. And the earth laughed under flashes of the bronze as they all passed along, and a din rose up under the feet of men. In their midst, noble Achilles put on his arms. There was gnashing of his teeth, and both his eyes glowed as if they were rays of light from a fire. In his heart was set unstoppable wrath. And he raved about the Trojans as he put on the gifts of the god, the things Hephaestus toiled to make for him. 368

First, he put the greaves around his shins. They were beautiful, fitted with silver ankle guards. Next he put the breastplate back around his chest. Around his shoulders he tossed the brazen, silver-studded sword. After that, he next grabbed the shield, both huge and stout. The rays of light that came from it were like those of the moon from afar. It was like when from the deep of the sea the rays from a burning fire are revealed to sailors who have been unwillingly carried far from their loved ones by storms come to them on the fishy deep. The fire burns high up in the mountains on a remote plantation. In such a way did the

rays of light reach the upper atmosphere from the shield of
Achilles, from its beautiful gleam. He raised up the heavy,
plumed helmet and placed it on his head. It glowed like a star
with its horsehair plume, set in a golden crest, which Hephaestus fixed tightly around the plume. Noble Achilles tried out the
armor. If he charged, would his magnificent limbs move freely?
He realized that for him it became like wings; the Shepherd of
the Troops arose in flight.   386

Next he drew a spear from his ancestral weapon-storage
tube, a spear that was huge, strong, and sturdy. None of the other
Acheans could handle it; only Achilles. It was of ash, and Chiron had given it to his father at his high station on Pelion so that
Peleus could visit death on heroes.   391

Automedon and Alcinous prepared the horses, yoking them.
Around their necks were beautiful collars. In the horses' jaws
they set the bits and pulled down the reins behind the chariot,
which was made of wooden pieces fitted together, while the
horses were in front. Automedon took the gleaming, fitted whip
in his hand to urge on the horses. And behind him went Achilles in the gleaming armor. He was like Hyperion Sun. In a terrifying way he called out to the horses of his father: "Xanthus,
and Balias, ever-famed children of Podarge, consider what we
might do differently this time so as to save the charioteer. When
we have had our fill of fighting we go back into the throng of
the Danaans, so that the charioteer is not left dead there, like
Patroclus!"   403

And from underneath the yoke the swift-footed horse Xanthus replied. Hera, the white-armed goddess, had presented him
with the faculty of speech. He immediately dropped his head,
and his mane spilled out from the bow of the yoke and fell to
the ground. Xanthus said: "Even though we will be very much
able to save you now, mighty Achilles, the day of your perishing is getting closer, and it will not be our fault. Instead the
blame rests with some god who is great, and a powerful Fate.
And it was not owing to our being slow or careless that the Tro-

jans took the armor from Patroclus's shoulders. Instead, the most eminent god, the son of lovely-haired Leto, killed him and gave Hector the glory. We would run with the breath of North Wind, which they say makes us fleetest of all. But your fate is that a god, and some powerful warrior will subdue you." 417

So the horse spoke in a human voice and the Furies stopped the sound. Greatly annoyed, Achilles, fleet of foot, replied: "Xanthus, why are you prophesying death for me? It's not necessary for you to do that. I very well know what my own fate is, to perish in this place far from my beloved father and mother. But even so, I shall not sleep until I will drive against the Trojans aplenty in the fighting." And, you may be sure, he gave a shout and drove the solid-hoofed horses into the front lines. 424

Book 20

A nd so the Acheans gathered around the son of Peleus, to arm themselves beside the beaked ships. And the Trojans back on the other side were on a ridge in the plain. Zeus ordered Themis to call the gods to assembly from a peak of craggy Olympus. And she went wandering around telling all to return to the palace of Zeus.   6

None of the rivers were absent, other than Ocean, nor the nymphs who dwell in the lovely groves, nor the springs that water the rivers and the grassy meadows. The gods went to the palace of Zeus the cloud-gatherer, which Hephaestus had fashioned for his father Zeus with great knowledge and skill. They sat on the gleaming, polished porches.   12

They gathered there on the order of Zeus, and neither the earth-shaker nor his goddesses ignored the order. He came up from the sea with them, and sat in their midst. He asked Zeus what his plan was: "Why, wielder of white lightning, did you call the gods to assembly? Are you considering something concerning the Trojans and the Acheans? Both are now as close as they could be to kindling mayhem and war."   18

And Zeus, the cloud-gatherer, answered: "You knew, you who hold the earth, my plan, and that I gathered you here because of it. I am concerned about the Trojans and the Acheans, even though they will perish. But let me tell you, I will remain seated on an outcrop of Olympus, watching there what pleases me. The others I summoned may go among the Trojans and the Acheans and render aid to both sides, whichever strikes the fancy of each one. If Achilles makes war on the Trojans by himself, they will hold the fleet-footed son of Peleus off just briefly. In the past they trembled at just the sight of him. Now, especially when he is so awfully angry over his friend, I am

afraid that he might even ransack the wall of Troy, though that
goes past fate." 30

So spoke the son of Cronus, and he raised up limitless war.
And the gods set off for the fighting with two different minds
in the matter. Hera went into the contest on the side of the ships,
as did Pallas Athena, and Poseidon, who holds the earth, and
the always useful Hermes, who excels in the prudence of his
mind. Hephaestus went with them, taking pleasure in his might,
but at the same time he was angry. His sprite knees spun around
underneath him. 37

Ares, of the helmet with a waving plume, was for the Trojans, and along with him were Phoebus, with unsheared hair,
and Artemis, who delights in archery, and Leto, and Xanthus,
and laughter-loving Aphrodite. 40

For as long as the gods were apart from the mortal men, the
Acheans enjoyed great glory, because Achilles had come into
view. For a long time he had completely withdrawn from the
calamitous fighting. A terrible trembling came underneath every
one of the Trojans when they charged on fleet-footed Achilles.
His armor gleamed like that of man-killing Ares. After the
Olympians went into the throng of men, mighty Strife, savior
of the troops, charged in. Athena stood and shouted as she
did when she was beside the trench dug outside the wall. Yet
another time she gave a loud shout that made a murderous
noise. Opposite her Ares shouted. He was like a dark hurricane,
calling at one time to the Trojans from the highest point of the
city and at another while running along the Simois to the little
hill, called Callicolone. 53

On both sides the blessed gods were roused up, hurling together, and among them was a desperate struggle. The father
of both men and gods thundered dreadfully from above, while
from beneath Poseidon shook the boundless earth and the highest ridges of the mountains. All the foothills of Ida, with many
springs, shook and the peak, too. And so did the city and the
ships of the Acheans. Underneath the earth, Hades, lord of the

underworld, was frightened. He shouted from his throne below, as he feared that Poseidon's earthquake might reveal his district to the mortals and the immortals, a terrible, wide-spreading dwelling, though such an event would be odious to the god Hades. So great was the commotion raised by the gods as they came together in the struggle.   66

You may be sure that opposite the Lord Poseidon stood Phoebus Apollo with his fletched arrows, and opposite Ares Enyalius stood the bright-eyed goddess, Athena. Against Hera stood the one with golden arrow shafts, with the terrifying cry, Artemis, lover of archery, and sister of Apollo. And against Leto stood the preserver, the always useful Hermes. Against Hephaestus was the huge, deep-swirling river the gods call Xanthus, but men call the Scamander.   74

And so it was that the gods were going against gods. Now, Achilles had an urgent desire to fight against the son of Priam. Achilles's spirit drove him on so that he might cause Hector's blood to satiate Ares, the warrior patient of blows. Apollo, savior of the troops, urged Aeneas to go straight against the son of Peleus, injecting him with the right strength. Apollo, son of Zeus, took on the voice and likeness of Priam's son Lycaon, and said to him: "Aeneas, counselor of the Trojans, where are the boasts you promised when you were carousing with the Trojan kings? Did you not claim that you would stand against Achilles Peleusson in the fighting?"   85

And Aeneas answered him, saying: "Son of Priam, why are you urging me in this way to fight against Peleus's son, even though I don't want to? Now will not be the first time I will stand against fleet-footed Achilles. For, already he put me to rout with his spear and ran me off Ida, when he came upon our cattle. He sacked Lyrnessus and Pedasus, though Zeus saved me. He gave me strength and made my knees nimble, or I'd have been taken down under the hand of Achilles and Athena, who was going with a light of inspiration, urging him to kill Lebeges and Trojans. A man doesn't stand just against Achilles, but against two,

for always there is one of the gods who protects him from calamity. At times when a missile was flying straight at him it has
been turned aside so the man's flesh didn't stop it. Even if there
were some god who balanced the outcome of war evenly, it
would not be easy for Achilles to win victory over me, not even
if he claims to be made of solid bronze."   102

And the Lord Apollo, son of Zeus, answered: "Come now,
hero. Even you yourself pray to the everlasting gods. They say
you were born of Aphrodite, daughter of Zeus, while Achilles
is from an inferior deity. Your mother is of Zeus, while his is of
the Old Man of the Sea. So, go straight for him with tireless
bronze, so that he does not turn you back with a tough threat."   109

So Apollo spoke and he breathed great strength into the
Shepherd of the Troops, who went through the front lines armed
in glowing bronze. And the son of Anchises did not escape the
notice of Hera as he went against Achilles in the close formation of men. She was standing with the gods and said this:
"Think about it, Poseidon and Athena, both of you, how this
thing will come about. Phoebus Apollo sent Aeneas, armed in
gleaming bronze, to take on Achilles. So come, will we turn
Aeneas around or go behind him, so that some one of us can
stand beside Achilles? It would give him great might, so that his
spirit wants for nothing, and so that he could see that the best
of the immortals love him. It was, after all, the blowhards, the
windbags of the group, who in the past were back behind the
Trojans, protecting them in the fighting and the conflagration.
Everybody came down from Olympus to stand in opposition in
the fighting, so that Achilles would suffer nothing while among
the Trojans today. Afterward again he will experience the fate
his mother spun with the thread of life when she bore him. If
Achilles believes that those things are from an oracle of the
gods, then he will be afraid, when some hugely powerful god
comes against him in war. The gods are harsh when they reveal themselves clearly."   131

At that, the earth-shaker Poseidon answered her: "Don't be

angry because of what you're thinking. It is not necessary.
I would not want to drive the gods together in the struggle,
either us or the others, even though we are much more powerful. Instead, let's us go off the path to a vantage spot and sit
down. The war is the concern of mortal men. If Ares might start
a fight or Phoebus Apollo, or one of them might hold Achilles
off, they would not be allowed to get away with it, for immediately we would be roused into a huge din of war. And I think
things would be sorted out very quickly and those gods would
go back to their gathering on Olympus, taken down under our
hands if we find it necessary."   143

So the black beard spoke, and he led them to a wall heaped
up by the divine Heracles that the Trojans and Pallas Athena
built for him. It was high so that he could escape discreetly
whenever the sea monster rushed on him from the shore to the
plain. Poseidon sat down there and the other gods as well,
clothed around their shoulders by an impenetrable mist. And
opposite them, the other gods sat near you, Phoebus and Ares,
sacker of cities, on the brow of Callicolone, the little hill beside
the Simois.   152

And so they sat apart considering plans. They were hesitant
to commence a painful war between themselves, even though
Zeus sitting above had told them to.   155

The men and horses completely filled the plain, and the
bronze glowed. The earth resounded under their feet as
they charged together. There were two men who stood out as
most excellent of all in the middle of both sides. They were impatient to come together for a fight, Aeneas Anchisesson and
noble Achilles. Aeneas was first to move threateningly, as he
lowered the visor on the front of his stout helmet and held his
shield defiantly in front of his chest, and brandished his brazen
spear. And opposite was the son of Peleus who charged against
him like a vicious lion that men gathered from the whole district are eager to kill. At first he goes around contemptuously,

but when one of the bellicose youths hits him with a spear, he crouches for a leap, and curls back his lips. Foam starts to show around his teeth, and he whips his flanks and loins on both sides with his tail. With glaring gray eyes, he allows himself to charge fiercely into the fight. Either he would kill some of the men, or he will perish in the front of the crowd. In such a way did Achilles rouse his strength and awesome spirit as he went against greathearted Aeneas. When they got close, noble Achilles, fleet of foot, was first to address Aeneas: "Why have you come from the throng to make such a show of standing here? Does your heart urge you to fight against me because you hope to rule over the Trojans, those noble horsemen, because of some honor from Priam? Maybe, if you were to strip me of my armor, Priam might not place such a prize in your hands, but in the hands of his sons. After all, he is not foolish, but sound of mind. Why would the Trojans divide off a plantation superior to all others with vineyards and fields for you to dwell on if you were to kill me? What you hope for is hard to do. To be sure, I tell you, my man, I will put you to rout with my spear yet again! Do you not remember when I drove you from your cattle speedily on the fastest feet down from the mountains of Ida, even though I was alone? Then there was no turning back as you took off. You fled from there to Lyrnessus, and afterward I charged in and sacked it with the help of Athena and father Zeus. I went from there leading captive women. Zeus and the other gods protected you, but I don't think they will this time and so you should get your mind around it. Instead, I am ordering you to pull back into the crowd; you must not make a stand against me before you suffer something evil. Even a fool learns from experience."   198

And Aeneas replied to him, saying: "You ought not to speak to me as though to a small child, since I hope to put fear into you. I know very well, and you do too, that we are supposed to say heartrending and nasty things. We know each other's ancestry and we know each other's parents, and that we know from hearing in the past the words of mortal men. But you might not have seen mine, nor I yours. They say that you were sired by the exceptional Peleus, and that you were born to a mother Thetis, a daughter of the sea who has lovely hair. But I claim that I am the son of greathearted Anchises, and my mother is Aphrodite. Now, different ones of those will weep for a beloved son this day, but I think that the matter of who will go home from this fight is not to be sorted out with childish words. But if you wish to learn our ancestry, many men know it.   214

"Zeus, the cloud-gatherer, fathered Dardanus first, and he founded a colony known as Dardania, since there was yet not sacred Troy, the city founded by mortal men, to be found anywhere on the plain. Instead, Dardania was settled at the foot of Ida, which has many springs. Dardanus fathered a son, Erichthonius, who became king, and also the richest of mortal men. He had three thousand horses pastured down on the marsh. Mares were taking pleasure in their spirited foals, and as they grazed North Wind pounded them. He took on the guise of a stallion with a black mane and serviced the mares. And they became pregnant and bore twelve foals, and when they went to the boundary limits, frisking on the fertile field, they did not break the seed heads off the sacred grain. And when, frisking near the wide back of the sea, they were galloping in the breakers of the gray Aegean.   229

"Erichthonius fathered Tros, king of the Trojans. Tros was the father of three illustrious sons: Ilus, Assaracus, and the godlike Ganymede, who was the handsomest child born of mortal men. The gods snatched him away to become a cupbearer to Zeus, because of his beauty, and so that he could keep company with immortals. Ilus fathered a celebrated son, Laomedon, and Laomedon fathered Priam, and Lampus, and Clytius, and Hicetaon, scion of Ares. While Assaracus fathered Capys, who fathered a son Anchises. And I am from Anchises. Priam fathered noble Hector. Those are my ancestries and bloodlines, I claim to you. Zeus both increases virtue and lessens it however he pleases, as he is most powerful of all.   243

"But come, let us talk no longer about such things like little children. Let us stand in the middle of the conflict that burns most brightly. Yelling the most intense threats at each other would create too big a burden even to be carried by a ship of a hundred rowers. It is the nature of men to turn the tongue, and say things to many people, many terms and words here and there. There are some that are spoken and some heard. But any such haggling between us would require one to win, standing against each other like women who are angry because of some soul-withering argument railing at each other in the middle of the street making lots of claims, some true, others not. Their anger demands it. But you could not turn my valor away with words, even ardent ones, before fighting against me with bronze. So, come, let us have a taste of each other's brazen spears."

258

And then, you may be sure, he drove his stout spear furiously into Achilles's terrifying shield. The shield gave off a loud clang when struck by the head of the spear, and the son of Peleus was stunned as he held the shield away from him in his beefy hand. He thought that the long spear of greathearted Aeneas would pass easily through it. What an idiot! He did not understand, either in his mind or in his spirit, that it is never easily that the ever-glorious gifts of the gods yield to mortal men. And the stout spear of warlike Aeneas didn't penetrate the shield at all. The gold held it back. See there, the gifts of the god! The spear drove through two layers of the shield, and there were still three more to penetrate. The lame one pounded together five layers, two of them bronze, two inside of tin, and one of gold. That was the one that held the ashen spear.

272

Next, Achilles again cast his long spear. And he hit the buckler of Aeneas that was balanced all around. It hit the front under the rim, where runs the thinnest bronze and the ox hide is also thinnest. The spear of ash from Pelion rushed through, and the shield shrieked under its assault. Terrified, Aeneas ducked and held the shield up away from him, and the spear made its way through, splitting apart the layers of the shield, which protects all around, over Aeneas and driving into the surface of the ground. Aeneas stood there, having escaped the long spear. He was stunned and under the strain, and a gush of immense grief welled in his eyes as the spear was fixed in the ground close to him.

283

After that, Achilles pulled out his sharp sword with a terrifying yell and ardently charged at Aeneas, who grabbed a stone in his hand. It was a huge one, such that two men couldn't carry it, but he handled it easily, even though he was alone. At this point might Aeneas have rushed on Achilles, hitting him with the rock on either his helmet or his shield, and delivered to him utter destruction, or might Achilles have come close to him and taken his life with the sword, had not the earth-shaker Poseidon taken keen notice of what was happening. Immediately, he spoke to the other gods: "What trouble comes my way from greathearted Aeneas, who will be quickly dispatched by the son of Peleus and sent down to Hades, because he believed what Apollo, who shoots from afar, told him! What an idiot! And there is nothing that god will do to ward off Aeneas's utter destruction. But, why now should he suffer pain when he is blameless, pointlessly carrying the burdens of others? He always delighted the gods who dwell in the wide heavens with his gifts. But, come now, we will lead him out from under death. Quite possibly even Zeus would be angry if Achilles were to kill Aeneas in this wrangle, and his fate should be averted, so that he doesn't die without issue and the line of Dardanus vanishes. The son of Cronus loved Dardanus most of all the children born to him by mortal women. And since now the son of Cronus despises the progeny of Priam, certainly mighty Aeneas could rule the Trojans, and his children's children, such as he produces in the future."

308

And the revered Hera, with lovely eyes, replied: "Earth-shaker, being virtuous, you know perfectly well in your own

mind whether to save Aeneas, or to allow him to be taken down
by Achilles Peleusson. But, you may be sure that Pallas Athena
and I have sworn many oaths before all the gods that we will
never give aid to the Trojans on their day of destruction, not
even when warlike sons of the Acheans set Troy on fire and the
fire consumes it all." 317

After he heard that Poseidon, the earth-shaker, set out
through the fighting and the clanging of spears and got to where
Aeneas and glorious Achilles were. Immediately Poseidon
poured darkness over the eyes of Achilles Peleusson, and pulled
the well-bronzed spear of ash from the shield of greathearted
Aeneas, placing it in front of Achilles's feet. He lifted Aeneas up
from the ground and tossed him over many formations of heroes and horses. Hurled from the hand of the god, Aeneas came
to rest at the outer limits of the toilsome fighting. There the
Cauconians were arming for the fighting. The earth-shaker,
Poseidon, went over very close to him and spoke with winged
words: "Aeneas, which one of the gods foolishly directed
you to fight against the haughty son of Peleus? Achilles is at
once more powerful and more loved by the gods than you are.
Instead, you should give him ground and back off whenever
you are thrown together in the fighting, so that you don't find
yourself in the House of Hades, even though that is not your
fate. Afterward, when Achilles has his encounter with death
and fate, then you should take courage and fight among the
front lines, for none of the other Acheans will strip your armor
from you." 339

Having explained everything in detail, Poseidon left him
there. Next, he quickly dispersed the darkness from Achilles's
eyes. Achilles was disturbed, and spoke to his own greathearted
spirit: "I see such a marvel! My spear is lying there on the ground
like that, and yet I see no man there. But I had made a spear cast
and was determined to kill someone. And, to be sure, he was
Aeneas, beloved of the immortal gods. I was telling him how
pointless his boasting was, and that he should get out of here.

He does not have the stuff to take me on yet, so he should be happy to escape from death. But come now, give orders to the war-loving Danaans to go out and take on the other Trojans."   352

And you may be sure, he vaulted into the ranks, and gave an order to each man: "No longer now ought the noble Acheans stand far back from the Trojans! Come, let man go against man, eager to fight. It should be such that neither Ares, though an immortal god, nor Athena would come close to the front of the brawling and the struggling. I will do what I am able to with my powerful hands and feet. I declare that I will not yet give in, not even a little bit. I am firm in the formation and I think that it will not please any of the Trojans to come within close range of my spear."   363

In such a way did Achilles urge them on. And glorious Hector called out to the Trojans, shouting in a loud voice: "Haughty Trojans, have no fear of the son of Peleus. I might fight against both his rumors and the immortals. It is hard to fight rumors with a spear, and it is hard to fight against the gods because they are much stronger. Achilles tells many fictions about how this will end, but in his telling, he leaves out the part in the middle. I am going against him even if his hands are like fire, and his might is like shining iron."   372

So he spoke and inspired them. The Trojans raised up their spears and mixed close in together with strength, charging forward with a shout. And at that point Phoebus Apollo stood beside Hector and said: "Hector, do not go against Achilles in the front lines at all, and do not get close enough to be hit by his cast or struck by his sword. Instead, remain in the throng to be seen among the clamoring soldiers."   378

So the god spoke, and Hector was stunned when he heard the sound of the god's voice, and went back into the crowd of men. Achilles jumped into the Trojans, focused on valor, bellowing a dreadful yell. First, he took Iphition, the worthy son of Otryntas, leader of the troops of war. A Naiad nymph bore him to Otryntas, sacker of cities, below snowy Tmolus, in the

rich district of Hyde. Feverishly, Achilles went straight for Iphition with his spear and hit him with his spear in the middle of
the head, which was cleaved completely in two. Iphition fell
with a thud, and Achilles boasted over him: "Lie down, son of
Otryntas, most magnificent of all men. Your origin was near the
Gygean lake, where your family's plantation is, near Hyllus, rich
with fish, and the flowing Hermus." So Achilles spoke in boast
as Iphition's eyes were enclosed in blackness. The horsemen of
the Acheans tore Iphition to pieces with the iron tires on the
wheels of their chariots in the front lines of the tumult.   395

The very next thing, Achilles took out Demoleon, worthy
protector in a fight, son of Antenor. Achilles struck him through
the bronze cheek-pieces of his helmet in the temple. But the
brazen helmet did not hold, and the spear point shot through,
smashing the bone. His brain within was completely jumbled
up, subduing Demoleon's ardor.   400

Next Achilles rushed down off his chariot at Hippodamas in
front of him who was taking flight. As he ran away, Achilles
hit him with his spear in the back, and as his breath rushed
out, he bellowed like a bull bellows as it is dragged around the
shrine of Lord Poseidon, the Heliconian, by the youths placat-
ing the earth-shaker. In the same way Hippodamas bellowed as
his manly spirit left his bones. After that Achilles went with his
spear toward the godlike Polydorus Priamson. His father had
not permitted him to fight at all, since he was the most recently
born of his sons and was loved by Priam the most. He bested
everyone on his feet, and at that time he was foolishly showing
off the virtue of his feet by darting around the front lines of the
fighting. Achilles hit him with a cast to the middle as he was
rushing by. He was hit in the back where the golden straps of
his girdle held together the two shells of his breastplate. The
point of the spear went straight through him beside his navel.
He let out a howl as he fell to his knees, and a dark cloud enveloped him as he clutched his guts that were pouring out.   418

When Hector realized that it was his brother Polydorus

holding his guts as they gushed out onto the ground, and that a darkness was pouring over his eyes, he realized also that he could no longer endure holding himself back. Instead he went against Achilles, brandishing his sharp spear like flames. When Achilles saw him that way, he raised up his own spear in his hand and said in boast: "A man comes close who is someone of great concern to me, as he is one who killed my highly esteemed friend. And no longer, for sure, will we hunker down like birds avoiding each other in the war formations." And he looked at Hector with a scowl on his face and said: "Come close, so that our duel to the death will come sooner." 429

But it was not with fear that Hector, of the helmet with the waving plume, replied: "Son of Peleus, don't speak to me as though to a small child, because you hope to frighten me. I know clearly as you yourself do, that we are supposed to speak harshly and savagely to adversaries. I know you to be worthy, and that I am much your inferior. But, rest assured, I leave such things to lie on the knees of the gods. Even though you are stronger, I might snatch your spirit in throwing my spear, since even my javelin has proven sharp before." Having spoken, he raised the spear in his hand and threw it. At that, Athena exhaled, and an especially soft breeze turned the spear back from glorious Achilles, and it came back to Hector, and fell in front of his feet. 441

After that, Achilles ardently charged, intent on killing Hector, letting out a dreadful yell. But, Apollo caught him, which is very easy for a god to do, and enclosed his mind in a dense fog. Three times noble Achilles, fleet of foot, charged Hector with his brazen spear, and three times he collided with the heavy fog. But on the fourth time, he rushed like a madman, and Achilles shouted in a dreadful voice and winged words came forth: "Now, again, you escape death, dog! Evil is coming close to you, but now again Phoebus Apollo saved you. You ought to be praying to him as you go into the clash of weapons. You may be certain that you will meet me later and I will finish you off,

if one of the gods is helpful to me. For now, I will go back to
the others and go against whomever I meet up with."   454

So Achilles spoke, and he hit Dryops in the middle of the
neck with his weapon, and he fell forward over his feet. Achilles left him, and hit Demouchus Philetorson, one who was
upright and big. He took the hit in the knees and it crippled
him. Achilles took away his breath with a strike of his huge
sword. After that he rushed on Laogonus and Dardanus, the
two sons of Bias, shoving both from their chariot down to the
ground. One of them he hit with his spear, while the other
he struck with his sword at close range. And then he got Tros
Alastorson, who came up to him clasping his knees, hoping
that Achilles might take pity on him because they were of the
same age and spare him, taking him alive. What a fool he was
to plead that way, for Achilles was not about to be persuaded.
There was nothing sweet-spirited about the man, nor was he
kindly disposed. Instead, he was very savage. As Tros held
tight to his knees, pleading and begging, Achilles hit him in
the liver with his sword. The liver slid out and dark blood came
down from it filling his bosom. Darkness enveloped his eyes
and he was deprived of breath.   472

Achilles stood beside Moulius and struck his ear with his
spear, and then the brazen spear tip went through and out from
the other ear. And he killed Echeclus, son of Agenor; Achilles
drove his sword, with a costly hilt, down through the middle
of Echeclus's head, and the entire blade was warmed by blood.
Porphyrean death and mighty fate seized Echeclus. Next Achilles punctured Deucalion's hand with his brazen spear, and as
Deucalion held his maimed hand together with the tendons of
his forearm before seeing death, Achilles slashed his neck with
his sword and the head with its helmet was propelled a ways
off. Marrow and the spinal cord spurted out of the vertebrae,
and Deucalion fell to the ground splayed out.   483

After that Achilles went against Rhigmus, the exceptional
son of Pires, who had come from Thrace, which has rich soil.

Achilles made a cast and hit Rhigmus in the middle, and the bronze stuck in his belly, knocking him off his chariot. Achilles got his attendant Areithous when he turned the chariot back. He was struck in the back by the sharp spear. Achilles shoved him off the chariot, and the horses circled around.   489

It was like when a huge fire rages furiously in the deep valleys lying at the bottom of a forest in the mountains during drought. The wind blows into a cyclone, fanning flames and making thunderous noise. Achilles was like that, darting in all directions with his spear like a madman, killing those he touched. Dark blood flowed over the earth. It was like when two harnessed bulls with broad foreheads pound the white barley on the sacred threshing floor. As they walk along, the grain becomes fine under the bulls' heavy feet. So it was beneath the feet of the horses of greathearted Achilles. They trampled both corpses and shields. The axle underneath was completely splattered with blood, and the horses and the frame of the chariot as well. Behind the horses' hooves a great cloud of dust shot out, and from the iron tires, as well. The son of Peleus charged on to win glory, but his invincible hands were stained with filth.   503

Book 21

Achilles was in pursuit of the Trojans when he reached a ford of the wide-flowing river Xanthus, which has currents, and which was fathered by immortal Zeus. There Achilles split them into two groups: one he pursued on the plain toward the city. It was there, though, on an earlier day when glorious Hector raged, that the stunned Acheans were put to rout and poured out there in their flight. On that day Hera magnanimously extended her help to save them.　　　　　　7

The other half of the Trojans were driven toward the river and packed tightly together beside the deep-running, silver-glinting stream; they fell in with a loud noise, which smacked on the deep currents. There was the greatest of shouting all around on the banks. They cried out as they were swimming around here and there, turning in the currents. It was like locusts hovering in the air that are thrust back by a sudden eruption of flames from an intense fire. They escape to a river and hunker down with their wings on the water. In such a way did the river of deep-swirling currents of the Xanthus fill with thunderous noise from the mingling of horses and men, driven by Achilles.　16

Noble-born Achilles left his spear leaning against some tamarisks near the riverbank and jumped in like a demon with only his sword, his mind filled with plans for evil deeds. He whirled around and struck, and there arose from his slashing sword a ghastly groaning, and the water ran red with blood. It was like when a great sea monster, the dolphin, comes and the other fish flee in fear and are driven to fill safe coves in a harbor. In such a way the Trojans crouched down from fear under the overhanging banks in the currents of the dreadful river. But when the killing wore out Achilles's arms, he counted out twelve living youths from the river to be a penalty for the death of Patroclus, and led them up and out of the river, and bound their hands behind them with the well-made leather straps they wore with their supple tunics. He gave them to his comrades to lead back to the hollow ships and returned to furiously charging around.   33

At that moment he came upon Lycaon, a son of Priam, descendant of Dardanus, as he was fleeing from the river. Achilles had himself once captured the man when going out maliciously at night. He had taken Lycaon by surprise when he found him in his father's orchard cutting young shoots from a wild fig tree with his sharp bronze to make rails for a chariot. Achilles led him off against his will and took him in a ship across to well-built Lemnos. There a son of Jason paid a price for him. Eetion of Imbros, a guest-friend, gave Achilles a lot for him, and Achilles let him loose. Eetion sent him to shining Arisbe. He fled stealthily from there and arrived back in Troy at the ancestral palace. For eleven days he pleasured his spirit with his friends, celebrating his return from Lemnos, and on the twelfth day, some god threw him back into the hands of Achilles, who was about to send him to Hades, not home as he wanted.   48

Noble Achilles recognized him because of their previous encounter, even unarmed, and without helmet, shield, or spear. All those things he had thrown on the ground as he fled from the river, tired and sweaty. He was exhausted and his knees were giving out under him.   52

Exasperated, Achilles spoke to his own greathearted spirit: "What a fantastic thing I see! I have killed many haughty Trojans, but has one ever come back from the murky darkness down below? Yet here comes one who escaped his day of reckoning when I crossed over to sacred Lemnos. But the deep of the gray sea did not hold him, though it restrains many who would rather escape. Get yourself together, let him taste our spear point, so that I can learn where he will go from here. For sure the Earth Mother, source of life, will restrain him. She restrains even the powerful."   63

So Achilles stood pondering over the problem. And Priam's son was also amazed as he came closer. He was eager to clasp Achilles's knees, wanting more than anything to escape evil death and black fate. And, you may be sure, as he raised his long spear, noble Achilles was ardent for a strike. Priam's son ran under and grabbed Achilles's knees in supplication, while the spear passed over him into a spot of ground, standing upright where it had been cast, though eager to be gorged with the flesh of men. Lycaon was holding Achilles's knees with one hand, while the other held fast to the spear as he pled with winged words: "Noble-born sir, I approach you reverently as a supplicant. I beg you at your knees, Achilles, to show me reverence and take pity on me. When first I was with you, I tasted the gifts of Demeter on that day when you captured me in the beautiful orchard. You led me far away from my father and my loved ones, crossing to sacred Lemnos, and I fetched for you the worth of a hundred oxen. Then, to be released, I paid three times as much. This morning was for me just the twelfth day since returning to Troy. But now again, deadly fate places me in your hands. I am doomed to be despised in some way by father Zeus, who gave me back to you.   84

"It was but for a short span of life that my mother bore me. She was Laothoe, daughter of old Altes, who rules the war-loving Lelegians and held the high fortress of Pedasus, beside the Satnioeis. Priam took his daughter to wife and many others as well. Two sons were born to her, and you will have slaughtered both. Count on it. One of them, godlike Polydorus, was among the first of the foot soldiers you killed. You hit him with your sharp spear taking him down. Now evil comes to me here, because I don't think I'll escape your hands, since some demon sent me close to you. But, understand that I am not of the same womb as Hector, so I ask you not to kill me, because he killed your friend, who was both kind and mighty."   96

So the glorious son of Priam pled. But the one who heard was altogether unmoved: "You moron, don't promise me a ransom and don't carry on so. Until Patroclus met his fated day, I was of a kinder spirit and would still spare some of the Trojans. I took many of them alive and carried them off. But, now none will escape death, certainly not one that some god has thrown into my hands in front of Troy. And of all the Trojans, least of all to be spared is one of the children of Priam. But friend, even you must die, so why are you bawling like this? Patroclus died, though he was much better than you. Can you not see how handsome and big I am? I am of a worthy father, and the mother who bore me was a goddess. Even so, death and black fate come even to me, as they come to you. It may be at dawn, or in the evening, or noon, whenever someone with Ares takes my breath away with the cast of a spear, or with an arrow from a bow-string." 113

So Achilles spoke, and the son of Priam released his knees and let go of his own will to live. He released the spear and sat with both his arms outstretched. Achilles pulled out his sharp sword and struck him on the collarbone beside the neck, and the double-edged sword went completely through. Lycaon fell prone on the ground, dead. Dark blood flowed from him, dampening the earth. 119

Achilles grabbed him by the feet and tossed him into the river to be carried off. And he spoke with winged words, boasting: "Now you will lie there with the fishes, and they will lick the blood from your wound. You get no funeral honors, and nor will your mother place you on a reposing couch and wail in mourning. Instead, the Scamander will carry you to a wide bay of the sea, and many a fish, jumping along, will rise up from dark foam on the waves to gorge on Lycaon's white fat. 127

"Die, all of you, as you beat a hasty retreat toward sacred Troy, while I am charging like a bull behind you. The river, even though it runs deep and has silver glints as it flows, did not protect you. For a long time you sacrificed many bulls and threw solid-hoofed horses in alive as sacrifices. But you all shall perish in an evil fate. You will pay the price for the murder of

Patroclus and for the destruction of the Acheans who were
near the ships while I was away from the fighting."   135

So he spoke, and the river was extremely angry. He considered how he might stop Achilles from his brawling and how he
might avert the destruction of the Trojans. In the meanwhile,
the son of Peleus raged, brandishing his long spear with the aim
to kill Asteropaeus, the son of Pelagon. Pelagon was fathered
by the fair-flowing Axios and born by Peribea, eldest of the
daughters of Ascesamenus, when the deep-running river coupled
with her. Achilles charged at Asteropaeus as he came out of the
river and stood against Achilles holding two spears. Xanthus,
angry over the youths killed as Achilles was mercilessly raging
in the currents, put strength in Asteropaeus's mind. When
they moved in closer to one another, noble Achilles, fleet of foot,
was first to speak: "Who are you, and from where, and from
which men, who dares to come against me? Unhappy are
those whose sons make a stand against my strength!"   151

And the glorious son of Pelagon responded: "Greathearted
son of Peleus, why do you ask about my ancestry? I am from
Peonia, which has rich soil, and is far from here. I command
Peonian warriors with long spears. And now, for me, eleven
days have passed since I came to Troy. As to the other, I am descended from the wide-flowing Axios. The Axios, the most
beautiful water on the sacred earth, fathered Pelagon, famed for
the spear. And, they say, he fathered me. Now, shall we return
to fighting, glorious Achilles?"   160

So he spoke tauntingly. And noble Achilles lifted the ashen
spear of Peleus. As for the hero Asteropaeus, he hurled both
spears at the same time, since he was ambidextrous. He made
a cast with one spear at Achilles's shield. But it didn't go through,
nor did it smash the shield. The gold restrained it, the gifts of
the god. He cast the other, and it grazed the beefy right hand of
Achilles, and dark blood spurted out. But the spear passed over
and fixed in the ground, longing to be gorged on flesh. Next,
Achilles hurled the ashen spear straight at Asteropaeus, intent

on killing him. But he missed, hitting the overhang of the riverbank, and the ashen spear was stuck halfway into the bank. Eager for Asteropaeus, Achilles pulled out the sword hanging beside his thigh. Asteropaeus shook Achilles's spear, intent on pulling it out, but three times it resisted his strength and he was unable to extract it. And he wished in his heart for a fourth try to bend and break the ashen spear of the grandson of Aeacus, but before he could, Achilles came close and took his life with the sword. He stabbed him in the stomach, near the navel, and all his guts poured out onto the ground. He gasped as a cloud of darkness enclosed his eyes.   182

Achilles jumped on his chest and stripped the armor, boasting: "Lie this way. It is hard to do battle against the children of the invincible son of Cronus, even for one descended from a river. You claimed that you were the progeny of a wide-flowing river, but I boast that I am the progeny of great Zeus. Peleus Aeacusson who rules over many Myrmidons fathered me. And Aeacus was from Zeus. In two ways this makes me stronger. Zeus is more powerful than the rivers, which pour into the sea, and also one that Zeus fathered is more powerful than a river. And so, since there was a great river beside you, had it been able, it would have helped you. But it could not fight against Zeus Cronusson; Lord Achelous, god of rivers, is not his equal. Nor is great, mighty, deep-flowing Ocean, though he is the source of all the rivers and all the seas, and all the springs, and the deep wells, which spill over. Instead, even he is frightened when the dreadful lightning and thunder of great Zeus reverberate from the heavens."   199

So it was. And Achilles pulled his brazen spear from the overhanging bank, and left Asteropaeus there, lying in the sand, having taken his life. Dark water sprinkled over him and the eels and fish commenced to feed on the fatty tissue and devour the inner organs.   204

And Achilles set off among the Paeonians, mounted warriors, who had watched as their best was brought down beside the swirling river under the hands of the son of Peleus and his mighty sword, but had yet to be put to rout. There, he took Thersilochus, and Mydon, and Astypylus, and Mnesus, and Thrasius, and even Aenius and Ophelestes. And at that point fleet-footed Achilles would have slain even more Paeonians had not the deep-swirling river spoken angrily to him. Taking the guise of a man, he spoke from his deep currents: "O Achilles, you are the most powerful, by far, of all men, but you do the most awful things, since the gods themselves always protect you. If the son of Cronus gave to you the destruction of all the Trojan sons, at least drive them onto the plain away from me. It fills my lovely currents with corpses, and I am unable to pour out my flowing water into the shining sea when I am choked up with corpses. An amazement holds me, leader of troops, because you kill so destructively. But come now, stop."   221

And fleet-footed Achilles replied to the river: "These things will be as you say, noble-born Scamander. I will not sleep before fighting against the haughty Trojans until I go against the city to take it, and make a try against Hector, and whether he will bring me down, or I him, is uncertain."   226

So he spoke and charged on the Trojans like a demon. And then, the deep-swirling river spoke to Apollo: "Silver bow, offspring of Zeus! You are not preserving the plan of the son of Cronus. Zeus gave you special orders to stand beside the Trojans and to protect them until late evening darkens the fertile land."   232

And Achilles, famed for the spear, jumped from the overhanging bank and sprang into the middle of the river. While Xanthus rushed forward brandishing a flood of currents that whirled all around, and pushing many corpses. There was an abundance of them in his bed that Achilles killed, and bellowing like a bull, the river threw them out onto dry land. Those Trojans who were still alive, he saved, hiding them in the swirls of his deepest currents. He sent a terrible swelling wave circling around Achilles. It shoved against his shield, knocking him down, and he could not keep a firm foothold. He grabbed a great and noble elm tree, but it was ripped up by the roots and completely pushed off the bank. It held back the beautiful currents with its thick branches and dammed the river itself when everything that had been ripped up fell in. Achilles rose up and charged onto the plain, flying fast on his feet in fear. But the great god did not let up on his attempt to make noble Achilles desist in his struggle and avert the destruction of the Trojans. A black-topped wave of the Xanthus swept toward Achilles.   250

And the son of Peleus rushed away as far as a spear cast, with the force of a black eagle in the hunt, who is at the same time the most powerful and the fastest of the creatures that fly. His rush was like that, and the bronze on his chest clanked in a terrifying way and down below he was turning this way and that to escape the flood. But Xanthus followed behind Achilles with a roaring of currents. It was like when the man who digs irrigation channels leads the dark water from the high place to his orchard with a hoe in his hands, and pitches the obstructions from the channel, so that the stream flows along underneath bouncing along all the little pebbles. It goes swiftly gurgling along on its way down to the plants. The stream gets there before the man leading it does. In such a way was the swelling wave of currents constantly coming upon Achilles, even though he was quick on his feet. The gods are better than men.   264

As many times as noble Achilles, fleet of foot, stood against it, and wondered whether all of the gods who dwell in the heavens were chasing him, just that many times the river, fed by the rains of Zeus, slammed down from above on his shoulders. He was leaping on both his feet underneath, but he was in distress. The river pressed down on his knees, and swirled violently above, and the mud dragged on his feet. The son of Peleus groaned as he looked to the wide heavens: "Father Zeus, how is it that none of the gods comes down to save miserable me from the river, as if I would suffer such a thing? Not one of the other heavenly beings is to blame for this. But my own mother

must have told me lies when she said that I was to perish under
the fortress walls of the well-armed Trojans by means of the fast
darts of Apollo. Oh, how I wish Hector, who was brought up
here to be the best, might kill me. Then the one slaying me
would be noble, and a worthy man would he have killed. But
now a miserable death is fated for me, to be taken into a huge
river like a swine-herding boy whom a mountain torrent sweeps
away as he is crossing it in winter!"   283

So he spoke, and both Poseidon and Athena quickly came
and stood close to him, taking the guise of men. They took his
hand in theirs consolingly. Poseidon, the earth-shaker, was first
to speak: "There is nothing much that should cause you fear or
trembling, for both of us gods are here to assist you, and Zeus
approves of this. I am here and so is Pallas Athena. It is not fated
that you be taken down by the river. Instead it will desist in
this soon, as you will see for yourself. If you trust us, we will
place great might in you. Do not restrain your hands from the
battle that is harsh to all the same, until you have bottled up
the Trojan troops inside the famous walls, at least those who
might escape. You are to take away the breath from Hector,
and go back to the ships. We give it to you to win glory."   297

So spoke the two of them and they went back to the company of the immortals. After that he went onto the plain, greatly
encouraged by the command of the gods. It was filled all over
with water that had poured out onto it. There was much beautiful armor from the youths killed in the fighting and corpses
floating on it. He went straight along against the current, leaping on his knees underneath him, and the wide-flowing river
didn't hold him back, as Athena had fixed enormous power in
him. And the Scamander could not stop him because of his
strength, but it was still very angry with the son of Peleus. It
raised up a swelling wave with a crest on top and called out to
the Simois: "Dear brother, we must hold this powerful man on
both sides, since he will surely sack the great city of King Priam
in short order. The Trojans cannot hold out against him. Instead,

come to their aid immediately, and having filled your currents
with water from springs, rouse them all into mountain torrents.
Send a swelling wave that raises a huge racket from timbers and
stones coming down so we can stop this savage man, who now
has grown so powerful, and who wishes to be the equal of gods.
I tell you that not his might, nor his good looks, not even his
beautiful armor will help him. We can make those things lie
somewhere in a very newly formed pool. I will encase them in
mud underneath it. And I shall wrap around him with sand
down below, and pour around it a huge pile of gravel and shells
that will be enough. I shall enclose him down underneath with
so much slime that the Acheans will not know where his bones
are and cannot lay him to rest. There, can be erected a marker,
but it will not be necessary to build a mound when they give
him funerary rites."   323

And he rose up, swirling around above Achilles, pouring
foam, and corpses, and blood. A brownish-purple swelling wave
of the river, fed by the rains of Zeus, shot upward, taking down
the son of Peleus. Hera let out a shriek of fear for Achilles, concerned that the great river, with deep-swirling currents, might
wash him away. At once, she spoke to Hephaestus, her beloved
son: "Get up, my lame son! Let us rush into battle. The swirling Xanthus is against you. Avert this as quickly as possible. Put
on a display of many flames. I will be rousing a furious storm
from the sea, driven by West Wind, and swift South Wind, that
will fan the flames onto the Trojan bodies and their armor. Burn
the trees on the bank of Xanthus, and throw fire at him. And
do not turn away from him, even if he tries sweet talk and do
not hold back your flames at all until you hear the sound of my
shouting. Then hold off the unquenchable fire."   341

So she spoke, and Hephaestus set off a major conflagration.
First the fire burned on the plain, and burned many bodies, as
there were enough of them down on it that Achilles had killed.
The plain completely dried up, holding back the glorious water. It was like when in autumn North Wind dries out a freshly

watered orchard, it delights the one who tends it. So, the whole plain was dried, and the corpses on it were completely burned. And he turned the resplendent flames on the river. He set afire elms, and willows, and tamarisks, and he burned lotus, and bulrushes, and sedges and the other things that grow in profusion along the pretty currents of the river. The eels and the fishes were exhausted; they went down in the currents, diving here and there, worn out by the breath of ever-cunning Hephaestus.   355

As it was burning, the spirit of the river spoke to Hephaestus and called him by name: "Hephaestus, none of the gods can compete with you, and I could not fight these flames. Stop the fighting, but then immediately would noble Achilles drive the Trojans out of the city. What is it to me, fighting and help?"   360

He was speaking as he burned with fire. And up bubbled the beautiful currents, like a cauldron boils inside when held up over a fire, and the fat from a gently raised and smoked sacrificial beast melts as it bubbles up from all directions, and underneath lie dry sticks of firewood. So it was with his beautiful currents in the flames of fire. The water boiled, and did not want to go forward, and instead was held back. He screamed as he was worn down by the might of cunning Hephaestus, pleading to Hera with winged words: "Hera, why is your son causing only my currents such pain? I am not so deserving of your blame, as there are many others who would assist the Trojans. I tell you: I will stop completely, if you command it, but you must have him stop this. I will swear to this absolutely. I will never avert the day of evil for the Trojans, nor will I assist them when the warlike sons of the Acheans torch all of Troy with consuming fire."   376

After hearing him, Hera, the white-armed goddess, shouted right away to her beloved son: "Hephaestus, stop, my famous child! It does not seem a good thing to completely overwhelm an immortal god for the sake of mortals."   380

So she spoke, and Hephaestus extinguished the huge fire,

and the river immediately flowed, its beautiful currents rushing along in a swelling wave.   381

After that mighty Xanthus was subdued, and stopped fighting altogether. And though Hera reined in her anger, a bitter squabble broke out among the other gods, as the two things fluttered back and forth in their minds. Their wrangling created a huge noise, which crashed on the wide earth, and the sound of trumpets resounded through the great heavens. And Zeus, sitting on Olympus, heard what was going on. He laughed in his own heart contentedly when he saw the gods coming together in a rumble. They had kept separate for a long time, but that was no longer to be. Ares, cleaver of shields, began it, and he charged first against Athena with his brazen spear, speaking to her tauntingly: "Why again, stable fly, do you drive the gods together into a squabble with such unbelievable audacity, to be swatted by your oversize spirit? Do you not remember that you set Diomedes Tydeusson to wound me? You yourself took the spear from him and pushed it straight on me in plain sight, tearing my lovely flesh! Now, though, I think it's payback time for both of us for your deeds."   399

So he spoke, and struck against the dreaded, tasseled aegis. But not even a lightning bolt of Zeus can harm the aegis. There, Ares, stained by murder, struck her with his long spear, but she backed off and snatched up a rock in her strong hand. Rough and huge, it lay on the plain. Men had earlier set it in place to be a boundary marker of a field. With it she hit furious Ares on the neck, loosening his limbs. He was knocked back seven hundred feet before coming to rest, hair covered in dust and armor made crashing around him. Pallas Athena laughed and spoke to him with winged words, boasting: "You oaf, even now, you try to equal me in might, though you forget how much better I claim to be at war. Payback time indeed! You have now completely paid back the Furies of your mother, who is annoyed with you and plotting evil against you for abandoning the Acheans and protecting the haughty Trojans."   414

So saying, Athena turned back her shining eyes, and Aphrodite, daughter of Zeus, took Ares by the hand, and led him off, with much loud groaning. He had difficulty catching his breath. When Hera, the white-armed goddess, realized that she was there, she immediately spoke to Athena with winged words: "Oh my goodness, Atrytone, child of Zeus who bears the aegis, yet again there is a stable fly. She is leading man-killing Ares away from the fighting along the clashing of arms. Go in pursuit!"   422

So Hera spoke and Athena set off in the chase, delighted at heart. She rushed on Aphrodite and hit her breast with her tough hands, and roughly loosened her limbs. Ares and Aphrodite both lay on the fertile ground, while Athena boasted with winged words: "It should be like this for all those who would assist the Trojans when they make war against the armed Acheans. They should be so brave and bold. So you, Aphrodite, came as an ally to Ares when he made a stand against me. But for the two of you, we would long ago have completely stopped the warring and sacked the well-built city of Troy."   433

So Athena spoke, and Hera, the white-armed goddess, smiled. Afterward, the lord earth-shaker said to Apollo: "Phoebus, why are the two of us standing against each other? It doesn't seem correct though the others are starting to do so. Maybe it would be more disgraceful if we both return to the bronze threshold of Zeus on Olympus without fighting. So you start it. You were born more recently than I was, and it would not be seen as worthy if I do it, since I was born earlier and I know more. Fool, you have might but you're stupid, and because of this you do not even remember what evil things we experienced around Troy when we were the only gods among them. It was when we went from Zeus to the distinguished Laomedon to work as hired laborers for one year at a fixed rate of pay. That was a sign of how things would turn out. You well know that I built the wall around Troy, wide and very beautiful, so the city would be impregnable. And you herded cloven-hoofed cattle with curved horns in the forested glades of Ida, which has many ridges. But when the end came, the happy times when we might carry away our pay, the magnificent Laomedon overpowered us, stealing the wages, and sent us away, threatening to bind us hand and foot, and send us in ships to a foreign country. He also promised to slice away both our ears with bronze. Both of us retraced our steps with heavy hearts, angry over the pay that was promised but not received. Certainly you now bring pleasure to the Trojan troops, and you do not try with us to make certain that the haughty Trojans are completely and horribly destroyed, along with their children and their honored wives."   460

And the Lord Apollo, who shoots from afar, answered him: "Earth-shaker, I am not all that smart, as you said, but smart enough not to fight against you on account of wretched mortals. They are like leaves. At one moment they are full of youthful vigor, eating the grain from the field, but at the next, they wither into lifelessness. Let us quickly put a stop to the fighting, and let them do their own quarreling."   467

So he spoke and turned around again. He honored his uncle instead of coming to blows with him. But his sister, revered Artemis, huntress of wild beasts, scolded him tauntingly: "One who shoots from afar, run off, and concede victory to Poseidon, giving him a cause to boast for no reason. You're an idiot. Your bow does nothing more here than a puff of wind. I will never again listen to you boasting among the immortal gods in our father's hall as you did earlier when you claimed you would go against Poseidon in battle!"   476

So Artemis spoke, but Apollo, who works from afar, said nothing in reply. Instead, Leto, the revered mistress of Zeus, shouted angrily in reproach to the one who delights in archery: "How is it that you have such a short memory of having your fill of battling me, prodigal daughter? Even though you are good, I outstrip you in archery and strength. Because Zeus

placed in you the soul of a lioness, and gave it to you to skillfully kill whichever mountain animals you wish. You kill wild
beasts and deer, or you can do battle with great might and fight
in the heated conflict if you want to, but know well that I am
much your better, and you do not surpass me in strength."   488

And, to be sure, Leto took Artemis's left hand by the wrist
and with the right she took the bow from her shoulders. She
smiled as she beat Artemis around the ears, and the arrows fell
from her quiver. From Leto the weeping goddess fled like a dove
that flies into a hollow safe haven in a rock under a hawk. So
weeping Artemis escaped, as it would not be in accordance with
fate for her to be captured, but she left her bow there.   496

And the messenger Argicide addressed Leto: "There is no
way I will fight against you, Leto. It is a hard thing to pick a fight
with the bed partners of Zeus the cloud-gatherer. Instead, go
right ahead and boast to the immortal gods that you defeated
me with your great might."   501

So he spoke, and Leto collected the curved bows where
they had fallen down amid a whirlwind of dust. Leto took her
daughter's bow and returned separately. Artemis arrived at the
bronze threshold of the palace of Zeus. Crying, she went to sit
like a girl on her father's knees. The son of Cronus lifted her up
and held her close to him, as his long, fragrant robe trembled
around him from her sobs. He laughed sweetly: "Which of the
heavenly beings has done you such foolishness? How could they
do mischief like that in plain sight?"   510

And the noisy one answered the one well crowned: "Your
wife roughed me up, Father, white-armed Hera. On her account
strife and quarreling cling to the immortals."   513

In such a way the gods talked to each other. Meanwhile, Apollo
entered sacred Troy. He was concerned about the wall of the
well-built city, anxious that the Danaans not sack it that day,
which would have been beyond fate. But the other gods, who
are everlasting, went to Olympus, where they sat down beside
their father's dark cloud, some nursing grudges, and some

greatly enjoying being themselves. At the same time Achilles was killing Trojans and their solid-hoofed horses. It was like when smoke goes up into the wide heavens and arrives in the starry beyond; it provokes the wrath of the gods, and they lay conflict on all, and send concern for many. In such a way did Achilles lay conflict and concern on the Trojans.   525

Old Priam stood on his excellent tower, and as he did noticed the monster Achilles. Trojans clamoring in the fight fled from him, and no one displayed any valor. Priam groaned and went down from the tower to rouse up the famous gate keepers along the wall: "Hold the gates open until the troops come toward the city in rout, for I tell you Achilles is coming close. I think ruin is imminent. When the men are packed tightly so they can rest, close the thick, fitted doors. I fear that man might jump inside the wall."   536

They pushed back the bolts, and flung open the gates, and flew around preparing for safety. Meanwhile, Apollo jumped down opposite Achilles so that he might avert the ruin of the Trojans.   539

The Trojans rushed straight for the city and its lofty wall, parched with thirst from sucking in the dust as they fled from the plain. Achilles was brutal in handling his spear, loosening their hearts. He was powerful as he raged to win glory.   543

And there might the sons of the Acheans have taken Troy had not Phoebus Apollo incensed a man, noble Agenor Antenorsson, who was both illustrious and powerful. Apollo thrust courage into his heart, and himself stood beside Agenor to ward off the heavy hand of death. He leaned against the oak tree, enclosed in a dense mist. Agenor recognized Achilles, sacker of cities, and stood still, his heart darkening as he waited there. Upset, he spoke to his own greathearted spirit: "Oh my, what a situation this is for me. I could flee from mighty Achilles, though the others are clamoring and running off from fright over there. If I do that, he will capture me, and cut off my

head like child's play. But if I permit these men to be thrown
into disorder by Achilles Peleusseon, I can flee on foot in another direction toward the Trojan plain, so that I would come
to the ridges of Ida and the wooded thickets on the west side,
and after bathing in the chilled water of a river, go back to
Troy. But, why is my heart in this dilemma? Were I to turn
away quickly, he would notice me, and Achilles would charge
at me immediately on his speedy feet. Not even then is it possible for me to avert death and fate. He is truly the mightiest by
far of all men, and if I go against him in front of the city, even
this man will, in time, have his flesh wounded with sharp
bronze. My mind is strong. People say that Achilles is to die, but
only after Zeus Cronusson grants him glory."   570

So he spoke and crouched down to wait for Achilles, and inside him his brave heart was charging up for war and fighting.
He was like a she-leopard who has come out of her lair to the
deep forest against hunters. There is nothing in her spirit that
said to be fearful or to rout, even though she could hear the
barking. Even if they were to get her first with a strike or a
throw, even pierced by a spear, she would not cease her bravery until she is completely wounded or brought down altogether. So noble Agenor, the fine son of Antenor, had no desire
to flee until he competed against Achilles. Instead, he held his
balanced shield in front of him and set his spear in place and
shouted loudly: "How much did you hope in your mind that today you might sack the city of the proud Trojans, fool! There is
still much suffering to be endured, more than anybody could
imagine. But we are brave warriors and we are many. We stand
in front to protect Troy and our beloved parents, wives, and
children. But here you may meet your fate, in this way, even
though you are magnificent and you are bold at warring."   589

At that, he hurled a sharp javelin from his sturdy hand and
hit the shin below the knee, and did not miss. A greave of newly
fashioned tin covered it. There was a dreadful crash, and the
bronze bounced back from it; the javelin did not pierce the

greave. The gifts of the god protected Achilles. Next the son of Peleus charged against godlike Agenor, but Apollo still didn't allow Achilles to win glory. Instead, he snatched Agenor away, enclosing him in a dense mist, and quietly sent him back home from the fighting. After that, Apollo lured the son of Peleus away from the troops with a ruse. He who works from afar, appearing exactly like Agenor, stood where his feet had been before. Apollo raced off, with Achilles chasing him on foot. He chased him across the plain, covered with grain, and turned beside the river Scamander, which has deep currents. Apollo outran Achilles by a little bit. With such a ruse Apollo confounded the one constantly trying to catch up with him on his feet. During this time the other Trojans welcomed the chance to flee in a mass toward the city, and the city was filled as they packed in together. And none dared to go outside the city and the wall. While they still remained with each other, they took stock of who fled and who had died in the fighting. Hurriedly, they poured into the city because of one who saved some of them using his feet and knees—Phoebus Apollo.   611

Book 22

Those who had fled into the city were like fawns sweating to cool off and drinking to slake their thirst. They leaned against the fine battlements, calling out, while the Acheans, coming closer to the walls, went around with their bucklers leaning on their shoulders. But Hector remained outside, shackled by ruinous destiny, in front of the Scaean Gate of Troy.   6

Elsewhere, Phoebus Apollo called to the son of Peleus: "Son of Peleus, why are you chasing me on your swift feet? You are mortal, but I am a god who eats no food! You have worked yourself up into a wild frenzy without realizing that. Have you now no concern for wrangling with the Trojans who fled back into the city, when you turned away to come here? You cannot kill me, because I am not destined for that."   13

Indignant, fleet-footed Achilles answered: "One who works from afar, you have tricked me now by turning me away from the wall. Otherwise, many would have chewed dirt without reaching Troy. Now you saved them handily and snatched great glory away from me, as you have no fear of reprisal in the future. I might avenge this on you, if the power were mine."   20

So Achilles spoke, and he focused his mind on going to the city, rushing like a prize-winning horse pulling a chariot that runs easily, stretched out on a plain. So Achilles moved, with his feet and knees lifted up high as he ran.   24

Old Priam was the first to see Achilles, gleaming like a star as he rushed over the plain, a star of a size that can be seen very clearly when it is revealed among the many stars of night at milking time. They call it by the name Dog of Orion. When it is at its brightest, it becomes a sign of evil, and brings intense, feverish heat to miserable men. So the bronze around his chest

gleamed as Achilles ran. The old man groaned and whipped his
head with his hands. He held them up and with a great groaning cried out pleading with his dear son, who stood motionless
in front of the gates, eager to fight against Achilles. The old man
extended his arms and begged: "Hector, dear son of mine, do
not make a stand against this man alone, and so meet your fate!
You would be taken down by Achilles, since he is much better.
That would be a disgrace. I wish that the gods loved him as
much as I do. For then quickly dogs and buzzards would dine
on him as he lay unmourned. Then dreadful grief would leave
my heart on account of it. That man has deprived me of many
excellent sons. Some he killed, others he transported in ships
to be sold in foreign places. And now I am unable to see two
sons, Lycaon and Polydorus, among the Trojans who have
crowded into the city. Laothoe, princess of women, bore them
to me. But if they are alive in the camp near the ships, certainly
we will ransom them with bronze and gold. We have much of
those in here. The old man Altes, with the famous name, provided many such things for his daughter Laothoe's bride price.
But if they are dead and gone to the palaces of Hades, there will
be grief in my heart and that of their mother. There will be grief
for the other troops, but their grief will have a shorter life, if you
are not overwhelmed and killed by Achilles. Instead, come inside the wall, dear child, so that you might save the Trojans and
the Trojan women. You should not secure great glory for the
son of Peleus. You would deprive yourself of your own share of
a long life. Take pity on me, who still ponders his misfortune
and is miserable. I am at the doorstep of old age, one to whom
father Cronusson has given the evil fate of withering away
while my sons perish, my daughters are ravaged, and my treasure chambers plundered, and the babies are thrown to the
ground in the burning conflagration, and the daughters-in-law
are dragged away by the murderous hands of the Acheans. The
end for me is to be struck with sharp bronze that will take the
spirit from my limbs, and then savage dogs will pull me to pieces

in front of the gates. The dogs who will drink my blood in a mad frenzy as I lie in the entrance chamber will be the very ones I have fed around the tables in the courtyard of my halls. It is proper that a young man who is killed in deadly conflict by sharp bronze be laid out in such a way that even though dead, he is made to look handsome. But it is quite another thing and a shame for an old man to be killed, and then dogs ravage his gray head, and gray beard, and genitals. This is a most disgraceful behavior for wretched mortals."   76

To be sure, the old man pulled on his gray hairs, tearing them from his head. But Hector's heart was unmoved. On the other side, his mother's eyes welled tears as she wailed. She loosed her bosom and held up a nipple in her left hand, and spoke to Hector, as the tears flowed: "Hector, my child, pay reverence to this that is mine and have mercy on me. If I ever held it out to ease your pain, remember that and protect our people against that man from inside the wall. Do not stand in front of it like this. It is disgraceful! If indeed he kills you, I will never weep beside your reposing couch for my beloved sprout, my own child, and neither will the wife you gave a large bride price for. Far from us, the swift dogs of the Argives will feast on you beside the ships."   89

So they both wept as they shouted to their dear son, earnestly imploring him. But Hector's heart was unmoved. Instead he waited on monstrous Achilles as he came closer. And he was like a snake near its hole in the mountains. As it waits for men to come near, it munches on evil herbs, and a dreadful anger enters it. It excites dread when it is seen coiling beside its hole. So Hector, with unquenchable strength, did not withdraw but propped up his gleaming shield against the solidly built tower. Annoyed, he spoke to his own greathearted spirit: "If I enter the gates to man the wall, Polydamas will surely be the first to reproach me, as he told me when noble Achilles rose up that deadly night to command the Trojans to return to the city. It definitely would have been a much better plan, but I did not listen. Now, since I wasted troops out of my own blind folly, I am ashamed around the Trojans and the long-gowned Trojan women, and I fear that at some time somebody might say that no one else was more timid than I. 'Hector trusted in his own might, and wasted the troops,' so they will say. Then, it would seem to me a better plan that either I return having gone against Achilles and killed him, or perish at his hand in a very public way before the city. Or perhaps, I could lay down my bossed shield and sturdy helmet, and prop my spear against the wall, and go myself to exceptional Achilles as he comes, and promise him that we will return Helen and her property with her, everything of what Alexander brought to Troy in his hollow ships that Agamemnon could carry back. She was the source of the quarrel. In addition, we would divide up what is in the city and what has been hidden elsewhere. Afterward I would swear a solemn oath that nothing has been kept secret, but that all the property has been divided in two parts, even what has been hoarded in the lovely city. But why am I debating this dilemma in my own heart? I'm not going to plead with him if I go. He will not have pity on me, and he will not respect me. Since I would be taking off my armor, he would kill me in my underwear like he would a woman. Nor is there any way that both of us might converse alongside the oak or the rock headland like a young girl and a youth courting her, exchanging intimate banter with each other. It is better then that we come together to fight as quickly as possible. We will know to which one the Olympian might grant glory."   130

So he pondered as he waited. Achilles came closer, equal to Enyalius, the helmed warrior. He brandished the frightening spear of Pelion ash over his right shoulder. Around him bronze gleamed like rays of a radiant fire, or of the rising sun. So he appeared when Hector caught sight of him, and was seized with trembling, and did not dare to make his stand there. He left the gate behind him and set off in flight. But the son of Peleus charged after him, trusting in his swift feet. He was like a peregrine falcon in the mountains, the fastest of winged creatures. It handily stoops on a trembling dove that flees below. Honing in on the shrill chirping, it rushes into the thicket and charges. Its heart directs it to seize the dove. In such a way did Achilles fly straight toward Hector, who trembled under the Trojans' wall, and then set his speedy limbs in motion. They raced past the lookout's mound and the wind-blown wild fig, constantly away from the wall, and from there they rushed along the wagon road and came to the spring that flows prettily. In that spot there are two fountains that rush out from the swirling Scamander. One pours warm water that gives off steam as though from a blazing fire. But the other even in summer pours forth water that is cold like hail, or the ice of winter. There between them were the wide wash tanks of fine stone where the pretty wives and daughters of the Trojans used to launder their shining garments during peacetime, until the sons of the Acheans came. There two men ran, one in flight, the other in pursuit. The one in front fleeing was fast, but the one chasing was faster. It was not about winning a sacrificial animal or a shield, prizes men win on their feet. Instead, noble horseman Hector was running for his life. It was like when prize-winning, solid-hoofed horses run fast around a racetrack, there is a huge contest underway. The prize is a tripod or a woman. The race is in honor of a warrior who has been killed. In that way both men ran around Priam's city three times on nimble feet.   166

As all the gods looked on, the father of men and of gods was first among them to speak: "I see clearly that a dear man is being chased around the wall. My heart fills with grief for Hector, who called to me often as he burned thighs on the peaks of Ida, with its many ridges, and also when he was at the highest point in the city. Now noble Achilles is chasing him on his swift feet around Priam's city. So come now, gods, think about this and give your counsel on whether we should save Hector from death, or vanquish him now using excellent Achilles Peleusson as our agent."   176

And Athena, the sharp-eyed goddess, spoke back to him: "O Father, you of white lightning and dark clouds, what nonsense you speak. The man's death was long ago fixed as his fate. Do you wish to lift him away from his death because you are feeling bad about it? Do it, but the other gods will not praise you for it."   181

And cloud-gathering Zeus responded: "Courage, dear child born of my head, I wasn't saying anything profound, and want to indulge you. Do as you please and don't hold back any longer." So saying, he urged Athena on, who had been eager for some time to go charging from his side down from the peak of Olympus.   187

And swift Achilles constantly pressed on Hector, badgering him. It was like when a dog chases a fawn in the mountains: he drives him from his den and through valleys and glades. And though the fawn cowers down to hide under a thicket, the dog tracks it relentlessly. So Hector could not hide from fleet-footed Achilles.   193

Every time Hector went near the Dardanian Gate under the well-built tower, hoping that his comrades would hurl down missiles from above, Achilles turned him toward the plain, outpacing him, though Hector himself was constantly fleeing toward the city. It was like in a dream: when being chased, one is unable to escape. On the one hand, there is one who cannot entirely escape, and on the other there is one who cannot quite catch the one pursued. How did Hector escape his deadly fate so many times? He would not have, had not Apollo come close to him just at the point of exhaustion. He increased Hector's strength and gave speed to his limbs. Noble Achilles nodded his head to his troops, forbidding them to shoot bitter arrows at Hector, lest one of them win glory doing so. If that happened, Achilles would win second place in glory. But when

Hector arrived at the spring for the fourth time, the father held
out his golden balance and placed on it two fates of death, which
causes a long sleep: one for Achilles and the other for Hector,
that noble horseman. He held it up by its middle. It tilted toward the fatal day for Hector. He was going to Hades, and Phoebus Apollo abandoned him.   213

Athena, the sharp-eyed goddess, came to the son of Peleus
and, standing close, spoke to him with winged words: "It is as
I had hoped, dear glorious Achilles. Both of us, with the blessing of Zeus, are to carry great glory to the Acheans in front of
the ships. We are to destroy Hector, even though his appetite
for fighting is insatiable. Until now it was impossible because he
always got away, but he would not have experienced so many
escapes save for Apollo, who works from afar. Apollo has been
prostrating himself before the feet of father Zeus, who bears
the aegis. So stand now, and take a breather while I go over there
and persuade Hector to fight against you."   223

So Athena spoke, and Achilles joyfully obeyed. He stood
leaning on the bronze-pointed, ashen spear. And she left him
and went to noble Hector, taking the form and likeness of
Deïphobus. Standing close to Hector, she spoke in Deïphobus's
tireless voice with winged words: "Older brother, while chasing you around Priam's city on his speedy feet, Achilles was
getting the better of you. But come on, we will stand and protect each other as we take him on."   231

And great Hector, of the helmet with the waving plume, answered: "Deïphobus, in the past, I knew you to be the dearest
by far of all the children born to Priam and Hecuba. And still
now I have great esteem for you that you would dare do this
for my sake, since you saw what was happening and came out
from the wall, while the others remained inside."   237

And Athena, the sharp-eyed goddess, answered: "Older
brother, when you were outside the gate, our father and revered
mother pleaded mightily, weeping and sobbing, for the comrades around them to remain there, while everyone trembled

with fear. But my spirit was worn down by grievous sorrow in
there. So now I am eager to go straight to the fight. There should
be no stinginess with spears. And we will see on that account
whether Achilles slays us and carries the bloody spoils back to
the hollow ships, or whether he is vanquished by your spear." 246

Having so spoken and carried off her deceit, Athena led
Hector off. And when they came close to Achilles, great Hector,
of the helmet with the waving plume, was first to speak:
"Though three times before I was put to rout by you around the
sacred city of Priam, I will not run away any longer, son of
Peleus. I did not dare to make a stand at all, but now again, my
spirit has been roused to stand against you. Either I will capture
or be captured. But come, we will yield here to the gods, for
they will be the best witnesses and monitors of agreements.
I will not treat you, who are magnificent, in a disgraceful way
if Zeus gives me enduring courage, and I take away your life.
Rather, I will strip your corpse of the famous armor, Achilles,
and I shall give the body back to the Acheans. And you do
likewise." 259

But fleet-footed Achilles scowled as he answered: "Enough,
Hector! Do not speak to me of agreements. It is not like there is
a solemn oath between lions and men, nor do wolves and lambs
have the same mind. Instead they are diametrically opposed
with regard to what is evil. In the same way, there is no friendship between me and you, and between the two of us there is
to be no oath, until one or the other falls in fighting that sati-
ates the blood of long-suffering Ares. Remember all your fighting skills, for now it is necessary for you to be a warrior and to
fight bravely. For you there is no escape. Soon Pallas Athena will
vanquish you with my spear. Now you will pay back for my pain
over the multitude of my comrades you killed with your spear
when you were raging." 272

Thus it was. And, taking the long spear in his palm, Achilles
hurled the missile. But glorious Hector saw it before it shot off
and avoided it. The brazen spear flew over him and became

fixed in the ground. Pallas Athena took it up and gave it back to Achilles, but concealed her action from Hector, Shepherd of the Troops. Hector said to exceptional Achilles: "You missed. And furthermore, there is no way that you would know anything about what fate there is for me from Zeus, as you claim. Instead you're a good talker, but what you say is nonsense! You did that to make me afraid, so I would forget my resolve, my valor. But I will not be someone you put to rout, so you can fix your spear in his back. You will have to drive it straight through my chest, if some god grants it to you. But now again, ward off my brazen spear or you will truly receive it all in your flesh. It would certainly make for a lighter load on the Trojans if you were to wither away. You are the worst curse for them."   288

And so, he held the long spear in his hand and then hurled it, and it hit the middle of the shield of the son of Peleus, and did not miss. But the spear glanced off a long way from the shield. Hector was upset that the speedy missile had fled from his hand in failure, and stood downcast. He did not have another spear, so he called loudly to Deïphobus, of the white shield, asking him for a long spear. But neither Deïphobus nor anything was close by. Hector realized what was happening and said: "Oh damn! It is true that the gods are calling death for me. I thought I spoke to the hero Deïphobus who was with me, but he is inside the wall. Athena tricked me. Now an evil death is not far off still and draws closer to me. And there is no escape! For a long time, this was the plan more loved by Zeus, and the son of Zeus who shoots from afar. In the past they were kindly disposed to protect me, but now deadly fate has found me. Yes, I am to perish without anyone's caring, and without glory. But I must try something huge and find out where things are headed."   305

So saying, he pulled out his sharp sword that was fixed below his flank. It was both big and stout. He charged into close combat, like a high-flying eagle that is going through dark clouds makes a stoop on a downy lamb or a jittery hare on the

plain, snatching it up. In such a way did Hector pounce, as he
brandished his sharp sword. But Achilles charged, having filled
his spirit with the strength of a wild beast. In front of him, his
shield covered his chest, beautiful and dazzling. The helmet had
its four plumes nodding. It was gorgeous with all the ethereal
gold that Hephaestus had hammered in around the mount for
the plumes. Like a star that is in the night sky at milking time,
that most beautiful evening star set in the heavens—in such a
way did the sharp-pointed spear tip that Achilles held in his
right hand gleam, plotting harm for noble Hector, looking
over his lovely flesh, looking for something like a gap in the armor. That intent was all the greater because Hector's flesh was
clothed in the sturdy, beautiful bronze armor that he had stripped
when he took the life of Patroclus. A gap was revealed where
the shoulder blades hold the neck and throat so that in the
quickest way might his life meet destruction.   325

At that moment noble Achilles forcefully drove the spear forward, and the spear point went completely through the soft
part of Hector's neck, though the heavy bronze did not cut off
the delicate windpipe, so that he could still speak to Achilles.
Hector fell in the dust, and noble Achilles boasted: "Whatever
you said to Patroclus when you stripped him now comes to you.
You were not afraid of me because I was separated from the
others. Fool! My great attendant whose limbs you loosed was
better than you. I left him behind near the ships. You, the dogs
and birds will pull to pieces without ceremony, while the Acheans will give him funeral rites."   336

Close to death, Hector, of the helmet with the waving plume,
said faintly: "I beg you, on your life and on your knees and your
parents' knees, do not allow the dogs of the Acheans to feast on
me by the ships. There is enough bronze and gold for you. Receive the gifts my father and revered mother will give you and
have my body returned back home so that the Trojans and the
Trojan wives can give me my share of the funeral fire."   343

Scowling, fleet-footed Achilles responded: "Dog, do not plead on my knees, nor those of my parents, as if somehow you could sway me, one who could cut off flesh and eat it raw, after what you have done. There is nothing that will protect your head from the dogs. Not even if a ransom ten times or twenty times a sum beyond counting were to be brought here, with more promised besides. Not even if Priam Dardanusson himself were to order that your weight be paid in his gold. And there is no way that your revered mother will place you on a reposing couch, to wail over the one she bore. No, the dogs and birds will divide up everything."   354

As he died, Hector, of the helmet with the waving plume, said: "I predict, and you know it well, though you will not believe me. There is an iron spirit in your mind. What is happening now is creating divine wrath for you among the gods. Think about it on that day when Paris and Phoebus Apollo destroy you, valiant though you are, at the Scaean Gate."   360

Having said that, the end of death enveloped him. His soul fluttered from the parts of his body and set off for Hades. Groaning, his fate left behind his manhood and his might. Though he was dead, noble Achilles said to him: "Die. I will accept then whatever fate Zeus and the other immortal gods produce for me."   366

And so it was. Achilles pulled his brazen spear out of the corpse and set it aside. He slipped the bloody armor from the shoulders. The other sons of the Acheans came running over, and they marveled at the large size and the handsome face of Hector, but there was not one of them who did not stab the corpse. Thus might one of them have spoken to another man close to him: "He's a whole lot more subdued than he was when he torched the ships."   375

And when he had stripped the armor, noble Achilles, fleet of foot, stood among the Acheans and spoke to them in winged words: "O friends, commanders, and counselors of the Argives, now the gods have granted the downfall of this man who did much harm. All the others put together could not have done as much. But come, let us make a trial with our arms so that we might know what the Trojans have on their mind, whether they will leave their high city to come down here because he has fallen and make a vigorous stand against us, without Hector. But why am I debating these things in my heart? Patroclus lies dead by the ships and has not received proper funeral rites. I shall not forget him, as long as I am among the living and my own limbs might lift me up. Even though the dead in Hades forget, even there I will remember my dear friend. Come, now we will return to the hollow ships so that the youths of the Acheans can sing the hymn of praise. We will lead them there. We have won glory. Noble Hector is dead. On that account the Trojans will come down from the city to pray to a god."   395

So it went, and Achilles planned abusive treatment of Hector. He slit the tendons of both his feet on the dorsal side to the ankle from the heel, and with ox hide ropes he suspended them from his chariot and bound them, so that it allowed the head to be dragged behind. He lifted the famous armor up into the chariot and mounted it. He cracked the whip and the two horses readily flew off. A cloud of dust rose up as the corpse was dragged along. On both sides, the black hair fell, and the head fell completely in the dust, the same head that had before lain with his wife in pleasure. And at that moment Zeus allowed Achilles to desecrate his enemies on the earth of their homeland.   404

So was Hector's head completely covered with dust. His mother tore at her hair, tossing away her glistening veil, crying loudly as she looked at her great child. His dear father gave out a great groan of lament. Around him the troops went down from the city with crying and groaning. So great was the welling of tears for him that it was as though the high, craggy city were consumed by fire. The troops were barely able to keep the grieving old man from going out through the Dardanian Gate. He was rolling around down in dung and begging loudly. The old man called to them, calling each man by name: "Stop this, my friends. And even though we are grieving, let me leave the city by myself and go to the ships of the Acheans. I will plead with this man who has done this savage, monstrous deed if somehow he will respect my age and take pity on an old man. Even now he has done such things for his father Peleus, who gave him life and brought him up to become a bane for the Trojans. He laid pain on me beyond that of all other men. Achilles has killed so many of my sons, who have fallen into the long sleep of death. But for them all, though there was much mourning and sorrow, there was not so much as for this one. The sharp grief of Hector being carried down to Hades is for me the worst. He ought to have died in my arms. Then we would both have our fill of crying and welling tears, both his mother who bore him to be unlucky, and I myself."   428

So he spoke, weeping. The citizens commenced the greatest groaning, and Hecuba started copious wailing among the Trojan women: "I am miserable because of your loss, my child. Why now am I going to live after experiencing the horror of your death? You were my pride, night and day. You were a great advantage for the Trojans and the Trojan women throughout the city. You were greatly renowned, and they welcomed you among them as though you were a god. But now, again comes death and fate."   436

She wept as she spoke. No one had gone to tell Hector's wife the true story of her husband earlier, when the message would have been that he was making a stand outside the gates. Knowing nothing about Hector, Andromache was weaving at her loom in the lofty inner recess of her chamber. Her loom produced a two-ply purple fabric, and as she sat in her chair she embroidered it with varied colors. And she called to her fair-haired maids throughout the palace to set up a large tripod around the fire, so there would be a warm bath for Hector when he returned from the fighting. How foolish she was; she didn't realize that he was a very long way from a bath. Sharp-eyed Athena took him down with the hands of Achilles. When Andromache heard the loud sobbing and wailing far away on the tower, she dropped her shuttle to the floor, her limbs whirling her around. She spoke again to her lovely-haired servants, saying: "Come here, you two. Follow me as I find out what has happened. I heard the voice of my respected mother-in-law, and because of that my heart is pounding in my chest and my throat and my legs are frozen beneath me. Something evil is close to the children of Priam, and I would like to get word of it. But I am especially worried that noble Achilles may have pursued my brave Hector on the plain and cut him off from the city and stopped him completely from the destructive valor that holds him. He always charges to the front and yields to the might of no one. He would never stay in the mass of men."

459

Having said that, she went through the halls like one possessed, her heart pounding, and with her went her chambermaids. And when they reached the tower and the throng of men hunkering down like frightened birds, she recognized Hector, as he was dragged before the city. The fast horses callously pulled him toward the hollow ships of the Acheans. Dusky night enveloped her eyes, and she fell backward. Her soul shrieked as it went out and away from her. The fall knocked her splendid hairpiece far from her head, her fillet, and hairnet, and the plaited mount for her veil. Golden Aphrodite gave that to her on the day when Hector, of the helmet with the waving plume, led her from Eetion's palace, having provided a bride price beyond counting. Her sisters-in-law were beside her, and around them her husband's brothers' wives in a gaggle. They feared that she would perish. But after a while she revived, and collected herself, mind and spirit. She spoke to the Trojan women, with intermittent spells of weeping and wailing: "Hector, I am wretched. We were both sent curses at birth, you in Troy, in Priam's palace, and I in Thebes, under forested Placus, in Eetion's palace. It was he who brought me up unlucky, with a terrible fate, when I was a little thing. Would that I had not been born! And now, you go to Hades, under the secret places of the earth, while you left me in a place of dismal grief, a widow in your halls. Your son is there, yet a baby, whom we conceived, you and I, to be unlucky. And Hector, you will be no use to him, since you are dead, nor he to you. Even if he might escape the war brought on by the Acheans, which brings many tears, there will for him, you may be sure, always be struggle and worry in the future. Others will encroach on the boundaries of his fields, shrinking them. This day has made our son an orphan, who has no contemporaries his own age. An orphan hangs his head in sadness and his cheeks are covered with tears. In want, the child goes up to friends of his father, and from one receives a cloak, and another a tunic. One of those who take pity on him extends a cup that he holds for a little while. There is enough in it to moisten his lips, but not to moisten the palate. The child with both parents still living, angrily excludes the orphan from the feast, beating him with his hands, and making abusive threats: 'Get lost! Your father does not dine with us.' And he would cry to his widowed mother. Before, Astyanax sat on his father's knees and ate things such as marrow and fat mutton. Afterward he would go to sleep, and that would bring to an end to his tired whining. He lay down in beds, lay in the arms of nurses, and slept in soft bedclothes, his heart satisfied. But now he will suffer much, missing the love of a father; Astyanax, the name the Trojans call him because, Hector, you alone protected the gates and long wall for the Trojans. Now, beside the beaked ships, far from your parents, wriggling worms will eat you, after the dogs have had their fill of your naked body. Your clothes still lie in the halls, soft and pleasingly worked by the hands of women. But, to be sure, I will throw them down onto the flames of a burning fire; they are of no use to you, since you will never wear them. They were to have been a glory for you from the Trojans and Trojan women." 514

So she spoke, weeping. And the women wailed nearby.

Book 23

And so the Trojans groaned and wailed throughout the city. When the Acheans arrived at the ships and the Helles-pont, they dispersed, each going to his own ship. But Achilles did not allow the Myrmidons to disperse. Instead, he spoke to his war-loving comrades: "Myrmidons, you with swift horses, my amiable comrades, we will not unhitch the solid-hoofed horses from the chariots yet. Instead, we will take them closer to Patroclus to weep. It is the mark of respect due the dead. And after we have taken consolation in groaning and wailing, we will loose the horses and have supper here." 11

So he spoke, and they all groaned together, with Achilles in the lead. Three times they drove the horses with beautiful manes around the corpse, their eyes welling with tears. And among them rose Thetis, longing to wail. The sand was soaked and the men's armor dampened by the weeping. They were filled with a great longing for that master of rout. The son of Peleus was chief among them in groaning, wrapping his man-killing arms around the chest of his friend: "Rejoice with me, Patroclus, even though you are in the House of Hades, over all the things that I accomplish for you before the end. I dragged Hector here to give to the dogs to divide up raw. Twelve mag-nificent sons of the Trojans are to be beheaded in front of your funeral pyre, because of my anger over your being killed." 23

And he planned even more disrespectful acts against Hec-tor, who was stretched out, facedown, beside the reposing couch of the son of Menoetius. And they all took off the armor they had fought in and loosed the whinnying horses, and sat down beside the ship of the grandson of Aeacus; they were beyond counting. And he set for them a sumptuous funeral feast. Many white oxen had their necks stretched and throats slit with iron in sacrifice, many sheep, many bleating goats, and many white-tusked hogs, amply fattened. They lay stretched out along the flames of Hephaestus. Blood flowed copiously around the corpse. 34

In the meantime, the kings of the Acheans led the fleet-footed son of Peleus to the noble Agamemnon, so that he might be persuaded by his advice to soften the anger in his heart over his comrade. They went, and when they arrived at Agamemnon's hut, he immediately ordered the loud-voiced heralds to place a large tripod around a fire, if the son of Peleus might be persuaded to wash off the bloody gore. When that was offered, Achilles adamantly refused, having sworn an oath on it: "No, by Zeus, who is the one of the gods who is highest and best. It is not right that I should wash my head before I cut my hair, place Patroclus in the fire, and set his marker. Even then there will never be any lessening of the grief that has come to my heart. That will be there as long as I am among the living. But truly, let us consent to the horrible feast, and in the morning, Supreme Commander Agamemnon, you order the men to the forest to bring as much wood as they can find, as much as it takes for us to give the corpse we have the flames of an un-quenchable fire to send this one to the misty darkness, so that he will sooner go away from our eyes and the troops can turn back to their work." 53

So Achilles spoke, and they listened to him intently and did as he asked. Each of them busied himself in preparing the food, and there was nothing the spirit found wanting in this proper feast. And after the desire for drink and food had gone from them, they set off, each to his own hut, and lay down to sleep. But Achilles lay groaning on the beach of the sea, where waves lapped up. It was a clean place, in the midst of many Myrmidons. When he let go of the cares of his heart, sleep caught up with him surrounding him with a sweet mist. His glorious legs were very tired from rushing after Hector in front of windy Troy. And the ghost of miserable Patroclus came to him, looking exactly like him. He was large, and had handsome features and his voice, and a garment was cloaked around his flesh. It stood above his head and spoke to him, saying: "You sleep, Achilles, and forget me. You cared for me when I was alive, but now I am dead. Give me funeral rites as quickly as possible so that I will be able to approach the Gates of Hades. The shades of those departed keep me far away from the gates, and the spirits do not allow me to mingle with those who are beyond the river. I wander around aimlessly through the palace of Hades, which has wide gates. Give me your hand. I weep from grief, because I will never come back again from Hades once you have given me my share of fire. And we will never again be alive, sitting apart from our beloved friends talking and making plans. Instead the horror consumes my heart in its jaws. But it was my lot when I was born, and even to you comes your fate of death, Achilles; you who are like the gods will perish under the wall of the rich Trojans. And I will tell you something else, if you will believe me. Your bones and mine will not be separated, Achilles, but in the same way as we were brought up in your palace when Menoetius brought me as a little thing from Opoeis, we will be together. On that day I came because of a miserable manslaughter: I had killed the son of Amphidamas. I was an idiot. I didn't intend to kill him, but I did it in anger over a game of dice. But the horseman Peleus received me into his palace, and brought me up humanely, and named me your attendant. And so the same urn should enclose the bones of both of us, the amphora made of gold that your revered mother gave you."   92

And fleet-footed Achilles answered: "My dear, honored friend, why have you come to me and told me all this? I shall obey you and do everything carefully. But stand closer, and just for a little while we can hold each other in our arms, taking consolation in crying and wailing."   98

So saying, Achilles reached out with loving arms, but he did not grab hold of the apparition. Departing with a shriek, it melted down to the ground like smoke. Astounded, Achilles got up and clapped his hands together, his eyes welling tears, and said: "Even though Patroclus is in the House of Hades, there was something there! It was a shade or an apparition, but it had no substance at all. All night long the ghost of miserable Patroclus stood beside me groaning and weeping, telling me how to do everything. It was wondrous!"   107

So he spoke, and roused in all of them a desire for wailing and weeping. Rosy-fingered Dawn appeared to them as they mourned around the corpse. The Lord Agamemnon rousted out the guards and men from all the huts to go fetch wood, and the most excellent of men, Meriones, attendant of manly Idomeneus, oversaw them. The guards went first, then woodcutters followed with axes and tightly twisted ropes in their hands. And many they were who went uphill, and downhill, and crossways, then askew. When they reached the ridges of Ida, with many springs, they immediately began to energetically cut lofty-crowned oak trees with their bronze axes. The branches fell with a huge crash. Then they limbed them and suspended them from mules. And the mules, straining for an open space, made a tattoo of their hooves through the dense thickets. As Meriones, attendant of manly Idomeneus, ordered, all the woodcutters carried branches in their arms, which they tossed down from the high places, one after the other. Meanwhile, Achilles planned a great tumulus for Patroclus, and for himself, as well.   125

And when the vast amount of wood they had brought had been put down, they sat there waiting, pressed close together. Achilles ordered the war-loving Myrmidons to gird themselves in bronze and to hitch up the horses under their chariots, and they rose up and put on their armor. They mounted the chariots and set out in them, chariot-warriors and charioteers, with their horses in front. Behind them followed the foot soldiers in a multitude like a cloud, there were so many. In the middle,

Patroclus's comrades carried him. They sheared off their hair
and tossed it on the corpse, covering it completely. Behind them
was noble Achilles with Patroclus's head in his hands—he was
sending his exceptional friend to Hades.   137

When they arrived at the place Achilles had decided on, they
set down their loads, and quickly began to heap up a suitable
pile of wood. And there noble Achilles thought back on another
time. He stood apart from the pyre and cut his red hair, which
had been nurtured into a dense growth along the Spercheius
River. Groaning in grief, he looked at the wine-red deep and
said: "Father Peleus, I swore to you in vain that I would lay my
cut hair beside the Spercheius on my return to my dear homeland, and make an offering of one hundred and fifty rams, and
make offerings of libations there in celebration, with fragrant
incense rising from the altar. So I promised the old man, but
now, since I am not to return to my dear fatherland, I would
make a present of my hair to the hero Patroclus, to take with
him to Hades."   151

So he spoke, and placed the hair in the hands of his beloved
friend. And that stirred the men's longing to wail in lament. At
that point, they would have remained in demonstrations of grief
until the light of the sun went down, had he not quickly said to
Agamemnon as he stood by: "Son of Atreus, it is you whose orders the Achean troops most readily obey. This is enough of
wailing and lament. Order them away from the pyre now, to
disperse and prepare their supper. Now those of us who most
especially cared for the dead will be working around here. They
and the leaders will remain with the body."   160

And when he heard that, the Supreme Commander Agamemnon immediately dispersed the troops to the balanced ships.
The undertakers remained by the wood pile, setting the corners
of the pyre at intervals of a hundred feet, here and there. Grieving at heart, they placed the corpse at the topmost place in the
fire. And they placed in front of the fire many fat sheep and
cloven-footed oxen with curved horns that had been led there

and flayed. Greathearted Achilles took the fat and completely
encased the corpse with it from head to toe, while leaning on
the reposing couch were amphorae of honey and fat. All around
the pyre flayed bodies lay. They groaned loudly from the effort
as they hurriedly threw on four long-necked horses. There
were nine household dogs that belonged to the king, and of
those Achilles slit the throats of two and tossed them on the
pyre. He did the same for twelve greathearted, excellent sons of
the Trojans, cutting their throats with gleaming bronze. He
had planned evil deeds for them, and he hurled a lump of smelt-
ing iron into the fire so that it might consume them. And then,
groaning, he called the name of his dear comrade: "Farewell,
rejoice with me, O Patroclus, even though you are in the House
of Hades. I have accomplished everything for you, those many
things are around you, among them are twelve excellent, greathearted sons of the Trojans who will all taste fire with you. But
to Hector, I will give no funeral rites at all. Instead, he goes to
the dogs."   183

So he spoke threateningly, but the dogs didn't get close to
Hector. Instead, Aphrodite, daughter of Zeus, kept the dogs
away from him day and night, and anointed him with ambrosial oil of roses so that he would not be shredded to pieces as he
was dragged around. And Phoebus Apollo brought a dark cloud
from the heavens to the plain near him, completely enclosing
the area around the corpse and increasing in density until the
force of the sun didn't wither the flesh on his tissues and limbs. 191

But Patroclus's funeral pyre would not burn. Noble Achilles,
fleet of foot, noticed, and standing away from the pyre, he prayed
to North Wind and West Wind, promising handsome offerings.
And there were many libations from the golden cup, and prayers
going up, in order that the flames of fire rush the wood into
burning and most quickly burn the dead. Hearing the prayers,
swift Iris, the messenger, went to the winds. They were gathered together in the home of furiously blowing West Wind,
drinking and feasting. Running Iris stopped on the stone

threshold. Seeing her, they all raised up, each one calling out to her to come in. But she refused to sit down there, and delivered her message: "I am going back over the currents of Ocean to the land of the Ethiopians. There they are doing sacrifices to the immortals, and I will feast at the sacred festival. But Achilles has called to North Wind and noisy West Wind, promising handsome sacrifices, praying for them to come so that they can urge on the burning fire in which Patroclus lies. All the Acheans have raised up groans of grief over him."   211

Having so spoken, she left. Roused by her, the two Winds made a thunderous noise that pushed a resounding cloud ahead of them. They shot over the deep, raising up a great wave with their shrill gusts. They reached fertile Troy and fell upon the fire. There was a wondrous noise as it exploded into flames. All night long flames shot up as the two winds howled, blowing together. And all night long swift Achilles poured libations onto the ground from a two-handled cup of gold that he filled with wine from the mixing bowl. And he dampened the earth as he called out to the soul of miserable Patroclus. His grieving was like that of a father who mourns for a newlywed son whose death has brought grief to his unhappy parents. So, walking slowly alongside the burning pyre, copiously groaning from wrenching grief, Achilles mourned as the bones of his friend burned.   225

There is a time the morning star, the light bearer, goes over the earth presenting light, after which appears a flowing gown of violet that Dawn spreads out above the sea. It was then that the burning pyre calmed down, and the flames were stopped. And the winds returned home over the Thracian deep, churning a rush of waves as they passed. The son of Peleus withdrew from the pyre. He lay down spent, and sweet sleep overwhelmed him.   232

Men approached, gathering together around the son of Atreus, and their murmuring increased to a loud roar that reached Achilles. He sat upright and spoke to them saying: "Son

of Atreus and others of the best of all the Acheans, the first
thing to do is to sprinkle dark red wine down on the whole pyre,
as much as it takes to stop the force of the fire. After that, dis-
criminating carefully, we will pick out the bones of Patroclus
Menoetiusson. Careful thought was given to assembling the
pyre. Patroclus lay in the middle and the others were on the
fire's outer edges, horses and men mixed together. And then
we will place his bones in the golden urn, with two layers of fat
for a seal. I will be buried in it myself, when I go to Hades. Not
so much should be done for the tomb, just what is suitable. And
then the Acheans can make it wide and high when I am the
second to be there, when they leave in their ships, which have
many rowers."   248

So he spoke, and they obeyed the fleet-footed son of Peleus.
First, they sprinkled the dark red wine where there were flames.
It drizzled down to the bottom of the ashes. They wept as they
picked up the white bones of their gentle comrade and placed
them in the urn with two layers of fat as a seal. They wrapped
the urn in soft linen and placed it in the huts. They scored out
a circle for a satisfactory monument, and set it near the pyre.
Then they heaped up dirt to form a tumulus, going back to heap
up more. After that was done, Achilles pulled the troops
back from it and commenced a wide range of games. From his
ships he brought out prizes: cauldrons, and tripods, and horses,
and mules, and oxen with fine heads, and buxom women, and
gray iron.   261

He set out magnificent prizes for a race for horses with
speedy hooves. For first place, he offered a woman who knew
how to do incomparable needlework and a tripod with handles
that had a capacity of twenty-two measures. That was for first
place. For second place, he offered a pregnant mare carrying a
mule. For third place he put down a handsome cauldron with a
capacity of four measures that had not been in a fire. It was still
untarnished all over. For fourth place he offered two golden talents. For fifth, he offered a two-handled bowl that had not been

in a fire. He stood up straight and spoke to the Argives, saying:
"Son of Atreus and you other well-armed Acheans, these prizes
lying in the place of assembly are for the horse race. And if there
were some other worthy man of the Acheans to compete with
me, you may be certain I would take the first prize to my hut,
since you know the virtue of my horses, the pair who pound
the earth faster than all others. They are immortal. Poseidon
granted them to my father Peleus, and he passed them on to me.
But be assured that I will hold back and the solid-hoofed horses
will, too. The glory is for one who is worthy of their gentle
charioteer, who often bathed those immortal horses in clear
water and combed their manes with damp olive oil. They stand
grieving at heart for him, not even able to keep their manes up
off the ground. You others get ready down in the camp, so one
of the Acheans might trust in his horses and wood-framed
chariot."   286

So the son of Peleus spoke, and the fast charioteers gathered
together. The first by far to charge forward was the commander
Eumelus, beloved son of Admetus, who distinguished himself
at chariot driving. After him was Diomedes Tydeusson, who led
Tros's horses under the yoke. Diomedes had taken them from
Aeneas, after Apollo snatched him away to save his life. Next
redheaded Menelaus Atreusson was roused, and he led fast
horses under the yoke, Agamemnon's mare Aethe and his own
stallion Podargus. Echepolus Anchisesson had given the mare
to Agamemnon as a gift, so that he would not be expected to
follow Agamemnon to windy Troy. Instead, Echepolus stayed
behind, enjoying himself. Zeus had given him huge riches, and
he dwelt in the wide space on Sicyon. Menelaus led Aethe under the yoke, restraining her eagerness for the great race.   300

And Antilochus was fourth to prepare his horses with beautiful manes. He was the glorious son of great-spirited King
Nestor Neleusson. The fast-hoofed horses were bred in Pylos for
pulling chariots. His wise and worthy father stood beside him
and explained to him, even though he was knowledgeable: "An-

tilochus, though you are young, it is for certain that both Zeus
and Poseidon love you, and you have been taught everything
about chariot driving. It is not especially necessary to teach you
or the horses anything, as you know well about rolling close to
the goalpost. But your horses run slowest and I think they will
lose. Their horses are faster, but they themselves have not been
coached to know as much as you yourself do."   312

B ut come, dear boy, I will fix in your mind a complete plan
so that a prize will not elude you. No big lumberjack is
better or more forceful than you, and nor again is a pilot on the
wine-red deep who steers a swift ship straight as it is tossed by
the winds. And there is no charioteer anywhere who knows
more about driving a chariot. But the one who puts his trust in
the horses and the chariot is foolish, as there will be for him
much rolling about here and there, and the horses will wander
about over the track, if he doesn't hold on to them. But the one
who might know how to drive lesser horses profitably, keeps his
eye constantly on the goal, turning as he gets closer. Nor does
he forget how he must first stretch the ox hide reins back and
hold them securely to excel in the chase. I will tell you about a
sign that you especially should be mindful of, and don't you
forget it. There is a wooden stump set in the track. It stands
about a fathom above the ground. It's either oak or fir and
does not rot in the rain. It faces a narrowing in the road, and
two white stones are set firmly on both sides of it. Either it was
some sort of sign of a mortal man long dead, or was set as a
goalpost by men much earlier. Now, noble Achilles, fleet of
foot, has determined it to be the turning post. You must get in
very close to it as you are driving the chariot and horses closer.
And lean yourself in the well-woven wicker chariot a little bit to
the left of your team. Then give the goad to the right horse,
easing the reins in your hands and shouting encouragement.
Going onto the post bring your left horse in so close that you're
not certain that the extreme edge of the hub of the crafted

wheel will graze it. Avoid striking a stone, lest you wound both horses and chariot as you drive along. That would be a disgrace for you but good sport for the rest. But dear son, stay alert and vigilant. If you are ahead of the others at the turning point, nobody is going to overtake you or pass you by even if he were to drive Areion, the fast horse of Adrastus, that was born of the gods, or those of Laomedon, that he raised to be excellent."   348

So Nestor Neleusson spoke, and having explained to his son every tactic, he went back to his place and sat.

Meriones was the fifth of those preparing horses, with beautiful manes, when they mounted the chariots. Achilles tossed their lots with his hand and the first lot jumped out, that of Antilochus Nestorsson; after his was the lot of Lord Eumelus, then Menelaus Atreusson, famed for the spear, and then the lot of Meriones for driving order. Again last in place was the son of Tydeus, though he was the best by far at driving horses. They stood in one line, and Achilles showed them the goal far away on the level plain. He positioned the godlike Phoenix, his father's attendant, near the lookout mound as monitor, since he knew about racing and was absolutely truthful in what he said.   361

And they all at the same time raised up their whips over their horses, and smacked the reins, and enthusiastically shouting words of encouragement, they speedily raced over the plain away from the swift ships. Under the horses' chests dust rose up into the air, like a cloud or a storm. Their manes fluttered in the breeze. At once the chariots were close to the fertile ground, but at another moment they rocketed skyward. And the drivers stayed on their chariots, the heart pounding in each one, shooting for victory. Each shouting encouragement to his horses, they flew, raising up dust from the plain.   372

But when they were finishing the final leg, and the fast horses were running back toward the gray sea, then was the skill of each man revealed, and immediately for the horses stretched out running. At that point the fleet-hoofed mares of the grandson of Pheretes were running off fast. Beside them, as they were running, were Tros's Trojan stallions driven by Diomedes. And they were very close together, and it looked like the stallions were trying to mount Eumelus's chariot. His broad back and shoulders began to heat up from their breath. Their heads were tilting down as they flew along, and now might the outcome have become doubtful for their race with Diomedes passing, had not Phoebus Apollo been peeved at the son of Tydeus. He knocked the gleaming whip from Diomedes's hands. Tears of anger welled up in his eyes because he saw the other going even faster while he was handicapped, as his horses were running without a goad. But Athena did not overlook Apollo's chicanery. With amazing speed she rushed to the side of the son of Tydeus, Shepherd of the Troops, and gave him his whip, and Diomedes urged on the strength in his horses. Annoyed by the incident, Athena went near the son of Admetus, and the goddess broke his horses' yoke, and as they ran in two directions along the road, the pole was loosened and it fell to the ground. Eumelus, himself, tumbled out of the chariot beside a wheel, receiving lacerations on his elbows, and his mouth and nose, and tearing his forehead near the brow ridge. Both his eyes filled with tears, but his vigorous voice was restrained. The son of Tydeus turned aside and pulled back his horses, but then raced ahead of all of the others. Athena arrived and placed might in the horses and in him, as well. And red-haired Menelaus Atreusson held the position just after him.

400

Antilochus called out, encouraging his father's horses: "Get on it, and that is for both of you! Stretch out into the fastest run possible. You may be sure that I am not at all ordering you to challenge the warlike horses of Tydeus's son. Athena now grants them speed and places glory on him. Instead, overtake the horses of the son of Atreus, and don't be left behind. Go fast! I suspect that Aethe might pour disgrace on your heads; she is a girl! Who is to be left the best? I will tell you how it will play out. For the two of you there will be no care and feeding near

Nestor, Shepherd of the Troops, and you will be slaughtered immediately with sharp bronze, if you are both careless and we carry off a lesser prize. Instead, follow them close on and speed up, you two, as fast as possible. I will execute on the things I myself am supposed to do, and I will recognize the narrowing in the road and steer through it. And it will not escape my notice!"   416

So he spoke, and put in them fear of their ruler. And in a short time there was a clamor as they ran all out. Right away Antilochus, firm in his valor, caught sight of the narrowing of the winding road. There was a fissure in the ground, which eroded during some winter storm, when water flowed over the road. It was a deep erosion. Menelaus directed his horses there in the belief that none would come alongside him for fear of collision of their wheels. But Antilochus turned aside and kept his solid-hoofed horses off the road, chasing along at a little bit of an incline. That frightened the son of Atreus, and he yelled: "Antilochus, you are crazy to drive like that. Instead, rein in your horses off the narrowing in the road and then drive faster where the road is wider. I worry that both the chariots will be damaged in a collision."   428

So Menelaus spoke, but Antilochus was still laying on the goad as though he had not heard Menelaus, driving awfully fast, as fast as a discus thrown from the shoulder in the proving trials that occur when a boy approaches manhood. That fast were the horses running. The horses of the son of Atreus swerved back because he himself was willing to hold back to prevent a collision with the solid-hoofed horses on the road, and overturning the well-woven wicker chariots. They themselves might have fallen into the dust, eager for victory. And red-haired Menelaus spoke, cursing him: "There is no one else more ruthless than you among mortal men. Get lost! On account of this the Acheans, who used to call you wise, will truly say that you have no sense. And there is surely no way that you will carry away a prize without an oath."   441

So speaking, Menelaus called out to his horses and said: "Do not be reined in by me, and do not grieve at heart. These horses got ahead of us, but their knees will weary before yours, for they lack the vigor of youth." 445

So Menelaus spoke, and the horses were fearful of their king and ran all out with a clamor, that they might quickly close in on Antilochus's horses. 447

The Argives were sitting in the gathering place looking out on the horses in the race as they flew, raising dust, on the plain. Idomeneus, commander of the Cretans, was the first to observe the horses, as he sat apart from the race on the top of the highest lookout mound. He recognized the shouting of encouragement that could be heard from far off, and he saw a horse that stood out very much in the forefront. It was roan all over except for a white blaze on the forehead that was round like the moon. Idomeneus stood up among the Argives and addressed them, saying: "O friends, chiefs, and counselors of the Argives, am I the only one to see the horses distinctly, or can you, too? Some other horses seem to me to be in the front, but then it appears to be another charioteer. The mares must somehow have been stricken there on the plain because they were stronger going out. You may be sure that I saw they were first to round the turning post, but now I cannot see them anywhere, though I have my eyes looking out everywhere over the plain. Maybe the reins got away from the charioteer or he was not able to hang on to reach the goal, or make his turn. I think he fell off there, and wrecked the chariot he was driving. Then the mares swerved off the course, when some anger seized their spirits. But, take a look, you should be standing up, for I cannot distinguish well. But it seems to me that a man is remaining on the track, a man of the Aetolian tribe, who rules among the Argives. It is the son of the noble horseman Tydeus, mighty Diomedes." 472

But swift Oïlean Aias scolded him sarcastically: "Idomeneus, why is it that in the past you have talked without thinking? The charioteer and the prancing horses are a long way off as they go across the wide plain. And you are neither the youngest among the Argives here, nor do your eyes look out from your head with the greatest acuity. But, you are constantly spouting nonsense, but it is not necessary for you to be such a babbler of stupidity, as there are others around who are better. The same horses are ahead as were before, those of Eumelus. And he is himself going along in the course holding the reins."   481

An angry leader of the Cretans answered back: "Aias, you are the best at nasty sarcasm, but you are the sorriest of all the Argives, mean spirited in whatever you do. Here now, let's us both put down a wager for a tripod, or a cauldron, and Agamemnon Atreusson can serve as the arbiter for both sides, determining whichever horses are first. In that way you might learn what it's like to pay up."   487

So, Idomeneus spoke and immediately swift Oïlean Aias rose up angry to make a catty reply. And now a row between both of them would have commenced, had not Achilles himself stood up and uttered: "No more nasty exchanges, you two! Aias and Idomeneus, this is not fitting. And you two would be annoyed if anyone else acted like this. Sit down and watch over the horses in their race. They will soon rush on to victory that will bring them here. Then all the Argives will know whose horses are ahead and whose lag."   498

So Achilles spoke, and the son of Tydeus came in much closer in the chase, constantly driving the whip down on the shoulders, and his horses underneath the whip, lifted their hooves high as they went leaping and bounding along the track. As they ran, the swift-hoofed horses constantly threw out a shower of dust onto their charioteer and the gold and tin ornaments encrusted on the chariot. But there was not much that came from behind the tires of the chariot wheels in the soft dust. The pair of horses flew, hastening on. And they stopped in the middle of the gathering place. Sweat popped out from the horses' necks and heavy sweat from their chests dripped onto the ground. Diomedes himself, glistening with sweat all over, leapt from the chariot to the ground, and then leaned the whip on the yoke. Brave Sthenelus wasted no time in claiming the prize, and Achilles gave the woman to be led off by Diomedes's greathearted comrade, and the tripod with handles, as well. And Sthenelus loosed the horses from under their yoke.   513

Next after Diomedes was Antilochus, grandson of Neleus, who drove his horses with cunning, not speed, edging in ahead of Menelaus. Though Menelaus was very close behind as he came in with his swift horses. The distance was as far as the horse pulling its king's chariot stretched out over the plain is from the wheel. They are so very close that the hairs of the tip of the tail touch the tires. By so much was worthy Menelaus left behind by Antilochus. At first, he lagged by the length of a discus toss, but Menelaus quickly caught up with Antilochus, as might increased in Agamemnon's mare Aethe. Next to return was Meriones, the virtuous attendant of Idomeneus, who was behind famed Menelaus the distance of a spear cast. His horses, with their beautiful manes, were the slowest, and he, himself, drove them slowly into the gathering place. The son of Admetus came in dead last, driving the horses ahead of him and dragging his beautiful chariot. Seeing him, noble Achilles felt pity on him, and, standing among the Argives, spoke to him with winged words: "The last man is the best of all at driving solid-hoofed horses. But come, I will give him a prize worthy of second place, though the son of Tydeus must take the first."   538

So Achilles spoke and they all praised his decision. And at that point would Achilles have given Eumelus a horse since the Acheans approved, had not Antilochus, son of greathearted Nestor Neleusson, stood up and answered Achilles on a point of right: "O Achilles, I shall be very upset if you fulfill your judgment in this way. After considering that this man was injured along with his horses and his chariot wrecked, you are about to take away my prize. He is himself an excellent man.

But I wish to pray to the immortals, because there should be nothing to one who comes in dead last in the race. But if you pity him and there is love in your heart for him, there is for him much gold in your hut, and bronze, and sheep, and servants for him and solid-hoofed horses. Give from that something he may then take away as a prize from a bigger contest, or give it to him immediately now, so that the Acheans will praise it. But I will not give up the mare. He should make a trial of men for her, if he might wish to fight against me with his hands."   555

So he spoke, and fleet-footed, noble Achilles smiled, delighted with Antilochus, his dear friend. And he answered with winged words: "If you tell me to give Eumelus something else from my household, I will make that happen. I will give him a breast-plate, one that I took from Asteropeus. It is bronze, with a dazzling rim of cast tin running around it. It will be very valuable to him."   562

And he ordered his dear friend Automedon to bring it out of his hut. He carried it and placed it in the hands of Eumelus, who received it with pleasure.   565

Among them Menelaus stood up, grieving at heart, angry at Antilochus on account of his greed. A herald placed a staff in hand, and ordered the Acheans to quiet down. And then Menelaus addressed them, a man who was like a god: "Antilochus, you used to be prudent, but this is outrageous! You disgraced my valor, and you rammed your horses who are far inferior in ahead of mine, injuring my horses. But come, chiefs and counselors of the Argives, make a judgment of both of us in your midst. It should not be for assistance, nor might any of the Acheans ever say: 'Menelaus got the better of Antilochus with lies, that he was going along driving his horses that were better with respect to both excellence and strength while those of Antilochus were much inferior.' Come, when I render a judgment, I swear that I would not denounce another of the Danaans over anything. I shall do it to render justice. Antilochus, if you are noble-born, come here. It is just. Stand in front of the horses and chariot, holding the flexible reins in your hand, as though about to drive, touching the horses, and swear by him who holds the earth, the earth-shaker, that you did not intentionally impede my chariot with your guile."   585

And prudent Antilochus stood opposite Menelaus and answered: "Hold on now! I am much younger than you, Menelaus. You are older and more worthy. You know how excessive exuberance takes over a young man. His mind is nimbler and more agile, but light on judgment. Bear up. But, though I won her, I myself will give you the mare. And if you now ask for something more from my household, I will give it to you immediately. You are always of noble birth, and I would not want to be considered churlish and to fall from your favor."   595

And to be sure, the son of greathearted Nestor led the mare and placed her lead in Menelaus's hands. Menelaus's heart was warmed, as if dew fell around the ears of standing, ripening grain, which wave over the fields. In that way your heart and mind turned warm, Menelaus, and you spoke to Antilochus with winged words: "Now, I must let go of my anger toward you, since nothing you have said in the past was crazy or stupid. Now this time has youth won a victory over the mind. But you should be more careful at avoiding deceit in the future. There is no other man of the Acheans who could have so quickly convinced me, since you and your worthy father have suffered a great deal and worked very hard on behalf of my brother and me. For both reasons, you have persuaded me with your entreaty, and I shall give you the mare, though she is mine, so that you and the Acheans, too, might know that my heart is never arrogant or vengeful."   611

So it was, and he gave the mare to Noemon, a comrade of Antilochus, to lead away, and then he took the cauldron that gleamed all over. Meriones lifted up the two talents of gold, since he drove in fourth. The fifth prize, the two-handled cup, was left unclaimed in the contest. Achilles gave it to Nestor, carrying it up to the leader of the Argives. He stood beside Nestor and said: "Take it now, let this be a precious object for you, old man, a memento of Patroclus's funeral rites, for he is no longer seen among the Argives. I give it to you on the occasion of the games, since you will not be boxing, and not wrestling, and not entering the javelin casting, and you will not run on your feet. Already, the harshness of age rushes down on you."

623

So speaking, he placed the cup in Nestor's hands, and he received it with pleasure. And he spoke with winged words: "Yes, indeed, my son, all those things you said accord with custom, for no longer are my own feet sturdy under my limbs, and there is no way for my arms on both shoulders to rush forward in a nimble way. I wish it were like when I was a young man, and had might and firmness in me. Like when the Epeans gave funeral rites for King Amaruceus at Bouprasium. The sons of the king held games for him. And there was nobody who came out my equal, none of the Epeans, or of the Pylians, nor of the greathearted Aetolians. In boxing, I won a victory over Clutomedes, son of Enops, and in wrestling Ancaeus Pleuronson stood against me. Running beside excellent Iphiclus in the footraces, I won victory over him. I won in javelin-casting against both Phyles and Polydorus, sons of Actor. They also drove against me in the chariot race. After much dashing forward, they drove toward a victory, because it was still the greatest contest there. Phyles and Polydorus were twins. One held the reins firmly while the other gave orders with a whip. That is how it was back when I pursued excellence among heroes, but now it is necessary for me to surrender to the misery of old age. Now again, it is for younger men to stand against each other in such doings.

645

"Continue conducting the funeral games for your friend. I receive this cup gladly; it brings my heart joy, and will always remind me of your kindness. I shall not forget you. It seems to me an honor to be so esteemed among the Acheans. May the gods give you abundant joy for doing this."

650

So he spoke, and the son of Neleus went through the great throng of the Acheans, after everyone heard the whole story of the son of Neleus. Next Achilles set out the prizes for the dangerous boxing match. A six-year-old mule, capable of hard work, was led out. It was not broken in and such mules are the most difficult to break. It stood tethered in the gathering place. For the loser Achilles selected a two-handled cup. He stood up and addressed the Argives: "Son of Atreus, and you other well-armed Acheans, let us call out two men for this. Though both are the best, they will both stand up under heavy beating. To the one Apollo gives perseverance, and all the Acheans will know about it, it is to him to return to his hut leading this mule, capable of hard work. After that, the loser will carry off the two-handled cup."   663

So Achilles spoke. And immediately Epeus, the son of Panopeus, rose up, one who was brave and huge, known for his boxing. He touched the mule, capable of hard work, and spoke in a resonant voice: "Let somebody come closer, who will carry off the two-handled cup. I declare that none of the other Acheans will be leading the mule, triumphant over me at boxing. I think that I am the best. And is it not enough that I am deficient in war? There was no way that a man could become knowledgeable in all skills. And so I will tell you how it will play out. I will completely shred flesh, and along with that I will smash bones. The undertakers who hang around together here will carry him away clobbered by my hands."   675

So Epeus spoke, and they all became silent, and speechless. But Euryalus, alone, stood up to him, a man equal to a god. He was the son of King Mecistes, and grandson of Talaus, who once went to Thebes for the funeral rites of the deceased Oedipus, where he was victorious over all the sons of Cadmus. The son of Tydeus, famed for the spear, wanted Euryalus to win, so he prepared him, and cheered him on. First he cinched the belt worn by boxers around him. Next he gave him well-made cords of the hides of oxen that live in the fields, to be wrapped

around the fists and so increase the damage inflicted by them.
Both the men prepared themselves for the match and went
into the middle of the gathering place.   685

They both held their sturdy fists up in front of them. Then,
at the same time their hands dropped, and they mixed it up
together with their heavy fists. The grinding of teeth was terrible. Sweat poured out on their limbs everywhere. Epeus charged
against Euryalus, and looking for an opportunity, landed a blow,
cutting the cheek. And Euryalus did not remain standing long.
His glorious limbs collapsed underneath him. It was like when
a fish leaps up from the froth as North Wind pounds on a shore
covered with seaweed; the fish is enveloped in a dark wave,
smacked down, and bounced back up. Greathearted Epeus took
his hand and set Euryalus upright. Friends and comrades carried him through the gathering spot with his feet dragging behind. He was vomiting thick blood and his head tilted to one
side, out of his mind as he was being carried off, so others took
possession of the two-handled cup.   699

The son of Peleus quickly set out three prizes, presenting
them to the Danaans for the dangerous sport of wrestling.
For the winner there was a huge tripod to be placed in a fire. It
would fetch the value of twelve oxen, and the Acheans there
knew it. For the loser he placed a woman skilled in needlework,
and her worth was four oxen. And he stood up straight among
the Argives and delivered his speech: "So, two of you get up
and you both may compete in this match."   707

So Achilles spoke, and then the huge Telamonian Aias rose,
and ever-cunning Odysseus stood up, a man with the mind of
a fox. They prepared themselves and went to the middle of the
gathering place. They took hold of each other's arms with their
sturdy hands like when beams alternate, those that a famous
builder sets in a roof truss to ward off the force of winds from
a lofty palace. There was a creaking sound from their backs as
they violently pulled on each other with daring hands. A trick-
ling of sweat poured down; their ribs and shoulders were thick

with bruises and they were reddened by blood as it spurted out. They were constantly aiming at winning the tripod. Odysseus was unable to take down Aias to bring about a victory, nor was Aias able to hold victory over Odysseus. But since they were not entertaining the well-armed Acheans very well, the huge Telamonian Aias said to Odysseus: "Noble-bred Odysseus Laertesson, ever inventive, either you lift me up or I you. As always, it will be the concern of Zeus."   724

So saying, he lifted Odysseus up. But Odysseus was not fooled by the trick. He struck Aias's calf from behind, and his limbs collapsed under him, and he fell backward. Odysseus fell down on his chest. The troops around them were both astonished and amazed. Next, noble, ever-daring Odysseus tried to raise Aias up and moved him a little bit but Aias was not quite rising up, when Odysseus bent his knee inside Aias's. They both fell down on the ground, close to each other, caked with dust. And then they might have made a third try, to charge on again with the wrestling, had not Achilles himself stood up and pulled them apart: "Do not continue this foulness, struggling like this. It is a victory for both of you. Select prizes that are equal as you go, so that the rest of the Acheans can compete." So he spoke, and they heard him clearly and obeyed. And then they scraped off the dust and donned their tunics.   739

And immediately the son of Peleus set out the prizes for the swiftest. For first he put out a mixing bowl wrought of silver. It would hold six measures. In beauty it surpassed everything in the entire world, since artisans in Sidon had extravagantly ornamented it, and the Phoenicians carried it over the dusky deep, and gave it to Thoas as a gift for harbor dues when they stopped there. Euneus Jasonson gave it to the hero Patroclus as the ransom for Lycaon, son of Priam. And Achilles set it out as a prize in the games for his friend. And it would be for the one who was nimblest on the fastest feet. For the second prize he set out an ox that was large and fat in its body. And he placed a half-talent of gold for the last-place runner. And he stood up and said to the Argives: "Get up now, those who are to compete in this contest."   753

So he spoke and right away swift Oïlean Aias stood. And ever-cunning Odysseus was up, and after him was the son of Nestor, Antilochus. He surpassed all of the young men on his feet. They stood in a line, and Achilles set the course for them from the turning point and showed them the boundaries. The son of Oïleus was fast off, and next rushed noble Odysseus very close to him. It was like when a distaff is some distance away from the breast of a buxom woman, but when she stretches her hands out to pull the thread from inside the spindle, the distaff is very close to her breast. That close was Odysseus as he ran. And behind him he stomped footprints in the dust they had mounded up earlier. Noble Odysseus panted against Aias's head as he ran, constantly lifting his knees up high. All the Acheans cheered for him, hoping for him to win. And they called out to him to go much faster. But when they were nearing the end of the race, Odysseus made a quick prayer to bright-eyed Athena for her encouragement: "Hear me worthy goddess, come to the aid of my feet." So he prayed and Pallas Athena heard him. She made his limbs nimble like those of a deer, and the feet below and hands above. But when they were about to race speedily for the prize, there Aias slipped as he was running. Athena thwarted him, spilling in his path some of the dung from the bellowing oxen that fleet-footed Achilles killed for Patroclus's funeral. Into it he fell, filling his mouth and nose with it. The ever-daring Odysseus held up the mixing bowl, since he got to the goal first. Glorious Aias, won the ox. He stood near the horns holding the ox with his hands, and spitting out dung, he said to the Argives: "Holy shit! A goddess got in the way of my feet. It was she who in the past stood beside Odysseus like a mother, and gives him aid now."   783

So he spoke, and they all laughed good-naturedly at him. And Antilochus carried off the prize for last place, smiling. He made a comment to the Argives: "Aias is just a little bit older than I am. But Odysseus is a generation older. But, they say that his will be a youthful old age, and it is hard for the Acheans to compete on their feet against him, except Achilles, that is." So he spoke, praising the son of Peleus. Achilles responded to him saying: "Antilochus, they will not say you are such a dreadful creep. Instead, I will add a half talent of gold to your prize."   796

So saying, he placed it in his hand, and Antilochus received it with pleasure. Next, the son of Peleus carried into the gathering place a long spear and set it down, and the shield, and plumed helmet, and armor of Sarpedon. Patroclus took them as prizes of war. He stood up straight and delivered his speech to the Argives: "We call for two men to come to this spot. Both must be the best. They will dress in armor that captures flesh-cutting bronze, and will compete with each other in front of the throng. Whoever first tears lovely flesh beneath skin and draws dark blood through armor, him I will give here a beautiful, silver-studded Thracian sword. I took it from Asteropaeus. The armor, they will share in common to carry off together. And, we shall set before both of them a worthy feast in my huts."   810

So he spoke, and after that huge Telamonian Aias rose and so did mighty Diomedes Tydeusson. And when they had armed themselves on opposites sides of the throng, both of them came together in the middle, eager to fight. The two were terrifying to look at, and all of the Acheans were awestruck. And when they got closer they went at each other. Three times they rushed on each other, and three times fought in hand-to-hand combat. There, Aias then struck against Diomedes's shield that was balanced all around, but it did not get to flesh. And he pulled it out of the breastplate. After that the son of Tydeus got above Aias's gigantic shield that he held constantly, and the spear tip lightly touched Aias's neck. And the Acheans were frightened for Aias, and clamored to get the fighting stopped, and that the two men

choose prizes that were equal in value. At that Achilles gave the
son of Tydeus a hero's sword, with its scabbard and a well-made
baldric to take away.   825

Next, the son of Peleus set out an iron discus that was just as
it was when the casting mold was broken away. That is to say,
it was neither finished, nor polished. It had in earlier times been
thrown by mighty Eetion. But you may be sure, noble Achilles, fleet of foot, slew him and carried in his ships this and
Eetion's other possessions. He stood up and announced to the
Argives present: "Let those of you who compete for this prize
rise. Even if the winner has many rich fields far from here, and
makes use of them for five revolving years, neither his shepherd, nor his ploughman will need to go to a city when he runs
short of iron, instead he who wins this prize will provide it."   835

So he spoke, and next thing Polypoetes, firm in the fight, rose
up. And Leonteus, with mighty strength like a god, was up. And
up stood both Aias Telamonson and noble Epeus. And they
stood in order. Noble Epeus took the discus casting and went
whirling around. All the Acheans laughed at him. Next, Leonteus, scion of Ares, hurled it, and third again was huge Telamonian Aias who threw it from his stout hand, and overthrew
the marks of all. But, then Polypoetes, firm in the fight, snatched
the discus casting. And as far as a cowherd throws his herding
staff, which he whirls around and lets fly through gathered oxen.
As far as that Polypoetes overthrew them all put together. And
they cheered him. And the comrades of mighty Polypoetes carried the prize of their king to the hollow ships.   849

Next Achilles laid out violet-colored iron for the archers: ten
battle-axes, and ten hatchets. He set up the mast of a dark-
prowed ship far off on the sandy beach. On it there was a timid
dove bound by its feet with light cord. He ordered that for the
archery contest: "The one who hits the timid dove will pick up
all the axes, and return home. He who might hit the cord, but
miss the bird, is less skilled, and he will carry off the hatchets."

So he spoke, and strong King Teucer rose, and up stood Meriones, worthy attendant of Idomeneus. Choosing lots, they shook them in a bronze helmet, and that of Teucer popped out first. Quickly, he went, the most powerful of all, but he did not swear to his chief that he would make a glorious sacrifice of a firstborn ram. He missed the bird, as Apollo was peeved with him. He hit the cord beside the bird's foot, and the sharp, pungent arrow cut completely through the cord. The bird rushed from the mast off toward the heavens, but the cord let go and dropped to the ground. At that, the Acheans raised up a ruckus.   869

Hurrying himself, Meriones snatched the bow from Teucer's hand, but he had held an arrow for some time, while Teucer took aim. He immediately vowed to his lord that he would make a glorious sacrifice of a firstborn lamb. He looked up and saw the timid dove under a cloud. Whirling around he shot the arrow off, hitting underneath the middle of the bird's wings. The missile went straight through, and came back down to earth and fixed in the ground in front of Meriones's feet. The bird was fixed on the mast, and its neck slumped over. A thick clump of feathers came out, and fell a long way from it. Its spirit flew speedily from its limbs. The troops were again astonished and amazed. And Meriones picked up all ten battle-axes while Teucer carried hatchets to the hollow ships.   883

After that the son of Peleus first set down in the gathering place a long spear, and then a cauldron decorated with flowers that had not been in a fire, with the value of an ox. These he led to the gathering place. The men who tossed javelins stood up. The emminent Prince Agamemnon Atreusson stood and Meriones, worthy attendant of Idomeneus, got up. Noble Achilles, fleet of foot, spoke to both him and them: "Son of Atreus, we know which of those who have presented themselves before everyone and demonstrated what they can do, which among us is the best. But this prize is for you to take as yours when you go to the hollow ships, or we might give the spear to the hero Meriones, if you would wish it in your heart. I heartily urge that this be done."

So he spoke, and the Supreme Commander Agamemnon did not disagree, and he gave Meriones the brazen spear. Next, the hero gave the herald Talthybius, the very beautiful prize of the cauldron.

894

897

Book 24

The assembly was dismissed, and the troops dispersed to the swift ships, each man to his own. They planned their supper and took pleasure in sweet sleep. In the meantime, Achilles wept as he remembered his beloved friend, and the sleep that conquers all did not lay hold of him. Instead, he turned this way and that, longing for the virility of Patroclus and for his solid strength. And he wistfully yearned for what he had done with Patroclus. Together, they had experienced the traversing of waves, destructive wars, and the pain of men. As he remembered the valor of those times, the tears trickled down. For a time he was on his side, at another time he was again faceup, and at another facedown. Then he stood up straight and turned around agonizing in grief as he walked along the seashore. And it didn't escape his notice when Dawn was revealed over the sea and the beach. For then he hitched his fast horses to the chariot, and dragged Hector bound behind it, pulling him three times around the grave marker for the son of Menoetius. He stopped and went back to his hut, but he allowed Hector to remain stretched out, facedown in the dust. But Apollo restrained all of the abuse to Hector's flesh, taking pity on the man, even in death, enclosing him completely in the golden aegis, so that he would not be lacerated as he was dragged along.

    The blessed gods looked on as Achilles was raging about, trying to desecrate noble Hector. It aroused their pity for Hector, and they urged Hermes, slayer of Argos, to steal him. That plan was satisfactory to all of the others, but never to Hera, nor to Poseidon, nor to her sharp-eyed daughter. They held off, since they were the first to despise sacred Troy, and Priam and the troops, on account of Alexander's blindness. He had insulted

19

the goddesses when they arrived at his courtyard, and praised
Helen who provided him with such outrageous lewdness.   31

But when the twelfth Dawn arose after Hector's death, Phoebus Apollo addressed the immortals: "You gods are disgraceful, evil minded. Did Hector never burn oxen or goats in
sacrifice? Now, you dare not save him, even though he is dead,
to be seen by his wife, and mother, and his child, together with
his father Priam, and the troops. Let them put him quickly in
the fire, and give him solemn funeral rites. But you gods want
to help destructive Achilles, who is not of sane mind, or right
in what he knows in his twisted heart. His mind is like a wild
lion that rushes toward the sheep of mortals in order to seize
them and feast on them. Likewise, Achilles has utterly lost compassion and pity, and there is engendered in him none of the
shame, that greatly harms men on the one hand and aids them
on the other. The fates dared to put shame in the hearts of men.
Achilles seems someone who would destroy another more
loved, or a brother from the same womb as his mother's, or even
a son. After taking away noble Hector's very life, Achilles will
eventually destroy his corpse. He attaches his horses, and drags
Hector around his friend's marker. But to be sure, Patroclus was
neither more handsome nor better than Hector. Though Achilles is worthy, we ought to chastise him, but here we wait while
he rages around desecrating the mute earth."   54

Growing angry, Hera addressed him: "What you said might
be so, silver bow, if Achilles and Hector were of the same rank.
But Hector was mortal and was placed at the nipple of a woman.
Whereas Achilles is the offspring of a goddess. I myself brought
her up and cared for her, and gave her to a man Peleus as his
wife. Peleus was the love of our heart, and their marriage came
about with the consent of the immortals. All the gods attended
the wedding, and among them at the feast was you playing the
lyre, and badly, too, chump! You are always untrustworthy!"   63

And cloud-gathering Zeus responded to her saying: "Hera,
don't be angry with the gods all the time. And this is not a mat-

ter of rank. Instead, Hector is the most loved by the gods of the mortals in Troy. And so by me, as well. It is because he never missed any opportunity for gifts. My altar never wanted for a balanced feast, and libations and the smoke of burned offerings. We received our share of his prizes. And, you may count on it, we will allow him to be stolen, but not in this way. Brave Hector could not be stolen without the notice of Achilles. Because of his grief, his mother has been at his side constantly night and day. But, I wish that some god would summon Thetis to come closer to me, so that I can tell her a wise plan. That way might Achilles obtain gifts from Priam for the release of Hector."

76

So he spoke and Iris, swift as a storm, rose, and went with the message. Midway between Samos and craggy Imbros, she dived into the black deep, and the cove resounded with a crashing noise. She sank to the bottom like a lead weight set on a fishing line, made from the hide of an ox that lives in the fields, which goes down to deliver fate to ravenous fish. She found Thetis in a hollow cave, and sitting around her were gathered the sea goddesses. She was in their midst, crying over the fate of her exceptional son, who was about to perish in Troy, which has rich soil, far away from his father. Iris stood close to her and spoke, saying: "Get up, Thetis. Zeus, devisor of imperishable plans, summons you."

88

And then Thetis, the goddess with silver feet, responded: "Why does that great god summon me? I am apprehensive about mixing with the immortals, and I have intense grief in my heart. But since whatever he might tell me will not be pointless, I am going." So speaking, she took her black veil and went through the goddesses, and no garment was darker than it was. And she set out, and Iris, swift as the wind, took the lead. And a wave of the sea parted around them, and they stepped out onto the shore and were rushed up to the highest point of the heavens. They found the wide-seeing son of Cronus, and all the others of the blessed, eternal gods were sitting, gathered around him.

Athena yielded her place and Thetis sat down beside father
Zeus. Hera placed a lovely, golden goblet in her hand, and
spoke kindly. Thetis drank and handed it back. The father of
both men and gods, commenced to speak: "Goddess Thetis, you
have come to Olympus, though you have cares. You have unbearable grief in your thoughts, and I know that myself. But
I will tell you what it was I summoned you about. For nine
days strife has arisen among the gods, concerning Hector's
corpse and Achilles, sacker of cities. They are urging the vigilant slayer of Argos to steal the corpse. This, after I laid glory
on Achilles in order to preserve your respect and love in the future. Go very quickly to the Acheans' camp and counsel your
son. Tell him the gods are angry with him that he has such
rage in his mind, and I most of all. He keeps Hector among the
beaked ships and won't release him. If he fears me, he will release Hector. I shall send Iris to greathearted Priam and I shall
say that he is to go to the ships of the Acheans since his beloved
son is to be released, and that he is to bring gifts to Achilles,
such presents as might soothe his heart."   119

   So he spoke, and the goddess Thetis, of the silver feet, obeyed.
She set out from the peaks of Olympus in a rush, and arrived
in the hut of her son. She found him there groaning in grief
without letup. His friends and comrades were around him carefully tending to things and preparing breakfast. For them a
large, shaggy ram was sacrificed. And she went very close to
him, and his revered mother sat down. She stroked him with
her hand and spoke to him, calling him by name: "My child, do
you not remember to eat bread and to sleep as you eat your
heart out in grief? It would be a good thing, though, for you to
make love to a woman. You do not have long to live, on my account. Instead, death and powerful fate stand very close to you,
and you will meet with them soon. But cooperate with me. I am
a messenger to you from Zeus. He says that the gods are angry
with you, and he most especially of all the immortals is furious,
that you are minded to rage and that you keep Hector beside

the beaked ships and won't release him. Instead, you ought to
receive a ransom for the corpse, and set Hector loose."   137

And Achilles, fleet of foot, responded: "If the Olympian himself in sound mind orders it this is the way it will be: whoever
might bring a ransom, may take the corpse."   140

So mother and son huddled near the ships, talking to each
other with many winged words. And the son of Cronus roused
Iris on to sacred Troy: "Leave behind the seat of Olympus, get
moving and go quickly, Iris. Take a message to greathearted
Priam that he is to go to the ships of the Acheans, carrying gifts
for Achilles that will soothe his heart, and his beloved son will
be released. No other Trojan man is to accompany him; he is to
go alone, except that a herald senior in rank may go along with
him to serve as skinner for the mules and wagon with sound
wheels, and would also carry back to the city the corpse of him
noble Achilles slew. He should have no concern for death, nor
should he be afraid, because we will make available the slayer
of Argos to be his guide. He will lead them along until he comes
near Achilles. After that, when Priam is led into the hut of
Achilles, he himself will protect Priam against all others. He
will not be slain, nor will there be animosity or thoughtlessness, and no injustice. Instead he should go as a supplicant to a
man who will be kindly disposed and will spare him."   158

So he spoke and Iris, fast as a storm, rushed off to deliver the
message. And she came to Priam, who was wailing and groaning, with his sons sitting around him in the courtyard. They
stained their clothing with their tears. In their midst, the old
man heaved with heavy sobs, convulsed with weeping. Around
him there was a lot of dung, on his head and also the old man's
neck. He was rolling in it and tossing it on his head. His daughters up in the palace and his sons' wives looked on as they
mourned those they remembered. There were many brave men,
who lay dead, their souls having perished at the hands of the
Argives.   168

The messenger of Zeus stood beside Priam and spoke to him

in a whisper, and his limbs were seized by fear and trembling: "Take courage, Priam, descendent of Dardanus, there is nothing to fear. I have not come because I foresee a portent of evil for you. Instead I am in a good humor. I am a messenger to you from Zeus, who is far away, but cares deeply and takes pity on you. The Olympian orders you to take gifts to Achilles that might soothe his heart to secure the release of noble Hector. None of the Trojans is to go with you except a herald of senior rank to serve as skinner for the mules and a wagon, with sound wheels, and to carry back to the city the corpse of him noble Achilles slew. You have no concern of death, nor should you be afraid, because we will make available the slayer of Argos to be your guide. He will lead you along until you come near Achilles. After that, when you have been led into Achilles's hut, he himself will protect you against all others. You will not be slain, nor will there be animosity, thoughtlessness, and no injustice. Instead you should go as a supplicant to a man who will be kindly disposed and will spare you."   187

Having said what she did, fleet-footed Iris went away. After that, Priam ordered his sons to harness mules to a wagon with sound wheels, and to lash a wicker box onto it. He himself went down into the fragrant chamber with high ceilings, paneled in cedar, which had held many precious objects. He called out to his wife Hecuba in his resonant voice: "Madam, a messenger from Zeus came to me. The Olympian says I am to go to the ships of the Acheans with gifts for Achilles that might soothe his heart, to secure the release of my dear son. But come now, tell me your mind in this matter? My own strength and spirit order me awfully to go to the ships in the wide camp of the Acheans."   199

So he spoke, and his wife sobbed loudly and answered him: "Oh my! Where has your mind gone? The mind that, in the past, gave orders to foreigners, and ruled over them, where has it gone? How could you want to go alone to the ships of the Acheans, to look into the eyes of one who killed your sons? Many and brave they were. Your heart is now iron! If he captures you, you will look into the eyes of one savage and untrustworthy, a man who will have no compassion for you, nor will he show you respect. Now we are crying away from the conflict, sitting in our halls. But, it happened as though a violent fate spun a thread for him when I myself bore him. It was his fate to satisfy the appetites of wild dogs far away from his parents, around a powerful man whose inner heart I wish I could gorge myself in eating. It would take that to avenge my son's death. Hector was not being cowardly when Achilles killed him. Instead, he stood to fight for the Trojans and the Trojan women with no thought of rout or a place of refuge."   216

And the old man, godlike Priam, answered her: "Don't hinder me; I wish to go. And do not talk about some bird of evil portent in the hall. You will not convince me. Were it anyone else on earth who had made such a claim, whether a soothsayer looking at leftovers from sacrifices, or a priest, 1 would claim that one false and would readily distance myself from him in the future. This time, though, I myself heard a goddess, and looked on her face. I am going and her prophecy will not prove useless. If it is fated for me to die beside the ships of the brazen-shirted Acheans, I welcome it. After I take my son in my arms and send away the desire for grieving, Achilles may slay me forthwith."   227

And he opened the beautiful lids of his caskets, and took out twelve very lovely long gowns, and twelve short robes, and as many rugs, and as many white shawls, and as many tunics for those shawls. He weighed out ten talents of pure gold. He took out two gleaming tripods, and four cauldrons. He took out a very beautiful cup, which Thracian warriors presented as a great gift when they came on an embassy. At that point there was no stinting in the halls, for the old man wanted most in his heart to secure the release of his dear son.   237

But he insultingly dismissed all the Trojans in the courtyard: "Get out of here, you disgraceful losers. Should you not now grieve in your own households? Why do you come bothering me with your concerns? Do you not realize that Zeus Cronusson has given me great pain with the destruction of my son, the best of them? Well, you will be aware of it, for it will be very much easier for the Acheans in their fighting with Hector dead. As for me, I would rather be on my way to the House of Hades, than to see the ravaging and destruction of our city." 246

And with his staff he directed the men, and because of the old man's raging, they went out of the courtyard. And he shouted abusively to his sons: Helenus, and Paris, and noble Agathon, and Pammon, and Antiphonus, and Polites, good at the war cry, and Deïphobus, and Hippothous, and lordly Dius. There were nine of them to whom the old man shouted his order: "Be quick about it, you degenerate, disgusting children. Oh, how I wish that the whole lot of you had perished beside the swift ships instead of Hector. Oh, damn! I am the most miserable of men, since I have lost my best sons—godlike Mestor, and the warlike horseman Troilus, and Hector, who was a god among men, and not like the son of a mortal. And, I declare Ares destroyed them and there is no one left, but all the disgraceful ones: liars, and dancers, and the best of choreographers who pillage the whole district for rams and kids for their feasting. Will you not harness a wagon for me, and be quick about it! Will you place all these things on it, so that we can get on with our journey?" 264

So Priam spoke, and they were certainly very much afraid of the loud abuse their father heaped on them. They pulled out a wagon for mule draft, with sound wheels. It was handsome, recently made. And they lashed a wicker box on it. They lifted a mule yoke from its wooden pegs, and took it down. It was of boxwood and well fitted with a knob and rings for reins to pass through it. And they brought down the leather ropes for fastening the pole, which was nine cubits, or thirteen and a half feet long, to the yoke. And, they carefully placed the front end of the well-smoothed pole against the yoke. And to the ring of the pole they pounded a ring bolt, and bound it three times around the knobs on both sides, and after that they bent under the tip. From the chamber, they brought to the polished wagon the extravagant ransom for Hector's head and heaped it up. And they hitched up mules with powerful hooves, capable of much work. The Mysians had given them to Priam as a magnificent gift. And the sons led under a yoke horses for Priam, which the old man had brought up, that were well cared for and well fed. 280

While the teams were being harnessed, the herald and Priam made careful plans for the journey in the lofty palace. Hecuba came close to them, grieving in her heart, with sweet-tasting wine in a golden goblet in her right hand, so that they might depart and get under way. She stood in front of the horses and spoke out, calling Priam by name: "You should make a libation to father Zeus, and pray for your return back home from the enemy warriors. I was not enthusiastic when you were roused in your heart to go to the ships. Instead, I pray you that you ask the cloud-gathering son of Cronus who watches over all of Troy from Ida, for a fast bird as his messenger, one that is very powerful and large, that is his most favorite of birds, to come on the right-hand side, so that you may confirm with your own eyes and trust that you might get to the ships of the Danaans, who have fast horses. If loud-thundering Zeus will not give you a messenger, I would urge you not to go to the ships of the Argives, even though you are eager to do it."   298

And godlike Priam answered her, saying: "O woman, I will not disobey you if he will not send what you describe. It is a worthy thing to raise our arms to Zeus to find out if he might take pity."   301

And the old man ordered the housekeeper to pour clean water over his hands. She stood beside him as a maid with her holding a basin and ewer. He held out his hands as she poured, washing them. And he received the goblet from his wife, and then he stood in the middle of the enclosure, holding the wine, and, looking up to the heavens he prayed: "Zeus, Father, who

rules from Ida, most glorious and greatest of all, grant to me
that I might go to Achilles amicably and that he might pity
me. Send a messenger, a fast bird, most favored, and very much
the greatest in might, to appear on the right-hand side so that
I might trust with my own eyes that I might get to the ships of
the Danaans, who have fast horses."   315

So he spoke in prayer, and Zeus, the counselor, heard him.
And, immediately an eagle came, the most reliable of birds for
auguries. It was a tawny predator they call the golden eagle. The
span of the wings spread on both sides of the bird was as wide
as the door of a high-ceilinged chamber built for a rich man that
is carefully fitted with a lock. It was seen by them on the right-
hand side, rushing through the city, and seeing it, they rejoiced,
and the heart in the breast of everyone was warmed.   321

Hastening on, the old man mounted his chariot and drove
out from the forecourt and the loudly resonating courtyard. In
front were the mules pulling the four-wheeled wagan. The wise
Idaeus drove them. Behind were the horses pulling the chariot.
The old man gave orders and cracked his whip and they went
speedily down from the city. All of his loved ones followed with
them, their eyes welling many tears and wailing as if he were
going to his death. And when they had gone down from the
city, and reached the plain, the sons and sons-in-law retraced
their steps, returning to Troy.   331

But, the two men did not escape the notice of loud-thundering
Zeus, as they were revealed to him on the plain. He felt compassion for the old man and quickly spoke to his dear son
Hermes: "Hermes, rendering help to men is the most especially
gratifying and pleasing thing you do, so listen for something you
might wish to do. Set off and lead Priam to the hollow ships of
the Acheans so that none of them are able to see him, or any
of the other Danaans recognize him, until he gets to the son of
Peleus."   338

So he spoke and the messenger, the slayer of Argos, did not

disobey. Immediately, then he bound his beautiful, ambrosial sandals of gold under his feet. They carry him over wet places, and over the boundless earth on the breaths of the wind. He seized his wand, with which he places trances on the eyes of men, and with it he again revives them from sleeping. Holding it in his hand, the mighty slayer of Argos flew, and quickly he arrived at Troy and the Hellespont. He went in the guise of a youth from a royal house, with just the beginnings of a beard coming. It is at such a time that a young man is at his absolutely most charming.

348

And when the two men were driving away from the great grave marker of Ilus, they halted the mules and horses so they might drink at the river. And, to be sure, dusk came to the earth. The herald saw Hermes as he came closer, and called out to Priam: "Think about it, son of Dardanus. I see a man, who I think might quickly destroy us. But come, do we flee on the chariot with the horses, or shall we clasp his knees and plead with him so that he might take pity on us?"

358

So he spoke, and so fear and dread poured out from his mind onto the old man, and the hairs stuck up straight on his slack limbs. Priam stood paralyzed, and the very useful one came closer and reached out and took the old man's hand, and spoke to him: "How is it, Father, that you are driving horses and mules through the ambrosial night when other mortals are sleeping? Do you not fear your enemies, the fury-breathing Acheans, or highwaymen who are close by? If one of them might see you taking such goods through the murky black night, what might your advice be? You are not young yourself, and this one who helps you is too old for protecting a man when somebody angry instigates something. But I liken you to a dear father and I will do you no harm, and would even protect you from anyone else who would."

371

And old, godlike Priam responded: "This way that you talk is like that of a dear child of my own. But, still one of the gods holds on to my hand, who has sent me a just traveler. How exceptionally handsome you are in body and face, and prudent in your mind. You are from blessed parents."   377

And the messenger, the slayer of Argos, answered him back: "Yes, for sure, everything you said accords with custom. But come, tell me this truthfully, either you are taking much and worthy treasure to foreign men for safekeeping, or you are abandoning sacred Troy altogether. Everyone there is very fearful because the best man perished, your son who was not at all hesitant to fight against the Acheans."   385

And then the old, godlike Priam responded: "Who are you, O best of men, and what parents are you from? Tell me how it is that you are handsome and how you can tell wretched me of the fate of my unlucky son."   388

And the messenger, slayer of Argos, answered back, saying: "Asking about noble Hector would be a test of me. I saw him very often in the fighting, which brings men glory, and when he was driving near the ships, slaying Acheans as he raged with sharp bronze. I stood in amazement, for Achilles would not allow us to fight while he was angry with the son of Atreus. I am his attendant; we came in the same well-ordered ship. And I am from the Myrmidons, and my father is Polyctor. He is rich, though he is also old, like you. It has been allowed for him to have sons, and I am his seventh. There was a casting of lots to determine which would accompany the Myrmidons here. And now I have come to the plain from the ships, as the sharp-eyed Acheans have set on a battle at dawn around the city. The men are restive from just sitting around, and the Achean kings are unable to restrain them from attacking."   404

And the old, godlike Priam next replied to him: "If you are the attendant of Achilles Peleusson, come, tell me the whole truth. Either my son is still beside the ships, or, indeed Achilles has sliced him limb from limb and tossed him to dogs. Tell me which is so."   409

And the messenger, the slayer of Argos, spoke back to him:

"Oh, old man, there is no way that the dogs and birds devoured him. Instead, that one still lies among the huts by the ship of Achilles, just as he was before. He has lain there twelve dawns, and his flesh has not rotted, nor have worms, which feast on men slain in war, eaten him. Certainly, Achilles drags him brutally around the grave marker of his dear friend when sacred dawn appears, but that doesn't disfigure the body. You yourself would look in wonder at how dewy he is as he lies, if you were to go there. The blood has been washed off all over, and there is no stain anywhere. All the wounds where he was stabbed have been closed over. There were many who drove bronze into him. It is true, you may be certain. Since there was the greatest love for the blessed gods in Hector's heart, they have taken care of their son, even though he is a corpse." 423

So Hermes spoke, and the old man rejoiced. And he replied with these words: "Oh child, it is a worthy thing and right to give gifts to the immortals. My son, if he was even my son, never forgot the gods who dwell on Olympus in our halls. For this they remember him even though he is in his destiny of death. But come, receive from me a beautiful cup that I have here, for protecting me. Guide me with the help of the gods, in order that I may reach the hut of Achilles." 431

And the messenger, the slayer of Argos, replied: "Old man, this would test me, a younger man than you, but you will not persuade me. You would have me to receive your gifts concealed from Achilles's awareness. I fear him greatly, and would be ashamed were I to steal from him, for it would portend evil in the future. But I am your guide, even were I to go to famed Argos. I will accompany you agreeably, whether in a swift ship or on foot, and no one will make threats against your guide, or fight against you." 439

And with that, the very useful one rushed onto the chariot and horses, and quickly took the whip and reins in his hand and he breathed special might into the horses and mules. But when they arrived at the fortified tower and the trench, the sentries had just recently prepared their supper. The messenger, the slayer of Argos, poured sleep on them. After that he opened the gates and pushed back the locking bars, leading inside both Priam and his magnificent gifts on the wagon.   444

The hut of Achilles was one that the Myrmidons built for their king. It had a high roof, built of fir timbers they cut. After framing it they covered it over with a dense thatching they mowed from grass growing on the damp meadows. Around its great courtyard they built for their king a thick palisade that had a single gate with a bolt of pine that locked it. It took three Acheans to lift the bolt into place to lock it, and three to unlock the great lock of the gate, though Achilles could lock it even alone. When Hermes and Priam arrived at the hut, the very useful Hermes opened the gate for the old man delivering the glorious gifts for Achilles Peleusson. He stepped down from the chariot and spoke: "O, old man, I must tell you truly that I am a god, not a man; I am Hermes and I have come because my father granted that I should go with you as your guide. But now I must go back again. I should not be seen by the eyes of Achilles. It would be distressing for an immortal god to receive affectionate treatment in front of a mortal. But you are to go in and clasp the knees of the son of Peleus, and plead with him for the sake of his father, and his mother, who has beautiful hair, and his child, so that you might with that appeal to his heart."   467

So speaking, Hermes left and went to high Olympus. Priam stepped down from his chariot. He parted with Idaeus, leaving him there to look after the horses and the mules. The old man went straight inside, and found the man himself, Achilles, beloved of Zeus, sitting there. His comrades sat apart from him. Priam knew both of them, the hero Automedon, and Alcimus, scion of Ares, accompanying Achilles as attendants. He had recently finished eating and drinking. And the table still lay beside him. Great Priam's approach escaped their notice, but he went closer, and clasped Achilles's knees in his hands and kissed the terrible man-killing hands that slew so many of his

sons. It was like when a dense blindness takes hold of a man
who runs into a man who has killed others in the family of a
rich man in the district. Shock holds those who look at him. So
it was that Achilles was startled on seeing godlike Priam. And
the others were shocked as well, as they looked at each other.   484

And pleading, Priam spoke to Achilles: "Remember your
father, Achilles, you who are very like the gods. He is the same
age that I am, poised at the threshold of ruinous old age. And
all those living around him as neighbors are weary from age.
There is no one to protect him from war and grief. But, I tell
you truly, that on hearing that you are alive, he rejoices in his
heart, and he hopes all the time most earnestly that he will
see his dear son coming from Troy. On the other hand, I am the
most wretched of men, since my child perished. I claim to have
had the best sons in wide Troy, but there are none left. I had fifty
sons when the Acheans came, and nineteen were from one
belly. The others were born to me by women in my halls. The
knees of many of them were loosed by violent Ares. And I had
just one alone to protect the city and the others. You recently
killed him while he was engaged in protecting his family—
Hector. And now I have come to the ships of the Acheans to
secure his release from you. I bring a ransom, beyond counting.
Respect the gods, Achilles, take pity on me, and remember your
father, though I am more to be pitied. And I dared do something
that no other mortal anywhere on the face of the earth would,
to touch with my mouth the hand of a man who was the murderer of my sons."   506

So Priam spoke, and roused in Achilles the desire to grieve
over his father. And then he touched the old man with his hands
and gently pushed him away. And they both remembered, the
one remembered man-killing Hector, after collapsing in front
Achilles's feet, and weeping without letup. While Achilles wept
for his father, and at another moment again for Patroclus, and
his groaning roared through the house. Afterward, when noble
Achilles had taken satisfaction in grieving, he immediately

rose from his throne, and raised up the old man with his hands. Looking compassionately on the gray head and the gray beard, he spoke to Priam with winged words: "Ah, you wretched man, you bear up under much trouble that weighs on your heart! How did you dare come to the Achean ships alone to look with your eyes at a man who has slain your many and worthy sons? Your heart must now be of iron. But come, sit on a throne. Pain has completely settled down in my heart, so we will ease off the grieving. One cannot continue with frigid crying indefinitely, since it is the gods who spin the thread of fate for miserable mortals with affliction for the living, while they themselves are carefree. There are two clay jars on the threshold of Zeus, one has gifts the gods give as they are creating trouble, the other has his good gifts. At some point, Zeus, who delights in thunder, mixes up gifts he would give, and one time it happens as evil, at another time as worthy. When that happens to those who are in misery he might place one to revile them, and he could drive an utter disaster over the whole earth. Such a one who reviles wanders around honored neither by gods nor mortals. And in such a way the gods gave Peleus magnificent gifts from his birth. He utterly surpassed all men in riches, ruling the Myrmidons. Even though he was mortal, they made a goddess his wife. But there was evil set on him, that there were no children born in the halls for the succession. Instead, there was just one son born premature, and I do not take care for Peleus in his old age, since I sit in Troy, far from my father, causing trouble for you and your offspring.   542

"And, old man, we heard earlier that you were happy since you were ruling over Lesbos, the island of the blessed, and received what it produced, and under your dominion were Phrygia, and the boundless Hellespont, and from those you had plenty, old man, and they say you even exceeded others in having sons. But then the heavenly beings brought you a fate, as there is constant warring and killing around your city. Bear up, don't allow senselessness to weigh down on your mind. You cannot accomplish anything by grieving over your son, and you could not call him back to life, before you might even suffer some other evil." 551

And the old, godlike Priam, replied: "Noble-born sir, there is no way I could sit on a throne while Hector lies in the hut without care. Instead, receive the entire, magnificent ransom I brought you, and release him as quickly as possible so that I might see him. And you may have the advantage of it and carry it to your homeland, after you allow me both to live and see the light of the sun." 558

Frowning, Achilles, fleet of foot, looked at him and said: "Do not quarrel with me any longer, old man. For my own reasons I intend to release Hector to you. My mother came as messenger to me from Zeus. It was she, a daughter of the Old Man of the Sea, who bore me. And thus I know what is on your mind, Priam. And it did not escape me that one of the gods led you to the swift ships of the Acheans. No mortal, not even one very swift and powerful, would have dared come through the camp, and he would not have been overlooked by the sentries. And he certainly could not so easily have unlocked the bolt in our gates. But you should not spur on my heart's pain, old man, because I might not spare you even though you have come here to the huts. If I did that I would disobey an order of Zeus." 570

So he spoke, and the old man became very frightened and did as he was told. Achilles leapt through the door out of the house like a lion. He was not alone. The two attendants followed him, the hero Automedon, and Alcimus. Achilles especially valued them as companions after Patroclus died. They loosed the horses and the mules from under their yokes and they led the herald, the crier of the old man, over and sat him down on a chair. From the well-scraped wagon, they took the ransom past valuation, for Hector's head. But they left two well-woven things from it, a robe and a tunic, so they might use them for dressing the corpse for the return trip home. Calling out to his servants, he ordered them to take the body a ways off, wash it, and anoint it with oil. This, so that when Priam saw his son he would not be angry at Achilles for not preserving his son. If he were to grow angry at Achilles on seeing his son because he killed him, Priam, too, would disobey an order of Zeus. And then, the servants washed the body and anointed it with olive oil, and slipped it into the tunic and the beautiful robe. And Achilles himself, lifted it up and placed it on the reposing couch, and with his comrades they lifted that onto the well-scraped wagon.   590

Afterward, he grieved, and called his dear friend's name: "If you learn, even in Hades, that I released noble Hector to his dear father, don't be angry with me, Patroclus, since Priam gave me a ransom that is not shabby. It is suitable for you, such as before we might have divided between us."   595

So noble Achilles spoke as he went back again into the hut. He sat on a very dazzling sofa situated along a wall opposite where Priam was sitting. He spoke to Priam: "Sir, your son has been released to you as you requested, and he lies on a reposing couch. With the revelation of dawn, you may see him yourself and take him. Now, we should take thought of supper. Even Niobe, with beautiful hair, remembered food, though at that time her twelve children perished in her halls. Six of them were daughters and six were adolescent sons. Apollo, of the silver bow, slew the sons over anger at Niobe, and Artemis, delighting in archery, slew the daughters because Niobe set herself as equal of sweet-cheeked Leto. She claimed that Leto had born but two children, while she, herself, had many. And even though there were only two, the both of them destroyed all that were from Niobe. They lay in death for nine days and no one performed funeral rites, because the son of Cronus turned the populace into rocks and stones. On that, the tenth day, the heavenly gods buried them. And Niobe remembered food, since she was worn out from shedding tears. Now, somewhere in the mountains is a high rock formation apart from others in Sipylus, where they say the sleeping places of goddesses and nymphs

are. They are strengthened and made more vigorous around the
sacred river Acheloïus. There, though Niobe is a stone, she ponders the woes sent her by the gods. 617

"But come, noble old man, we will give some thought to
food. After that you may weep as you take your dear son back
to Troy; there will be many tears for you." 620

And swift Achilles rose himself and slit the throat of a white-
fleeced ram. His comrades flayed it and went about preparing
it properly. They cut it into small pieces and pierced them, putting the pieces on spits. They roasted them with care and skill,
and pulled them all off. Automedon parceled out bread into
beautiful baskets on the table, and then Achilles distributed the
meat. And they stretched forth their hands to the proper feast
that lay before them. When the want for drink and food had
gone from them, Priam Dardanusson truly looked with awe at
Achilles, how remarkable he was. It was like being in front of a
god. And then Achilles looked with wonder at Priam Dardanusson, looking at his handsome face, and hearing him speak. And
after they were satisfied at looking at each other, old, godlike
Priam was first to speak, saying to Achilles: "You now should
lay me to rest most quickly, noble-born sir, so that I may indeed
delight in sweet sleep, lying down. I have not closed my eyes
anywhere, from the moment my son's spirit perished at your
hands. Instead, I have constantly groaned with grief and brooded
over countless cares, falling down and rolling in dung in the stable enclosures of my courtyard. Though earlier I had tasted
nothing, now I have tasted bread, and deep red wine has passed
down my throat." 642

At that Achilles ordered his comrades and servants to place
beds under the porch. And they went from the halls with torches
in their hands and quickly busied themselves in setting up
two beds and spread out carpets over them. And they threw on
beautiful crimson woolen sleeping rugs. And they placed woolen
sheets to wrap around them. 648

And fleet-footed Achilles spoke sharply to Priam: "Surely,

I must go to bed apart from you, dear old man, lest one of the Acheans come in here to confer about some plan of the sort they constantly come to me for, and properly so. But if one of them might see you, in the dusky, black night, he would immediately report that to Agamemnon, Shepherd of the Troops, and that would put a stop to the release of the corpse. But come now, tell me this truthfully, how many days do you want for the rites for noble Hector, so that for that many I myself will hold back, and restrain the troops."   658

And old, godlike Priam replied: "If you wish me to complete the funeral rites for noble Hector, you will make me glad, Achilles, for allowing me this. You know that we are cooped up in the city, and we will have to carry wood a long way from the mountain, and the Trojans are very much afraid. We would mourn him for nine days in the halls, and on the tenth, set the funeral pyre, and on the eleventh, we would build a mound. On the twelfth, we will fight if we have to."   667

And noble Achilles, fleet of foot, answered him back: "You may be sure that these things will be even as you said, old Priam. I shall hold off the war for as long as you ordered."   670

So saying, he took hold of the old man's right arm at the wrist to alleviate any fear in his heart. And the herald and Priam contentedly bedded down there in the vestibule of the house. Afterward, Achilles slept in the inner chamber of the well-constructed hut, and beside him slept sweet-cheeked Briseis.   676

And the other gods and horse-driving men lay the entire night subdued by soft, gentle sleep. But sleep did not capture ever-useful Hermes. He thrashed about in his mind how he could guide King Priam away from the ships without the notice of the sacred doorkeepers. He stood over Priam's head and spoke to him saying: "O old man, there is not supposed to be evil for you, since Achilles spares you even though you sleep among warring men. Though you gave much for the release of your dear son, the ransom for you alive would be three times as much for your remaining sons to pay in the future. If

Agamemnon finds out you are here, all the Acheans will
know."

So he spoke and excited fear in the old man, and he stood
the herald up. Hermes harnessed the horses and mules for them,
and drove fast across the plain with the horses trotting along
briskly, and none of the Acheans knew a thing about it.

But when they reached the ford of the wide-flowing, swirling river Xanthus, that immortal Zeus fathered, Hermes then
departed for high Olympus, and Dawn spread her long, purple
gown over all the earth. And they proceeded toward the city,
grieving and groaning in sorrow, Priam driving the horses, with
the herald driving the mules pulling the wagon bearing the
corpse. And none of the other men or the buxom women was
aware of them. But Cassandra, like golden Aphrodite, having
gone up to the high citadel, saw her dear father standing on the
chariot and the herald, the town crier, with Hector on the wagon
drawn by the mules. When she saw him lying on the reposing
couch, she burst into tears, sobbing loudly, and yelled out to the
whole city: "Trojans and Trojan women, you will see that Hector is coming. Whenever anybody saw him return alive from
fighting, he was pleased and there was great joy in the city and
the entire district!"

So she yelled, and there was no one left inside the city, not a
man or a woman. An enormous load of grief came on all of
them as they crowded together close to the gates as the corpse
came along. In the front were his beloved wife and his revered
mother. They rushed onto the wagon, with sound wheels, and
clasped his head, and both pulled out hair from their heads,
and the crowd around them was weeping. And at that point
might they have remained the whole day until the sun went down,
had not the old man spoken to the troops from his chariot: "Make
way for me; make room for the mules to come through. You
will have your fill of weeping and wailing afterward, as soon
as I take him to the palace."

So he spoke, and they stood apart, making way for the

wagon. And when they got to the famed palace, they next placed
the body on a bored-frame bed, the kind that has ropes tied
through holes bored in a frame, used by the rich for sleeping.
Alongside it they seated the singers, who began the dirges. They
chanted their mournful song for him, and next the women commenced their wailing, and white-armed Andromache led their
lament, taking the head of man-killing Hector in her hands: "My
husband, in the short life span of a young man you perished,
and thereby you leave me a widow in the halls, and a son who
is still an infant, one that we produced, you and I. How unlucky
we were. And I do not think he will take his seat as youthful
men do at the council. Before that time, the city will have utterly perished. You, its guardian, have been destroyed, you who
protected him and protected me myself. You were holding in
your protection the circumspect wives and young children. You
may be sure that soon they will be taken away on the hollow
ships. Then, either our child follows with me and would toil at
unworthy work, competing on behalf of some nasty tyrant, or
perhaps one of the Acheans, seizing his hands, will throw him
from the tower to a wretched death, because the man is angry
over someone Hector killed at some time, a brother, or a father
or even a son, since there were a great many Acheans that Hector took into his hands who clinched their teeth around immea-
surable amounts of dirt. Astyanax's father was not kind when
he was in the deadly fighting. On account of you the troops
grieve miserably down in the city. You placed a curse on your
parents who now mourn and grieve, Hector, and for me you
have left behind the most miserable pain. As you are dead, you
will not stretch out your arms to me in our bed, and say the
dear things lovers say, and I will know nothing in the nights and
days, but tears."   745

So she spoke, weeping, and the women began their wailing.
And again, among them Hecuba commenced unstoppable wailing: "Hector, you were by far the most loved of all my children
while you were alive, and as you were dear to me, you were to

the gods, as well. They care for you even in death, though that is as it should be. Achilles, swift of foot, sold my other sons, whom he captured at the limits of the baron sea at Samos, and Imbros and Lemnos, which has no harbor. But when he snatched out your spirit with his long-pointed spear, he dragged you abusively many times around the grave marker of his friend Patroclus, whom you slew. Then the gods held you up so that he would not destroy you. And, now you are displayed before me lying dewy fresh in the halls, just like someone Apollo, of the silver bow, has slain with his gentle arrows."

759

So she spoke, and roused up intense wailing. Next, then, Helen was the third to commence grieving: "Hector, you are the most loved in my heart of all my brothers-in-law. Certainly, godlike Alexander is my husband, who brought me here to Troy. Oh, how I wish that I had perished before that. It is now the twentieth year since I went from there, leaving my father behind. But I never heard an unpleasant word from you, nor were you ever condescending. But whenever any of the brothers-in law, or sisters-in-law, or the long-gowned wives of your brothers might snipe at me, you would always restrain that one, saying kind words on my behalf. My mother-in-law, and father-in-law, your father, were consistently kind to me as well. I weep for both you and me together and am grief stricken over my misfortune. But no one was ever so gentle and kind to me in wide Troy as you. All of the others shuddered at the sight of me."

775

So she spoke, weeping. And there was wailing and groaning of the greatest sort in the district. But old Priam addressed the troops, saying: "Trojans, now you are to bring wood to the city. And have no fear of a devious ambush by the Argives. You may be sure that Achilles sent a message to me, that he has ordered that there is to be no harm from the black ships until dawn arrives on the twelfth day."

781

So he spoke and they harnessed up the oxen and mules under the wagons, and then quickly set off from the city. For nine days they brought a huge amount of wood back, you may be sure. But when on the tenth day, Dawn, who brings light to men, revealed herself, then weeping, they brought out brave Hector, and placed him at the top of the pyre, and thrust him in the fire. When Dawn, born of the morning, next revealed her rose-red fingers, the troops gathered around the pyre of famed Hector and sprinkled dark red wine down around the burning coals, enough to take away the force of the fire. Afterward, then Hector's brothers and his comrades collected the white bones, bawling with an abundance of tears rolling down their cheeks. And picking them out, they placed them in a golden urn and wrapped around it a soft crimson cloth. They quickly placed it in a hollow grave, and covered it over with close-set stones. They pushed up a mound over it and speedily set up a funeral marker. Around the mound they placed sentries to watch for the Achean onslaught. After setting the funeral marker, they went forth for an extravagant funeral feast in the palace of noble-born King Priam.

And this is how they went about the funeral observance for the noble horseman, Hector.   804

ACKNOWLEDGMENTS

My deepest thanks to philologist James H. Tatum, professor emeritus at Dartmouth College, for his encouragement and genial communications (some enlivened by expressions in Old High Texan, a dialect different from my own of the Deep South but comprehensible nonetheless); and to Victorian poet Matthew Arnold's essay *On Translating Homer,* which, along with the criticism published by the eminent Homerist Charles Rowan Beye, Distinguished Professor of Classics Emeritus at the City University of New York, shaped my ideas on how the poem should be translated. And to Professor Beye himself, who has since been uncommonly generous.